Dispelled

A Null for Hire Novel

By Terri L. Austin

Praise for Terri L. Austin

"Austin infuses her characters with relatable problems and hot chemistry that will keep readers turning pages." - *Publishers Weekly*

"Austin never fails to deliver engaging, complex and refreshingly unique characters whose journeys are full of smart banter and delicious chemistry."- *RT Book Reviews*

Books by Terri L. Austin

The Rose Strickland Mystery Series
Diners, Dives and Dead Ends
Last Diner Standing
Diner Impossible
Diner Knockout
Heartache Motel

The Beauty and the Brit Romance Series
His Every Need
To Be His
His Kind of Trouble
His to Keep

Copyright

Dispelled
Copyright © 2016 Terri L. Austin
All rights reserved.
No parts of this publication may be reproduced, stored in a retrieval system, or transmitted in any form or by any means, electronic, mechanical, photocopying, recording, or otherwise, without the prior written permission of the copyright owner.
This book is sold subject to the condition that it shall not, by way of trade or otherwise, be lent, resold, hired out, or otherwise circulated without the author's prior consent in any form of binding or cover other than that in which it is published and without a similar condition including this condition being imposed on the subsequent purchaser.
Under no circumstances may any part of this book be photocopied for resale.
This is a work of fiction. Any similarity between the characters and situations within its pages and places or persons, living or dead, is unintentional and co-incidental.
Cover art © Renu Sharma | www.thedarkrayne.com
EBook ISBN: 978-1-946066-00-8
Paperback ISBN: 978-1-946066-01-5

PROLOGUE

Friday was a scorcher. The weatherman said Oklahoma hadn't seen a summer this hot since 1936. Temperatures had spiked well into the hundreds every day for the past three weeks. Not a drop of rain in the last nine. Farmers worried, tempers flared, and I felt a little pissy myself. This was my fifth wedding in a month, so I'd had my fill of blushing brides and all the drama that went with them.

I snapped off the radio and pulled my car onto an unpaved road, dodging four Texas-sized potholes to park behind a slew of pickups. I dragged myself out of the car, and as I stepped into the swirling dust and oppressive heat, I received a few angry glares from my fellow wedding guests. I didn't let it bother me. After all, I was the paid party pooper. And speaking of poop, I gazed across the field to realize the bride's backyard was a cow pasture. The heat added a special piquant bouquet to the fly-covered cow shit that surrounded me. Fortunately, the cows were fenced off to one side, their lazy tails swishing to and fro as they people-watched and chewed their cuds.

I was going to kill my soon-to-be-former assistant. Sunny had to have known about this venue when she booked the job. Sunny knew everything.

I almost turned and hopped into the car, ready to speed back to Tulsa. To hell with the five thousand-dollar fee.

But then I'd never hear the end of it. Sunny could hold a grudge longer than anyone I'd ever met.

Since going home wasn't really an option, I cautiously stepped off the dirt road and into the field. My glittery Ann Taylor pumps weren't any happier to tromp across the scorched grass than I was. Cursing under my breath, I wobbled on my heels as I sidestepped cow pies. A man in a mustard yellow shirt and too-tight brown slacks watched me struggle to keep my balance. Asshole didn't even offer to help. Just gave me a smirk and moved on.

Typical. Others didn't like me much. *Understatement.* Although my business card claimed I was an event consultant, in actuality I was a glorified babysitter for magical folk. My name is Holly James, and I'm a null for hire. The couple getting married—werepossums. I know, all the movies and books portray shape shifters as scary, sexy wolves that will rip out your throat or steal your heart, sometimes simultaneously. And while that's not inaccurate, they come in the marsupial variety as well. I'm sort of a supernatural bodyguard. My magical void would render them incapable of shifting into possums and ruining the wedding. Especially the pictures. I'm sure you haven't seen weres post-shift, but it's not pretty. Let's just say drippy, viscous fluids and leave it at that.

Of course, even with my presence, nothing would prevent these two squabbling families from beating the crap out of each other in human form. But that, my friends, was not my problem.

So here I was, trekking through a damn pasture on one of the hottest days of the year when out of nowhere a blast of frigid air teased the hem of my blue skirt and tickled the backs of my knees. Goosebumps rose along my heated skin.

I stopped in my tracks. Normally, that type of wind came with cloud cover and an impending rainstorm. But all was clear in the cornflower blue sky. The early evening sun hovered near the horizon, shining bright enough to make me squint behind my oversized sunglasses.

As abruptly as the wind came, it went.

I gazed at the group moving toward the arched trellis planted in the middle of the field. No one else seemed to notice that sharp, icy gust.

I shrugged off a hint of foreboding and chalked it up to my imagination. I shouldn't have.

That breeze was the wind of change.

And if I ever feel it again, I'm going to run like hell in the opposite direction.

CHAPTER ONE

Fucking redneck werepossums.

Wearing only one shoe, I stumbled into my two bedroom ranch in South Tulsa. Pink frosting coated my hair, and I'd stupidly used my vintage Chanel purse as a shield against a flying rib. *Vintage. Chanel.* The silver leather bore a barbecue splotch right on the logo.

The ceremony had gone off without a hitch unless you counted obscene hand gestures thrown back and forth while the bride and groom exchanged vows. But the reception was another story. The groom's daddy downed too many shots of Jack, so when the bride's mama started mouthing off about the white trash possum her daughter married, it was game on. The families battled it out using potluck side dishes as weapons. That's right, a potluck wedding reception. At a bingo hall.

And the final classy touch? The bride got hauled away in a police cruiser while her groom chased it down the street, screaming her name.

Never again. No more shifters. No more weddings in the middle of shit-filled pastures. I'd reached my limit. Sunny was going to get an earful come Monday morning. She set up all my gigs and wasn't as picky as I was. In fact, as long as the check cleared, she wasn't picky at all. That needed to change.

Kicking off my remaining shoe, I glanced at my once beautiful bag. I'd do what I could to remove the stain, but I wasn't holding my breath. After laying it to rest on the hall table, I shucked my clothes, tossed them in the laundry room, and headed for the shower.

I didn't come out until I'd used up every drop of hot water. With my skin scrubbed pink and my shoulder-length brown hair squeaky clean, I pulled it into a wet ponytail. Not bothering with a bra, I threw on a t-shirt and a pair of shorts before padding to the kitchen. I needed a serious amount of wine.

I had just curled up on the sofa with the remote and was about to take my first sip of New Zealand Pinot Noir when a knock sounded at the door. Since it was after eleven, I wasn't expecting company.

Emptying my hands, I tiptoed to the front door. The motion-activated porch light flooded the stoop. I glanced out the peephole, and a stranger stared back. A hot grimacing stranger.

"Open up, Null."

I jerked away, my eyebrows sky-high, my heart pounding. Had to be an Other. How else would he know my null status? And how did he find my address? I wasn't listed. I didn't know what he wanted with me, but showing up at my home? Unannounced? It couldn't be good.

I snatched the old aluminum baseball bat I kept in the corner for protection. "Who are you?" I yelled, spying through the hole once again.

"Cade McAllister, here on Council business."

That made me pause. I lived on the periphery of the magical community. Even so, I'd heard rumors over the years. Mainly from my Gran, but still. According to her, the Council was a powerful, corrupt governing body. They policed Others and managed to line their pockets at the same time—just like your run-of-the-mill Norm politicians. The big difference: one did not screw with the Council and live to tell the tale.

So what did they want with me? I simply provided a service for Others who couldn't control themselves. Funerals, birthday parties, reunions. The world was full of feuding families. When you added the supernatural element, a spat could turn ugly quick.

I licked my dry lips, adjusting my grip on the bat. "How do I know you're not lying?"

I heard some mumbling.

"What was that?" I yelled.

"I'm showing you my badge. Look through the peephole."

I peered out, but couldn't see it clearly through the distorted glass. "I can't read what it says."

"Goddamn it, woman," he rumbled. "Open the door."

I hesitated. If he were an Other, I'd already nullified him. But even if he couldn't use his magical powers, he could still do awful, human things to me.

"If you don't open up, Null," he said so quietly I could barely make out the words, "I'm going to bust it down."

Shit.

With a frown, I undid all three locks, still holding the bat in my right hand. When I cracked the door open a few inches, Cade McAllister loomed over me. I'm on the short side, so most people are taller than I am, but this man's height made me feel downright petite. Propping both hands on either side of the brick façade, he stared down at me with pale hazel eyes.

Those eyes slid up my body like a caress, taking in my coral polished toes and bare feet. They skimmed my lightly tanned legs to my blue dolphin shorts—the ones that showed a little too much ass, which is why I only wore them around the house—and my pink *I heart ninjas* t-shirt, sans bra. He grunted at my chest. His gaze lingered on my breasts longer than was necessary before tracing up to my face. He finally stopped at my eyes, which I narrowed in irritation.

"Holly James?" His voice was rough and deep and sent the tiniest shiver through me. My nipples stood at attention.

I held the bat up, ready to swing for the fences if I had to. "What are you?"

"Sorcerer. At least I *was* before you sucked all the magic out of me. So, you suck anything else, Null, or am I safe?"

Sorcerers were top dog in the witch world. They could tap into Others' powers and hijack them, harness those powers for themselves. They had a reputation for being arrogant pricks.

Anyway, I didn't zap an Other's mojo permanently. He'd be fine once we went our separate ways. And I didn't dignify his innuendo by responding either. Not so much as a blink. "Let me see your ID."

He shoved the badge under my nose. It looked official. Council seal and all that. And he didn't smile for the photo. He scowled like he was ready to kick the camera's ass.

I glanced from the photo to the real deal. My gaze swept over him, then traveled the length of him once again at a more leisurely pace. In his early to mid-thirties, he wasn't handsome. His features were too interesting for that. His nose was a tad crooked at the bridge, his cheekbones high and sharp. He was sexy in a masculine way despite the fact that the scowl seemed permanent. Tanned skin with red undertones said he spent a lot of time outdoors.

His dark hair was super short, almost buzzed, and sort of melded with his five o'clock shadow. The odd thing was, he had an old jagged scar about an inch and half long on his right jaw. Most sorcerers would have aided the healing process with magic, left no trace of an imperfection. But he'd let it heal and scar on its own. I wondered why.

Broad shoulders stretched the knit fabric of his green t-shirt. What looked to be a colorful, tattooed dragon wound its way out of his collar and around the side of his neck. The red, green, and gold scales appeared fluid in the dim light. Tight, faded jeans molded over long legs and muscular thighs. I finally dragged my gaze from his brown, worn shit kickers up to his eyes. "You'd better come in before we attract the moths."

"No. Someone wants to speak to you. Follow me." He spun and sauntered down my porch steps. That's when I saw the limo idling on the curb in front of my house.

"Forget it, Sorcerer," I called after him. "I'm not getting in a car with you." Voluntarily ride off with a strange Other? A *Council* Other at that? Not even.

McAllister's shoulders stiffened. Turning on his heel, he slowly strode back to me, stopping at the threshold. I tightened my clutch on the bat.

He moved closer and, as his chest brushed my knuckles, I caught a hint of some exotic scent. I'd never smelled anything like it, and it was heady. He jerked the bat from my hands and tossed it behind me. It landed with a clatter on the tiled floor of the entryway.

I gaped at him. "Hey, what the hell?"

He didn't argue, just bent to grab my knees and tossed me over his shoulder in one swift move.

Son of a bitch. On the short walk to the car, I punched his ass. I pinched his side. I bit the back of his arm. Other than a grunt, he didn't seem to notice.

After he dropped me onto the limo's leather seat, he shut the door in my face, leaving me trapped inside. I pulled the handle, but it wouldn't budge, so I pounded on the window. "Let me out, McAllister. Let me out, now!"

When the interior light switched on, I was struck silent by the presence of an elderly man sitting across from me. His dark, three-piece suit and snowy white shirt were impeccably tailored. His red silk tie rocked a double

Windsor. A shock of long, white hair trailed past his shoulders and contrasted with his tanned skin. And those eyes. *We shared the same light blue eyes.*

"Hello, my dear. I'm terribly sorry Cade was so cavalier with you. He's a bit of a throwback." Across his lap laid a polished walking stick, its gold handle cast into the shape of an owl with sparkling red stones for eyes. "I'm Wallace Dumahl. I'm your grandfather."

At Wallace's pronouncement, I was too stunned to move. I had a grandfather? And he was *here*. Sitting across from me.

I'd never met my father, knew nothing about him. Not even his name. All these years I'd assumed he and his family never knew about me either—so you can imagine my shock. After a long moment, the rusty manners Gran tried to instill kicked in. "I'm pleased to meet you, Mr. Dumahl." My voice didn't rise above a whisper.

He smiled, causing deep wrinkles to crease his cheeks. "You may call me Grandfather if you wish. May I call you Holly?"

I couldn't breathe. Questions swirled around my head, but I didn't know what to ask first.

"You're probably wondering why I'm here?" he asked, gently.

I nodded. *Why now? Why come at all? What did he have to do with the Council?* Too many questions. But the most important one loomed large. Who the hell was my father?

"We have much to discuss, you and I," he said. "Shall I give you the condensed version until we can talk properly?" I noticed for the first time that he didn't have an Oklahoma accent. It was Southern, but more of a genteel drawl than a twang.

"Sure. Condensed will work." Better than nothing, which was what I'd been operating on for the past twenty-five years.

"I didn't know about you until six months ago," he said. "My son, your father, left me a letter upon his death, telling me about you. He was killed in a plane crash. So young." He stopped speaking, his grief almost tangible. After a minute, he cleared his throat and resumed. "It's my regret and shame that he never did right by you, Holly. But you must understand the position he was in. Your father was a very powerful enchanter. He felt he couldn't claim you as his own. He'd give up too much of himself. Too much of his heritage."

Of course he would. Enchanters were heavy hitters in the Other world, specializing in indirect magic. Imagine a pair of tricked out Nikes that let you run at hyper-speed. Or a cell phone that allowed you to teleport. Only uber wealthy Others could afford such enchanted luxury items. I'd have nullified my father's powers, made them inert. As I was now doing with Wallace. As I'd done with Gran. The difference was, she'd sacrificed her power to raise me.

"What was his name?" I asked.

When he reached out to grasp my hand, Wallace hesitated slightly. That one, brief pause spoke volumes. His hand was cold and dry. "Samuel Dumahl, of the Alabama Dumahls. We come from a very long line of enchanters. A few precogs. Or black sheep, as we call them." He smiled at what was probably an old family joke, but I didn't share his amusement.

If a precognitive was a black sheep, what did that make me? The family freak? Nulls were rare. Some said we were abominations. So I wasn't surprised my father pretended I didn't exist. But it still hurt.

"I am a member of the Council," Wallace said, "although that's not why I'm here. I wanted to meet you." His eyes darted over me. "You look a lot like my Sam. Same dark brown hair, same proud chin. And you've got my eyes."

I wanted to ask him all about Samuel. Every detail, from his favorite food to his college alma mater. Pride kept me from doing it. "Why did you wait six months to come?"

"I've been busy getting Sam's estate in order. His poor wife is falling apart."

Wife? My father had been married. *Of course he had, idiot.* He'd lived a full life that didn't include me. "Does he have other children?" The question was out before I could rein it back.

"Two boys and a girl. Fourteen, twelve, and eight." Wallace beamed when he talked about Sam's kids. The legitimate ones. He must have realized he was acting a mite insensitive because when he looked at my face, he sobered. "We can talk about all that some other time. Holly, I'll admit my main reason for being here is to meet you, but I have a personal favor to ask, as well."

My heart, so hopeful a moment before, fell to my stomach. Of course he needed something. Why else would he be here? A powerful enchanter suddenly had a hankering to meet the illegitimate granddaughter who turned out wrong? Not likely.

I pulled my hand from his and placed it in my lap. "What do you want?"

His white brows lowered at my blunt tone. "I know you must feel cheated, but your grandmother, Eloise, she took good care of you?"

I stared at him with an unflinching gaze. Yes, Gran had taken perfect care of me. Had gone above and beyond. But he wasn't here to make sure I was okay. So I asked again. "What do you want from me?"

"There's been a murder here, a young witch about your age. Her name was London Sanders, and her family and ours go back a ways. She died by touching a cursed object." He placed his hand on the walking stick, stroked the polished wood with one finger.

"Dark magic?" I asked.

"The darkest. This type of curse requires blood. A lot of it. No one's been able to touch the amulet. They're afraid it might still be active. That's where you come in. I want you to nullify the amulet and avail yourself to Investigator McAllister. The scene's been left in stasis. It's going on two weeks now, and he doesn't have a single lead. We need to give this girl's parents a measure of peace."

I suddenly knew the truth. This witch mattered more to him than I did. I didn't like being played, and I had a zero tolerance policy for bullshit. "You're not here to meet me at all. You never would have bothered if this situation hadn't popped up."

"Of course I would have." His honeyed voice sounded so sincere. "You're family."

"Why should I help you? What have you and the mighty Dumahls ever done for me? Or for my Gran? You may not have known about me, but Samuel apparently did." Until three minutes ago, I didn't even know my own father's name. Pain, familiar and sharp, slashed at my insides, tried to claw to the surface. I tapped it down, let the anger wash over me instead. How dare this old man come here and ask me for a favor. He and his whole enchanter clan could go to hell. I didn't want anything to do with him.

"Holly." He leaned forward. "We can't go back and change the past. We can only move forward from here."

"Oh? Great. I'm all about moving forward. What should I bring to the Dumahl Thanksgiving dinner?"

He opened his mouth, then closed it just as quickly.

"Yeah, I didn't think so." I jerked on the door handle again with the same frustrating result.

"I could find your mother for you."

His words stilled my frantic movements.

"I know she disappeared right after your birth. I have money, resources."

My heart stuttered. Hope sparked to life once again.

When she was nineteen, my mother was supposed to be in college, studying romance languages and playing beer pong on the weekends. Instead, she got knocked up with me. My poor Gran didn't have a clue until Brianna showed up one night, cradling me in her arms. The next morning, she was gone. Like disappeared-off-the-face-of-the-earth gone.

Gran tried everything to find my mother. Because I obliterated all her magic, Gran couldn't perform any rituals or spells herself, so she sought out other witches, psychics, and even trackers. When that didn't work, she broke down and hired Normal private detectives. Years of searching yielded nothing, not one clue. It was as if my mother had vanished into thin air.

"In exchange for your help with this murdered girl," Wallace said, "I'll do everything I can to find your mother."

I let go of the handle and glanced at him. "And all I have to do is nullify the amulet?"

Pursing his lips, he tilted his head to one side. "Yes, and assist Cade. This murder must be solved. Quickly."

"Solved?" I echoed. "I'm not an investigator. I don't know anything about solving murders and working cursed…whatevers."

"Cade's getting nowhere on this. He won't like your interference—he'll fight you. But this murder, there's something different about it."

Agitated, I shifted in the seat. "I don't know what you expect me to do."

"People aren't talking to Cade, but they might talk to you."

I laughed, but it sounded loud and off to my own ears. "Others hire me—grudgingly—but they're not going to answer questions about a dark magic curse."

His look was appraising. "I think they will. You're just a null. They'll have nothing to lose by talking to you. Speak to the girl's friends, ask if she had any enemies. Report it all back to Cade, and he'll take it from there. Do we have a deal?"

Yeah, we did. On one condition. "I want your oath that you won't stop searching until you find my mother." As a girl, I used to dream about her coming home to live with Gran and me. We'd be a family. I thought that dream had died a long time ago, but Wallace's offer made me realize it never really left. This dead witch's parents wanted peace? Well, I wanted that for Gran, too. She'd been in limbo about Brianna for far too long. She deserved some closure.

Wallace stared into my eyes for a moment. "I give you my solemn, binding oath. If you help Cade solve this case, I'll do everything in my considerable power to find your mother."

Others took their vows seriously. Being an oathbreaker was a punishable offense—probably not against a null—but it gave me some slight assurance that he'd keep his word. "Fine. I'll do it." *For Gran.*

Reaching into his jacket's inner pocket he withdrew a silver case, and from it, handed me an embossed card with his name and number. "It was a pleasure meeting you, Holly. I look forward to getting to know you better."

"Sure you do."

"You may not believe it, my dear, but it's true." Wallace rapped his knuckles on the window three times, and McAllister opened the car door.

I hopped out and marched toward my house, clamping onto Wallace's card so tightly, it crumpled between my fingers. I noticed the sorcerer had gone back to shut my front door. I'd have called it considerate if he hadn't already hauled me over his shoulder, caveman style.

McAllister silently followed me. I strode inside, and when I tried to slam the door in his face, his hand shot out to keep it from closing.

"I'll pick you up at eight tomorrow morning." His gaze flicked down my body. "Don't keep me waiting."

CHAPTER TWO

At seven-thirty the next morning I paced the living room, fueled on coffee and nerves. Wallace had mentioned that the murder scene had been left in stasis. Frozen in time. That meant a dead body.

Needless to say, I hadn't gotten much sleep the night before. Between my apprehensions about seeing a corpse, thinking about my dead father who never once contacted me, and the need to find my missing mother—I tossed and turned.

Plus, I had to face the sorcerer again.

McAllister was hard to read. With that harsh, impassive face and imposing height, he made me antsy. And while I was used to dealing with Others, I did it on my terms, not theirs.

When he arrived a few minutes early, I smoothed my hands over my hips. I'd decided to wear my office clothes—a navy pencil skirt and a white, frilly sleeveless blouse. It made me feel professional, more in control. It was an illusion, but I clung to it.

When I opened the door, the wall of heat and humidity almost took my breath away. McAllister wore the same clothes from the night before. His five o'clock shadow was now more beard than stubble. I could feel his eyes, hidden behind sunglasses, dancing along my body. Not that he gave any indication he liked what he saw.

"There's been another murder. Let's go." He turned, walking to his pickup.

"Wait!" I shut the door behind me and struggled to keep up. "What do you mean there's been another murder? Like a cursed amulet murder?"

Stopping, he watched me over the truck's black hood. "No, like a cursed grimoire murder. This one's relatively fresh, so hop to it."

"Am I going to have to nullify the spell book, too?"

"That's the idea."

Two dead bodies in one day. I swallowed the lump in my throat and attempted to get into the truck.

Stepping onto a Ford 150 running board in a pair of three-inch heels was a challenge. Then I had to finagle my way inside because the narrow skirt didn't want to cooperate. "Who's the victim? This is related to the first murder, right?"

He sighed as I wriggled, lifting my ass to adjust the skirt for the third time. "Are you almost done?"

I refrained from snapping at him—barely—and buckled my seat belt. "Fill me in. Is this another witch we're talking about?"

"Yes. Stephanie Carson, aged twenty-seven. Satisfied?"

"At least tell me how they died? By simply touching the amulet and grimoire? Or is there more to it than that?" I stared at him, but he kept his profile to me. That scar taunted me. Why had he kept it? "Have you traced the cursed items to their source?"

"You're going to be one giant pain in my ass, aren't you?" He backed out of the drive.

"Most likely. So, where did the cursed objects come from?"

One hand on the wheel, he reached beneath his glasses with the other and rubbed his eyes. "The items were wrapped in plain brown paper. No postage."

"Hand-delivered?" I asked.

"Apparently. Although none of this is your concern. You have one job, and it doesn't involve asking a million questions. You're here to nullify the objects, then stay the hell out of my way."

I wondered if he knew about my deal with Wallace. The old man told me to assist McAllister and help solve the murder. If the sorcerer had a problem with that, tough shit. I'd do just about anything to find my mother, and if that meant putting up with this foul-tempered investigator, it was a small price to pay. "Who wanted these girls dead?"

"No one."

"And yet they've been murdered. Ergo, *someone* wanted them dead."

"They were average witches, nothing special about them," he said more to himself than me. "If there was a motive, I sure as hell haven't been able to find it." That admission must have cost him. Cade McAllister came across as a guy who was very competent at his job. For him to admit he had no clues, no leads, he must be very frustrated. And desperate.

I dug into my sassy blue Botkier handbag and pulled out a pen and notepad. I wrote London Sanders' name at the top of the first page. "Who were London's friends?"

He glanced over at me. "I thought I was very clear about your role. You're not here to play detective, Null."

"That's not what Wallace said."

"I don't give a shit what Wallace said."

Time to set some parameters. "Let's get one thing straight, McAllister, I'm in this. And if you get in *my* way, I'll stick to you like Velcro, keeping close enough that you won't be able to perform any of your little magic tricks. Now, who were London's friends?"

He refused to answer my question and chose to grind his molars instead. Very mature. Well, if he didn't want to help me, I'd find out on my own. Somehow.

After fifteen minutes of uncomfortable silence, Cade turned into one of the most exclusive neighborhoods in Tulsa. The homes—estates almost—were built to impress.

"Whose house are we going to first?" I asked.

"London's."

"She must have been filthy rich. What did she do for a living?"

He offered no response as he pulled into a circular driveway, stopping behind a white van. I pressed my nose to the truck's window and glanced up. London Sanders had turrets, for God's sake.

"How far?" he asked.

"How far what?" I couldn't stop looking at the house. It was old-worldly with arches and thick wooden doors and an S-shaped clay tile roof.

"How close do you have to get to an object to nullify it?"

I tore my gaze from the mansion. "I don't really know. The stronger someone's power, the closer I have to be. For weaker Others, I can wipe them out at fifty yards. The same is probably true with spells. But once I've nullified a spell, it dies and has to be recast. Same goes for wards."

He rubbed his forehead. "I felt my powers leave when I stepped onto your porch." Fifteen feet. McAllister was very powerful. Quelle surprise.

He moved to get out of the truck, and I did the same. "Stay right behind me," he said, "and don't touch anything. Your only job is to neutralize the amulet, got it?"

I stopped, placing a finger near my bottom lip. "Gee, I don't know, it sounds so complicated. Can you go over it one more time? My tiny brain is having trouble with the concept."

He bent down and got in my face. "Do you think this is funny? Two girls are dead." He stretched out his arm and pointed at the house. "One of them is in there right now."

That took the piss out of me, and I was immediately contrite. "You're right. Sorry."

He strode toward the front door, removing his sunglasses and tucking the earpiece into the collar of his shirt. Feeling a little green around the gills, I slowly followed him.

When we stepped inside, he pointed at me. "Stay here. I'll call you if I need you."

So I stood there alone, in a dead woman's entryway. Foyer? What did really rich people call it? Whatever the name, it was covered in gray and white marble. Green shadows flickered along the walls and floor. I took off my sunglasses and tilted my head back, looking up two stories to an enormous, round stained glass window set into the roof. A tree with differing shades of green and yellow leaves, surrounded by a pale blue glass sky. Beautiful.

"You must be the null I've heard so much about. Nice to meet you."

I lowered my gaze to a man in his fifties with gray tufts of hair shooting around his head in a horseshoe pattern. He wore white paper coveralls and nerdy glasses.

"I'm Herbert Novak, MME. It's such a pleasure." He grabbed my hand and gave it a few hearty pumps. "This is absolutely fascinating. I thought you might have to touch an object to nullify it, but Cade assured me that your mere presence does the trick."

"MME?" I tried to subtly pull my hand away. Herbert wasn't having it and held on tight.

"Medical and Magical Examiner," he said. "It's a blend of science and magic. I'd love to explain it in further detail."

Cade emerged from the hallway and walked toward us. "Quit flirting, Herb. And you, Null, I need you closer to the amulet. I'm still getting a charge from it."

Herbert smiled at me and took two steps forward, right into my personal space. He must have had onions for dinner because his bad breath had me holding mine. "I want to get to know you better," he whispered as if Cade couldn't hear him from a foot away. "I have so many questions."

"Herb." McAllister made it sound like a warning.

Herb unzipped his coveralls and, reaching into his shirt pocket, pulled out a card. He pressed it into my hand before hightailing it down the hall. Once he was out of sight, I tucked his card away then wiped my palm on my skirt. Very creepy guy.

"The spell on the amulet is a powerful one," Cade said. "You're too far away."

I took a deep breath and nodded. I really didn't want to go anywhere near the murder victim.

We followed Herbert down the hallway. I glanced into each room we passed—two bedrooms, a bath, an office—and tried not to think about the fact that London Sanders was lying dead in one of them.

Cade stopped outside the last door. "Let me check it out. If this doesn't work, you're going to have to go in."

I stared at his Adam's apple. "Sure." *Please let it work.*

Cade left me and entered the room. I waited, my mouth dry, my heart beating rapidly.

He popped his head out a moment later. "The amulet's still hot. Come inside."

I gripped the strap of my bag a little tighter and, step by halting step, walked into a large bedroom. McAllister stood on the far side of the sleek, four-poster bed, looking down. Herbert and some other coveralled guy stood close to the headboard, six feet away from the sorcerer. I knew what lay between them. The witch's body.

I gazed down at McAllister's foot. Next to it, a pale hand gripped the amulet.

I shut my eyes for a minute, took a deep breath, then opened them. Her nails were painted neon pink and looked frivolous in comparison to the worn, carved silver. A thumb-sized, oval bloodstone rested in the center of the pendant.

I forced myself to look away, take in the room. Two photos in silver frames stood on the bedside table. The black and white shot of a couple in wedding attire appeared to be from the nineteen-twenties. Her grandparents maybe? The second pic was probably London with her parents. She must have been about six or seven with light brown hair and a bright smile that showed off two missing upper teeth. That little girl was gone. Murdered.

This was no longer just an anonymous witch. London Sanders had a life, friends, a family who loved her. It was too awful. I started growing a little dizzy.

"Null."

I flinched at McAllister's harsh tone and snapped back into the moment. Since I was oblivious to all magic, I didn't know if I'd nullified the amulet or not. "Am I done here?"

"Step into the hallway so I can get a read on it. I'll let you know if you need to come back."

Taking a deep breath, I nodded and scampered out of the room. I stood next to the bathroom door and placed my palm against my heated cheek, praying the amulet was inert.

"You're good," Cade called out. "It finally worked." I breathed a sigh of relief. "Now, go wait for me in the truck." He dismissed me like I was irrelevant. No word of thanks. No acknowledgment that this had been a gruesome job. Just a command to wait outside in the brutal heat. McAllister was beginning to work my last nerve.

I slowly made my way to the front door and leaned against it for a moment, letting it hold me up. I just needed a second to feel steady again. As I stood there, my gaze flitted around the foyer. That's what I'd decided on. Foyer, not entryway. A small ornately carved credenza stood along one wall. It was obviously an old piece. I pushed off the door and walked to it, trailed one finger along the flower etched into the wood.

I peeked over my shoulder to make sure I was alone and pulled open the doors. Inside was a pen, a pad of paper, and a basket filled with disposable footies. Hmm, London was a neat freak who didn't want people to wear shoes in her pristine mansion. Not exactly a clue.

I figured I may as well snoop in a few more rooms since I was here. Perhaps McAllister had overlooked something. And what would he do if he found me snooping? Scowl harder?

I peeked into the tastefully decorated formal living room on the right. The cream armless chairs and modern black sofa screamed money. Not one personal item in the room.

I moved on to the kitchen. It was spacious and made me want to cook, even though I hate cooking. Aged, white cabinets reached to the ceiling. A huge island took up most of the space. Stainless appliances and black granite countertops gleamed. Dust must not accumulate under a stasis spell. I wished for the millionth time I could do magic, but shoved the thought out of my mind and began opening cabinets. Not much in the way of food. Rice cakes. Cans of soup.

In the adjacent family room, I found a DVR in a mahogany cabinet, along with the remote control. The only unusual thing about London was her lack of shit. There was nothing here, nothing personal, nothing cluttered. Maybe McAllister had cleaned it all out. But then why leave photos on the bedside table?

As I walked back to the foyer, I heard voices drifting from the hallway. While McAllister was occupied, I decided to check out the second floor. As quietly as I could, I snuck up the thickly carpeted steps and repeated my search. More nothing. Not one item out of place.

Then I walked into an empty bedroom with ultra-white walls. It was completely bare except for the circled pentagram painted on the hardwood floor. This was obviously where she practiced her craft. Had Cade taken away all of her paraphernalia?

London was quite a puzzle. There was no evidence that anyone else lived in this huge house. The place was beautifully decorated and immaculately clean, but sterile, like a model home.

I crept out of the room and headed toward the top of the stairs, but I was too late. Herbert Novak and the other man pushed a gurney loaded with a body bag into the foyer. I paused on the landing, nausea welling up inside me. I'd been sneaking through this dead woman's house while these men were taking care of her body. It felt wrong.

From the bottom step, Cade glared up at me. He didn't say anything as I descended. Then he opened the door so Herbert and his companion could remove London from the house. When they cleared the door, Cade slammed it shut and strode toward me.

"What did I tell you?" That husky voice dropped a notch.

"The empty bedroom upstairs, that's where she practiced?"

His lips compressed into a straight line. "No," he ground out. "And this isn't your business."

"But there was a pentagram on the floor."

He rubbed his eyes and tilted his chin in the air as he addressed the stained glass skylight. "What the hell did I do to deserve this shit?"

"I don't know who you're talking to, McAllister, but maybe you should ask for patience. And better communication skills. And maybe a razor."

He lowered his head, watching me through narrowed eyes. "There was no aura in the room with the pentagram."

He pointed toward the stairs. "No signature, no indication that she'd done any magic there."

"I never knew magic had a signature." I thought I knew most everything about Others. Gran had taught me from an early age. Normal kids listened to fairy tales. I listened to Other tales. But being able to see a magical signature? That was pretty cool. "What exactly does it look like?"

"Like magic," he bit out.

Mr. Helpful. I glanced around the foyer once again. "So, if she didn't practice upstairs, where did she practice?"

He hesitated before answering. "From the beginning, I've only detected one signature in the entire goddamned house, and it didn't belong to London. The woman who found her body attempted to cast a healing spell. Other than that, this place is clean."

That didn't make sense. Witches practiced. And not only practiced, they performed magic for simple, everyday tasks. It'd be impossible for London not to have left some kind of trace. "So what does that mean?"

"I don't know. Yet. And by the way"—he walked toward me until his broad chest touched my chin, forcing me to crane my neck to look into his eyes—"when I tell you to go to the truck, you'd better damn well do it."

"Or what?" That exotic scent hit me again. I ignored it.

"Or I'll tie your ass up and toss you there myself. Rule number one." He held a finger in front of my face. "Don't fuck with the evidence." Then he spun and stomped out of the house.

As far as I could see, he didn't have any evidence. I hoped McAllister had performed all of his spells and rituals before I arrived on the scene. That healing spell he talked about—the one cast by the person who'd found London's body—I'd wiped out that signature permanently.

I took a final glance around. London's place was empty as if she'd never practiced the craft. I didn't know what it meant, but I found it interesting.

Walking back to the truck, I noticed a lawn service van parked across the street. I wished I could afford a lawn service. In this drought, my yard looked like crap.

As gracefully as I could manage, I climbed into the cab. It took a few minutes to situate myself.

McAllister impatiently tapped his fingers on the steering wheel, but he turned his head toward me, watching as the skirt inched its way up my thighs. "Next time, wear pants."

I batted my eyelashes. "Oh golly, Sorcerer, you mean we get to do this again?" As I fastened my belt, he did what he did best. Ignored me.

CHAPTER THREE

Stephanie Carson's house sat on a quiet, residential street with mature trees and charming homes. Her place wasn't palatial as London's had been, but with pale yellow paint and white trim, it was cozy.

McAllister parked at the curb. "Got a call about the victim after I left you last night. She's been dead for a few days. We searched the house, but haven't been able to touch the body because of the grimoire." I shuddered at his words. I really didn't want to know what "dead for a few days" looked like. "Why don't you stay put? We'll see if you can nullify the book from here."

"Yeah. Good idea." I was more than happy to avoid dead bodies, even if that meant I couldn't search the house. I hadn't found anything in London's, probably wouldn't find anything here either. Good theory. I was sticking to it.

He left the truck's engine running, and I watched him disappear inside before switching on the radio. Turns out the sorcerer was a classic rock fan—Van Halen, the David Lee Roth years. I was fiddling with the scan button when a knock on the window almost made me leap out of my skin.

Clutching my heart I hit the window button, and hot air filled the cab. "Jeez, Sorcerer, you scared me."

"You're going to have to get closer to the grimoire."

"Like how much closer?" I asked.

"As close as it takes. Now let's go." Cade opened the door for me, and as I scampered down, I stumbled a bit.

He reached out and caught hold of my upper arm to keep me from falling. His knuckles brushed the side of my breast. His grazing touch sent an unexpected shiver through me. I wasn't sure why I reacted that way, but I didn't like it. I jerked out of his grasp and hustled off the grass and onto the sidewalk.

"You all right?" he asked.

"Let's just get this over with."

"You don't have to go inside," he said, keeping pace with me up the walkway, "just step onto the porch. That should work."

I nodded, staring straight ahead. "Yep."

The same white van that had been at London's place sat in the driveway. We passed it, and eight rose bushes, flanking either side of the front path.

McAllister stood at the door while I placed one foot on the porch then immediately made a U-turn. I was almost to the truck when Cade's voice stopped me mid-stride.

"Stay there. Let me see if it worked this time."

Please work.

I heard the door creak open, but kept my back to the house.

"Sorry." His voice was gruff. "You're going to have to come inside. I can still sense the spell. It's stronger than the one on the amulet."

Everything in me wanted to bolt. I squared my shoulders, and before facing him, donned my tough girl mask that got me through numerous unpleasant Other events—like that horrible *quinceañera* where the clairvoyant birthday girl decided to beat me instead of the piñata filled with twenty dollar bills.

"No problem." I retraced my steps. "I've seen dead bodies before." *At funerals.* I had to walk past him to cross the threshold. I was very careful about not touching him.

The front door opened directly into a small living room where Stephanie Carson lay sprawled in the middle of the floor. The smell of decay hit me, and I stifled a gag.

With large, filmy eyes, she stared through me. I covered my mouth with one hand, staggering backward into the sorcerer's chest.

McAllister gripped my elbow. "Easy," he whispered. "You're not going to faint on me, are you?"

I shook my head. Somewhere in my brain, I noted that Herbert Novak and his companion weren't in the room. Just the sorcerer, the dead witch, and me.

"Why don't you touch the book, just to make sure it's inactive? Then you can leave."

Biting my lower lip, I moved forward with halting steps. McAllister held onto my arm, which I found comforting. Bending down, I hesitantly reached out and barely brushed the cracked, leather-bound cover. Narrow with thick, off-white pages, the spell book was obviously very, very old.

I tried hard to focus on the grimoire and not the dead girl who clutched it. I failed. Wearing a white t-shirt, jean shorts, and cork-heeled wedges, she would have looked adorable if her skin hadn't been grayish or her lips blue. On the floor next to her lay an open white cardboard box and the brown paper wrapping McAllister had talked about. No postage, he'd said.

I stood, and he pulled me backward to the front door. Yet I couldn't quit staring into those dead, unseeing eyes.

Suddenly I pivoted, pushed past him, and ran out of the house. For once the scorching temperature was a welcome distraction. It helped me concentrate on something other than Stephanie Carson's body. I watched the waves of heat shimmer off the road. Even with the sun beating down on me, I shivered.

The screen door behind me banged shut, and a hand squeezed my shoulder. "You all right, Little Null?"

McAllister asked, his voice close to my ear. His compassion surprised me.

I cleared my throat. "Yeah." I removed my sunglasses from the top of my head and shoved them on my nose. Then I stepped away from him. "How much longer are you going to be here?"

"I'll take you home. There's no need for you to stick around."

I walked with him to the truck. This time, he actually opened the door and helped me inside. Then he slid in the driver's seat and stared out the windshield. "I know it's hard, seeing a body like that. But you did okay, Null. You handled it."

I wasn't feeling enough like myself to offer a sarcastic retort, so I just nodded.

Stephanie's house was ten minutes from my own. My brain sort of shut down on the drive, but once McAllister parked in my driveway, I turned to him. "Who discovered the body?"

"Her boss notified us when she didn't show up for work two days in a row. We think she's been dead between forty-eight to seventy-two hours."

"Is there a magical signature in Stephanie's house, or was her place clean, too?"

"What does it matter?" He rubbed at his jaw, his hand lingering over the scar. "You're out of this as of right now."

Of course I wasn't. I was his little helper whether he wanted me or not. It wasn't just about finding my mother anymore. Not completely. From the moment I'd looked into Stephanie Carson's eyes, this felt personal. If these girls' friends would talk to me, give me a clue as to who sent the cursed objects, I'd sleep a little better at night.

I had more questions, but McAllister would simply ignore me, so I didn't waste time asking them. "It's been real, Sorcerer." I opened the truck door and hopped out.

I'd like to say I exited gracefully. But that'd be a lie.

#

Growing up, Gran taught me everything about Others and the powers they wielded. I didn't comprehend when I was little, but as soon as I could read, I pored over her grimoires. I'd ask her repeatedly why I couldn't whip up a potion or cast a spell. She was always very patient with me. *"You're a null, Hollyhocks, there's no magic in you. You're more precious than magic."*

I grew up in a smallish town devoid of Others. Throughout grade and middle school, I was obsessed with softball, hanging with my best friend, Rita, and Tommy Bridgerton—the cutest boy in my class. Once puberty struck, all I wanted was a coveted spot on the pep squad and a dose of popularity. Gran and I didn't talk about my mother much anymore, but her absence was always there, like a specter hovering over every holiday, every birthday. I knew Gran continued her search, we just didn't discuss it.

At college, I encountered Others for the first time. I didn't realize what they were, of course—everyone looks like a Norm to me. Never would have known if they hadn't taunted me, spat at me, and yelled "go home, null bitch" every time I walked by. There were only a few hundred out of thousands, but I seemed to encounter them everywhere.

I couldn't even go to a party without causing trouble. Other girls used glamours to spackle over the freshman fifteen and bad skin. Telepathic creeps misused their powers of compulsion to mindfuck girls at parties—like a mystical roofie. But the moment I entered the room, my anti-magic incinerated all spells. That didn't exactly make me the most desirable girl on campus.

There were even a few physical fights, but I gave as good as I got. Those four years toughened me up. Made me stronger. Others feared me because I took away everything that made them special. Can you imagine possessing supernatural powers your whole life, then having them disappear in an instant? It downright pissed them off.

By the time I graduated, I understood why they hated me.

And for every vicious thing they'd done to me, I hated them back. Now when they came to me for help, it gave me a sense of smug satisfaction. The fact that my personal assistant, Sunny, charged through the nose for my services didn't suck either.

But right now, I had nothing but empathy for these Other girls. No one deserved to die the way London and Stephanie had. It was horrible, senseless. What had happened to them was evil. I desperately wanted to find the bastard who'd cursed them. However, since Cade wasn't going to cooperate with me, I'd have to figure it out on my own.

I kicked off my shoes and booted up my laptop. When I Googled London's name, the first hit was a New Age shop on the east side of town called Blessed Be. The website showed a pic of a blonde standing next to a woman with a wild mane of curls. The caption read *Owners London Sanders and Jasmine True*. I trailed my finger over London's face. Long blonde hair. Perfect skin. Infectious smile. She'd been a knockout.

The second hit turned up a social networking site. I navigated around and found a picture of London and a girlfriend at a nightclub. They held cocktails and, with glazed eyes, smiled into the camera. The girlfriend was tagged as Tamara Dermot. With a little more searching, I found her home number and address.

I searched for Stephanie Carson but didn't get as many hits. She had a membership to a lone social site which was closed to public viewing. I couldn't find anything else other than her addy, which I already knew.

So, London it was.

I called the New Age store first. I'd heard of Blessed Be. They sold crystals, tarot cards, and love spells to the Norms, but carried real deal items for Others in the back.

"Blessed Be, this is Jasmine speaking."

"Hi, my name is Holly James." There was no way to break the news gently, so I jumped in with both feet. "I was wondering if I could ask you a few questions about London Sanders. I'm looking into her death."

There was a very long pause. "I know who you are. You're that null who hires herself out like a party clown. Fuck off." She hung up.

Blessed Be yourself, bitch. I hit redial. When she picked up, I didn't wait for her to answer. "We can meet at Starbucks, or I can come to your shop. I'll permanently wipe out every magical item you have. Your choice."

She gasped, but still didn't speak.

"This is a limited time offer," I said.

"You can't do that. The Council—"

"The Council hired me." Okay, that was a bit of an exaggeration. My newly found grandfather, who happened to be a Council member, wanted me to ask a few questions. Same dif.

"Fine," she said, "I'll meet you in half an hour on South Yale."

I hung up and entered Tamara Dermot's home number into my phone before changing out of my skirt and into shorts, an orange top, and a pair of sandals. Then I walked back outside into the sweltering heat and drove toward the center of town.

When I arrived at Starbucks, it was filled to capacity, but I spotted the woman from the *Blessed Be* website at a table near the window. She was around my own age, maybe a little older. Tight brown ringlets fell to her bare shoulders, and the blue peasant blouse showed off her cleavage. Her features were overly large for her long, narrow face. Her attitude toward me had been less than pleasant, so I was disinclined to like her on sight.

As soon as I walked in, she looked bewildered, as if she'd forgotten something important. I skirted over to her table. "Hi, you must be Jasmine."

"My power is gone." Her brown eyes widened. "I thought what they said about you was all bullshit, but it's true."

"Yep. Hence the term null." I parked in a chair across from her and tugged the notebook and pen from my purse. I decided to skip the coffee and get right down to business. "So, you and London were partners?"

"Will I get my powers back or have I lost them forever?" There was an edge of panic in her voice.

"It's only temporary. The sooner you answer my questions, the sooner you can get out of here. You'll be feeling like your witchy little self in no time. London?" I prodded.

She took a deep breath. "Right, London is...was my business partner in Blessed Be."

"Who found her body?"

She blinked. "I thought you said you worked for the Council. Shouldn't you already know this?" She had a tone. A snotty, Other tone.

I pinned her with a glare. "I'm going over everything again. Starting with the basics. Now, who found her?"

"I did. If you don't mind, I really don't want to talk about that day. It was awful."

I immediately grew contrite. Maybe she had a reason to be bitchy. She'd just lost her partner in a very gruesome way. My voice softened. "I'm sorry. I can't pretend to know how hard this is for you, but please walk me through it."

She took a gulp of coffee, then looked down at the table and nodded. "She didn't show up for work Friday. I tried calling her several times, but I kept getting her voicemail. After closing, I went to her house and used the key she'd given me." She paused and inhaled deeply. "London was in her bedroom. Dead. Clutching this old amulet. I cast a healing spell, but she was already gone. No aura, no signs of her life force. Just…gone."

"Had you ever seen the amulet before?"

"No." She stared out the window.

"How did you know not to touch it?"

"I don't know. I don't remember touching anything. I just ran out of the house and called her parents."

If Jasmine were a Norm, I'd have reached out and patted her hand, but I knew she wouldn't appreciate my attempts at consolation. She'd made her feelings about me pretty clear. I waited her out.

"Anything else or can I go?" she asked.

"Did she have any enemies?"

"None that I know of."

London obviously had at least one enemy. A deadly one. "What about boyfriends, frenemies, or anyone who wanted to harm her?"

Jasmine's eyes shifted left before drifting back to mine. Hello. Total lie coming up. And I didn't even need psychic powers to catch it, just Psych 101.

"No, everyone loved her." With her thumbnail, she flicked the edge of her plastic lid.

"You're lying. Someone wanted to hurt her. Enough to use blood magic. Don't you want to help catch the son of a bitch who did this?"

"Yeah, I do." She rolled her lips inward. "You didn't hear this from me, agreed?"

"Agreed."

"London broke up with her boyfriend about six or seven weeks ago. He was pretty pissed about it. He's the only person who had a grudge against her."

"Who is he? Was he angry enough to kill her?"

"James Sharpe, but I doubt he killed her. He sure wouldn't use blood magic at any rate," she said with a scoff.

"Why is that? Is he a Norm or something?"

She curled her lip. "Yeah, like London would ever date a Norm. James Sharpe is a vampire, okay? He wouldn't kill her by sending a cursed object."

Jasmine threw it out there like it wasn't huge news, but dating a vamp was a big, honking deal. All the vamps I'd met—not that many, but still—they were really old, set in their ways, and very territorial. Once a vamp marked you, you were his bitch forever. Plus, their mojo was stronger than most witches'. They could turn you into a virtual slave with their voice alone. I shuddered. London not only dated one, she'd dumped him. That took balls. Had it also gotten her killed?

I leaned across the table and whispered, "That's some serious shit. Why would she do that? Risk tying herself to a vampire for the rest of her life?" Witches lived a long time. Not as long as vamps, but a witch's lifespan could last centuries. We were talking major commitment.

Jasmine leaned as far away from me as she could manage. "That was typical London."

I straightened. "Did her family know?"

"Are you serious? Of course not, and I don't want them to find out. They'd be devastated. Again. London had a history of making really bad decisions. Anyway, James wanted her back, not dead."

"Had he already marked her?" That mystical bond could easily be detected by Others. At least that's what Gran said. If London had been marked, surely her friends and family would have seen the evidence with their own eyes.

Jasmine shook her head, and her springy curls bounced. "No, she wouldn't let him. But he was constantly pressuring her. A few weeks after London broke up with him, he almost drained her. She wouldn't go to the hospital. She wouldn't even let me call a more powerful witch to help cast healing spells. She nearly died."

"Did you mention this to McAllister?"

"The investigator?" She hesitated. "Look, I told you, I don't think James did this. He would have just killed her outright. Besides, I don't want to get involved. Don't let anyone know you got his name from me. The last thing I need is to be on a vamp's radar."

"Did you know Stephanie Carson?" I flipped through my notebook and wrote her name at the top of a page. When I glanced up, Jasmine stared at me with her mouth wide open.

"What? What do you mean?"

I'd handled this badly. I'd blurted it out instead of easing into it. "She's dead, Jasmine. I'm sorry. How did you know her?"

"Dead? She came into the store last week."

"Was she a customer? A friend?"

"Customer. Not a frequent one." She rubbed a hand over her mouth. "But she was really nice. What happened?"

I wasn't sure how much I should tell. Cade might want to keep the details to himself. "Her death is suspicious." That's the best I could come up with, and it was lame.

"Did she die like London? A cursed amulet?" Her voice was faint, and she paled, making the freckles scattered across the bridge of her nose seem more pronounced.

"No. Not like London." Not a complete lie.

She pushed back from the table. "Are we done here?"

"Yeah," I said absently, then glanced down at my notes. "Wait, no. What do you mean when you said London had a habit of making bad decisions?"

Jasmine rose from her chair and grabbed her drink. "I met with you, and I gave you a name. Now leave me alone." She squeezed past two moms with strollers and marched out the door.

I wrote James Sharpe's name on my to-do list. So I was going to have to find and question a vamp. Gee, that didn't sound like a suicide mission. Of course he couldn't drain me since my presence would give him a bad case of limp fang, but he could probably beat the ever-loving snot out of me.

I sighed. Deeply.

I watched Jasmine walk across the parking lot. As soon as she got about five or six yards away, I could tell my null powers stopped working. I didn't feel any different, but apparently she did. Her posture became straighter, and she lifted her face toward the sun. With confident steps, she strode to a yellow SUV, hopped in, and sped off.

CHAPTER FOUR

I decided to worry about the vamp later and instead called Tamara Dermot. She answered on the second ring. "'ello?" Sounded like she had a cold.

"Tamara? My name is Holly James. I'm looking into the death of London Sanders. For the Council," I added. I was almost starting to believe it myself.

"I've already talked to the investigator," she said with a sniff.

"I'm new to the case and trying to play catch up. Do you feel like meeting with me today?"

"Yeah, whatever."

Such enthusiasm made me feel all warm and tingly inside. She mentioned the name of an overpriced outdoor café. While I promised to meet her in half an hour, I also questioned her sanity, wanting to sit outside on a day like this. It was hotter than a by-God—Oklahoma speak for sweating your balls off.

The Saturday afternoon traffic was heavy and the heat merciless. Even with my air cranked up all the way, every time I idled at a red light the interior of the car warmed up.

I found a parking spot on the street a block from the café and hot-footed it—literally. The blacktop, sticky and melting from the high temps, jacked with the bottoms of my new sandals. Damn, now I'd tread tar everywhere I stepped.

Wilted and damp after the short walk, I scoped out the round tables shaded from the sun by green umbrellas. I spotted the woman tagged on London's social media page. She wore a pretty pink sundress and a sleek dark ponytail. As I approached, her brow furrowed, and she clutched her throat with one hand.

"Tamara?"

"Are you Holly? I knew your name sounded familiar. You're that null, aren't you?" she whispered the last bit. Then she rubbed a tissue against her raw, red nose.

"Yeah." I pulled out a chair and sat. I ordered iced tea with lemon from the waiter. Poor kid looked like he was melting in the heat, too.

"So I get 'em back right?" she asked when he walked away. "My powers? It's just a temporary thing?"

"Yeah."

"Do you want anything to eat?" she asked. An untouched iced coffee sat in front of her.

"No, it's too hot."

"It's weird that you called when you did. I've been crying over London all day. I miss her." Her brown eyes welled with unshed tears. "She was my best friend."

"How long had you known her?"

"Since we were babies. I can't remember not knowing her. We'd always been super tight until about a year ago. Around the same time she opened Blessed Be."

The waiter returned with my tea. I nodded a thanks and pulled out my notebook and pen. "What do you mean until a year ago? What happened to your friendship?"

She waved her soggy tissue in the air. "I don't know. She just started acting weird, like she had secrets or something. But I knew all her secrets, and I never judged. She started pulling away from me. And her aura...wait, you know what those are, right? They're like these pretty, sparkly colors that surround a person. I can't read yours since you took my magic and all."

Tamara was sweet—unusual for an Other—but not exactly a gold medal winner in the brainiac Olympics. "Yeah, I know what an aura is. What happened to London's?"

"She used to be bright blue, but it dimmed to this gray color, and then started getting darker. Dark gray is bad just so you know. I asked her all the time what was going on, but she denied anything was different."

"You must have some idea of what she was up to?"

She glanced toward the street, watched an SUV drive by. "London had a boyfriend—"

"James Sharpe?"

Her eyes flew to mine. "Oh, my gosh. How did you know?"

Jasmine had asked me to keep her name out of it. I'd honor her wish for as long as I could. "I can't reveal my sources."

Glancing at the few patrons at the other tables, she leaned toward me. "He wasn't the only person she was dating."

I bent my head closer. "Really? Who else?"

"A shifter."

I reared back in my chair. "Whoa."

Tamara nodded. "I know, right? But that was London for you." Shifters had a certain sexual reputation. Vanilla wasn't on the menu. They played rough and were even more possessive than vamps. Animal instinct, probably.

So, London had been dating a territorial shifter and a vamp that pressured her into taking his mark? If one found out about the other, all three of them might have ended up in a ménage-a-mangle.

"What the hell was she thinking? And who was the shifter? Do you know?"

"She wouldn't tell me his name. Look, London was a doll, but she had another side to her. She played games and got reckless. She fed on adrenaline. Sometimes—" She hesitated and swallowed like it was hard to reveal this about her friend. "Sometimes she'd get a little crazy at this certain club."

"The Raven?" It was the most popular Other hangout in town, a sort of neutral territory enforced not by magic, but by the owner, sorcerer Mick Raven. His zero-tolerance-for-bullshit attitude held most Others in check. I heard rumors about what happened at The Raven. It wasn't a place for sweet little witches with New Age shops, that was for damn sure.

"Well yeah, but other places, too. And she liked swap meets." She saw my frown and explained. "You know. Black sheep parties."

I shook my head. "Sorry, I'm still not following."

"Sex parties," she whispered. "From what little she told me, they sounded pretty hardcore. No safe words. I'm talking scary, nonconsensual stuff."

Apparently, London Sanders had a taste for living fast and wild. Interesting. "Where were these parties?"

"No idea. One of the many things she wouldn't share with me."

"What else can you tell me about her life? Anything might help."

Tamara played with the small diamond pendant resting in the hollow of her throat. "London was the center of everything. She was popular in school. Everyone liked her. She was smart. And she was a good witch, powerful." She raised her shoulders.

"What about these games she liked to play? What exactly was she into?"

Tamara nibbled her lips. "She liked bad boys. And she liked to be on display, you know. But sometimes she'd let things go too far. James almost killed her."

"On display?"

"She was an exhibitionist. There were a couple of times in the past few months when she got real moody and shut everyone out. She'd stay locked up in her house for days, wouldn't answer the phone, wouldn't let anyone inside. I had no idea what was going on with her."

"Was she into drugs?" That would explain a lot. The recklessness. Dating not just bad boys, but predatory Others. Shutting herself off when she needed a fix.

Tamara laughed. "Gosh, no. She was holistic."

"Then how do you explain the mood swings?"

"I can't. She wasn't always like that." Her eyes became clouded. "Something changed. I wish she would have talked to me."

"What about dating a vamp appealed to her?"

Tamara's face lost some of its sadness, and she smiled. "Said it was the best sex she ever had. When he took her blood during"—she rotated her hand—"*you know*, she almost passed out from pleasure."

More like blood loss. The thought of a vamp draining me during sex was repulsive. "What did she like about the shifter?"

"They have a rough reputation. London had bruises all over her body."

I frowned. "He beat her?"

She shook her head, and her ponytail slid across her neck. "Rough sex," she mouthed. "London was really into it."

I didn't understand that either. Everyone liked a little slap ass now and again, but bruises and exhibitionism? Getting sucked during the act? Not for this prudish null. London definitely had a couple of kinks. Especially if she kept the bruises instead of healing herself or using a glamour to cover over them. Jeez.

"I heard about another witch. Stephanie Carson?" I tried to use more tact this time, and not blurt it out the way I had with Jasmine.

Tamara twirled her ponytail around one finger. "Yeah, I know her. Sort of. What did you hear?"

"I'm sorry to have to tell you this, but she's dead."

"That's sad. How'd she die?" Her gaze drifted to a cute guy driving by on a motorcycle.

"Home accident. Were Stephanie and London friends?"

She looked back to me. "No. We never hung out with her. I've seen her around at Sabbat celebrations and inter-coven dinners. Stuff like that. But I think she mostly practiced solo."

I couldn't get a handle on Stephanie, so I went back to my original line of questioning. "What about London's other friends? Was there anyone else she might confide in?"

"No." Tamara grabbed the phone out of her bag, tapped the screen, and handed it to me. "These were taken a few weeks ago at her Summer Solstice party. That's the last time I saw her. If she didn't spill her secrets to me, she wasn't going to tell anyone else. I'm sure about that."

I scrolled through the pics of London and a group of people, both male and female, buck ass naked and covered in body glitter. London looked beautiful with a wreath of fresh flowers entwined in her hair.

"Who's this?" I showed her a pic of a blond guy with his arm wrapped around London's waist.

"That's Brant Braxton. He does our hair and makeup before every party. He's kind of amazing. We've known him forever."

"Would London have confided in Brant?" I gave her back the phone.

"No. Brant's a gossip. He's fun and all, but he can't keep a secret." Despite her doubts that London had taken Brant into her confidence, Tamara gave me his number.

"Was London close to Jasmine True? I didn't see her in any of the party pics you showed me."

Tamara rolled her dark eyes. "I can't remember if she was there that night. After a few glasses of honeyed wine,

I don't remember much. But Jasmine's a trip. She's very picky. I worked in the store when they first opened, but I couldn't take her. You shift a crystal two inches, and she's right behind you, moving it back in place."

"You don't like her?"

"No. I think she's a bitch, but she's a smart businesswoman. Blessed Be is booming."

I couldn't think of any more questions, so I said goodbye and packed it in for the day.

As I walked to the car, I checked my phone. Sunny left a message demanding details on the possum wedding. She was on my shit list since she hadn't told me about the cow pasture, so I didn't bother calling her back.

The second message was from Gran. I'd decided to put off talking to her for a bit longer, too. I didn't think I should mention the Wallace Dumahl situation. Even if my new-found grandfather used every resource he had, it didn't mean he'd find Brianna. I didn't want Gran to get her hopes up again.

The real problem was keeping all this Council business under my hat. Gran was a human lie detector. She'd know something was wrong the minute she clapped eyes on me. Since I was having brunch with her tomorrow, I'd have to come up with a plausible story and fast.

Once I got home, I tried to do a little research on Stephanie Carson and James Sharpe. I didn't find a thing on either one. Not so surprising in the vamp's case. They were very protective of their identities. Only a newbie or an idiot would plaster his business all over the internet. But not finding any info on Stephanie Carson irritated me. I even ran her name through the County Assessor site, looking for a deed to her house. Evidently, she was a renter.

I also checked out the Other club Tamara had talked about. You wouldn't know from The Raven's website that deadly Others played there. I pitied the Norms who wandered in unintentionally. Mick Raven's badass reputation would probably keep them safe—probably being the operative word.

I called The Raven and asked to speak to Mick. I was put on hold for ten minutes and tortured with house music until I finally gave up. Chances were, I'd have to show up at the club unannounced in order to get any information. Not the best case scenario, seeing as I wasn't a real big fan of getting my ass kicked by Others. Well, to be honest, I wasn't fond of getting my ass kicked by anyone.

Last, I tried Brant Braxton, leaving a brief message before zapping myself a frozen dinner. I wasn't hungry and wound up poking at the limp green beans with a fork, unable to get Stephanie Carson out of my head. Her still body, her cloudy eyes...I'd never forget it.

I'd just tossed my uneaten dinner in the trash when my phone rang. "Hello?"

"Good evening, Holly." Wallace's accented voice dripped with southern charm. He was good, the old man. That sweet tone, the slower cadence—I almost bought his concerned grandfather act. However, I suspected he wanted an update rather than a chit-chat. "How did you do today? You and Cade rubbing along all right?"

I flashed back to Cade's hand brushing the side of my breast. His touch had unsettled me. I was usually cucumber cool, not the type to get flustered over a guy. Why should the sorcerer be any different?

"Holly?"

"Um, yeah, today was fine. Amulet and grimoire deactivated."

"Grimoire? What on earth are you talking about?"

"Guess you haven't heard. They found another body last night. Stephanie Carson. She was killed by a cursed grimoire."

"Dear Lord," he said softly. "Are you talking to London's friends? Are you helping Cade solve this thing?"

"Yeah, I am, but I imagine it's going to take some time."

"We don't have much time. We need to find the person sending these items. Soon. Do you hear me?" The accent was still there, but the sugar had evaporated.

"Don't pressure me, Wallace. I'm doing the best I can."

"Of course you are, dear," he said, softening his tone. "I didn't mean to be so brusque. But these murders are a blight on our community. They can't remain unpunished."

"I have to go."

"I appreciate all you're doing. We'll talk again soon."

I hit the end button and laid the phone on the counter. I had no clue what I was doing, and little pep talks like that weren't going to turn me into an investigator.

To distract myself, I tidied up the house and sat down to watch a movie, but I couldn't focus. London Sanders had secret boyfriends and lived a triple life. Stephanie Carson was still a mystery. Their deaths must be related somehow. Same killer. Same cause of death. What tied the two girls together? Stephanie was a Blessed Be customer. Was it as simple as that?

Someone pounded on my front door, and I jumped. "Open up, Null."

Oh hell, not this again. I switched off the TV and walked to the door. Jerking it open, I stared at Cade McAllister. "What now?"

Shouldering past me, he advanced into my living room. With his hands propped on his hips, he openly took in his surroundings.

I glanced around my living room and liked what I saw. Light blue walls and mounds of throw pillows on the off white sofa. Vases of fresh flowers on side tables. It was home.

He spun and faced me. "Jasmine True. What the fuck?" That demanding alpha act wasn't going to work on me.

When I didn't answer, he began pacing behind the sofa, all the while rubbing his thumb along that mysterious scar.

"Come on in, McAllister. Make yourself at home." I shut the door and leaned against it.

He stopped pacing and pinned me with a glare. "Explain yourself."

I didn't think he'd leave until we had this out, so I crossed to a blue chintz chair and sat. "I asked her a few questions. What's your malfunction?"

"What was the one instruction I gave you today?" He held up his forefinger. "The. One. Instruction."

I gaped at him, momentarily dumbstruck. "Are you for real? You never stopped giving instructions, McAllister, so you'll have to be more specific. I'm not sure you're aware of it, but you are really bossy."

He worked the muscles in his jaw. "Rule number one: Don't fuck with the evidence. No one breaks rule number one. Especially short, little nulls who never shut up."

I sat back and affected a bored-to-death look. "First of all, a rule is not an instruction. It's more of a guideline. Also, short and little are the same thing. You're repeating yourself."

He stalked to my chair and towering over me, growled. He honest to God growled at me. "Jasmine True called my office and threatened to file a complaint against you."

I gasped. "Oh no! Not a complaint."

As his chest rapidly rose and fell, his eyes turned glacial. *Danger: Thin ice.*

"Fine." I held up my hands in surrender. "I won't talk to Jasmine anymore. Happy?" Besides, I didn't think she had anything else to tell me.

It took a few seconds, but he visibly relaxed. His lips tilted up ever so slightly at the corners. That passed for a smile in McAllister's world. "Good. You leave the detective work to me. You're not cut out for it."

I blinked. Twice. Did the sorcerer just talk down to me? "You're kind of a dick, McAllister. And why shouldn't I have a go at it? You haven't exactly been successful in this investigation."

His eyes never left my face. "Remember rule number one?"

"Have you checked out London's boyfriend?" I watched him closely. Except for the tiniest narrowing of his eyes, he didn't move.

"Tell me," he said.

So, the sorcerer didn't know about the vampire, James Sharpe. I splayed a hand on my chest. "But I'm just a simple null. What could I possibly know that you don't?"

His cool eyes shuttered for an instant, and the muscle in his jaw jumped. Without warning, he snatched me up by my shoulders; my toes barely skimmed the floor. Even without his powers, he was fast and dangerous. My heart quickened its pace to a gallop.

"You will tell me what you know." He looked intently into my eyes as if he were trying to impress his will on me.

I could feel my pulse fluttering at my throat like one of the moths at the front porch light. But if he thought he was going to intimidate me, he didn't know who he was dealing with. "Let me give you a tip, Sorcerer. Your little mind fucks don't work on me. You can try to enthrall me all day long, but I'm a null, remember?"

"I'm not known for my patience." His rough whiskey voice rolled over me.

"I'm not scared of you." *Like hell.* I was totally scared of him. But I'd buy a knockoff Fendi before I let him know it.

His hands squeezed my arms tighter. "You're hurting me," I said, calmly. I couldn't believe my tone sounded so reasonable because inside I was quivering like Gran's apple jelly. "Do you like it rough, Sorcerer?" I asked in a husky whisper.

Just as quickly as he'd plucked me up, he dropped me to my feet, though he didn't step back. With the chair grazing the backs of my knees, I didn't have anywhere to go. We stood there glaring at each other, our bodies barely touching.

"Now, do you want to trade information? Or do you want to keep acting like a jerk-off?" I raised my brows.

He said nothing, just continued to burn me with his icy hot gaze. "Tell me."

I sank back down in the chair. "Uh-uh. It's not going to work like that."

The scar stood in white relief against the dark stubble. For a minute there, I thought he might toss me across the room. Instead, with precise movements, he sat on the coffee table in front of me, his knees pressing against mine.

I flicked a hand in his direction. "You're going to tell me one thing you found out, and then I'll do the same. That's the deal."

I knew it was foolish to poke a bear, but when McAllister tried to intimidate me, all the horrible memories from college rose to the surface. I'd had my tires slashed, my room tossed, had been followed and harassed—two girls from a mountain lion shifter sorority jumped me. I broke one's nose and punched the other bitch in the throat before managing to get away. Those experiences turned me into a fighter. So backing down to this sorcerer? Not happening.

He took a deep breath and his wide chest rose. My gaze drifted toward the pecs outlined through his tight t-shirt and back up to his face.

"The amulet held traces of black magic," he said.

I shook my head. "I already knew that. Tell me something I don't know."

"That wasn't the deal," he ground out.

"It was implied."

"If I had my powers, I'd make you spill everything you know. I might leave your brain intact. If I was feeling generous."

This guy was too much. Sorcerers—so full of themselves. When you're capable of manipulating the powers of Others around you, it must go straight to your ego. I gave him a wry smile. "Moot point. Are you going to tell me something interesting or what?"

He looked like he was about to lose what little patience he had left. Crossing his arms, he glared at me. "Three weeks before her murder, London disappeared for a few days. No one knew where she went, and when she came back, she refused to tell anyone where she'd been. Now you."

"She dated a vampire who almost sucked her dry. I suspect it was around the same time she went missing. She was probably recovering."

His expression gave nothing away, but tension ran through him like a live wire jumping from his body to mine where our knees touched. "How do you know this?"

"Your turn," I said.

"She was a dabbler."

My jaw fell. "As in black magic?"

His chin lowered a fraction. I took that as a yes. "Go."

"Wait." I held up a hand. "You can't just drop that and not give an explanation. Besides, you said you couldn't see her magical signature or whatever. How do you know she was dabbling?"

He didn't move. Didn't blink.

I sighed. "Fine, she was also dating a shifter."

He dropped his arms and ran his hands over his legs. Back and forth, his tapered fingers slid across the faded denim. My eyes lingered on his thighs. They were as thick as tree trunks. "Fuck," he said.

"Yeah, they were doing that, too. That's a freebie." I threw him a saucy wink.

He gave me a black look. "How do you know this?" His voice became whisper soft. "Did Jasmine tell you?"

"Sorry, McAllister, it's your turn."

"Fuck turns." His nostrils flared.

"How do you know she was a dabbler?"

One truly pissed sorcerer sat before me. The atmosphere in the room felt explosive while I waited for him to speak. And waited. And waited.

"Look," I said, "you obviously need my help, and I could use some backup in my investigation." I knew I'd pushed him too far.

In one swift move, he pulled me off the chair and had me on the floor, his big, muscular body pinning mine. He felt almost feverish. Heat radiated off him, searing me. Our hips were flush, and his cock stiffened against my hip. "If you don't tell me everything—"

"You'll what?" I pushed against his chest, but he didn't budge. I left my hands where they were, and we stared into each other's eyes. Barely aware of what I was doing, I acted on instinct, my fingertips lightly tracing over his hard nipples. A shiver visibly ran through him. And I wasn't scared of him at all. On the contrary. My skin felt sensitive and tingly, anticipating his next move. "What will you do, Sorcerer?" I whispered.

He grabbed both my wrists in one of his large hands and held them above my head. Then leaning down, he spoke against my lips. "I'll make you beg for it."

CHAPTER FIVE

He kissed me, and my entire body sprang to life. The exotic scent that belonged only to Cade wrapped itself around me. Ensnared me. Made me want to rub myself against him.

His lips were firm, and when his tongue stroked mine, I responded, angling my head to give him better access. I tried to yank my wrists from his hand, but he was too strong. I didn't want to get away though. I wanted to touch him. I wanted to feel that scar on his cheek, run my lips over it, taste it.

Breathing hard, he pulled his mouth from mine and followed the seam of my lips with his thumb. I arched my back, letting my aching nipples rub over his chest. God, he felt good. So big. So hard.

Cade softly kissed his way across my chin, along my jaw. His stubble was coarse and scratchy, and I loved the sensation. Then he ran the tip of his tongue along the shell of my ear. When he ground his hips against mine and bit my earlobe at the same time, I almost shattered.

"Tell me everything you know, Little Null. I promise I'll make it good." It took a few seconds for that to register. But when it did, my ardor fled, and anger quickly slid in its place. Trying to sex me for info? That was low, even for Cade. This arrogant sorcerer was going to pay.

When I gazed up at him, my smile promised seduction and heat. My smile was such a liar.

I leaned up, and taking his chin between my teeth, gently bit down. He groaned in response. I dragged my lips down the column of this throat, over his colorful tattoo, and sucked on his salty skin. Then I nipped his neck, not so gently this time. Bucking his hips against me, he let me know just how much he liked it.

Yeah, I could take this jerk, make him putty in my hands. He'd be begging *me* by the time I was through with him. But I realized that if I played him, I'd be caught in the trap as well. I was too attracted to remain unscathed. Damn.

"Sorcerer," I whispered.

He looked down at me with glazed eyes, his heart pounding so hard, I could feel it between us.

"Go fuck *yourself* because I'm out of your league. I'm going to keep asking questions, and you can get on board or get left behind."

It took a few seconds, but as his eyes went from dreamy to hard, he released my hands. Raising his torso slightly, he leaned on his forearms and continued to stare into my eyes. "Two girls are dead. Do you want to be the third?"

I curled my fingers into claws, lightly ran them down his massive chest. "Cursed items don't affect me."

"A bullet to the head would."

"Are you threatening me, McAllister?" I dug my nails into his stomach.

He sucked in a breath and shifted his hips. His rigid cock prodded my upper thigh, causing me to dig my nails in a little deeper. "Just stating a fact. You're human. You're fragile. This is a murder investigation. I don't want you to get hurt."

This sorcerer, an Other, was worried about me. Something in my heart broke open. Just a crack, but it felt like a fault line had shifted. I wrapped my arms around his back, stroked his broad shoulders, felt his defined muscles contract beneath my touch. His hot gaze raked my face, resting on my lips.

"I can take care of myself, Cade. I've been doing it for a long time. But thank you for being concerned about me."

His eyes slammed back to mine. They'd been languid and filled with sexual promise a moment before. Their iciness now chilled me. "Not concerned. I just don't want to be saddled with a shitload of paperwork if you die on my watch."

I balled my hands into fists. "You're such a dick." I pounded his shoulder blades.

His face dipped closer to mine. "You're repeating yourself, Little Null."

I stopped my pummeling since it hurt my hands and had no effect on him whatsoever. The sorcerer was rock hard everywhere. "I'm not going to stop investigating. My grandfather said we needed to wrap this up fast. He's not going to be happy with your lack of cooperation." Empty threat. I wasn't going to tattle to Wallace. I wasn't anxious to talk to the old man again. He brought up feelings I'd buried a long time ago. Abandonment and inferiority to name a couple.

Pressing his lips into a thin line, Cade scowled. "Okay, but whatever you find out, you'll tell me."

I noticed he hadn't agreed to be as forthcoming. "That goes both ways."

He literally gnashed his teeth. "Fine."

I gave his shoulders another experimental push. Still immovable. His body heat warmed my hands. The man was a furnace. "Promise you'll keep me in the loop."

His lips hovered above mine, and even though he was a jerk, I wanted him to kiss me again. What an idiot I was, going soft over an Other.

"Promise," he whispered against my mouth.

"We're equal partners in this thing?"

"Yes." His lips barely moved.

I waited for him to get off me, but he didn't seem inclined. Finally I asked, "Did you know London liked to hang out at The Raven?"

He shut his eyes. "Shit."

"Thought I might drop by there tomorrow night. Wanna come?" I'd be glad for the escort. I really didn't want to head into Other central by myself.

"You'll get yourself killed, walking in there. You'll piss off every Other faction in the state."

I smiled. "Not with you to protect me."

"Who will protect you from me?"

I didn't have an answer for that one.

Slowly, he slid his body along mine. His chest grazed my belly, while his prickly chin skimmed my breastbone. He moved down the length of me, inch by agonizing inch. When he scraped his rough cheek against my bare upper thigh, I gasped. Then balancing gracefully on the balls of his feet, he stood and didn't bother to offer me a helping hand.

"I won't be responsible if you're harmed. Pick you up at ten." He slammed the door on his way out.

I lay there, too stunned to move.

#

The next morning I'd decided on a story for Gran. One that didn't venture too far from the truth. No, I wasn't going to tell her about Wallace and his promise to look for my mom. I didn't want to break Gran's heart if he failed.

I drove out past newer housing developments in Bixby and cruised the highway to the secluded 1920's farmhouse in Wagoner County. After Gran got saddled with me, she moved us all the way out here. With no Others for miles, she figured it was a safe place to raise a null.

Pulling into the gravel driveway, I passed a profusion of colorful flowers. Even without using her magic, Gran's green thumb thrived despite the heat and drought we'd been having. Sky blue Bachelor's Buttons lined the drive. Purple coneflowers and clusters of Naked Ladies filled the yard. Gran's favorites, Hollyhocks, in shades of pink, peach and coral towered over the white picket fence.

Walking through the front door, I was treated to the smell of blueberry pancakes and fresh sausage. My mouth watered.

I hung my black Furla tote on a hook by the door and walked down the short hallway. The walls were lined with framed photos of my mom and me. Mostly me. My short history was well documented. Class photos, every softball team I'd ever played on, and cheerleading poses. She kept the trophies on the mantle in the living room, refusing to take them down even after all these years.

I wandered into the blue and white kitchen. The dated country goose wallpaper was comforting and reminded me of my childhood. Gran had always made me feel loved, wanted, in spite of everything.

She stood at the stove, flipping pancakes. "Hey." I gave her a hug, and she kissed my cheek. I swiped at it, my fingers now smeared in orange lipstick.

"I called you yesterday, Hollyhocks. Left a message."

"Sorry, Gran."

She pursed her lips. "You getting too big for your britches? What was so important that you couldn't call your grandmother back? The woman who bought you those expensive tennis shoes you just *had* to have, the ones that got stolen a week later?" She had a flair for the dramatic and a very long memory.

"Shitballs, Gran, I was eleven years old. And I was busy yesterday." I washed my hands at the sink and dried them on a nearby tea towel.

"Who taught you to talk that way, Holly James?"

"You did when you broke your toe on Christmas Eve." I was fourteen at the time, but if she wanted to take a walk down memory lane, I'd play.

She sniffed. "Smart ass. And I'm sure it didn't sound quite so vulgar when I said it."

Although she'd be seventy next year, Gran appeared no older than fifty. For reasons I'd never figured out, she chose to dress like a semi-slutty cocktail waitress. She teased her chin-length bright red hair and shellacked it to withstand the strongest wind or the highest humidity. It contrasted with her rhinestone-encrusted purple glasses. She lived for animal prints, and today was a short-sleeved giraffe tee that showed a little too much cleavage and a black bra strap.

She turned from the stove to eye me. "Busy with what? Another shifter wedding?"

"No, just work."

Her blue gaze tore right through me. Like a laser. "So, what were you up to? Something's wrong."

"Nothing's wrong, Gran." I would have sworn I hadn't given myself away, but she could always tell. I never got by with anything as a kid. Not much had changed. Leaning against the counter, I shrugged. "Things are good."

"What work stuff? And don't you lie to me. You're not too old for the switch." She was all bluster. The woman had never laid a hand on me.

"Okay, but you have to promise to keep your cool. I don't want to upset you."

She flipped off the stove with an angry click and pointed her spatula at me like a six shooter. "Just who do you think you're talking to, Missy? I'm not an old lady; I'm a vibrant, active woman." She was an old lady, though. Since she'd spent the last few decades with a null, the lack of magic had shortened her lifespan. My presence literally cut years off her life. Yet another sacrifice she'd made to raise me.

"Sorry, Gran."

"Now, what don't you want to tell me?"

I took a deep breath, then let it out in a rush. "I'm working with a Council Investigator."

The only sound in the house was the hum of the air conditioner and the whirl of the ceiling fan. Without saying a word or showing any emotion, she walked past me, out the door and into the backyard.

Oh no. The freeze out. I'd expected her to give me a million reasons why associating with the Council in any way was a bad idea—at the top of her lungs. But the silent treatment was worse.

I followed her outside. Gran stood in the garden and viciously twisted tomatoes from her plants before gently placing them in the basket at the crook of her elbow.

"Gran, please…" She worried about me. I understood why—she'd lost her daughter, and I was all she had left. She hated my business. Gran thought I should keep my head down and stay as far away from the magical world as I could. Working for Others wasn't exactly a healthy occupation. Every event I attended was like walking into hostile territory. Now the Council.

Gran turned her back to me and headed for the peppers.

I squinted against the bright sun, could feel it burning my skin. I'd have a farmer's tan in another few minutes.

The silence stretched as she moved further down the row to pull a couple of onions out of the ground.

"Two girls were murdered, Gran. The Council needs my help."

She slapped her hands together to rid them of dirt. Then placing them on her hips, she looked out over her bountiful garden. "After everything I've told you about the Council, about Others, everything that happened to you in college—you deliberately choose to put yourself in their path? I knew you'd draw attention with that business of yours."

"You know I didn't plan any of this. It just happened." Loaning myself out to desperate Others had been an accident. After I graduated from college one of my old classmates, a coyote shifter I barely remembered, came looking for me. She had a big job interview the morning after a full moon. But turning furry and chasing rabbits all night leaves a shifter drained. So I stayed with her, kept her from changing. She paid me a boatload of cash. Word spread and the next thing I knew, I had myself a little business.

It wasn't like I *enjoyed* working for Others. But I charged them a small fortune, which paid the mortgage and kept me in handbags. Everybody won.

"The girls were around my age, Gran. I saw one of them. Her dead body, I mean." I dreamed about Stephanie last night. Her filmy eyes followed me around her living room. No matter where I moved, they watched. Then Cade stormed into the house and made me touch the grimoire over and over. I finally crawled out of bed and went for a walk just before dawn to try and clear my head.

"Why does this investigator need your help?" Gran finally asked.

"The girls were killed by cursed objects."

"Who were they?"

"London Sanders and Stephanie Carson."

She glanced at me then, her eyes full of pain. "I knew London's grandmother, Mary Ann, forty years ago. She must be heartsick."

"That's why I'm trying to help. I nullified the cursed objects, and I'm looking into who killed them. It's important, Gran."

"No, it's stupid. You can't get involved. What happened to these girls is a tragedy, but I don't know what

I'd do if I lost you, too. You're all I have left, honey. If anything happened to you, it would kill me."

Tears stung the backs of my eyes, but I refused to give in to them. I headed toward her through the narrow rows of plants, my hips brushing past the large, fragrant tomato leaves. "I promise I'll be careful." I wrapped my arms around her and hugged. "And Cade will protect me." That was a big, fat lie. His paperwork comment still hurt.

Gran squeezed me tight before pulling away. With the back of her hand, she wiped her eyes. "The Council has too much power, and they wield it like a blunt instrument to get what they want. Get out of this while you still can. Please."

To hear Gran tell it, the Council was comprised of Machiavellian Others, each member with their own personal agenda. And like the Mafia, once they had you, you were a pawn forever. But Cade didn't seem like the type who'd work for a Star Chamber of power whores. Besides, I was doing this to find my mom. Whatever attention it brought from the Council, it'd be worth it to give Gran some closure.

I gave her a reassuring smile. "I'm not dealing with them, only with Cade."

She pursed her lips in displeasure. "Who's this Cade? A sorcerer?"

"Yeah."

"Arrogant. Every last one of them. Your grandfather was the biggest pain in the ass I ever met. Worth every ounce of trouble he gave me, though." My granddad had died when my mom was a baby. Tanked up on Jim Beam one night, he didn't buckle his seatbelt. So, when he hit a tree and sailed through the windshield, it whacked his head clean off. No amount of magic could fix that.

I let her tell me an often repeated story about how they met. Throughout the morning, I only had to endure three more lectures about staying away from the Council. All in all, I got off pretty easy. Most importantly, I managed to keep quiet about Wallace and our deal.

CHAPTER SIX

I spent most of the day with Gran, helping her put up twenty jars of salsa. Six hours in a hot kitchen had taken its toll on my hair.

As soon as I got home, I hopped in the shower. I needed to look spectacular tonight. For The Raven, of course, not McAllister.

Then I thought about his long, muscular body stretched out on top of mine. All of his heat and that heavenly, exotic scent. After he left me last night, I could still smell him on my skin.

Okay, so maybe I wanted to stun the sorcerer with a hot dress.

By the time Cade showed up, I'd changed my outfit three times. Although tonight was all about business, I wore something that I hoped would make him sit up and pant. A little forest green number that brought out the red highlights in my dark hair. Sleeveless and tight, it was prim in the front but left my back completely exposed. Heels and a Ralph Lauren classic clutch completed my "you-know-you-want-a-piece-of-this-Sorcerer" look.

When he knocked at ten after ten, my heart skipped a beat. Laying a hand over my pounding chest, I took a deep breath, blew it out, and assumed a nonchalant air before opening the door.

Cade stood on my front porch looking good enough to eat. He'd shaved, and his irregular features were even sexier now than when they'd been surrounded by stubble. The scar was more pronounced, too.

Dressed in a white button-down, he'd rolled up the sleeves, showing off his tanned forearms. Leaning one hand against the doorpost, he crossed his long legs at the ankle.

My gaze slipped over him, taking in his jeans, worn and faded in the right places. My eyes *may* have lingered on the bulge at his fly for the briefest second. His scuffed, black cowboy boots had seen better days.

He looked perfect.

"We need to talk," he said, moving past me.

"Let's talk in the car." He didn't respond, so with an eye roll, I swung the door closed and turned around.

Before he could bank it, I saw the heat in his gaze. He'd been checking out my backside. Mission sit-up-and-pant: accomplished.

"I've changed my mind," he said. "You're not going."

"Au contraire, I am going."

He squinted. Fine lines framed the outer corners of his eyes. "The only reason you're alive, Null, is because you don't present a threat to Others. The minute that changes, you're dead."

"I've been dealing with Others for a long time, Cade. I keep telling you, I can handle myself. Now, did you find any information about the shifter London was dating? Or that vampire, James Sharpe?"

"Did you hear me?"

"Yeah, yeah, dead null."

He twitched his lips, baring clenched white teeth. If we were animals, that look would have sent me packing in the other direction. But I was all human, baby, and I wasn't budging.

"Also, I need to take a look at London's file." I wanted to see pics of what he'd found in her house. Surely it hadn't always been as sterile as the day I snooped through it.

"Forget it. That's evidence."

Of course, precious rule number one. "I'll barely look at it. You can even turn the pages so I won't sully it with my little null fingers."

"No."

McAllister was a stickler for his details and rules. He wouldn't let me touch the original, but... "Didn't you at least make copies? That's not evidence. Technically speaking."

He closed his eyes for a second and sighed. "Fine," he ground out. "If it shuts you up, you can look at a copy."

That was almost too easy. Still, there was a hint of smugness in my grin. "See, that wasn't so hard, now was it?"

He took a step toward me, narrowing the space between us. Heat rolled off him, and his delicious smell, mixed with the fresh scent of laundry soap, teased my nose. "Do you really want to play games with me, Little Null?"

I could think of a couple that might be fun. Instead I said, "I could easily kick your ass at Twister. I'm very limber."

In the dim entryway, most of his face was cast in shadows. But those eyes. They glimmered greener than normal and were full of strong emotions. Anger. Irritation. Sexual frustration. Maybe a dangerous combination of all three? "You want to fuck with me, I'll fuck right back. But I don't recommend it."

His words conjured up images of him moving on top of me, sliding inside me. I felt a little lightheaded from the thought. Clearing my throat, I placed my hands on my hips. The tips of my breasts brushed his shirt, making my nipples hard. His prolonged gaze at my chest told me he noticed. I couldn't allow myself to get distracted this way. I had a job to do, a reward to collect. Screwing the sorcerer didn't play into it.

"What I want is a look at your file and a trip to The Raven," I said. "Since I'm the one who brought all this information to the table, the very least you can do is provide protection."

He held my gaze and nodded. "One condition."

"Look, McAl—"

He pressed his finger to my lips, silencing me. "We do it my way. It's the only shot you have of getting out of there alive."

I may be reckless at times, but I wasn't an idiot. I liked living as much as the next girl. I nodded, but he didn't remove his finger. Instead, he used the pad to slowly trace around my lips, robbing me of expertly applied pink gloss. My knees almost buckled when he put the same fingertip in his own mouth, sucking it.

"Tastes like peppermint," he said in a low, rumbling voice.

If I'd let things continue last night, I'd have had that mouth all over me. Heat suffused my body as I stood transfixed, unable to look away. Not too full, not too thin. Those lips were just right. And they knew how to kiss.

My gaze slowly trailed up his face. As I stared into his amused eyes, my cheeks felt like they were on fire. He knew exactly what I was thinking. "What is your way, Sorcerer?"

"Tonight, we're a couple. You're going to keep that smart mouth shut and let me ask the questions. Oh, and one more thing."

I raised a brow.

"You're crazy about me."

"If I were dating you, McAllister, I'd have to be crazy."

#

After we climbed into the truck, Cade flipped on the overhead light then leaned in my direction, stretching his hand toward my legs. When the back of his knuckles brushed over my bare calf and his chin nudged my knee, I jerked away.

"What the hell are you doing?"

He scrounged under my seat and straightened, holding an accordion folder. "You said you wanted to see a copy of London's file. Change your mind?" He offered it to me with the tiniest of smirks.

"Of course not." I grabbed it, and lowering my head, let a curtain of hair cover my embarrassment. So he wasn't trying to grope me? Good. All good.

He let out a noise that sounded suspiciously like a chuckle, but since I didn't think McAllister was capable of laughter, I let it go and flipped through the disappointingly thin file. I'd found out more information in one day than McAllister had in almost two weeks. For some reason, people didn't want to confide in him.

As Cade backed out of the driveway, I held up a snapshot of London. Unlike the nude, glittery pics Tamara Dermot had shown me, here London was casually dressed. It was a candid photo where she grinned at something off camera. Long golden hair, lightly tanned skin, and bright blue eyes—she was brimming with life. Her risky dating behavior provided motives for her death. But how did it tie into poor Stephanie Carson?

Turning my head toward Cade, my gaze swept his profile. I reached out and lightly fingered his scar. "Why did you leave this?" His skin was warm; the scar felt smooth. I continued to slowly trace it. Once. Twice. On my third pass, he slid me a look that said "mind your own damn business" before tilting his head to the left and severing our contact.

I dropped my hand and focused my attention on the file. I wasn't sure what impulse possessed me to touch him. Did he hate the feel of my fingers on his skin? He didn't act like it last night, but that hadn't been about attraction.

That had been manipulation. In truth, he probably hated being stuck in the same room with me. Very few Others tolerated me unless they were hiring me for a specific reason. Then I was seen as the help. I couldn't name any who actually liked me—besides Gran. But in some cosmic joke, I found myself attracted to one.

This was ridiculous. A doomed romance with an Other was not on my to-do list. Gorgeous, cranky sorcerers with colorful tattoos and facial scars didn't have a place in my life.

I realized I was beginning to crumple the evidence photos in my fist, so I quickly glanced through them. I shuffled past the ones featuring London's dead body and concentrated on a picture of a large carved wooden box. It held a host of magical supplies. According to Cade's handwritten notes, the evidence of London's dabbling in black magic had been tucked away in this case hidden beneath her bed. There were vials of blood, black candles, dirt—probably from a graveyard—and an athame, a sacred ceremonial knife used in spells.

"London had all the paraphernalia for black casting work, but there was no trace of it in her house?" I asked. Gran had taught me that black magic left a stain on your aura. A big one. Took a lot of cleansing to get rid of it. Getting the stain off your soul was even harder. Maybe that's why London's aura had turned gray?

"Her bedroom contained residue," Cade said, "but it all leads back to the amulet. Nothing from London's body, the items in the box, or the room with the pentagram. Not a goddamned thing." His muscles tensed from his forearms to his hands where he gripped the steering wheel.

I wasn't sure how all this signature/residue stuff worked. I knew about the black magic stain, but that was as far as I got. Never having seen it, I had trouble picturing it. "What is this signature thing? What's it look like? Explain it to me."

"A signature is like a fingerprint," he said. "Every Other has one. Different color, different texture, and pattern. It's unique to each practitioner. Black magic residue is like soot after a fire, covering everything. Evil leaves its mark. That room was coated in residue but, like I said, it was coming straight from the amulet."

"And you couldn't trace the amulet back to the spellcaster? It didn't have a signature either?"

"No, and I can usually find a trail, a pattern as well. Backtrack the spell and find the source. It may take a while, but the signature's always there. Not this time."

I shuffled through the photos once more. "What happened to the magical signatures in London's house?"

"I think the killer might have wiped them clean. Used magic to remove any traces of himself."

"How is that possible?"

He hefted one shoulder. "A very powerful practitioner could do it. With dark magic and more blood."

"What about Stephanie Carson's house? Did you find any signature there?"

"Just hers. The grimoire contained residue, but that was it."

I thought for a moment. "Could a vampire wipe out signatures?"

He paused, his expression grim. "They don't advertise their powers, and the Council pretty much leaves them alone. They're secretive as hell, so yeah, maybe."

I glanced back at London's smiling face. Little Miss Oklahoma wasn't what she seemed. She loved rough, kinky sex. She was sleeping with a vamp and a shifter. Either one could have turned her or killed her. That was more than enough trouble, but for some reason, she took it further by dabbling in dark magic.

"Whoever cast the curse on the amulet and grimoire is extremely powerful," I said. "How many Others could pull off something like that? Should be easy to pin down. You can tell who's practicing dark magic, right?"

"Some Others hide their power. They can swipe at the stain and glamour over the rest. It's not always easy to tell who's powerful and who's not. If they're using blood magic, it makes it even more difficult."

That was something Gran had never mentioned. "I want to see the amulet."

"There's a picture of it in the file."

"Why can't I see the real thing?"

"You know why."

"Just out of curiosity, McAllister, what are your other rules?"

"Rule number two: don't piss me off. Since you do that constantly, I figured it wasn't worth mentioning."

"Rules are for suckers." I stuck the photo back in the accordion file and wrapped the band around it before tucking it under the seat. I reached up and turned off the cab light. "Do you think one of the guys she was dating had something to do with this?"

"Don't know." While I was busy thumbing through the file, Cade had driven downtown. He swung a left into a parking lot of an old building—four stories, light brick exterior, every window painted black. I didn't hear music spilling out onto the street, didn't see smokers loitering at the entrance. If it weren't for all the cars in the lot, The Raven would look like an abandoned building.

Cade parked along the back row then turned to look at me. "Last chance to back out, Null."

I waved him off. "I'm ready."

CHAPTER SEVEN

I wasn't ready.

The building must have been magically muted because it was as quiet as a church on Saturday night. Until I stepped within five feet of the door. Then bass-pumping techno music hit us like a wave.

Cade grabbed my hand and laced his fingers with mine. His palm was warm and rough with calluses. I guessed he didn't mind touching me after all. I squeezed his left hand as he opened the door with his right.

The instant we entered the room, everyone froze. Literally.

The girls on tall, circular daises, wearing nothing but g-strings and hot pink fur boots stopped mid-head shake. Bartenders over-poured drinks from cocktail shakers. Customers, bouncers, people on the dance floor halted their movements. Even a spiky-haired guy at the bar paused in the middle of licking his body shot partner, his tongue clinging to her bare breast like it was stuck to a frozen popsicle. The house music blared on, but it was as if the moment was suspended in time.

Then I noticed movement on the stairs leading to the second floor. A tall man with chin-length, straight black hair glided sinuously downward, never taking his dark, almond-shaped eyes from mine. Dressed in a suit without a tie, he looked club casual, but at the same time, I never doubted for a moment he was in charge. His skin was dusky, his lips sensuous. This had to be Mick Raven. With his hands in his pockets and a hank of hair framing either side of his preternaturally handsome face, he made his way toward us.

Cade dropped my hand and clenched his own into a fist at his side. The heightened tension running through his body was palpable.

When the man stopped in front of me, he smiled. The brackets on either side of his mouth deepened as he reached out to take my hand, raising it to those full, upturned lips for a brief kiss. He was sex on two legs, and the effect of that smile knocked the breath clean out of me.

With his eyes still on mine, he spoke to McAllister, raising his voice to be heard above the music. "Such interesting company you keep, Cade." Next, he spoke to me. "I'm Mick Raven. Welcome." He carried the trace of an accent, something dark and crisp that wove its way around the consonants, softly lilted over the vowels. Where Cade's voice was rough and deep, this man's was smooth like silk sheets.

Cade's hand found its way to my bare back. His fingers softly charted my skin, rubbing circles along my shoulders. Between Cade's gentle touch and the pretty man stroking my palm, it was all I could do not to shiver from head to toe.

He shifted his gaze to Cade. "She belongs to you exclusively?"

I didn't like that. Not one bit. I was no one's property. I opened my mouth to tell him so when Cade's hand clamped onto my nape and squeezed. This was his little reminder to keep my mouth closed. Since I was in over my head and surrounded by hostile Others, I decided to let it slide.

"Yes." Cade released my neck. His fingers drifted down, tracing light patterns over my spine. I craved those fingers on other parts of my anatomy as well.

Mick looked back at me with a wicked smile. "Too bad. What is it like to fuck her without your powers? Does it heighten the experience, or lessen it?"

My eyes widened. And here I thought McAllister was a dick. This asshole redefined the word.

"You'll never find out," Cade growled.

Mick dropped my hand, threw back his head and laughed. Suddenly, everyone in the club resumed their lives like they had been on pause and his laughter hit the play button. "Come." He turned, making his way back toward the stairs.

Cade slid his hand to my hip and pulled me closer to his side. I didn't take any of this personally. Despite his earlier denial, this was Cade's way of protecting me. All that touching and stroking—it was just for show.

But then he turned and faced me, roughly thrusting his hand into the hair at the base of my neck. Using it as leverage, he tugged me closer and lowered his lips to mine. And when he kissed me it felt very personal, a blatant display of possession. That bruising kiss had heat pooling in my lady bits and told everyone in the room that if they messed with me, they'd wind up with a bad case of Cade McAllister.

I clutched at his shirt, bunching it in my fists, completely forgetting we were within eyeshot of everyone in the room. There was only now. Only Cade.

His other hand rubbed one of my ass cheeks. Oh, my Lord. What would it feel like to be kissed by this man for real? Not because he was making a point, not to get his own way, but just because he wanted me? It would probably ruin me for good.

Abruptly, he released me. I felt a little woozy for a second before remembering where I was. With my head lowered, I licked my lips, savoring his taste and cast my gaze toward the bar. Everyone stared at us, some with taunting smiles, some with expressions of disgust.

Cade ignored everyone, grabbed my hand and pulled me behind him as he pounded up the stairs. I trotted along after him, avoided looking anyone in the eye.

All throughout the second floor, round tables were framed with curtains that could be closed for privacy. I saw very few closed, red curtains. Seemed most people here didn't mind who saw them having sex on curved black booths, giving handies under the table, or in one case, a girl bent over some old guy's lap, getting her naked ass slapped. But they all stopped what they were doing to glare at Cade and me.

Cade didn't care. He yanked me toward the back of the room and down a hallway, first left then right. He was very familiar with this place. Don't think I wouldn't be asking him about it later.

We stopped in front of a black lacquered door. In fact, the entire hallway was black. Black marble floors, black walls. The only illumination came from tiny yellow pin-lights beaming down from the ceiling. This place was creepy. I was very glad I hadn't come here alone.

Without knocking, Cade opened the door and strode in. He led me to his side and without turning, kicked the door closed with the heel of his boot.

Mick Raven smiled. "Cade, always making the dramatic entrance, yes?" He sat behind his large mahogany desk, puffing on a thin cigar, his eyes narrowed through the smoky haze. The sweet-sharp smell wasn't unpleasant.

Without letting go of my hand, Cade strode to a black club chair in front of the desk. He dropped into it, smoothly pulling me onto his lap. My skirt rode up, revealing all of one thigh and a hint of midnight blue lace that decorated my panties.

I gritted my teeth and refrained from jerking down my skirt. *Play it cool, Holly.* As if lounging on top of McAllister while I flashed my underwear was an everyday thing, I slung my arm over his shoulder and crossed my legs.

"Why are you here, Cade?" Mick asked. He motioned to a guy in the corner, one I hadn't seen until now. A thick-necked bouncer type in a dark suit and black t-shirt. "Get Cade a drink, Jasper."

"I'm fine," Cade said.

"Nonsense."

Jasper ignored Cade's refusal and handed him a drink. Notice *I* wasn't offered a glass. Sexist jerks.

Putting the tumbler to his lips, Cade gulped it in one swallow, then handed the glass back without ever taking his eyes off Raven.

Mick shook his head in disapproval. "That was a fifty-year-old scotch. But I am glad to see you appreciate *some* of the finer things." His gaze swept over my bare leg, traveled slowly to my breasts and finally made it north to my eyes. "And what can I give you, Miss James? Anything at all, you've only to ask."

I wasn't surprised he knew my name. My reputation for magical suckage preceded me. I thinned my lips at his sexually frank suggestion. "I'm fine, thanks."

"Very much so." He stuck the cigar in his mouth and puffed, his appreciative, seductive gaze fixed on mine. This guy was good.

Cade's hand tightened on my thigh. "Cut the bullshit."

I stroked the tattoo on Cade's neck with one finger and placed my other hand on top of his, where it gripped my leg. He immediately loosened his hold, brushing his thumb along my skin. Tingles followed in its wake.

Mick grinned. "I see time hasn't mellowed that temper of yours."

"I want to know what London Sanders was doing here."

Mick raised a brow. "Heard you were looking into that." He shook his head. "Sad, a beautiful girl dying in such a way. But this is a club. What do you think she was doing here?"

"Do not fuck with me. Who was she here with?" Cade's voice deepened, sounding harsher than usual. Anger and frustration frayed the edges of his vocal chords. It was pretty obvious my sorcerer didn't like Mick Raven.

Wait, *my* sorcerer? No. Just *a* sorcerer. One I'd shared a couple of kisses with and now used as a recliner.

Mick raised a shoulder. "How should I know? I don't keep tabs on everyone who walks through my doors."

Cade grunted. "Like hell you don't."

Mick puffed away in silence. Finally, he said, "As I'm sure you know, the girl had an affinity for, shall we say, men who are a little rough around the edges?"

"Which men?" Cade asked.

Mick took the cigar from his lips and jabbed it out in a marble ashtray. "Part of my success is my ability to keep what happens in the club quiet." As his agitation grew, the accent became thicker. He leaned back in his chair, brushed a thumb over his upper lip. "What can you give me in return for this information?"

The muscles of Cade's neck became rigid beneath my hand. "I'll let you live."

Mick laughed. "You could have killed me long ago, and you chose not to."

Cade remained silent.

What the hell was going on with these two? There was some deep, treacherous undercurrent that I didn't understand. A conversation *underneath* the conversation.

"Fine," Mick said. "She ran with Vane Aldridge."

Cade's thumb on my leg stilled. "Anyone else?"

Wait, who was Vane Aldridge? I'd never heard of him.

"Nick Alpert, werewolf enforcer. James Sharpe, vampire prick."

"Who else?"

Mick sighed. "That is all I know."

"What about you?" I asked. "Were you with London?" The questions popped out of my mouth before I could stop them. Once again, Cade's grip on my leg became almost painful. But the theory made sense. She liked dangerous men, and Mick Raven was lethal.

Although Mick smiled, the look in those dark eyes had me on alert. He watched me with tolerant, predatory amusement like a cat watches a mouse before it decides to pounce. "Not I, Miss James. I don't seduce women who like to *play* at being bad. My tastes run to something more unique." He drew the word out as his gaze shifted over my body, taking in every inch of me. I felt a rising tide of heat suffuse my cheeks. Then his glance drifted to Cade. "Are we done? I do have a business to run, as lovely as this has been."

Cade scooped me onto my feet and stood. "We're through. For now."

Grasping my hand once again, he strode to the door, flung it open and marched through the upper story of the club back to the stairs. I tried to wrench my hand from his grasp, pulling as hard as I could. He finally took notice and turned to glare at me.

"What?"

I hiked my thumb over my shoulder. "What the hell was that back there? What's going on with you and Mick Raven? Who is Vane Aldridge? Why do you know this club like the back of your hand?"

His facial muscles tightened. "Later." Spinning, he jogged down the stairs, pulling me along for the ride. When he got to the bar, a tall, spindly man with curly brown hair stepped in front of him.

"McAllister, we need to talk."

Cade shifted a sideways glance at me. He dropped my hand, dug around in his front pocket, and pulled out his keys. "Go wait in the truck."

Really? Relegated to the truck like an annoying child? No, more like a pet. Stick the null in the front seat and don't forget to crack a window. Un. Be. Lievable.

I hesitated for a moment, grabbed the keys and stomped to the door, ignoring the nasty looks I received from everyone I passed. As a null, I was a second class citizen. But tonight, Cade and Mick had made me feel like a piece of meat they were fighting over. I would tolerate this type of bullshit from my clients. After all, they paid for the privilege, but I didn't have to take it from a sorcerer with a stick up his ass. This partnership was over, off. *Finito Benito.*

Walking outside, the humid air was thick and soupy. I'd almost made it across the lot to the Ford, when out of nowhere, a pair of arms wrapped around me from behind, one at my waist, one at my chest, tightening painfully across my breasts. Before my brain could register what was happening, my assailant pulled me to the ground and sank his teeth into the side of my neck.

"Agh. Stop!" With my Ralph Lauren clutch, I beat the side of my attacker's head. With my free hand, I grabbed a fistful of his hair, scraping my elbow and forearm on the asphalt in the process. Over and over, I slugged and tugged as he sucked on my neck like a sixteen-year-old boy during his first make out session.

Finally, he released me, pulling his mouth from my skin with an audible *pop*. "Stop hitting me," he yelled in my ear.

In a flash, I hopped to my feet, whirled around, and kicked him as hard as I could in the balls. He screamed like a little girl.

Short and slight, he curled into a fetal position and cupped his crotch. His sharp features scrunched together in pain. "What's wrong with me?" he whined.

"Yeah, that's what I want to know." I kicked him again in the forehead.

"Would you please stop kicking me?" His wavy hair looked wonky from where I'd been yanking on it, and he now sported a red welt between his eyes.

I slapped my hand over my neck. "You bit me, you asshole."

"I was hungry, okay? But something's wrong with me. I feel weird. It's not just the ball pain, either."

"Oh, my God. Are you a *vampire*?"

"No. Ha, ha, ha." His voice cracked on the last syllable. "That's crazy. Vampires aren't real." He moved to stand, but I bent and pushed his shoulders, making him lose his balance. He fell to the ground again.

"You are," I accused, pointing at him with my purse. "You're a vampire."

He scowled at me. "So what if I am? I'm hungry. I have a right to eat, too."

"Not from me you don't. I am so telling Monty about this." Monty Ridgecliff was the go-to vampire in Oklahoma. I'd met him at a couple of cocktail parties. As personal assistant to the state's Master vamp, Sebastian, Monty didn't take a lick of shit from anyone. All requests, complaints, and introductions filtered through him up to the Master. While unfailingly polite, Monty wouldn't look kindly on a pussy vamp running loose, trying to bite humans in the parking lot of The Raven.

He struggled to sit. "No, please, not Monty. I'm sorry. Look." He bared his teeth at me. "I'm not even a vamp anymore. See?"

"That's because I'm a null, numb nuts."

"What's that?"

I rolled my eyes. "How old are you? In vamp years, I mean?"

He leaned his back against the front tire of a gray sedan and tried to play it cool. Hard to do when he was still clutching his package with both hands. "Old enough."

"You're just turned, aren't you? Where the hell is your sponsor?" I hadn't met any young vamps, but to hear Gran tell it, all new vamps had a sponsor that kept them from spinning out of control. And this dipwad was spinning like a pinwheel.

The door to the club opened, letting music and voices swell out into the night before being muffled once again. Since I'd nullified the mute spell, it would have to be cast again to shroud the building in silence.

Cade walked across the parking lot and came to stand beside me. His hot glance took in the hand I held over my neck and the goofy kid at my feet. Putting two and two together, he summed up the situation pretty fast. So fast, I hardly followed his movements as he jerked the vamp up by the collar of his t-shirt and dangled him off the ground. "Did you bite her?"

"Dude, I'm sorry. Okay? I didn't mean to."

"You just violated rules two and three, motherfucker. I'm going to have to kill you." Cade's features appeared harsher in the dim lights. His voice didn't contain emotion as it had when he spoke to Mick Raven. It was deadly cold and detached. Even the hot night air turned a little cooler from his frigid tone.

"Cade," I said, "I'll take care of it. I'll call Monty as soon as we get in the truck."

The vamp's wide, frightened eyes focused on me. "Yeah, call Monty. Great idea." I guessed getting punished by the Master's personal assistant wasn't as bad as getting killed by a pissed off sorcerer.

"Please." I tentatively stroked McAllister's bicep through the soft cotton of his button down.

Cade shook the little guy, making his de-fanged teeth rattle. "If Monty doesn't take care of you, I will."

Killing a vamp, even a young, stupid one like this, would be a disaster. Cade would have a bounty on his head. It could spark an inter-species war. "Cade."

He dropped the kid to the ground, and the vamp stayed low, covering his head with his arms. "Please don't hurt me."

Cade didn't spare him another look. He turned to me, pulling my hand away from my neck to examine the bite. "Going to have one hell of a hickey, Little Null." With a whisper soft touch, he brushed his fingers over the sore skin. Then he leaned forward and pressed his lips to my temple. "Let's get you home."

CHAPTER EIGHT

Cade sat next to me on the sofa, his huge body practically wrapped around mine while he held an ice pack to the far side of my neck. "You should have a doc look at that. A human bite can get infected, so I've heard."

"I'll be fine." I'd called Monty Ridgecliff on the way home. I explained the situation and described the vamp who'd attacked me. Monty assured me it would be dealt with, and I believed him. Vamps didn't like bad publicity. Actually, they didn't like any publicity.

"So, who's Vane Aldridge?" I glanced up at him. His expression gave nothing away.

"Before tonight, I'd never heard of him."

"Oh, really?" I didn't buy that for a second. Cade knew him all right. He just wasn't going to share it with me.

He removed the icepack and glanced at my neck. "How are you feeling?"

"Who is Vane Aldridge?" I scooted away, leaving a foot of space between us. When he touched me, my brain felt a little scrambled, and I needed all my faculties right now.

I faced him, twisting my legs to the side which hiked my dress up, exposing a good deal of thigh. Cade's gaze lingered there before he reached out and drew a finger along my knee, up my leg. It disappeared beneath my dress.

"He's just one more piece of the puzzle that was London Sanders."

I smacked his hand away. "We're done."

"We haven't even gotten started, Little Null." His gravelly voice sent a shiver through me.

To steel myself from this crazy pull he had on me, I scooted further away. "I mean this partnership we had going. You're not keeping me in the loop. And you treated me like a piece of meat tonight."

He raised a brow. "I kept you safe."

"Now you won't tell me who Vane Aldridge is. You're holding back. So, I'll continue this investigation on my own."

His cold eyes met mine. "No. You won't."

I smiled. "I think it's time for you to leave, McAllister. I'll find out who Vane Aldridge is and question him myself."

"No, you won't," he repeated.

"Yes. I will."

Cade moved closer until I was huddled in the corner of the couch. His body hovered inches above mine as he wedged his knee between my thighs. Slowly, he leaned down until our mouths almost touched. "No. You. Won't." He punctuated that statement with a swift, harsh kiss. Before I could kiss him back, he broke it off and suddenly became gentle, almost tender. His lips lightly danced across my jaw, taking time to explore my cheek, my fluttering eyelids, my brow. Occasionally, his tongue darted out to flick my earlobe or taste the corner of my mouth.

With so little effort, the man had me melting into a puddle. It was hard to catch a breath, and my body felt like it was on fire. Although I craved him, he was doing this to shut me up. Again. Seducing me to get what he wanted. Maybe it was time to do a little seducing of my own.

Reaching up, I swiftly unbuttoned his shirt. He stopped kissing my forehead and looked at me with unfocused, lust-filled eyes. The light hazel color had darkened and appeared deeper, greener than before. Locking my gaze on his, I took my time as I peeled the shirt from his shoulders and down to his elbows.

Bulging muscles. Well-defined chest. Eight-pack abs. These were a few of my favorite things.

I got a good look at the tattoo that started on his left pec. A snarling, fire-breathing dragon stared at me with red eyes. Its body swirled and writhed up over his shoulder and the upper edge of his bicep, coiling its long tail around his neck. I slid my finger over the red, gold, and green scales, following the path of its body all the way to Cade's nape, where the tail ended.

He bent over me again, biting my earlobe—a particularly sensitive spot—and shifted his hands under me to knead my ass. I was throbbing in time to the pressure of his hands, thrusting my hips toward him in response. His cock twitched against my leg. Long and hard and thick.

I shoved at his shoulders and got him to raise slightly so that I had room to explore his chest. With my fingertips, I caressed the curve of his pecs. Then I took a winding, lazy path over the contours of his firm belly, feeling my way along the ridges of hard-packed muscle. He let out a soft moan when I fit my thumbs into the V-shaped indentations above the waistband of his jeans.

God, his body was a work of art. The smooth, heated skin. The controlled strength in his taut muscles.

When I lightly slid my fingers back up his chest to pinch a nipple, his breath faltered.

He began nibbling the unbitten side of my neck, causing goose bumps to rise along my skin. I stroked his arms and licked the column of his throat. The weight of him felt good, solid. Cade's scent enveloped me, distinct and intoxicating.

His hand moved under my dress, his thumb traced over the edge of my panties. "Holly. You feel so damn good."

I slid my hands to his face and stroked his smooth cheeks, playing with his scar a bit before running my fingertips over his buzzed hair. "Cade?"

His thumb was under the elastic now and working its way over my damp, swollen lips. It felt so good I didn't want him to ever stop. But I forced myself to focus. "Who is Vane Aldridge?"

He kissed me in response, twirling his tongue in my mouth while his thumb circled my clit. One more minute. Then I'd ask him again.

But this felt so delicious I couldn't think clearly. All I could do was kiss him back.

Cade used just the right amount of pressure and within seconds, a sudden, intense orgasm burst through me. I closed my eyes and grasped his shoulders, riding it out as his tongue tangled with mine. But he never let up, kept that thumb working its magic. And when I thought it was over, another wave hit me.

I tugged my mouth from his and arched my back. "Cade. Oh, God." I shuddered as he continued to work me. Eventually, I drifted back down to earth while Cade still played with me, softly gliding over my slick lips, slipping the tip of his thumb inside me.

With my eyes still closed, I reached for his shaft just as he moved away, slipping his hand out of my panties and down my leg. I flicked my eyelids open and watched him sit up and slide to the other end of the sofa. When he began buttoning his shirt, I knew playtime was over.

Scrambling up, I tugged at my dress and stared at him in disbelief. Gone was the tender expression that softened his features. The bad ass sorcerer was back, seemingly unaffected by our romp on the couch, even though his dick was still hard, distorting the fly of his jeans.

"You're leaving?" I was annoyed that my voice sounded breathy and disappointed.

He stood and stared down at me. "Yeah. I'll check in with the werewolf, Nick Alpert, tomorrow and give you a call. Look, Holly." He tracked his scar with a finger. "I shouldn't have let things get so out of hand. Sorry."

I shot up from the sofa. "Excuse me?" I didn't know if I was more pissed off that he'd just given me not one, but two, orgasms then *apologized* or the fact that he planned to question the werewolf without me.

Not true. I knew which pissed me off more. The orgasm and subsequent regret. And to imply our hooking up was a bad idea? No shit. I didn't need that spelled out. But I wasn't the one who'd started it. He had. The whole damn fiasco was humiliating.

Taking a deep breath, I pushed away the pain his words inflicted. He could reject me all he wanted. I had to speak to Nick Alpert myself. London hadn't been banging just any werewolf. According to Mick Raven, she'd been doing an enforcer. Enforcers were right below the Alpha in a pack. They meted out punishment and pain. They were brawn to the Alpha's brain.

I wasn't looking forward to meeting this wolf, but he might have killed London. Nailing his shifter ass to the wall for these murders would solve all my problems, including never having to see McAllister again.

"I'm going with you to question the werewolf," I said.

He shook his head. "I doubt I'll get much out of him. They aren't known for their cooperation."

"I'm coming, Cade. Deal with it."

"This isn't your concern. You have no place in Other business." He narrowed his eyes, and a white line appeared around his compressed lips. "You're a liability. I can't investigate and watch out for you, too."

I stiffened in anger. "I don't need you watching out for me. I can do this on my own."

He stepped into me, pressed his face closer to mine. "Don't kid yourself, sweetheart. You'd have never made it through the front door of The Raven if I hadn't been there."

"Maybe not, but even with all of your sorcerer's tricks, you've gotten nowhere on this case. Have your little mind fucks had any effect at all?"

He clenched his jaw.

"You intimidate people, McAllister, and they don't want to confide in you. I *will* be there when you question Nick Alpert, even if I have to chain myself to your side. Is that clear enough for you? You gave me your word that you'd keep me in the loop. Are you a liar?"

His nose flared slightly as he glared at me. After a long moment, he took a step backward. "I agree with you about one thing. After we question the wolf, we're through."

"Pick me up at my office. I'm sure you can find it, being such an astute investigator and all."

"Fine. Then I've more than fulfilled my obligation to your grandfather. I don't have time to babysit your ass."

"What do you mean? What did Wallace tell you?"

Without sparing me another glance, he strode to the door and slammed it on his way out.

At least now I knew how McAllister felt about me. *A liability.* What happened on the couch meant less than nothing. It was just sex.

Well, almost sex.

And it would never happen again.

CHAPTER NINE

The next morning, exhausted and feeling high-strung, I dragged myself to work. Much to my irritation, I'd lain awake and thought about McAllister all night long. The feel of his hard body pressing against mine. The way he touched me. The way his thumb slid inside me. The way he left me high and dry after two orgasms and dismissed me, calling me a liability.

I needed to talk to Wallace and figure out what the hell was going on. I didn't need babysitting, thank you. I'd been holding my own against Others for years now and had gotten along just fine.

On top of all that, I sported a hickey the size of a grapefruit. I tried, unsuccessfully, to cover it with makeup and wound up wearing a black wool scarf to hide it. It was the only one I owned.

It was a Monday morning, which was bad enough, and already over ninety degrees.

This was shaping up to be a shitty day.

My small office was situated in a strip mall off Harvard, wedged between a day-old bread store and an insurance agency. I didn't have a title on the door or a listed phone number. My clients found me by word of mouth. Mostly I took cases where I acted as a magical wet blanket, but sometimes Norms got mixed up in Others' business, and I helped them out, too.

As I walked through the door, Sunny Carmichael peered at me through oval, black-framed glasses. She wore her brown hair in a low ponytail, her plain white blouse wouldn't dare show a wrinkle, and I knew without question she had on a long, black skirt and flats beneath the desk. Sunny had the fashion sense of a Mormon missionary.

"You're late."

I glanced at my phone. "By six minutes."

"Which is late. And save your breath. I'm not interested in excuses."

"I wasn't going to offer any."

Sunny—who's the opposite of everything her name implies—is a perfectionist, which is why I hired her. She's a no-nonsense, efficient, office-running machine, who always makes sure the check clears. Although I'd be lost without her, I wouldn't own up to that fact if you waterboarded me.

With her fingers flying over the keyboard, she nodded at my neck. "What's with the scarf? It's ninety-seven degrees, and with the heat index, it feels like one hundred and three."

Leaning down, I tugged on the wool material and showed her my hickey. "This is why."

"I see teeth marks. Do you know how many germs are in the human mouth?"

"I got attacked by a newbie vamp."

That shut her up for all of three seconds. "A vamp did this? Have you called Monty and reported it? This type of thing shouldn't happen, even if you are a null. There are rules."

Supposedly, vamps only tapped willing donors. Yeah, and the tooth fairy was a harmless little creature who left money under the pillows of small children. I'd met that bitch, and there's no way I'd let her near innocent, defenseless kids.

"Monty's aware. Before I forget, I have an assignment for you."

"Am I in high school now? Unlike you, I have important work to do. Quarterlies are coming up in three weeks, you know."

I didn't know. I paid her so I wouldn't have to. "Vane Aldridge. Find out who he is."

She continued clacking on the keyboard. "You have an appointment at ten."

"Cancel it. I'm taking a few days off. I just stopped by to check in."

Staring at me with unblinking brown eyes, she finally stopped typing. "How do you think we're going to pay the rent if you take a few days off? You didn't clear this with me."

"First of all, we're not going to go broke in a few days' time. Second, I don't have to clear it with you because I'm the boss. Third"—I walked to the half-full coffee pot next to her desk and grabbed a mug—"I'm doing a job for the Council, and it's not the type of thing I can blow off. So, deal."

She rolled her shoulders. "How much are they paying? Don't quote them a price. You always undercharge."

I doctored my cup with sweetener and powdered creamer. "I'm not charging them anything."

"I beg your pardon?" She spun in her chair and straightened her glasses a millimeter. "What do you mean you're not charging?" Nothing angered Sunny more than pro bono work. I still didn't know what her issue *was* with money, but she had one. If a check bounced, she was on the phone in a hot minute. If she thought I charged too little, she wasn't afraid to call the client and demand a bigger payment. Sunny was a straight up null pimp.

"It's a personal thing." I took a sip of coffee, hoping it would wake me up. I felt sluggish after too little sleep and too much Cade on the brain.

Sunny pursed her lips. "What's going on? You don't deal with the Council. In fact, I've worked very hard to keep you away from the Council."

I blew out a breath. "Cliffs Notes version, I'm looking into the murders of two witches. Kind of important. Now do you get why I can't take a client today?"

"No. And frankly, I don't understand why you didn't tell the Council that you charge ten thousand for that kind of intense job. You never think about the bottom line."

I slammed my cup on her desk, slopping a few drops of coffee onto the polished wood surface. "Two young women are dead. Jeez, Sunny."

She grabbed a tissue and wiped up my mess. "Fine, but the least you can do before you go tearing off is meet with this client. It's an easy one. Shouldn't take you any time at all."

I rubbed a hand over my forehead. I wasn't sure when Cade was picking me up. I probably had time for a quickie. "Give me the details."

"The client was given a voodoo doll, and now she's losing her hair."

"She's a Norm, I take it?" Even a weak witch would have been able to break that kind of spell without much trouble.

"Sounds like it. She seemed desperate, so I charged her an extra thousand."

"You price-gouged a helpless Norm? You're shameless. And who sends voodoo dolls these days? Very seventies, hippie crap. Honestly." I leaned against her desk and sipped my coffee.

"My grandmother was very fond of them." Sunny's mother was a full-blooded witch, but she'd married a Norm. While Sunny grew up in a mixed-race household, she learned all about witchcraft from her mother and grandparents.

Sunny and I both straddled the world between Others and Norms. Though she couldn't perform magic, she wasn't affected by it either. She was immune. Spells and charms just rolled right off her. She saw through glamours, would never get fooled by a prank-playing imp, and if she was bitten by a werewolf, she might die from blood loss, but she wouldn't turn.

"By the way, how was the shifter wedding on Friday?" she asked.

"Not just shifters. Werepossums. Did you know they were getting married in a cow pasture?"

"I believe the correct term is were*o*pposum. And what does it matter? They paid on time."

"I believe the correct term is *never again*."

She gave my butt—which was perched on the corner of her desk—an irritated glance. "You may have the luxury of taking a few days off, but I have work to do. Shoo."

Rolling my eyes, I meandered to my office and closed the door. I'd already tried to get hold of London's hairstylist friend, the man who'd been at her Solstice party, Brant Braxton. I'd even left two messages. As I eased back in my ergonomically correct chair and rang him again, I hoped I wouldn't have to hunt him down. I had enough on my plate as it was.

He answered on the fifth ring and groaned. "Who is this?"

"My name is Holly James. I'm investigating the death of London Sanders."

"Oh," he said through a yawn. "I thought that hot sorcerer was investigating?"

"We're colleagues." That'd be the day. "I thought maybe you and I could meet up. I'd like to ask you a few questions."

"I told him everything I know. Even gave him my phone number. Rowr." If he had ever grieved for London, he'd gotten over it.

"Why don't I buy you a drink and you can tell me?"

He paused. "They do a mean mojito at The Factory." A hot bar downtown, The Factory attracted office workers after five p.m., partiers after ten.

"Great. Meet you there at five?"

"Sure. How will I recognize you?" he asked.

"Don't worry, I'll find you."

I checked in with Gran, let her know that I was still alive. She gave me another lecture on the evils of the Council. I told her I loved her before hanging up.

Then I called Wallace.

"Hello, Holly," he answered. "Have you discovered any new evidence?"

"I'm doing great, thanks." I ran my finger over the grain of wood on my desktop.

"I do apologize, dear. You're absolutely right, where are my manners? I just naturally assumed your call had something to do with London." He didn't seem bothered by Stephanie's death at all.

"What is your deal with this girl?" I asked. "Why are you pushing so hard on this?" He had an ulterior motive here. I felt it in my bones.

"I told you, our families have been friends for years. Don't you think that young girl's killer deserves punishment?"

"Yeah, of course I do. But you're not telling me everything. For instance, why does Cade think he's babysitting me?"

He scoffed. "I have no earthly idea what you're talking about. You and Cade are supposed to be working together. If he's resistant, that's just his way. You can win him over, darlin', you're a Dumahl after all. We're very persuasive."

No, I wasn't a Dumahl. My father was a donor, not a dad. And Wallace only tolerated me because he wanted something from me. Well, I wanted something, too. "Have you started looking into my mom's disappearance?"

"I haven't had the time. Once this case is solved, I'll do as I vowed."

Hurt and anger stirred within me. "And not a minute before, huh? I guess I don't hold as much clout as London Sanders and her wealthy family." Stupidly, I'd expected him to start looking for Brianna immediately. Never trust an Other. I'd learned that lesson over and over. Not as well as I should have though, because I was astonished by his lack of give-a-damn.

"Holly, don't be that w—"

I hung up. I was tired of his genteel, coaxing tone. He probably never intended on keeping his vow to me. Well, we'd see about that. *Bastard.* He would find my mother, or I'd make his life a living hell, and I had the nullifying power to do it.

Before I could sit and brood, Sunny knocked once on the office door and ushered in a woman wearing a green and yellow silk turban. Enormous sunglasses covered half of her face.

"Holly, this is Mrs. Pascoe. She's the client I mentioned earlier." Then Sunny removed herself, shutting the door to give us some privacy.

The woman and I shook hands, and I offered her a seat.

She fondled the edge of her glasses and gracefully slid into the chair in front of my desk. Her white slacks, white blouse, and gold pumps reeked of money. But it was the white Prada calfskin bag that made me almost swoon.

I didn't know when my love of handbags became an obsession, but when I was fourteen, I saw a black Calvin Klein purse I *had* to have. I saved up my babysitting money for two years and bought it from an online discount store. I'd been adding to my collection ever since. And that white Prada was the most delicious thing I'd ever seen.

Feeling lightheaded, I swallowed and traced my brow with one finger. With difficulty, I pried my eyes from that beautiful, beautiful bag. "How can I help you?"

The woman straightened her shoulders. "I know this is absurd, but I was shopping last week, and before I got to the car, I saw this hanging from my driver's side mirror." She reached into her purse—the one I wanted to jerk out of her hands and clutch to me like a long lost child who'd been ripped from my bosom—and plucked out a naked Barbie doll. A red ribbon hung from its neck like a noose, and its head had been shaved bald so only stubble remained.

Ridiculous. I'd seen voodoo dolls hand-sewn to look like their victim, down to a mole. This shit was just lazy.

Her free hand strayed to the turban, her fingers grazing over the material. "I started losing my hair that same day. Big clumps of it."

I nodded sympathetically. Her hair would start growing back immediately. My null status couldn't reverse the spell, just put a stop to it.

"Are you able to help me?" she asked. "Someone from my tennis club said you banished a poltergeist. She swears by you."

"Definitely, but I'm going to need to perform a ceremony." Of course the spell had been broken the second she walked into my office, but I had to put on a show for the Norms.

I reached into my bottom drawer and pulled out a Ziploc bag of lavender, wood shavings, and dried rose petals, snagged a box of matches, and a glass ashtray.

"Let's go out back." The alley behind the strip mall was the best place to burn this stuff. Otherwise, Sunny complained endlessly about the stench and would run around the office with a can of air freshener for the rest of the day.

I placed the glass on the pavement and bending down, reached into the plastic bag, grabbing a handful of dried flowers and wood chips. Slowly, I crumpled them in my hand, letting them sift through my fingers and into the ashtray. I struck a match and lit it. Waving my hands in a circle over the burning flowers, I uttered some nonsense. Then I picked up the doll and waved it over the smoke, continuing to chant. After about three minutes, I took a cleansing breath and clutched the doll between my hands, as if to sense any lingering curse vibes. I smiled at Mrs. Pascoe. "It's done."

She flattened her palm over her chest. "Are you sure. My hair will start growing back?"

"Immediately. Would you like me to keep the doll?"

"Please. I never want to see that thing again."

"Go in peace." Okay, I was a fraud. A fraud who provided a highly specialized service.

When I walked her back inside and to the front door, my gaze tripped over Cade McAllister lounging in a chair in front of Sunny's desk, his long legs stretched out before him. His eyes flew over Mrs. Pascoe before landing on the doll in my hands. I couldn't tell what he was thinking. His features were inscrutable, as always.

After Mrs. Pascoe left, Cade stood. "Do you have any other bullshit rituals you'd like to perform or are we good to go?"

CHAPTER TEN

The set of his jaw told me he was angry. He plucked the sunglasses from his shirt and sauntered out the door.

"Is he always like that?" Sunny asked.

"You caught him on a good day." I hustled back to my office, dropped the doll on the desk and grabbed my black DVF purse and phone. I wasn't sure what had put the sorcerer in such a foul mood. Not sure I cared. Last night's drive-by finger-bang hadn't made me very chipper, either. Taking a deep breath, I shook it off.

When I climbed into the truck, Cade sat stony-faced behind the wheel. REO Speedwagon was cranked to annoying decibels. Cade sped down the highway, refusing to acknowledge me when I asked for the third time where we were headed. Annoyed, I reached out and snapped off the radio. Cade tried to turn it back on, but I slapped his hand.

"Are you sure you want to meet with Nick Alpert today, Null?" He said the word like it was an accusation. Last night he'd called me Holly. Last night had been a mistake.

"Yes, I still want to talk to him. London was having an affair with that werewolf, and she met him at The Raven. Maybe he's the one who sent the cursed amulet."

He paused for so long I thought maybe he was giving me the cold shoulder again. "Then why did he kill Stephanie?"

He appeared more tanned today, his profile harsher. Stubble covered his jaw. Except for the scar. This time, I squashed the temptation to touch it and kept my hands to myself.

"Stephanie was a client at Blessed Be. Maybe she saw something or overheard something. He had to take her out, too."

Cade shook his head. "Doesn't sit right. I talked to the neighbors and her coworkers. Stephanie was a quiet witch who kept to herself. Her powers were so weak, she could barely cast a protection ward on the front and back doors. A child could have broken through them. She was harmless. And for the record, talking to this shifter is a stupid waste of time. You do not want to be on a shifter's bad side. But hey, it's your funeral."

"You'd better hope so, and then I'll be out of your hair for good. No more liability."

"That's not funny," he said quietly, his eyes on the road.

"You brought it up."

"Sorry. I shouldn't have said it."

An apology? This was a landmark event. I opened my mouth to say something snarky, but when I scanned his profile, a muscle jumped in his cheek. Whatever I'd said struck a nerve.

On the surface, Cade appeared quiet, intense. Underneath, his emotions swirled turbulent and deep. Even if I wanted to delve in there, he wouldn't welcome it.

In an effort to get this relationship back on a professional footing, I changed the subject. "Where are we meeting this guy anyway? At a restaurant or something?"

He barely moved his head to the right. "Pack territory."

"Oh." Shifters, especially predators, were a volatile bunch, even in their human form. Three things drove them: the hunt, sex, or a good fight. And if they could do all three at the same time, so much the better. I'd had my fair share of dealings with weres at social events. You do not want to get between a seven-year-old shifter and ice cream cake, trust me. I still carried the scar on my knee as proof. So meeting on shifter land seemed like a very bad idea to me. "Why did you agree to this? Why not neutral ground?"

"Wouldn't talk anywhere else. I tried to warn you."

Sighing, I stared out the window as we drove toward Collinsville, about twenty miles from Tulsa. My palms felt clammy, so I reached over and cranked up the air conditioner. It didn't help. The sun beat down on the blacktop as the Ford ate up the miles between safety and pack territory.

Cade exited the highway and drove onto an outer road. It took another fifteen minutes before he made a turn down a long, unpaved drive. We passed a NO TRESPASSING sign, and I felt it was speaking directly to me.

I unbuckled my seat belt as he pulled to a stop in front of a large, modern house covered in taupe stucco. It sat back about three hundred yards from the road, surrounded by trees on one side and a field being used as a parking lot on the other. There were twenty or so vehicles here, the sun glinting off their windshields. We weren't just dealing with Nick Alpert today; we got to face the whole pack. Oh, goody.

"You don't have to do this, Little Null."

With an angry push, I shoved open the door. "Can we please stop having this discussion? I don't have a choice."

"What do you mea—"

I slammed the door on his words. Slinging the chain purse strap over my shoulder, I walked toward the house.

Cade emerged from the driver's seat and grabbed my arm. "What do you mean you don't have a choice?"

"Just forget it."

He jerked his glasses off with his free hand but kept hold of me. His fingers pressed into my skin. "What the hell are you talking about?" He lowered his brow and squinted against the sun. "I know your grandfather asked you to help me investigate. Did he threaten you or something?"

The front door of the house opened, putting an end to our conversation. A tall, lean man who appeared to be in his late twenties trotted down the porch steps, and in a few long strides, met us in front of the truck.

He had strong cheekbones with hollows beneath. A square jaw and ice blue eyes tinged with gold at the pupils gave him a regal air. But that face was completely at odds with his shoulder-length, sun-streaked hair, faded Abercrombie tee, and ripped jeans frayed at the hems above his bare feet. Surfer Dude meets Disney Prince.

"McAllister."

Cade let go of my arm and shook his hand. "Dawson."

The man turned his gaze on me. "Null." He tipped his head almost imperceptibly.

"This is Holly James. Holly, Dawson Nash, Alpha of eastern Oklahoma."

"Pleased to meet you," I said.

"We're extending you a courtesy, Holly. Violate that courtesy, and you'll be dead." His unusual eyes bore through me. In spite of the heat, a chill raced up my spine.

Cade smoothly angled his body, inserting his broad shoulder as a barrier between the Alpha and me. "Save your threats, wolf. She's no harm to you."

Dawson's gaze slid back and forth between the two of us, and then he threw out a wide smile. He seemed more approachable, friendlier. But I didn't trust it. He probably smiled that way before he changed into a wolf and ripped out an innocent squirrel's jugular.

"Make sure she keeps it that way." Dawson ambled toward the house and jogged up the steps, expecting us to follow.

He held the front door open, and without thinking, I walked in first. Cade quickly pulled ahead, shoving me behind him before entering the spacious living area off the entryway.

A pretty young woman popped out of a hallway and parked herself in front of us. She whipped her light brown hair over one shoulder. "You're not welcome here." She flicked a glance at Dawson. "Letting her come was a mistake, big brother. Now she knows where we live."

Dawson moved so quietly, I didn't know he was standing next to me until he spoke. "My mistake to make, Tessa."

"It should have been a group decision. We're all affected by her, we should all have a vote." She may have been talking to Dawson, but her blue eyes slowly dissected me, starting with my Steve Madden sandals and working up. She must have taken particular offense at my wool scarf because her scowl deepened considerably.

"If you ever become Alpha, darlin', you can install democracy," Dawson said. "In the meantime, if you don't like the way I do things, you can always leave."

Tessa's narrowed gaze returned to her brother. She lowered her head a touch, and her upper lip curled back, showing a hint of teeth.

Next to me, Dawson growled deep in his chest. He may have been human at that moment, but he sure as hell sounded like a wolf.

Tessa blinked and snapped out of it. Raising her brow, she gave him a one-fingered salute. "Fuck you, loser." Then she stomped off to the living room, her hips swaying in time to her swinging mane of hair.

Dawson bent and whispered in my ear, "Little sisters. Can't live with 'em, can't eviscerate 'em. Well, you can, but you wind up grounded for six months. Come on in."

He led the way to a room that was as big as a barn; comfortable oversized furniture filled the space, giving it a cozy feel despite its size. A faint whiff of lavender air freshener mingled with lemon furniture polish. Sunshine poured in from tall windows and cast a glow on honey-colored wood floors.

About twenty-five adult shifters sat before us. Their low chatter stopped as soon as we walked in.

Dawson Nash took up residence at the wide, stone fireplace, looking relaxed as he propped one hand on the mantle, the other on his hip. He nodded to two empty chairs in the center of the room, facing him.

As Cade and I sat, I glanced at our audience. The pack, men and women from late teens to early bird specials, all had one thing in common. Despite their various casual postures, distrust and animosity flashed from every pair of eyes. All directed at me.

A man in jeans and a tight black t-shirt that clung to his overdeveloped muscles stepped forward and stood near Dawson. From his sharp, bladed nose and deeply tanned skin, I suspected he was part Native American. A skeletal Cherokee warrior inked on his bicep confirmed it. His dark hair was shaved almost completely bald, and his eyes were so brown they appeared black. He had a hot, scary, unpredictable vibe going on. This was the bad boy your mama warned you about—and she was right.

"I'm Nick Alpert. You wanted to talk to me?"

I glanced at Cade, but he said nothing. Since he'd insisted on taking the lead with Mick Raven, I was a little surprised. Apparently, this was going to be The Holly Show.

I clasped my hands together in my lap. "Thanks for meeting with us. We're here about London Sanders."

Nick crossed his arms over his massive chest. "No shit."

He wasn't going to make this easy. "What was the nature of your relationship?"

"We drank tea and ate cupcakes." Scorn dripped from his deep voice.

There were a few titters around the room.

"Muffin more like," a male voice called.

That ticked me off. Where was their respect? "Funny," I said over my shoulder. The smug asshole stood in the corner, wearing a smirk. "Would you like to make any more sex jokes at the expense of a *murder* victim?" The laughter abruptly stopped, and the culprit skewered me with a glare.

I focused on the enforcer once more. "Why were you so rough with her, Nick? You left her covered in bruises."

His flat, brown eyes flashed with emotion. "What London and I did was our business."

I shook my head. "Not anymore. She was murdered, and that means her life is an open book. Reports say you left her bruised after a bout of rough sex. I know shifters lack self-control…" Everyone in this room already hated my guts so I had nothing to lose by laying it out there as bluntly as I could. Might as well see if I could antagonize Nick into revealing something.

He slowly uncrossed his arms and took a step toward me. Dawson Nash's hand on his chest stopped him.

"Shut up." Nick extended his arm, pointing his finger at me. "You don't know what the hell you're talking about. I never hurt her. And I was very careful not to bruise her. What we did together was entirely consensual, you bitch."

"Watch yourself," Cade said.

I flicked a glance at McAllister. Why was he defending me? Because he felt responsible for my safety? He was an honorable guy with a strong sense of duty, whether he liked me or not. I stupidly felt myself softening toward him. Just the tiniest bit.

My eyes returned to Nick. What he said didn't ring true with the little I knew about London. Tamara Dermot said London liked rough sex and being on display. It sounded to me like she wore those bruises as a badge of honor. But if Nick was telling the truth about leaving her unharmed, who marked her?

I decided to push him further, see if I could get him to crack. "How did you feel about the fact that London was dating someone else while she was eating cupcakes with you? Maybe that pissed you off enough to kill her."

Silence. Not a sound in the room.

Nick's lips thinned, and his hands balled into meaty fists. "Bullshit. We were exclusive. I wouldn't hurt London, and I sure as shit didn't kill her."

Dawson lost his casual position. Dropping his hand from the mantle, he took a step toward Nick.

"So you didn't know she was dating a vampire?" I asked.

"What? You're crazy."

"No, it's true."

He glanced at Cade. Whatever he saw there made his shoulders inch toward his ears. "What's the vamp's name?" he ground out.

I ignored his question and asked another one of my own. "How well did London know Vane Aldridge?"

"What the fuck?" Nick spun, punched a round stone in the fireplace, and immediately cradled his hand. "Goddamn." Looking back at me, his nostrils flared. "She was cheating on me? For real?"

I lifted a shoulder. "She was definitely dating the vamp, and she was seen publicly with Aldridge."

He breathed audibly through his nose, noisy gusts of air. In and out. "That bitch."

Dawson wrapped his hand around Nick's forearm. "Be calm." His voice was low and soothing. I wondered if it was an Alpha technique, using his voice to soothe the pack.

If so, it wouldn't work in my presence. In fact, the whole mood of the room had changed. Every shifter seemed tense, ready to pounce.

"Did you know London dabbled in black magic?" I asked.

At hearing the news, Nick's face became a mask of anguish. Taking his shirt in both hands, he ripped it down the middle and let out a god awful howl. Then he ran from the room and flung himself out the front door.

I whispered to Cade, "Guess not."

Except for Dawson, the other pack members followed him. They shed their clothes as they fled. I tactfully stared at the ceiling beam instead of bare butts, breasts, and balls.

Once they were gone, I lowered my eyes. My gaze landed on a very annoyed Dawson Nash.

Hands shoved into the pockets of his faded jeans, he shook his head. "Great job. You really know how to work a room, Null."

CHAPTER ELEVEN

Cade didn't say one word until he parked at a rest stop twenty minutes from Nash's house. He unbuckled his belt and ripped off his sunglasses, throwing them on the dashboard. "Do you know what happened back there?"

"I—"

"You just pissed off an entire goddamned werewolf pack."

"But—"

"You told Alpert his girl was fucking two other men. You accused him of murder on top of it. Are you out of your mind?" His darkened eyes were fixed on mine. "Well?"

"Oh, do I get to talk now? Look, he wasn't going to tell me anything. That whole pack resented me being there. I thought by provoking him, he might let something slip."

Cade rolled his eyes. "You definitely provoked him, so good work. And what did you mean when you said you had no choice but to talk to the wolf?"

I blinked at his sudden change in topic. Nervously chewing off my lip gloss, I weighed the idea of telling him everything about Wallace, my unknown father, my missing mother. Then decided against it. I didn't want to lay open my life, reveal all my secrets any more than he did. "I didn't mean anything. I just want to find the killer."

"I can't help you if you're not honest with me." His rough voice softened just a smidge. "And I can't have your personal agenda interfering with my investigation."

I raised a brow. "Your investigation?" Nothing was more important to Cade than his job. God, I was stupid. When was I going to get it through my skull that Cade didn't care about me? As soon as we found the killer, he'd be gone. I'd never see him again.

"If you keep me in the dark, I can't guarantee your safety," he said.

I faced the window and looked out at the picnic tables dotting the rest area. "I don't need your protection."

Cade's laugh was rusty. "The hell you don't. Entire wolf pack. Pissed off. Remember?" He brushed the hair off my shoulder and fingered the scarf at my throat. "Let me see your hickey."

I ignored him.

He gave the long scarf a tug. "Come on. Let me see."

It was the gentle tone that did it. In spite of everything, I liked him. Cade was gruff and angry one minute, gruff and sexy the next. But if I didn't keep my guard up, I'd end up heartbroken when all this was over. I really liked my heart in one solid piece, thank you.

I swiveled in my seat to face him. He lowered the scarf with one finger. His gaze landed on the vamp's bite, and his features hardened.

"That little fucker is going to pay." He slid his finger from the scarf and ran it along my jaw. "Tell me what's going on with Wallace. Your secret is safe with me. I give you my oath."

My breath caught in my throat. I knew Cade wouldn't make an oath lightly. And if I didn't trust him completely, I trusted in that. But I wasn't prepared to tell him the whole truth. "Wallace promised me a favor in exchange for helping find the murderer."

He scoffed. "You're not an investigator. No one expects you to find the killer. That's ridiculous."

"Wallace does."

"Must be a damn important favor."

"It is," I said. "It's vital."

"How can you trust him? He's a politician. He wouldn't know the truth if it blew him. And he's up for reelection this year. London's family are powerful backers."

"Ah. That explains why he cares about London's death, but not Stephanie's." Figured. I finally met my father's family, and they turned out to be politicians. So damned typical.

"Sorry, I shouldn't have said that. He is your grandpa."

"It doesn't matter. He made a vow to help me. I'm holding him to it."

Once again, Cade reached out and caressed me, brushed his warm fingers over my cheek. "I could help you with this favor. If you'd let me."

Before I could answer, my phone rang. *I'm Only Happy When it Rains.* Sunny's ringtone.

"Sorry." I dug my phone out of my purse. "What's up?"

"I haven't found out anything about Vane Aldridge. Either he's a ghost or you have the name wrong. I'm betting on the latter. And I canceled all of your appointments for the rest of the week. Dr. Fischbein was most displeased."

"He'll get over it." I worked with an empath couples' counselor on a case by case basis. He was a decent guy, and I'd make it up to him. I ended the call, glad that Sunny interrupted when she had. The conversation with Cade had been getting too serious for me. I was sorely tempted to tell him my life's story and accept his offer of help. But if Wallace had his own motives, Cade did, too. His first obligation was as an investigator, and he wanted me off this case in a bad way. Still, he needed my help. I had no skills and no experience, but I'd learned more in a couple of days than he had in two weeks. Wallace had been right. I was a nonentity in the Other world. People didn't care what they said to me.

I faced forward and remained silent, felt Cade's eyes on me. But he didn't make the offer to help again.

Retrieving his sunglasses from the dash, he re-buckled his seat belt and got back on the highway. We didn't speak for a long time. Finally, Cade stopped at a fast food place and ordered a late lunch from the drive thru.

We ate in silence as he drove. Fifteen minutes later, he stopped at a rundown Mom and Pop convenience store in North Tulsa. Not the safest neighborhood. I'd have questioned him about it, but I knew he'd pay zero attention to me and crank up the Pink Floyd. So why bother?

When he left the truck, I pulled out my Bobbi Brown lip gloss and turned down the visor to stare into the mirror. When Cade opened my door, I was so startled, I almost glossed outside my natural lip line.

"Come on. Don't have all day, Little Null."

"I don't need to go inside. I'm good." I raised the pink-colored wand to my lips.

Cade plucked it and the tube from my hands.

"Hey, what the hell, McAllister?"

He held them aloft. "Out. Now."

I sighed. Deeply. Once I climbed out, he handed them back, then grasping my elbow, led me into the building. He nodded at the young guy manning the counter and walked past the cigarettes, the refrigerated beer section, the SlimJims, all the way to the swinging employee door in the back.

"Is this your day job?" I asked as I stumbled along, my toes barely touching the ground. "You know you have a very bad habit of hauling me around."

"Shut up."

We blew by shelves of paper products, stacked cardboard boxes of breath mints, and a mop bucket to the final door on the right. When Cade knocked, I stuck the lip gloss back in my purse.

A short, bald man opened the door, grinning when he saw Cade. "Ah, my friend, how have you been?" He glanced at me. "This is something very interesting you've brought me today." He showed me his white, even teeth.

The man stepped aside and allowed us to enter the janitorial closet. With the three of us in there, the room seemed even smaller than it actually was. Gallon bottles filled with green, pink, and blue liquid lined up neatly on metal shelves. A sharp chemical stench made my eyes water.

Cade finally released my arm. "Amit, this is Holly. We need to get her hooked up."

"Nice to meet you, Amit." I glanced up at Cade. "What's going on?" I mouthed.

Cade propped his hands on his hips. "I'm thinking something small, but effective."

Amit took one of my hands in his. "Yes, very delicate." Then he wrenched a cardboard box the size of a microwave from the bottom shelf. As he opened it up, I peeked inside, gasping in surprise at the pile of guns.

I looked up at Cade. "No. No way. I'm not getting a gun."

Amit bent over and dug through them, pulling out a tiny revolver.

Cade shook his head. "That one's for pussies. She needs something that will make a statement."

"No," I said. "Thank you so much, Amit, but I don't need to make a statement."

Amit pulled a Cade and ignored me as he dug through the box a little more. "Ah." He came out with a semi-automatic. He caressed the butt of the gun lovingly. "This little beauty will do very nicely. Sig Sauer P225. Can't find these puppies anymore." He handed it to Cade.

Cade weighed it in his hand, made sure it was empty of bullets. He gripped the gun, and extending his arm, aimed it at the floor. "Yep feels good. Load us up."

I tugged on Cade's sleeve. "Listen up, Sor...," I glanced over at Amit, who shoved the box back on the shelf.

"He knows what I am."

"Oh." I wondered what type of Other Amit was. And why he needed guns.

Amit grabbed another box, a smaller one, and extracted a magazine. "Standard nine millimeter."

Cade loaded the gun then he grabbed my purse, which was barely big enough to hold all the stuff I had crammed into it.

"I don't want this, Cade."

He began extracting items from my bag—my wallet, makeup, Always panty liners with wings, my phone—and tossed them at me. I caught them, fumbled a couple of times, but recovered. With my belongings in the crook of my arm, I tried to pull the bag out of his grasp.

He gave me an icy glare, and I knew he wasn't going to let go. If he thought I was willing to damage my DVF just to make a point, he was sadly mistaken. I glared at him and released the strap.

Amit grinned like this was the most entertaining thing he'd ever witnessed. "Normally I'd charge one thousand but for you, my friend, seven hundred with the ammo."

Cade hung my purse from his wrist, which should have looked ridiculous, but instead, he made it into a tough guy accessory. He plucked his wallet from his back pocket and removed a few bills. "I'll give you five."

Amit scratched his brow, but after a second, he snatched the money from Cade. "Only for you. But you owe me."

"No. I don't."

Cade took my elbow, strode through the store and back to his truck. He opened the passenger door for me and placed the bag on my lap. Once he climbed in the cab, I let loose.

"I am not carrying a gun, Cade. I don't know how to get that through your stubborn head, but I am not. Carrying. A gun."

He started the ignition. Putting the truck in gear, he squealed out of the parking lot.

"I'm throwing it away. Hope you know that."

"If you're going to go around pissing off Others, you had better be able to protect yourself. And at the rate you're going, you're going to need that gun sooner rather than later. Now, if you decide to throw it away, we'll just buy another one. On your dime."

He drove the highway and sped past my office exit.

"Where are we headed now?" I asked, not really expecting an answer.

"I overheard your secretary on the phone. She can't find anything on Vane Aldridge. I know where his great-great-granddad lives. I'd take you back to your office and go it alone, but you'd probably just follow me or worse."

"True." This felt like a small victory. Cade wasn't prattling on about how I shouldn't be a nosy null, I shouldn't be questioning Others, blah, blah, blah. He was almost treating me like a partner.

"And after we're through I'm going to teach you how to shoot that gun."

I didn't want to learn how to shoot. But a part of me knew he was right. Others may not be able to use their magic on me, but they could put a bullet right through my brain. Would be nice if I had a fighting chance.

#

Thaddeus Aldridge was a loon. What else would explain hubcaps and rusted mufflers hanging from a tree in the front yard like ripened fruit? Or the army of ceramic gnomes lined up in formation on the sparse brown lawn, waving gardening implements like weapons?

His ramshackle property stood six miles from the highway. The narrow, two-story house was missing more paint than not. Faded red shutters hung cockeyed next to filthy windows. On the sagging porch sat a ripped, floral sofa. On that sofa sat an old man wearing overalls—no shirt—chain smoking and using a Folgers coffee can for an ashtray.

Cade parked in front of the house and we stepped out into the heat. No wind moved the heavy, humid air.

Before we took two steps toward him, the old man stood, flicked the butt in the can, and grabbed a gnarled wooden wand from his pocket. "Get off my land. This here is private property." He raised the wand, pointed it toward us, then looked at it with a frown. His eyes shot to me. "What the Sam Hill?"

"I'm a null."

Surprise flashed across his features as he made a move to dash inside but Cade was there before him, blocking the screen door. "Sit down, old man. We're just here to talk."

The heavy scarf draped around my neck itched, and I rubbed at it while I climbed the weathered, rickety porch steps to get a better look at the loon in question. Thaddeus Aldridge could be summed up in one color: gray. Gray hair, gray stubble, gray skin.

His sunken brown eyes shot angry daggers at Cade. "I don't have to talk to you."

Cade crossed his arms. "According to section three-thirteen, subsection B of the Code—"

"Don't quote the Code to me, son, I wrote the damned book." He stomped back to the sofa and fell onto it.

"My name's Cade McAllister. I'm a Council investigator."

"I don't give a hot goddamn who you are. This is my house, and you brought a null here. Now I'm gonna have to redo all my wards. You know how long that'll take?"

Cade walked from the door to perch his ass on the porch railing. I copied his move.

With a sigh, Aldridge lit up a smoke, squinting as he inhaled. He ran a thumb over a groove in the wand.

Wands were passé. Even Gran didn't use a wand back in the day. They were a crutch. If you rely on your wand and find yourself without it, you're screwed.

"Where's Vane?" Cade asked.

The old fart puffed away. Soon his head was enveloped in a cloud of smoke. "How should I know? That boy don't inform me of his comings and goings."

Cade turned to me. "Go check inside. See what you can find."

On the one hand, I really didn't want to go into the house. Who knew what disaster lurked there? On the other hand, I was suspicious that Cade might discover some clue and not share it with me. No matter which hand I chose, it was a lose-lose proposition.

I looked into Cade's eyes, widened mine in warning, and poked his chest with a finger. "We're partners, don't forget."

When I walked inside the house, letting the screen door slam behind me, I heard Aldridge's wheezy laugh. "I reckon she's a handful."

"You have no idea," Cade rumbled.

The place reeked with sixty years' worth of stale smoke that was probably embedded into the walls and scarred wood floor. Newspapers, old coffee cups, and dust covered every surface. I walked to the kitchen. It was even grosser in there. Years of food had been cooked onto the stovetop. It made the burger I'd eaten earlier rebel in my stomach.

I took in the kitchen and spotted the phone. He had an old-fashioned, yellow rotary attached to the wall. Rotary, for God's sake. No redial, no phone history.

But next to the phone, I found a number written in ink on the peeling wallpaper. I didn't use my cell because I didn't want it to show up on caller ID. So with two fingers, I gingerly picked up the receiver and spun the dial.

A deep voice answered. "Hey, Gramps, what's up?"

"Um, hi. Is this Vane?"

"Who the fuck is this?"

I swallowed. "My name is Holly James. Cade McAllister and I are—"

He hung up on me. Son of a bitch.

I grabbed my phone, entered the number in my address book, and walked back outside.

Cade had his chin propped in one hand as he nodded, listening to the old man.

"Probably using some ancient black spell to mask the signature," Thaddeus said around a cigarette. "But when you run into the caster, you should find a trace of it on his aura." He stopped to hack before spitting into the coffee can. "Sorry 'bout that. Anyway, you can't hide a dark aura for long. Not without a continual supply of sacrificial blood and blowing through a lot of power. It always leaves a stain somewhere."

Cade glanced at me, his eyebrows shooting up. "Find anything?"

"I called Vane, and he hung up on me."

Thaddeus sniffed. "Yeah, he don't like to talk on the phone none. Especially to strangers. And if'n he knew you was a null, he'd be even less inclined."

"Well, thanks for your time." Cade held out his hand, and the old man shook it. "Good to talk shop with you."

"Come back and see me, son. But don't bring this one." He jerked his head in my direction.

I rolled my eyes and made my way to the Ford. As I did, I held the ends of the scarf up to my nose. I stank of cigarette smoke. Blech.

Cade took the gravel road leading to the highway. I slid my gaze to him. "I have Vane's number."

"Good."

I waited a beat. "What did you mean back there about talking shop?"

"Thaddeus used to be an investigator himself. He's still sharp."

"Learn anything new?"

"Not really."

"Did he tell you about Vane?"

"No." He turned on the radio to block my questions.

I reached out and hit the search button. I was tired of classic rock. I stopped on a country station. "So what is Vane Aldridge and how did he know London? Why would he want to kill her? Bigger question, why would he want to kill Stephanie?"

"He didn't kill anybody, Holly. Vane works for the Council."

I stared at him in silence for a full minute. "What the hell, Cade? Did you know this all along?" I smacked my forehead. Of course he did. That's why he'd tensed up when Mick Raven said the name. "How long were you going to keep this from me?"

"I'm telling you now."

Seething, I stared out the window. What else was McAllister hiding? Probably a whole host of things. That just jacked my anger up even further. "What does Vane Aldridge do for the Council?"

"He enforces their decisions."

I turned to him. "What does that mean?"

He twisted his lips to one side and remained silent.

"You know what? Forget it. Take me back to my office, please." It was after four, and I was supposed to meet Brant Braxton for mojitos at five. After a day in the sorcerer's company, I deserved two.

I didn't need McAllister. He held back more information than he shared, and it was starting to chap my hide. I'd done pretty well on my own without his help. I'd continue doing so until I found the murderer. Then Wallace would start searching for my mother, and I'd never have to endure Cade's company again.

That last one stung just a bit.

"We should go to the range," he said. "You need to practice shooting that gun."

"I have an appointment at five." I'd been planning to let him tag along, but now that I'd discovered his latest deception, forget it.

"Fine," he ground out, "I'll pick you up at your place at seven."

I thought about skipping out on him. He must have read my mind because he added, "You don't want to make me hunt you down, Null. Trust me."

That was just it. I wanted to trust him. But he made it so damned hard.

CHAPTER TWELVE

The Factory used to manufacture buttons until the early 80s, and then the building sat vacant for years. Now it's a club. Lots of brick. Lots of young professionals stopping for a drink or two before heading home. Lots of crappy appetizers. Things would pick up after seven or eight but in the meantime, I got scoped out by Norm bankers and real estate brokers as I wended through the room.

I glanced around, looking for a guy who seemed on the verge of a panic attack. Ah, there he was, sitting at the bar.

I walked up to him and tapped his shoulder. "Hello, I'm Holly James." I held out my hand. "Brant Braxton?" He was all beefy, muscled goodness with highlighted hair. A turquoise V-neck tee nicely displayed his waxed he-vage.

He nodded. "I can't stay. Something's wrong with me. I don't feel well."

I hopped onto the stool next to him. "I'm a null. You'll be fine when I leave."

Brant looked at me with wide blue eyes. "I thought that null stuff was just talk."

I shrugged. "Let me buy you a drink." I nodded at the bartender and ordered two mojitos. While we waited, I pulled the notebook out of my purse. In the truck, I'd stuck it and my phone back in the bag, wedging them around the gun. Now I did my best to pretend the Sig wasn't there.

"Love the handbag," Brant said.

"Thanks. Diane Von Furstenberg."

"She's an icon for a reason. But that scarf you're wearing is a mess."

"I know." In a self-conscious move, I adjusted it, twisting the black material around my neck. "I'm really sorry about London. Her death must have come as a shock."

He nodded but as soon as the bartender set down his drink, Brant winked and smiled at the man. "Call me," he mouthed. The bartender rolled his eyes and walked away. Color me a wackadoo, but Brant didn't seem that bummed his friend was dead.

"How did you know London?" I took a sip and flipped the notebook open to a fresh page.

"I was her hairdresser. She came in at least twice a month. I specialize in hair potions and tonics. You'll never see one of my clients with split ends." Brant eyed me critically, tilting his head this way and that. "Who does your hair by the way? It's good, but I think I could make it better."

"What would you do?"

Reaching out, he ran a hand through it, pulling it away from my face. "I'd give you a few more layers. And maybe put in mahogany lowlights?" He pushed his lips out. "Of course I'd have to hide my charmed scissors and put foil in your hair the way the Norms do, but I'm good enough I could still make it look amazing."

I pulled a dark brown strand in front of me, staring at it until my eyes crossed, then dropped it back in place. "Maybe. So, you and London were pretty tight?"

Brant shrugged and sipped from his straw. "Not very. She had a weird side. Kind of kinky, kind of hot. We hung out some, but more as acquaintances, you know?"

"How kinky?" I thought I knew the answer from the information Tamara Dermot had shared, but wolf enforcer, Nick Alpert, swore he never left marks on London. So who was telling the truth?

"She liked it rough," Brant said. "Had the bruises to prove it. She acted like it was no biggie, but girl, why not glamour over those black and blue marks? I'm all for raising the freak flag, but sometimes you need to keep your shiz locked down. Know what I mean?"

I nodded. "She seemed proud of the bruises?"

He thought for a second. "I don't know if proud is the word. More matter of fact. She wore those bruises like she would a pair of earrings."

I made a few notes in my book. "I saw a picture of you at the Summer Solstice party."

"That was a fun night. London's parents came back to organize it—they live in Florida now. Anyway, it was amazing. Best food ever. Sushi flown in from Cali. So fresh, it was practically swimming." He spun on his stool and scoped out the place. Smiling coyly, he winked at someone standing across the room.

"Did she mention a boyfriend?"

Brant swiveled back around and smiled. "Sweetie, hairdressers are like priests. We hear all the dirty details." He leaned toward me and spoke right in my ear. "She was dating a vamp." He pulled back, his eyebrows raised over wide eyes. "Said it was the hottest sex she'd ever had. Like multi-orgasmic. You girls are so lucky."

"What about the werewolf?"

Clapping, Brant let out a laugh. "You know about that, too? Good for you. He's the one who roughed her up. But like I said, that was her thing. She never apologized for who she was. You've got to admire that in a person." He stared into his glass and frowned. "I'm going to miss her."

"According to the wolf, he didn't leave bruises on London."

Brant appeared startled. "Maybe he's lying? Because she had definitely been roughed up. And if he didn't do it, then I have no clue who did. London told me she was dating a werewolf who liked to mark his territory. That's all I know."

"Was Stephanie Carson a client of yours, as well?"

"Is she a mousy little witch? Keeps to herself?"

"That's her," I said.

"No, but she should be. Wait, you said *was*. Is she dead, too?" He grabbed my wrist. "I saw her the night of the Solstice party."

Now, this was news. London's former bestie, Tamara, hadn't said a word about it. "Stephanie was there? For how long? Did you talk to her?"

"No, she wasn't a guest. I saw her in the kitchen on my way to the bathroom. She was part of the catering staff. I remember feeling sorry for her. What a way to spend Solstice, plating tempura rolls for other witches."

Maybe Stephanie had overheard something at the party. Saw something she shouldn't have? Did that mean the killer was at the party, too?

"I really want to catch the person responsible for this. Brant, do you have any idea who would want to kill London?"

"Other than those two crazies she dated? No idea. And who would hurt little Stephanie? She wouldn't holler at a ghost. Sad." He drained his glass. "Seriously, that is just sad."

I stared at him closely. "Did you know London was a dabbler?"

His face went slack. "You're shitting me? You think you know a person."

We talked a few minutes more, but I didn't find out anything else. Brant gave me his card and made me promise to call. I thanked him and threw a twenty on the bar.

#

When I got home, I changed into jeans and a t-shirt but kept the scarf. I transferred everything, including the damned gun, out of my small purse and into a blue Coach tote. I barely had time for a frozen dinner—chicken with fiesta rice—before Cade showed up.

He looked exactly as he had a few hours ago. *Sexy good.*

His gaze slid up and down my body, stopping long enough to read my shirt—*Boys Are Stinky*—and hitched his thumb over his shoulder. "Let's go."

So we weren't going to talk about this afternoon? Or that he kept important information from me? Perfect. Maybe I'd keep the news about Stephanie Carson being at London's party to myself, too.

I waved him out of the house and locked the door. I said nothing on the way to the truck. He said nothing on the drive to the range. We let AC/DC do the talking for us.

Cade drove to a freestanding building off Harvard Avenue. The parking spots in front of the range were full, so Cade pulled to the far side of the lot.

Inside was a cool respite from the humidity. About ten customers wandered around the store. Unfortunately, it was also crammed to the brim with guns of every size and style. I didn't like guns or violence. Words and a snarky attitude were my weapons of choice. Still, I didn't think a well-stated put-down would stop a pissed off Nick Alpert in his tracks.

Cade strode forward where a tall man and an older, white-haired guy stood behind the counter. Cade lifted his chin in greeting. "We need gear, two boxes of nine millimeters, and a couple of targets."

The tall guy nodded. "Sure thing." He reached under the counter and pulled out two pairs of shooting glasses and noise-reducing headphones. While we showed our IDs and signed release forms, the older guy set an extraordinary amount of bullets in front of us.

I nudged Cade with my elbow. "Why do we need so much ammo?"

"Because you're going to miss. A lot." He whipped out his wallet and paid the guy, then scooped up the ear muffs and dropped them over my head. Carefully, he placed the glasses on the bridge of my nose.

"How do I look?"

His eyes scanned my face before putting on his own gear. "Hot," he mouthed. Then he took off through the door that led to the range.

He thought I looked hot? Feverish or sexy? Considering I'd been out in the blistering heat and humidity all day and wore a seasonally inappropriate scarf to cover my vamp hickey, it was probably the former.

With reluctance, I walked onto the range. There were eight other shooters lined up in little booths. Cade waited for me in one. When I stopped in front of him, he reached out and gently unknotted my scarf and slid it from my neck. Then tugging my purse from my shoulder, he thrust the bag at me and gestured that I should remove the gun.

I reached into my purse and plucked it out. Holding the gun's barrel by my thumb and forefinger, I carefully handed it to him.

Cade rolled his eyes and, grasping it firmly, showed me how to pull back the slide to make sure there wasn't a live round in the chamber. He lifted the edge of my ear muff. "There's no safety, just a hammer lock." He showed me that, too, and how to load it.

"Your first shot will be a double action. It will require a stronger finger pull. After that, it's easy." He held the gun in both hands, turned toward the target, adjusted his stance, and shot until he was out of bullets. He hit the button to bring the target forward. Cade had shot a smiley face, and the rest of the bullets hit the center of the chest.

"Show off."

He reloaded the clip and held it out to me. With shaking fingers, I took it. Cade stood back a pace, allowing me to step in front of him. When he moved behind me, heat radiated off him, making my own body temperature rise. I closed my eyes as he wrapped his muscular arms around me, cradling my forearms in his big hands. His delicious scent mingled with the gun smoke.

When his fingers slid down to my wrists, my eyes popped open. Every time he touched me, little waves of pleasure zipped through my body. I fought the feeling, but it was useless. I was hopelessly attracted to the sorcerer.

He leaned down, his breath fanning the side of my neck. "Gently squeeze," he said, loud enough so I could hear through the headphones.

I took a deep breath and tried to focus on the target guy who'd never said a bad word about me. Then I squeezed the trigger. He was right, I had to squeeze hard that first time, but after that, the shots came fast. *Boom, boom, boom.* I felt the recoil all the way up to my shoulder.

Even after I'd shot all the bullets, Cade remained glued to my back. As the target man fluttered toward us, I noticed that I had almost hit him once, near the left shoulder.

"Okay, can we go now?"

"No. Do it again. You load it this time."

We spent the next hour reloading and shooting the gun. Eventually, Cade moved away from me, and I shot on my own. I could aim better when he wasn't plastered against me. I managed to shoot the silhouette man in his intestines. I didn't know whether to feel proud that I'd made a hit or repulsed because I'd just used a deadly weapon. Pride crept over the finish line by a nose.

At the front of the shop, only two other customers milled about. We dropped off our safety gear, then Cade led me into the one person bathroom, shutting the door behind us.

I looked up at him with a raised brow. "I can manage on my own, thanks."

"You need to wash the lead residue off your hands. Cool water."

When I realized he wasn't leaving, I turned on the faucet, pumped some soap into my hands, and glanced up in the mirror. My eyes met Cade's. He stood behind me as he had in the range, his wide-spread legs framing my shorter ones. He stuck his hands under the water and grasped my fingers, rubbing them gently. His thumbs pressed little circles over my palms, but his gaze never veered from mine.

The moment stretched out. I stopped breathing for a second. Without thinking, I pushed my ass backward, rubbing it along his zipper.

Still keeping eye contact in the mirror, Cade lowered his head and nuzzled my cheek. As his hips moved forward, his hard-on prodded my lower back. The combination of his five o'clock shadow gently abrading my skin and the enticing feel of his cock made me ache. I angled my head so I could trace my tongue along the line of his scar.

One of his wet hands caressed my wrist, while his other hand brushed the bruise along my neck. The cold water felt soothing against my tender skin. Cade captured my mouth in a hot kiss, his firm lips taking control of mine. I swayed against him, and his solid body held me upright.

Cade's touch made me long for something I could never have. This attraction between the two of us would fizzle out. I was an anathema to everything he was. It would be very stupid to get tangled up with him. Every self-protective instinct I had told me to run. But my damned emotions—they wanted to tangle with him in the worst way.

A knock jerked us apart. Cade released my wrist and, reaching past me, yanked the door open.

The tall guy smiled at us. "Doing okay in here?"

"Fine," Cade growled.

The guy held up his hands, began walking backward. "Just checking."

Cade snagged a paper towel and stormed out of the bathroom. I watched him go, taking a second to compose myself. I glanced in the mirror and wrapped the scarf back around my neck, tying it in place with shaky hands.

I hastened to the front of the store where Cade stood at the glass door. When I approached he held it open, and we stepped out into the heat. "We're going to have to come back. You need practice. Your aim sucks." He stared down at me as he hit the starter on his key fob.

"My aim doesn't suck. I made a perfectly decent gut shot."

Then an explosion rocked the night.

CHAPTER THIRTEEN

I didn't have time to react as the truck's hood catapulted high into the air. Immediately, Cade began moving his lips and swirling his fingers in an incantation—probably a protective spell to shield us from the fallout. A confused expression crossed his face until he realized that he couldn't perform magic around me. As glass and fiery metal rained down on us, Cade quickly shoved me to the asphalt and landed on top of me, knocking all the air out of my lungs. My knees and palms stung from slamming into the ground.

Cade covered me completely, making it hard to breathe. Finally, he rose and snaked an arm around my torso, jerking me to my feet. Then he spun and carried me around the corner of the building.

My heart raced. Fear flooded my system. "What the hell?"

"Are you all right?"

"Yeah." My hands shook as I clung to his t-shirt. There were cuts along his neck and a slash below his ear. "Who did this?" Sirens sounded in the distance.

"I don't know," he growled. "But I'll find out."

It finally dawned on me that we were standing next to a building filled with ammunition. "Oh, my God. The bullets. We have to get out of here."

Cade peered around the corner. "The truck wasn't close enough to the store. They're not going to blow. It was a shock, not being able to raise a protection shield, but the fire's already dying down, and we're still alive." He peered down at me. That's when I noticed a jagged gash on his forearm. It looked deep. Blood poured down his elbow.

"You're hurt." I unwound the scarf from my neck and began wrapping it around his arm.

"Stop, Holly, I'm fine."

I kept winding, over and over, until it was a bulky bandage. I had to stop the bleeding. I pulled the material tight, tied a huge knot. "It's not near an artery, is it?" Panic filled my chest. Pressing my trembling hands to his wound, I gazed up at him. "I'm sorry. I'm so sorry, Cade."

His hand cupped my chin, and I noticed scrapes along his knuckles. "Not your fault. You're bleeding, too, Little Null." His thumb grazed my jaw. "I don't think it will scar. Too shallow."

I didn't care about scarring, and it *was* my fault. If I hadn't been here, he could have protected himself and shut down the fire. My presence put his life in danger.

Minutes later, two fire trucks parked on the street in front of the shop. Three police cruisers and an ambulance drove into the lot. Cade kissed my forehead before taking my hand and leading me around the corner to the front of the store. Our feet crunched over shards of broken glass, and I sidestepped larger pieces of debris.

The truck was still on fire, but the flames were low. Thick, black smoke rose from the remnants. The foul smell was nausea-inducing. I was just so grateful all the ammo in the gun store hadn't blown up.

The two employees stood on the far side of the building, soaking wet. I glanced through the window to see they'd triggered the sprinkler system. Water rained down from the ceiling, making everything a drippy mess. The black finish on the guns looked oily slick.

In just minutes, the fireman doused the truck. The police had pulled us toward the street, and one EMT doctored Cade's arm while the other dabbed at my face.

I felt numb, shocky. Someone tried to fucking kill us. If Cade and I had gotten in the truck instead of using his remote, we'd be charred ash.

Without warning, my knees buckled and I collapsed to the ground. The EMTs tried to coax me onto a gurney, but Cade bitched at them. Sitting on the grass next to me, he engulfed me in his arms.

"It's okay. We're okay," he whispered.

The police questioned us, asking the same things repeatedly, and we gave them the same answers. No, we didn't know why someone would want to blow up Cade's truck. No, we didn't have any enemies. No, we didn't sell drugs. Why were we at the gun range?

"Because we wanted to practice shooting," Cade snapped for the third time. "Why the hell else would we be here?"

I was just glad the cops hadn't looked in my purse and found the illegal Sig. That would have landed us in deep shit.

When the news crews showed up en masse, one of the officers drove us to my house. We climbed out of the cruiser, but the cop idled in the driveway until Cade waved him off.

After he left I asked, "So, who did this? The killer? One of the werewolves?"

"Don't know."

"Vane Aldridge?" I asked.

"Definitely not. I told you, he works for the Council."

"Then why is he so hard to find? Is he hiding?"

"No. His job requires a certain amount of secrecy. Look, let me worry about Vane. I'll find him, Holly.

Promise." He threw his arm around my shoulder, and we made our way to the front door. Cade entered the house first. "Wait here."

Stepping inside, I watched him flip on the kitchen light, then stalk off down the hall where he checked every room. He strode back to the entryway. "Clear. You can come in now. And lock the door."

"Lock the door? I never would have thought of that."

Ignoring my smartass remark, he walked to the kitchen, jerked open the refrigerator, examined its contents. "Where the hell's the beer?"

Feeling icy from shock and still freaked out, I slogged to the kitchen. I didn't feel safe. Well, with Cade here, I felt marginally sa*fer*. But what if someone decided to torch my house? My business? I didn't know if the killer was targeting Cade, me, or the both of us, but I needed to call Sunny, tell her to take the rest of the week off.

"No beer. There's wine, and I think I still have some tequila."

"Tequila." He leaned against the fridge, arms crossed as he watched me pull the bottle from a cupboard next to the sink. Although the medics tried to give Cade pain meds, he'd refused. He wouldn't go to the hospital either. His arm must hurt like hell.

"How are you feeling?" I asked.

"Been worse."

I reached in the top cabinet and snagged two hot pink shot glasses with *Diva* etched in silver glitter. Cade raised a brow as I set them on the counter.

"Do you own anything that isn't girly?"

I poured us each a shot. "Only my penis."

He must have thought that was hilarious because he actually huffed out a laugh. He slammed his drink, then set the glass down with a thud. "You realize you could have been killed tonight?"

I drank my shot, savored the alcohol burn all the way to my stomach. "Back attcha. Which is why we should split up. That way, you'll be able to protect yourself."

"Not the point, Null. You should be out of this completely. Whatever Wallace promised you, I'll match it. Just pack a bag and get the hell out of town."

"Boy, I *missed* not having this conversation in the last hour." I left the kitchen. Walking into my bedroom, I kicked the door closed behind me. I hadn't eaten much for dinner, and the tequila was giving me a nice buzz.

I whipped off my clothes, threw them at the hamper and missed. With a shrug, I tugged on a strand of hair, took a deep whiff. Torched truck smell was disgusting.

In the small master bath, I carefully climbed into the shower stall and let hot water warm me on the outside. The tequila was doing a great job of warming me on the inside. I washed myself once and my hair twice.

As I threw on some clothes and whipped my hair into a ponytail, I thought over my suggestion that we should split up. I knew Cade didn't like it, but he needed to practice magic. He was right—I was a liability to him. My presence could easily get him killed. We needed to part, for his safety and my heart.

I walked into the living room to tell him that, but the words didn't come. Cade stood near the entryway, arms at his sides, hands clenched into fists. The white bandage on his forearm seemed bright against his tanned skin. "You have visitors," he said, his voice low and gravelly.

Slouching on my couch was the loser vamp who'd bitten me the night before. Beside him sat a girl with straight blonde hair and bright blue eyes. A strapless romper exposed her spray-tanned shoulders, including the tops of her rather large, very perky breasts.

"Hi," she said with a pageant wave. "I'm Abby."

I glanced at Cade, but his hawk-like stare remained on the couple. "They came over to apologize."

I was not in the mood for this. Cade and I were about to argue—that was a given. Now I had the dick and the chick to contend with. My gaze returned to Abby. "Who are you?"

Her eyebrows pulled together. "I just told you, I'm Abby."

"What I mean is, who are you in relation to fangboy?"

Her brow cleared. "Oh, I'm his sponsor." She rolled her eyes. "I know, so embarrassing, right? Someone like *me*, siring someone like *him*." With a long red nail, she poked him in the shoulder. "Don't just sit there, Neil. Tell her how sorry you are."

Neil raised his eyes but kept his head lowered. With his wavy hair and scrawny frame, I wondered how in the world he wound up a vampire. I'd never met any who were less than gorgeous and very old. Was this some kind of weird experiment gone awry?

"Sorry," he mumbled.

"I don't think she heard that, Neil. Louder."

He cleared his throat. "Sorry, I tried to bite you."

Cade moved from the wall and stood at my back. "Correction, asshole, you did bite her."

"I said I was sorry. Jeez."

"Actually," Abby said, "this was kind of my fault." She lifted her fingertips to her bare shoulder. "I went to a party last night, and I was supposed to take him with me. It's just that he's such a fang block, you know? But still, I'm sorry, too. I shouldn't have trusted him to stay home alone."

Fascination quickly replaced any lingering anger I felt over getting hickeyed. It wasn't every day I got to quiz a vamp. I sank down on the chintz chair, pulling my feet underneath me. "So, you're his sponsor? That means you made him, right?"

Abby leaned back against the sofa. "Yeah, it was an accident. I was at a frat party—one of those geeky engineering frats. I'm thinking, easy pickings. Next thing you know, I'm stuck with him. Monty was wicked pissed last night when he found out Neil was roaming around on his own." She glared at him. "I told you to stay put. That I'd bring someone home for you to eat."

"You were gone forever. I was hungry," he said, baring his teeth.

She gasped and leaned toward him, her finger an inch from his eyeball. "Don't you try to dominate me, Neil Stratton. I will kick your candy ass from here to Little Rock, do you hear me?"

He immediately hung his head.

God, I almost felt sorry for him. I didn't know which was worse, spending the rest of a very long life with a sire like Abby or a having a drip of a child like Neil. Tough call.

"So, how old are you, Abby? I know it's a personal question, but you seem so…youthful."

She preened. "Oh, my God, you are so sweet. I'm only thirty. My sponsor finally let up and gave me a little independence." A frown marred her pretty face. "But then I got too hungry one night, and this is the result." She tilted her head in Neil's direction. "Monty ripped me a new one when he found out I'd sired a child. Last night was like, strike two. So, we're here to tell you that if you need anything from us, we're totes up for it." She elbowed him in the arm. "Right, Neil?"

He nodded.

I thought for a minute. "Can you tell us where to find James Sharpe?" We needed to pin down the vamp who almost sucked London Sanders dry. Who better to help us than these two?

Behind my chair, Cade shifted slightly, and I sensed his disapproval at the question. But the sooner we uncovered who sent the cursed objects to London and Stephanie, the sooner I could stop being a hindrance to Cade, and people would quit trying to blow us up.

"Listen, Holly," Abby said. "Can I call you Holly? You do not want to fuck with a guy like James Sharpe, m'kay? Just take my word on that one. Even my sponsor's afraid of him, and she's like, super scary."

"Could you at least keep your ears open, let me know if he turns up? It's kind of important."

She didn't look happy about it but nodded. "All right. Monty said make you happy, so…" She shrugged.

"I'll give you my cell number."

She twisted a blonde strand around one finger. "Monty already gave it to me."

I retrieved my purse from the entryway and pulled out my cell. "What's your number? I'd like to check in every once and a while." She told me, and I entered it in my address book.

Abby stood and smoothed down her romper, tugging at the hem, which gave us an almost completely unhampered view of her braless titties. Time to put those girls away before someone lost an eye.

"Can I use your bathroom?" she asked. "I can't tell you how long it's been since I looked in a mirror. Actually, I can. It's been eleven years, three months, and four days."

"Sure. First door on the left."

After she trotted out of the room, a weird silence descended over the three of us. Cade wore a stony expression, and Neil stared at the hickey he'd given me. *Awkward.*

A couple of minutes later Abby returned with a huge smile on her glossy lips. "OMG, I look amazing. I mean, I knew I did. You can tell by the way a guy stares at you, but to see myself." She clasped her hands to her chest. "I look even better than I remember." She gave me a quick hug. "Thanks, Holly. It was awesome to see me again."

"Glad you enjoyed it, Abby." As I pulled out of her embrace, her eyes zeroed in on my bruised neck.

"God, Neil, you are such a fuckwad. You couldn't tell there is something completely different about her?" She shook her head. "For a smart boy, he's so dumb. Listen, next time, stick a spoon in the freezer, then put it on your neck. I did that after junior prom. It totally worked. My mom never saw a thing. Of course she liked to get buzzed on mimosas every Sunday morning, so maybe she just didn't notice, but whatever."

"You need to leave now," Cade said. He hadn't moved, just shifted his head to keep both vamps in his line of sight.

"Kay. See ya." With her back to Neil, Abby snapped her fingers. "Door."

He shuffled to the door and held it open for her. Abby tossed back her hair, giving me another little wave before she sailed out with Neil trailing behind.

I peeked up at Cade. "Do you think those crazy kids will make it?" I smiled.

He didn't smile back. "You're out of this."

Let's get ready to rumble. "You'll be safer if we divide and conquer. You go your way, Cade, I'll go mine. We'll stay in touch and share what we learn."

"You're done, Null."

I reached up, stroked my fingers across his stubbled jaw. His hazel eyes deepened to golden brown. I realized they changed color when his emotions ran high. He may not be showing me anything other than irritation right now, but he felt something. "I couldn't stand it if anything happened to you, Cade."

He scoffed and pulled away. "You'd get over it."

My hand fell to my side. "I'm worried about you."

He leaned down, got in my face. "I don't need your concern. And I don't need you fucking up this investigation any more than you already have. Is that plain enough for you?"

I was tired of arguing with him, tired of his lectures about steering clear of this investigation. I wanted to stay the hell out of it, but I'd made a deal with Wallace. Mostly for Gran, but also for myself. I needed to find my mom and nothing, not even McAllister, was going to stop me.

No matter how much he protested, Cade was worried about me. After the truck explosion, he'd thrown me to the ground before I even had time to react. This afternoon at the werewolf meeting, he'd shoved me behind him until he knew it was safe to enter the room. The guy bought me a gun and taught me how to shoot it.

McAllister may not care about me as a person, but he was a protector all the way to his core. Splitting up, letting me question people on my own? He wasn't going to go for it. So, I decided to lie.

With a sigh, I cast my eyes to the floor. "Fine, we'll do it your way. I'll quit inserting myself into your business." I glanced up at him. "Will you at least let me know if you find the killer?"

His eyes widened a fraction, then he scowled. "I'm not fucking around, Null."

"Me neither."

With the palm of his hand, he cupped my cheek. "You've been bitten by a vamp, pissed off a pack of werewolves, and you came this close to getting killed tonight. I won't allow you to stay in town. I'll pack your bags myself if I have to. Staying here is too dangerous."

His concern would have melted me if his words hadn't been so arrogant. Sorcerer wouldn't *allow* me to stay? I narrowed my eyes in defiance. "Too bad you don't get the final vote." So much for pretense.

"Goddammit, Holly. I could force you to stop."

"I'd love to see you try, McAllister."

CHAPTER FOURTEEN

"Do not test me," he ground out. Something dangerous shifted behind his eyes and suddenly, he drew me up by the waist and slammed his mouth over mine. He'd kissed me before but never like this. This went beyond passion. There was something feral and reckless in the way he claimed me. That was it. He was claiming me.

With one arm encircling my waist, his free hand twisted itself in my ponytail. He laid siege to my lips, thrusting his tongue against mine. He didn't just taste me, he devoured.

Wrapping my legs around his waist, I clung to his shoulders. He was wild and untamed and smelled so freaking good.

I'd never felt this way. I barely knew him, but it didn't matter. Even as my body throbbed for more of his touch, something deep inside my chest burst open. What was this? It felt mindless and maddening. It felt *right*.

He pulled his mouth from mine to rain scorching kisses down my neck. His lips slid over the bruise, and the pain felt good. He could do anything to me right now, and I'd be down for it. My life distilled to this moment. Being in his arms, feeling his dick hard against me. I was needy hunger. Aching desire. All for Cade.

His exotic, earthy scent filled my senses. The prickly stubble scratched my neck, my jawline. I'd have a beard burn, but I didn't care.

I vaguely heard a noise in the background. Whatever it was, I wished it would shut up. It pulled me out the moment, brought me back to myself. I resented the hell out of it.

I'm Bringing Sexy Back.

Gran had picked her own ringtone. Totally inappropriate. Just like her.

I groaned against Cade's cheek. "I have to answer that." I softly kissed his scar. "It's Gran. If I don't, she'll worry." I unwrapped my legs from his waist.

Panting, Cade lowered me to the floor. "Hurry."

I snatched up my phone. "Gran. What's wrong?"

"I was going to ask you the same question. I haven't heard from you since this morning."

I couldn't stop watching Cade. His broad chest heaved with each breath. My gaze drifted to his. His eyes were different now, the green flecks more prominent. He reached toward me and worked one finger beneath the collar of my shirt. His touch made my heart skip.

"I...I should have checked in again. Sorry, Gran." My voice sounded thready. I batted at his hand and spun around, giving Cade my back.

"What's wrong with you, Holly? Why do you sound so out of breath?"

"I ran to answer the phone. I'm fine, I promise." A little white lie. So someone tried to incinerate Cade's ride. I was unharmed, right?

"I've been worried sick since you told me about working for the Council. I need regular updates, you hear me?"

"Please don't fret about this. It's just another job." I did my best to keep my tone light. "You're worrying for nothing."

Cade stared a hole through the back of my head. He was close. I could feel him, his warmth, his frustration.

"All right, Hollyhocks." Gran sounded resigned. "Do what you have to. And remember, I love you, my precious girl. Be careful."

"Love you, too, Gran. I'll call tomorrow and check in." I hit the end button, tossed the phone in the chair before turning back to Cade.

"That favor Wallace promised you, it has something to do with your Gran, doesn't it?"

I couldn't meet his eyes and instead, wound up staring at his chin.

He remained silent so long, I dragged my gaze back to his face. His expression was locked down, gave nothing away. "I'll sleep on the couch tonight," he finally said. "Mind if I take a shower first?"

"I'll get you a fresh towel."

On shaky legs, I walked down the hall. In the main bathroom, I paused, covering my face with trembling hands. Too much had happened today. The stress of it all was starting to wear on me.

On top of that, the emotions Cade's kiss had churned up were still there, bubbling below the surface. I needed to get a handle on them but having him under the same roof didn't help. Taking a deep breath, I forced my feet to move.

I laid out a spare toothbrush and a towel before returning to the living room. "You can go ahead. Toothpaste is in the drawer."

Cade stared out the window, into the darkened back yard. When he faced me, he looked as exhausted as I felt. "Thanks." Passing me on the way to the bathroom, he paused.

I tensed, waiting for his touch, but it never came.

The shower started running, and as quickly as I could, I placed a pillow and blankets on the couch. Then I locked myself in the bedroom before he emerged. If I saw even a bare ass cheek, I'd be all over him like a duck on a June bug.

I couldn't trust myself around him. It was a good thing Gran interrupted. She stopped me from making a terrible mistake. Sleeping with Cade would only make these feelings stronger.

I had to shut this off somehow, but whenever he touched me, I melted. Still, I couldn't get distracted by sex. I needed to fight this. I wasn't a slave to my emotions. I was tougher than that. And it was time I started showing it.

#

At eight-thirty the next morning, I awoke to silence. I hadn't bothered to set my alarm since I never slept in. But I'd spent most of the night imagining McAllister naked on my sofa, so when I finally drifted off toward dawn, I slept hard.

Tossing aside the covers, I grabbed my short, cotton robe and slipped it over my Wonder Woman pajamas. Cautiously, I opened the bedroom door, listening for any hint of movement. Nothing.

I crept down the hallway, tying the strings of my robe. The only sound in the house came from the thrum of the air conditioner. In the kitchen, I found half a pot of cold coffee and a note. *TOOK YOUR CAR. HAVE A LEAD ON ALDRIDGE. BACK TONIGHT. STAY PUT OR ELSE.* Succinct words, all caps. Even his notes were terse.

Did the sorcerer really think I would sit around and wait on him like some helpless little female? After four days of working this case together, did the man not know me at all? Yes, dealing with Others on my own had become more dangerous than usual, but I was determined to keep going. I had too much to lose. If I could uncover something that would lead to a resolution, Cade and I would both be better off. But where could I go to uncover more clues? Hmmm.

I grabbed the Coach tote I'd used the night before. It reeked of smoke and blown up Ford. I was down two handbags in less than a week. Things were definitely not going my way.

From my wallet, I pulled out the card Herbert Novak had given me. He said he wanted to learn more about nulldom. Well, I wanted to know more about this case. There was a lot Cade wasn't sharing. Maybe I could charm Dr. Novak into being a little more forthcoming.

Also, it had occurred to me that everyone kept talking about London. London dated vamps. London had bruises. London liked it rough. What about poor Stephanie? She was a shadow of a girl, but she had to have friends. I needed to find them and get some answers.

First, I called for an Uber to pick me up in an hour, and then I dialed Herbert. He was thrilled to receive my call and agreed to meet me at IHOP. Whatever. I just wanted information, and if I had to eat Belgian waffles to get it, I'd fall on that sword.

After grabbing a quick shower, I threw on a pair of shorts and a blue blouse. I transferred all my personal stuff and the gun into a Michael Kors silver satchel.

When the cab arrived, its air conditioner wasn't working. By the time I made it to the car rental place five miles from my house, I was a hot, steaming mess.

From the fleet of cars, I chose a boring silver sedan. The interior smelled of fake pine air freshener and onions. But it was a ride. I also stopped at Target and picked up several colorful scarves. I wrapped a lavender one around my neck, letting the ends drape down my chest.

By the time I made it to the restaurant, it was almost noon. The place was busy, nearly every table full, but I spied Herbert Novak against the far wall.

He watched the door with a look of excited anticipation, not unlike a five-year-old on Christmas morning. When he saw me, he stood, his eyes wide. He wore a wrinkled button-down and khaki pants. His belt missed two loops, and he'd buttoned his shirt wrong. Dr. Novak was every inch the absent-minded academic.

"Miss James. Remarkable. Extraordinary. Come, sit. So good to see you again." He waited until I scooted into the booth then pulled a small notebook from his shirt pocket. "Do you mind if I take notes?"

I shook my head and pulled out my own notebook. "Not at all."

When he grinned, his ears wiggled slightly, causing his nerd glasses to wobble on the bridge of his nose. "So, what was it like growing up a null? Did you always know what you were? What were your experiences when you encountered an Other?"

"Can I order some coffee first?"

He looked chagrined. "Oh, yes. I'm sorry. I just get so excited about new discoveries."

That's what I was? A discovery? I thought about it for a second. Okay, I could live with that.

The waitress came over, took my order for waffles and coffee. As soon as she walked away, he leaned forward.

"I want to know everything about you. *Everything.*" Herb was a wee bit intense.

"All right, but I'd like to ask you a few things, too."

His brows rose, causing a series of horizontal lines to crease his wide forehead. "Indeed? I'm intrigued. Ask away, fine lady, and I'll do my best to answer."

I stifled a laugh. What an odd duck. "I'll answer your questions first. You wanted to know what it was like growing up a null?"

He waved one hand. "Please, spare no detail."

"I grew up with my grandmother—she's a witch, by the way—and I always knew what I was. I didn't have any contact with Others until college. And now of course, I run my business."

He scribbled furiously. "And what business is that, dear?"

"I'm a null for hire."

The scribbling stopped, and he peered up at me, his head tilted in confusion. "But who would hire you?"

I tried not to take offense. The waitress saved me from saying something completely rude when she came back with a carafe and a cup. I sweetened my coffee as I looked at Herb. "Others hire me when they need crowd control. Rowdy Other family reunions, weddings, bar mitzvahs. Sometimes, Norms come to me with ghosts or curses. I help them out."

"That's ingenious."

"I like to think so."

"But what about your parents? Where are they? How did your grandmother practice the craft around you?"

I blew out a breath. This was going to be one long ass brunch. "I never knew my father, and my mother abandoned me." Ouch. When I stated the facts baldly, without any qualifiers, it hurt like hell. "My grandmother gave up the craft to raise me."

"That was quite a sacrifice. It would be like amputating an arm."

Now came the guilt. "Yes."

"They used to kill nulls at birth, you know." He said it so casually, I winced. "Occasionally, they'd keep them alive to be used as a weapon. It's good you live in the modern age."

"Guess I got lucky."

Herb seemed oblivious to the pain his words caused. They were just another reminder that I'd turned out wrong.

Abnormal. Mutant. Abomination. All the old taunts rang through my head.

"How about distance," he said. "How close do you have to be in order to nullify a person? Is there a quantifiable distance? I know you had to touch the grimoire at the young girl's house, but you didn't have to touch the amulet. Perhaps we should perform a few tests."

The waitress approached with two plates. She set one before me, and I thanked her. "I think it's my turn to ask you a few questions." This screwball would experiment on me when hell froze over.

When he opened his mouth to argue, I asked, "What does a Magical Medical Examiner do, anyway?"

Setting his notebook aside, he saturated his pancakes with syrup. "Oh, it's fascinating, really. I consider myself something of a mystical forensic specialist. For instance, in the case I was just working on, four Norms had been killed, their hearts crushed to a pulp. Looked like a can of tomatoes had been dumped inside the chest cavity."

I pushed my plate to the side. So much for waffles.

"Turns out, a telekinetic had used his powers to literally squeeze the hearts of his victims."

"Why?" I scratched the side of my white ceramic mug with a fingernail.

"He was paranoid, thought the Norms were out to get him." He smiled and forked a bite of pancake into his mouth. "I'm a postcog, you see. I can touch a person, relive the last few moments of their life. I'm not as successful with objects, though." Postcogs were rare. Precogs—clairvoyants—not as much. As Wallace informed me, I had a few of those on the branches of my family tree.

"Do you know what the victims felt as they died? What was going through their minds?" I asked.

"I get an impression of their emotional state if what they were feeling was strong enough to resonate." He paused to douse his pancakes with more syrup. "With unexpected deaths, I don't experience much of their emotions at all. I can occasionally pick up a random thought."

"What about Stephanie Carson?"

"I saw the last five or six seconds of her life as she pulled the grimoire from the box."

I shivered and cradled the coffee cup with both hands. That had to be awful, seeing through a dead person's eyes. "Do you know what she was feeling?"

He wiped his mouth with a paper napkin. "She seemed very surprised that someone sent her a gift. However, I didn't sense any of London Sanders' emotions."

"So you see *how* the victim died, and Cade sees magical signatures of the killer?"

"Quite so. McAllister can usually tell right away what kind of spell has been used. Just last month, he uncovered a clever murder scheme. A woman summoned an evil spirit and had it temporarily take over her sister's body. Then she instructed the spirit to kill her husband, laying all the blame on her poor sibling. She thought she'd get off scot-free. But she hadn't planned on a powerful sorcerer seeing her magical signature woven around her sister's aura."

He shoved another bite into his mouth. "Cade claims all spells have a certain sweet odor and black magic, like the cursed amulet, has a burnt smell. But they all contain a pattern. Cade unweaves the pattern, like a tapestry, and then he finds the signature."

"But how does he recognize the signature?" I asked. "I mean, how does he tell if a witch's signature matches up to the spell unless he's seen signs of their spell-casting before? Like the police have a fingerprint in their database, doesn't Cade need to see the signature beforehand, have it on file, so to speak?"

"You think like a null." He pointed his fork at me. "Witches are full of magic. They always have a spell near them, on their clothes or a protection spell on their home." He picked up a slice of bacon and nibbled on it like a rabbit with a carrot. After taking a sip of coffee, he continued, "A signature is unique to each individual. A powerful sorcerer can trace a signature as easily as you, my dear, can detect that water falling from the sky indicates rain."

Herb stated it in more condescending terms, but that's exactly what Cade had told me. I leaned my elbows on the table and frowned. "Tell me about the amulet."

"Ah, the amulet. Beautiful. Sixteenth century, silver with traces of lead, hand-carved runes. European in origin. Probably used as a protective talisman. Impossible to read now, because the carvings have been rubbed down through the years."

"Where would someone get an amulet like that?"

He shoved the last of the pancake into this mouth. "Easy. Get it from an online auction, a catalog, anywhere really."

"So why haven't you been able to find the girls' killer?"

"The practitioner who sent those items is using black magic to erase all traces of himself. Like wearing gloves will keep a burglar from leaving fingerprints."

"So, what does that tell you?"

"Whoever cast that curse, Miss James, is extremely powerful."

I sipped my coffee, letting all the information he'd given me digest in my brain. "What about the grimoire? Ever seen anything like it before?"

"Oh yes, they're very common. Every family has one. In fact, I was performing a few tests on it this morning. It's old, but there's nothing special about it." He reached into his leather briefcase and pulled out a plastic evidence bag containing the book.

My heart started beating a mile a minute. "Can I see that?"

Smiling, he handed it over. Boy howdy, we were violating the hell out of Cade's rule number one. Herb and I were fucking with the evidence.

"Herbert, I'm going to take this for a few hours. I'll give it back to Cade when I'm done." There. I'd said that with confidence and authority.

Herb blinked like an owl behind his glasses. "I don't know. We don't really do things that way. Chain of evidence is important."

"So is finding this killer." I leaned toward him, lowered my voice. "Why do you think they brought me in on this case?"

"Why?" he whispered.

"Because this isn't a run-of-the-mill murder investigation. A null working with a sorcerer? You do the math." I gave him a mysterious smile.

I could see him trying to work it out and let him draw his own conclusions. I sat back in my seat. "By the way, something's been nagging at me. Why was the curse on the grimoire stronger than the one on the amulet?"

As his confused expression cleared, he waved one finger in the air. "Now that is an excellent question. The amulet was more powerful than a simple grimoire. Like a battery that hadn't discharged all of its energy, it needed less power poured into it. The grimoire contains simple, household spells. It needed more power to create the curse."

"Do you think the spell-caster used whatever items he had on hand?" I asked. "That maybe the amulet and the grimoire weren't actually that important, but just handy? Or did they hold special significance?"

He nodded slowly. "I'm not sure, but your theory is plausible. Items of convenience. Yes, there may be some merit in that."

"What happens to someone when they use that much black magic? Is it draining? Do they have to recharge their own magical batteries after a curse like that?"

"You're very bright." He studied me for a moment through narrowed eyes. Now I knew what a lab rat felt like. "It depends, of course, on how powerful the spell-caster is. And we've already concluded in our little hypothesis that this particular caster is indeed powerful. Perhaps the most powerful practitioner I've ever come across. Did it drain this person? I don't know. Normally, yes, it would deplete the caster for several days, if not weeks. Black magic takes its ugly toll, Miss James. But this case is different. No signature. No pattern. Very interesting."

I dug out a few bills from my purse and tossed them on the table before grabbing the grimoire. If Herb wanted it back, he'd have to wrestle me for it. "Thanks for meeting with me."

"Wait. I need to set up a time to test the distance of your power."

I quickly rose from the table, made a beeline for the exit.

"We'll talk later," he called after me.

CHAPTER FIFTEEN

I got on the road and dialed Blessed Be. I wanted to talk to Jasmine True again. I had a ton of questions for her, and I wanted her opinion about this grimoire.

"Blessed Be." Jasmine's voice sounded light and serene.

"Hey, Jasmine, it's Holly James. I was wondering if we could meet today."

"I'm busy, okay? Just leave me alone and quit calling."

"Come on, Jas, it won't take long." I wasn't taking no for an answer. "And you know I can't come to the shop."

She muttered under her breath, calling me a foul name. I'd been called worse. "I can meet with you this evening. I'll give you ten minutes."

"I was thinking more along the lines of right this minute. I've got something I want to show you."

Even her silence felt angry.

"Don't you want to find London's killer?" I wasn't above using a little guilt.

"Fine, I'll meet you at the Soho Bakery on Hamilton in ten minutes."

I raised my brows at her choice of eateries. The Soho Bakery was a coffee shop owned by latter-day hippies and reeked of incense. A cup of free trade coffee came with good vibes and a napkin made of recycled wood chips. The bagels didn't look half bad, but having a woman with dirty dreadlocks and armpit hair serve them to me was a deal breaker.

The place was crowded when I arrived. Scrunching my nose at the smell, I stood in line, bought a cup of expensive coffee, and poured a bit of raw sugar into it. I snagged a two person table near the restrooms while I waited for Jasmine.

She arrived dressed in tight jeans and a tank top. Her wild, curly hair was twisted on the back of her head, anchored in place with two enameled red sticks. As soon as she walked through the door, a look of unease crossed her features. She absently rubbed her stomach and scoped the room. When she spotted me, she made her way to the table and sat, leaning her forearms on the chipped Formica top. "I forgot how nauseous you make me."

Feel the love? I sure could. "Sorry about that."

"What did you want to show me? I need to get back to the shop. Now that London's gone, I've been putting in a lot more hours."

I looked at her curiously. "She's not gone, Jasmine, she's dead."

"I know that, okay? I just mean I have more on my plate now." She scanned the tables with a sniff.

I pulled the grimoire out of the evidence bag and handed it to her.

She turned it over and studied it. "A grimoire? This one's pretty old, but what's so special about it?" She flipped through the pages. "Standard stuff for a beginner or a witch who's not very powerful. How to diminish wrinkles; how to make your cow give more milk."

"Yeah, those spells seemed pretty mild to me, too," I said. "What kind of spells does a powerful witch perform?"

She glanced up, meeting my eyes. "All kinds. At the shop, we sell love spells, sleeping tonics, prosperity charms. But a powerful witch can change her eye color, her appearance. A witch with evil intent can cast mild curses.

Not like the one that killed London, of course, just annoying stuff, like zits or a string of bad luck. But they say casting with malicious intent comes back threefold." She read a page and chuckled. "Some of these herbs are really old school. Dew of the Sea. That's Rosemary. You probably never had to learn any of this stuff, not being a witch and all." She sounded smug.

I didn't bother correcting her. I may not have performed spells or brewed potions, but Gran kept a kick ass herb garden and made me learn all the names, both old and modern. I knew their magical properties, too.

Jasmine set the book down, crossed her arms. "Is this why you called me? To look at an old grimoire?"

"Where would something like that have come from?"

She shook her head, making an escaped curl dance next to her ear. "Who knows? This shit is a waste of my time. Don't call me again." She straightened and moved to get up.

I clamped my hand onto her arm. "Take a guess. Where would someone get a book like this? You own an occult shop, surely you have an idea."

Shaking me off, she settled back in the chair. "I really don't know. You could buy something like this online. Could be a family heirloom. Where did *you* get it?"

"It's the cursed grimoire that killed Stephanie Carson."

"What?" she yelled. She realized that everyone in the place heard her and visibly struggled to pull herself together. She looked at the book with a mixture of horror and disgust. "You let me touch that?"

I stretched my lips into a fake smile. "You don't look any worse for the wear. Hey, speaking of weres, why didn't you tell me London was seeing a werewolf named Nick Alpert?"

Her mouth gaped open. "How did you find out?"

"I'll find out all of London's secrets, Jasmine, you can be sure about that. Why didn't *you* tell me? You filled me in on James Sharpe. Why tell me about the vamp, but not the shifter?" I kept my voice low. Didn't want the Normals to overhear things they shouldn't.

"I...I..." She took a deep breath, then her shoulders sagged. "London and I had a fight over Nick. I dated him first. I didn't want you to think he had anything to do with her death. He was crazy about her. And I didn't want to be cast as the spurned, jealous ex."

I pulled my trusty little notebook out of my bag. "Details, please." She didn't look happy. But she did look like a possible suspect.

"Nick and I dated a year ago." She glanced at a woman wearing Birkenstocks, clomping to the bathroom door. "I was more into him than he was into me."

"Did London know?"

She scoffed. "Of course she did. But just like always, she took what she wanted. She knew how much I cared about him. I mean, what we had was over." She squared her shoulders. "But London knew I still had feelings."

"Sounds like London was pretty cruel."

"She could be. She could also be very kind. Now, if you don't have any more questions for me—"

"Actually, I do. What about Stephanie Carson?"

Jasmine rolled her eyes. "What about her? I already told you, Stephanie was a client, a weak witch who bought trinkets from the front of the store every once in a while."

"Why do you think she was killed?"

Jasmine canted her head to the side. "It's your job to find that out, not mine."

"Did she have any boyfriends? Girlfriends? Where did she work?"

"I don't know who she was seeing. And why am I the source of all your information? You are really horrible at your job."

I smiled. "Oh, Jazzy. You'd best watch yourself before I turn up at Blessed Be to buy a packet of tarot cards and nullify your entire stock. I've forgiven you for filing a report against me with Cade McAllister." The smile slipped from my lips. "But don't push it. Now, where did Stephanie work?"

She smirked. "Why don't you ask Tamara Dermot?"

Tamara, the aura reader. When I met her at the outdoor café and asked about Stephanie Carson, she hadn't given me any information. But according to Brant Braxton, Stephanie was at London's Solstice party, acting as a caterer. And Tamara knew where Stephanie worked? Why the hell couldn't everyone just tell me what they knew the first time around?

"Vane Aldridge." I threw the name out, carefully watching Jasmine's reaction.

"Don't know him."

"Really? London was seen hanging out with him at The Raven."

"He was probably some bad boy she picked up. Like I said, she had a habit of making terrible decisions."

I looked into her eyes. "I don't picture you with the baddest badass of the pack. You and Nick Alpert? Together? I thought you were all New Agey peace and harmony."

"That's just for the Norms." She shook a stray curl back from her face. "And Nick's a nice guy."

"For a pain-inducing enforcer?"

#

When I didn't have any more questions, Jasmine hightailed it out of the bakery so fast, I nearly got whiplash. As I sweltered in the heat schlepping to my rental, I put in a call to Tamara Dermot but got her voicemail. I left a message, said it was urgent, and then called Gran to assure her I was A-Okay.

I decided to drive by the office, make sure it was still standing. I'd texted Sunny last night, giving her the rest of the week off. With pay. So I was more than a little irritated when I saw her Toyota in the lot. I parked next to her car, then strode inside.

"What are you doing here?" she asked. "Checking up on me? You should know by now I do not require supervision."

"What are you doing here? I told you to stay home." I propped my sunglasses on the top of my head.

"I had a few things to do, so I came in. What's got you worked up?" Her tapping fingers never let up on the keyboard.

"Cade's truck was rigged with a bomb last night. What if the same person targets the office? It's not safe to be here."

Immediately she stopped typing and stood. "Why didn't you say so? I swear, I should get hazard pay for this job." She shut down her computer before waving a hand toward my office. "A package came. It's on your desk."

"I didn't order anything." I hustled to my office. Standing upright on my desktop was a large rectangular box bearing the Nordstrom logo with a small card taped to the outside. After the cursed amulet and grimoire, I was wary of unknown boxes, but this one hadn't been wrapped in brown paper. At least it wasn't ticking.

"Who delivered this, Sunny?"

"Some guy named Jasper."

Mick Raven's sidekick. How many other Jaspers could there be running around Tulsa? I grabbed the card, keeping one eye on the box. When it didn't go boom, I took that as a good sign.

I hope you enjoy this small token. Have dinner with me tonight. Mick Raven. He'd jotted down his number. His handwriting was an elegant scrawl compared to Cade's blunt letters.

Curiosity overrode my caution. What would Mick have sent me—and why? With tentative steps, I approached the box and untied the white string binding it. Peeling back the tissue paper, I shrieked when I saw the red Valentino bag. I snatched it up, held it to my nose. With my eyes closed, I inhaled. Mmm, the smell of leather filled my senses. I ran my hands along the studs dotting the seams. The pads of my fingers trailed over the bumps and ridges of each one. It was exquisite. Gorgeous and functional. How did he know my weakness?

Sunny stepped into the office behind me, picking up the card I'd dropped. "Even I know who Mick Raven is. I don't think having dinner with him is a very good idea."

"It's a terrible idea. Cade McAllister and Mick Raven have a past."

"You are returning the bag, right?"

I swung to her, shoved the purse under her nose. "Are you nuts? This is a Valentino. Smell it."

She pushed it away. "No. Let's get out of here. If someone tries to blow me up, I'm blaming you." She straightened her glasses as she fled the room.

I'd follow her. In just one second. I clutched the bag to my chest. I didn't know what Mick Raven wanted—other than to tweak Cade—but boy, he knew how to tempt a girl.

I tucked the card in the bag. By the time I walked into the outer office, seconds later, Sunny was already gone. I set the alarm and locked up. When I climbed in the rental, I caressed the Valentino's handle. Such craftsmanship.

I set it gently in the passenger seat and started the engine. Before I could back out, my phone rang. *Caller Unknown.*

"Hello."

"Did you receive my gift?" Mick Raven asked, his sensuous voice gliding over me. How did he get my number?

I was rarely tongue-tied, but Mick had me grasping for words. "Yes. It was beautiful...I thank you much for the kindness." Shit, that didn't make sense in my head, let alone falling out of my mouth.

He chuckled. Even that sounded seductive. "I'm so glad you enjoyed it." His accent tickled my ear, and little ripples of pleasure danced over my body. "I'd like to have dinner with you. If this evening's not convenient, then tomorrow will suffice."

"I appreciate the offer, but no."

"No? I am unfamiliar with this strange word. What does it mean?" His teasing tone surprised me. Sorcerers had a reputation for being serious, sullen. Cade fit the profile. Mick Raven was a different breed. I doubted people said "no" to him very often. They were probably too scared or too in awe of him to ever use it.

A trickle of laughter escaped me before I could stop it. "It's the opposite of yes."

"Is this because you're fucking Cade?"

Good Lord, these sorcerers had bigger balls than a prized steer. "That's rather personal," I snapped.

"It is of no import. I would like to see you anyway. I find you very attractive, Holly James. What night would work for you?"

I chose my words carefully. I didn't want to cause offense. "I don't think it's a good idea. But I thank you for the opportunity." Mick Raven would make a very bad enemy.

Cade McAllister was a scary guy. Tall, brooding, too hot for words. I had little doubt he could rip someone to shreds, if not with his magic, then with his bare hands. Mick Raven, on the other hand, was more serpent in the garden than striking cobra, but just as deadly. His accent seduced, coerced, where Cade's drawl and clipped sentences told you he had a low threshold for bullshit. Both were dangerous, but they used different methods.

"I won't give up," he said. "You are now in my sights." Mick's laugh sent shivers down my spine.

Uh oh.

CHAPTER SIXTEEN

Driving home, I wondered how Cade was doing. I missed his scowl. His scar. That deep, sexy voice issuing stupid rules. I hadn't heard from him all day and realized I didn't even have the sorcerer's phone number. How ridiculous was that? I'd practically climbed into bed with him, but I couldn't text him. The man was infuriating.

I scampered into the house and sucked down a bottle of cold water before placing the Valentino at the top of my closet. I wasn't hiding it—exactly. I just didn't want Cade to see it yet.

I grabbed a quick, cool shower. While drying my hair, I mentally reviewed everything I knew about London and Stephanie, their deaths and their lives. London had secrets—dating a vamp, a werewolf, the mysterious Vane. She liked rough sex, but Nick claimed he'd never left bruises. Did James Sharpe come back to deliver a beat down? If so, why did she wear them publicly? I didn't think we'd scratched the surface of London's private life.

And poor Stephanie. She didn't seem to have any friends at all. She was a witch without power. She occasionally shopped at Blessed Be. She worked as a caterer. Had Stephanie seen something she shouldn't have? Did she know secrets about London? I had far more questions than answers, and that was frustrating.

After dressing in fresh clothes, I made myself comfortable while I thumbed through the cursed grimoire. The book was old. The papers had been stitched in place, each spell hand-written. I knew theoretically that results yielded from such simple spells depended on the power of the practitioner. The stronger the witch, the more effective the spell.

I trailed my finger over a drawing of mugwort, a key ingredient in a nine herbs charm—a standard potion for infections back in the day. I read over the instructions, glad for once I didn't have to rely on magic and could count on my friend, penicillin, instead. There was some serious preparation involved in this spell. Lots of cooking. *Shudder.*

The grimoire didn't offer me any clues to Stephanie's death. I finally stuck it back in the evidence bag and placed it on the coffee table. Cade would have a cow when he found out I'd taken it, but he'd get over it.

I made a microwave dinner, ate half of it, and then paced the house, willing the phone to ring. Had Cade found Vane Aldridge? If so, what did Aldridge know about London? Question after question. My brain wouldn't stop chasing its tail.

Around eight, my doorbell rang. I thought it might be Cade, then remembered he didn't ring. He pounded on the door, demanding to be let in.

I found Sunny on my porch with a handful of papers. Despite the heat, her white blouse retained its crisp, starched appearance.

"What are you doing here? Just seeking the pleasure of my company?"

She slipped past me to enter the house. "Hardly. You need to sign the monthly expense report."

I quirked a brow. "Really. Why didn't you have me sign it at the office?"

She shifted slightly, poked at her glasses. "I was in a hurry to leave. I'm doing it now. That's all that matters."

I grinned. "You forgot, didn't you?" Sunny prided herself on many things, most of them absurd. Like the fact that she refused to wear contact lenses—which conformed to society's idea of beauty. Or that she'd never stepped foot in a Hooters—they didn't employ flat-chested girls because of society's rigid notions of womanhood. Sunny had a real beef with societal standards. I think her nouveau hippy parents did a number on her. Even with the awful clothes and lack of humor, she was incredibly pretty. Her makeup-free skin was flawless. Her long dark hair had a silky sheen that didn't come from a salon. And I suspected, but couldn't prove it, that beneath those bland blouses, she had a decent rack. She either didn't view herself as attractive or didn't give a damn about her appearance. Her massive ego was entirely based on her efficiency, and I liked to give it a jab once in a while.

"I didn't forget," she insisted. "I simply got sidetracked by your personal life. Which will never happen again because your personal life is—"

"Oh, just give it." I held my palm up. When she shoved the papers at me, I wagged a finger. "I hope this isn't going to become a bad habit, Sunshine."

Her lips pressed into a tight seam. "Do not call me that."

I grinned as I trotted to the desk and grabbed a pen. Sunshine was her real name. I used it sparingly for greater impact.

Before I could slash my John Hancock to the report, my phone rang. I hoped it was Cade, although he didn't have my number. Nevertheless, he was a resourceful Council investigator, so anything was possible. I glanced at the screen and, to my surprise, it was Abby, the perky vamp.

"Holly, you'll never guess who walked into The Raven."

"You're right. Why don't you just tell me?"

"That vamp you were looking for, James Sharpe."

"Are you sure?"

"Totes. He's talking to Mick Raven right now."

"Oh." I was kind of hoping Cade would be by my side when I confronted Sharpe.

"You'd better come now if you want to talk to him," Abby said. "I don't know how much longer he'll be here."

"If he tries to leave, stall him. I'll be there as soon as I can." I hit the end button, grabbed my silver purse and hauled ass to the front door.

Sunny traipsed after me, shaking the expense report in my face. "I'm not leaving until you sign this."

"No time. I have to go."

"Then I'm coming, too. I don't know what is so important that you can't—"

Grabbing her hand, I pulled her out of the house. She was no Cade, but she was better than nothing. *By a hair.*

"Where are we going?" she asked, buckling her seat belt.

"It's a surprise." I hopped in the car and started the engine.

"You know I hate surprises."

With Sunny clutching onto the ceiling handle to steady herself, I zipped through stop signs, red lights, and drove fifteen miles over the speed limit to get to The Raven in record time. In the lot, I parked illegally near the front door. After shutting off the car, I sat behind the wheel, my hands shaking slightly.

"No," Sunny said. "I'm not going inside. This is not in my job description. Do you know what kind of debauchery goes on here?"

"Yep. Saw it firsthand. If you want me to sign anything for the rest of the month, you're going in. That includes your paycheck." Bringing out the big guns.

"I can forge your signature, you know."

"But you won't." I dialed Abby's number. "Is he still here?"

"Yeah, he and Mick went into the VIP room."

I took a deep breath. "Can you come outside and meet me? I don't want to go in alone."

Sunny huffed. "What am I? Invisible?"

"Sure, I'll be out in a sec," Abby said.

The door of the club opened. I'd parked close enough to nullify the soundproof spell. Music poured out of the building. A deep pumping bass shook the ground. The lights flickered, piercing the dim parking lot. Abby, dressed in a white micro-mini skirt connected to a halter top by one long, thin strip of material, sauntered toward the car. Neil, hands shoved into the pockets of his ripped jeans, shuffled after her.

I glanced over at Sunny. "If I were you, I'd come inside. Sitting out here is not a smart move. Even if you're immune, you don't want to be Other bait, do you?"

She slid an irritated glance in my direction. "Fine. But I'm getting a ten percent bonus for this."

"Five," I countered.

"Eight. And I get next Monday off. With pay."

"You drive a hard bargain. Sunshine."

We stepped out of the car, and I led the way to Abby and Neil.

"Hey, Holly." Abby waved. Then she fixed her sights on Sunny. "Who are you?"

Sunny held the report in front of her like it was a textbook and pushed at her glasses. "I'm Holly's executive assistant."

Executive? Since when? I hoped this new title didn't come with a pay raise.

"You girls ready to go?" Abby asked.

"Sure," I said, "lead the way."

"First, we need to rally." Abby stretched her arm out in front of her.

Sunny, Neil and I cast each other looks of confusion.

Abby rolled her eyes and sighed. "Everybody put a hand in."

With a shrug, I placed my hand on top of Abby's. Sunny reluctantly settled her hand on mine. Neil shook his head and muttered, "Whatever. So dumb." He slammed his hand on top.

"Let's do this bitch," Abby yelled.

"Yeah, let's do it." I started clapping and nodding, trying to get myself pumped up to work past the fear that sat like a lump of un-risen bread dough in my stomach. "Let's do this bitch."

Sunny tilted her head. "What are you even talking about?"

"We're talking about going in there and kicking some ass," Abby said as she shoved a hand into the halter top and adjusted her left boob. "Are the girls even?"

I gave them a critical squint. "Yep."

When I'd come to The Raven with Cade, I'd received a cold reception. Still nobody wanted to mess with him, therefore they didn't mess with me. This time, I had a slutty vamp cheerleader, a shy, nerdy girl, and a spaz, thrown together for one common goal—to keep me from getting ripped apart. Teen movie rejects from central casting were hardly the bodyguards of choice, but they'd have to do.

Abby spun on her thigh high boots and strode inside. Wanting desperately to do anything but confront a mob of Others, I fought the urge to turn around and run back to the car. But I didn't. *Let's do this bitch.*

I strode inside right behind her, trying to appear confident. Abby strutted boldly past the bar, down three steps and turned right. I matched her stride, not looking back to make sure that Sunny and Neil followed. Either they did, or they didn't, but if I looked over my shoulder, I'd get overwhelmed by hateful, possibly violent, Others. So, I kept my eyes on Abby's head and kept moving.

We stopped at a velvet rope designating the VIP area. A no-neck bouncer stood to the side of the entrance. He barely glanced our way.

Abby faced me. "Here you go." She took my shoulders in both hands. "Good luck, Holly." Then she turned to leave.

"Wait. Aren't you staying with me?"

"No way. You're on your own. I don't want to be on James Sharpe's shit list." She snapped her fingers. "Neil." She glided away, melted into the crowd with Neil trailing after her. Well, there went my guide.

I gazed at Sunny. "You don't have to go in there with me. Here." I dangled my keys from one finger. "Take the rental and go."

She took a deep breath and lifted her nose in the air. "I'm fine. But the next time we do this, we're getting paid double. This pro bono stuff is bull. "

I smiled in relief. "Thanks." Sunny's gumption, despite her obvious fear, spurred me on. I unhooked the rope from the silver post, handed it to the bouncer, and walked in the room. Almost as dark as a movie theater, lines of neon blinked blue, pink, and red along the walls. About fifteen people lounged on plush sofas next to mirrored square tables.

I peered through the dimness, spotted Mick Raven. He stood and prowled toward me. Long, lean, and gorgeous, he moved with easy grace. Raw male sexuality surrounded him like an invisible cloak. When he reached me, his dark eyes sparkled. Bending down to kiss my cheek, he murmured, "You couldn't stay away, I see. Decided to have dinner with me after all?" He smelled of cloves and cedar.

In spite of myself, I took a deep whiff. "I'm here on business."

He leaned away. "That is a disappointment." His gaze swept over Sunny. "Who is this? And why is she dressed like that?"

"Sunny Carmichael, this is Mick Raven." He took one of her hands, brought it to his mouth, but she snatched it away before his lips could make contact.

"I didn't give you permission to touch me."

He burst out laughing—a dark, seductive rumble. Mick placed his hand on my hip, rubbed his thumb along the hem of my blouse. "My apologies, Sunny Carmichael. Let me make it up to you." He crooked the index finger of his free hand, and a waiter appeared. "A bottle of champagne to my office, immediately."

His dark eyes raked over me. "No Cade tonight?"

I moved away, brushing at his hand until he no longer touched me. "I'm here to speak to James Sharpe."

Mick glanced at the corner where he'd been sitting. A man with dark, shaggy hair and two gold hoop earrings held up his glass. He mockingly toasted us before taking a drink.

"Tell me, what do you want with James?" Mick asked.

"You already know the answer to that. London Sanders."

Mick's dark eyes became shuttered. "I think not. He's rather ferocious and not fit for polite company. Like a vicious dog one keeps for protection, but not to pet."

"The thing is, Mick, I'm not leaving until I speak to him, and the longer I'm here, the more restless your clientele is going to get. If they decide to take their frustration out on me? Well, Cade will be all kinds of pissed."

Mick stepped toward me, planting his foot between mine. "You should be very careful about making threats, darling." He grabbed my nape and gave a tug until my chest was pressed flat against his. "I don't respond well to them."

CHAPTER SEVENTEEN

My mouth went dry, and my heart tripped in fear. So this was the real Mick Raven. Hiding under the mask of sophistication lived steely arrogance and a hot temper. I found myself preferring Cade's surly disposition. I knew where I stood with McAllister—most of the time.

Releasing me abruptly, Mick turned and jerked his head towards James Sharpe, who stood, drained his glass, and moved in our direction.

He wasn't as tall as I'd imagined. An inch or two under six feet. But he had broad shoulders and lean muscles. When he reached us, his eyes were full of amusement, but there was a cruel twist to his mouth.

"James Sharpe, this is Holly James and Sunny Carmichael. They would like to speak to you. And they are under my protection while they are in The Raven."

Whoa, that was quite some caveat. I raised my brows and gaped at Mick. "So, what? He can attack us the second we leave the building? I don't think so."

Nodding, Sunny clung to her paper. "We need to define the scope of protection," she said, her voice shaking. She cleared her throat. "Broaden the parameters."

A smile played on Mick's lips. "You're right, Sunny Carmichael." He glanced at James Sharpe. "These ladies are under my protection, both in and out of the club. If you harm them, you'll answer to me." Mick's eyes found mine. "I vow it." His hot gaze packed a sexual promise. How was I still standing after being on the receiving end of that smoldering look? I was kind of surprised I wasn't flat on my back with my legs in the air.

Although he was pretty to look at, and that accent had my stomach in a tizzy, he wasn't Cade—the taciturn sorcerer who would never truly be himself as long as I was around. Wasn't life a kick in the pants?

"Thank you, Mick," I said.

He angled his head toward mine. "That wasn't so hard, now was it?" he whispered.

He took my arm, leading us out of the VIP section to the main room of the club and up the stairs. I felt James behind me, and it sent goose bumps up and down my arms. His presence was how I imagined a ghost would be, hovering, silent, icy.

As I walked up the steps, I glanced at the angry faces below. People weren't glad to see me. Same old, same old.

On the second floor, we walked past the booths again. I heard moans from behind a few closed curtains, but like before, most were open, giving me a window into the world of Others. One woman had a bite mark on her neck, and the vamp who gave it to her looked like he wanted to kill me. Until he saw who was walking behind me. He lowered his head in submission and held out his hands, wrist side up. James Sharpe must be the shiz to get that kind of reception.

Wandering through the maze of hallways, we stopped in front of Mick's office. Inside, Sunny and I found our way to the black leather sofa angled in the corner. James pulled up a chair and sat across from us, casually draping one leg over the other. His gaze rested on Sunny and me in turn. For such a warm honey color, his eyes were cold and calculating.

Mick removed the champagne from an ice bucket, filled glasses, and handed them out. Sunny primly shook her head and refused to accept it.

Mick settled himself on the arm of the sofa, his thigh resting against my shoulder. I forced myself not to scoot away. He wanted to play protector for the evening, I'd let him. "Mr. Sharpe—"

"Just Sharpe, love." The vamp had a working-class British accent. He looked like he was about thirty, but I wondered at his true age. For all I knew, this guy could be a relic. "And what should I call you? Freak?"

Mick's body became still. "Watch yourself," he said softly. "You are in my house. Play nice."

I shrugged. "It's fine. You can call me whatever you want. Just tell me about London Sanders."

James shot Mick a look. "Is she having a laugh, mate?" Then he glanced back at me. "You want to know about my sex life? Get off on hearing the details, do you, love? Want to hear about my favorite positions, then?"

He drained his glass and set it on a side table. When he gazed at Sunny, his eyes moved over her in an insultingly thorough way. "And what's the story wiv you? You're a timid little rabbit, you are. I'll bet your blood tastes like fear and virgin. Fuck me, but I love that combination." He kissed the tips of his fingers like an Italian chef. "Delicious."

Sunny shifted uncomfortably and stared at the floor. The poor crushed expense report fluttered in her trembling hands.

"Hey." I brought James' attention back to me. "Over here, White Fang. London Sanders."

Mick drew his finger along my arm. I didn't want to show weakness in front of either of these men, so I ignored it.

"She is inquiring into London's death," Mick said.

Sharpe's dark brows shot up. "Why the fuck is a null getting into Others' business, eh?"

I looked him square in the eye. "Did you kill London because she broke up with you?"

"If I did, do you think I'd tell *you*?"

"I know you bit her so hard, took so much blood, that she almost died."

In an instant, his face went from a mocking smile to a snarl. "Wha'? What the bloody hell are you on about? I never hurt her like that."

"You didn't know?" I was silent a moment. "If not you, who?"

Breathing deeply, he stroked his chin. "When did this happen?"

"A few weeks before her death."

He glanced away, remaining silent.

"I've always heard vamps were territorial," I said. "If she was your girlfriend, why did another vamp bite her? Hard enough to kill her even? Were they sending you a message, James?"

The look he gave me chilled me to the bone. Those light brown eyes were emotionless and flat. Not an ounce of mercy in them. "People don't send me messages, love. Not if they want to live to see another moon."

I held his gaze though my insides were quivering. "You have quite a reputation, but I'm thinking it's unfounded. I mean, another vamp poaching on what's yours? And you did nothing about it. That's a pussy move. Love."

"You're a brave one." He smiled, but there was nothing joyful in it. "And for your information, no one touches what's mine and gets away wiv it."

I shrugged. "You may want to tell that to the shifter she was banging behind your back."

"What did you say?" Sharpe became statue still, not blinking, not even breathing as far as I could see. Then he stood so abruptly his chair toppled over, and he lunged at me.

Before he could wrap his hands around my throat, Mick grabbed his shoulder and hauled him back. "Calm down." Mick's words were clipped.

"*You* calm the fuck down." He flung an arm in my direction. "She's lying about London. I won't have it, you hear me?" He shoved at Mick, who finally released him.

Mick gave his jacket sleeve a casual tug. "She's not lying. I saw her with him, here in the club."

Sharpe straightened, his breath coming in short bursts. "Who? What is this bastard's name?"

Before Mick could answer, I stood and so did Sunny. I'd never seen her so pale. Swallowing, I faced Sharpe. "Why did London break up with you?"

He stepped toward me, but Mick jumped in front of him. "Stop this at once. Why don't you two exchange information, like civilized beings?"

Sharpe glared at Mick's hand resting on his gray t-shirt.

"There's apparently a lot you didn't know about your girlfriend," I said.

Sharpe turned to leave.

"How well did you know Stephanie Carson?" I asked.

He didn't answer as he stormed from the room.

Mick crossed his arms and shook his head. "I see you have been learning interrogative techniques from Cade. Really, Holly, a softer touch might work more effectively. Next time, use your femininity. You'll catch more insects with sugar than not, hmm?"

"Probably. I guess I should warn Nick Alpert that one very angry vamp could be gunning for him?"

He nodded. "It may be wise, yes."

"What about you? Did you know Stephanie Carson?"

"That is an interesting question."

I froze. "What does that mean?"

"You're fumbling in the dark, Holly." Mick leaned down and caressed the side of my face with his large hand.

I pulled back. "Then why don't you shed some light and help me out?"

"Because it's more entertaining this way." He smiled so brightly, I was dumbstruck for a second.

Sunny sniffed, sidestepping her way to the door. "Let's go, Holly. He's not going to answer any more of your questions."

"Of course I will," he said. "For a price."

I wasn't willing to pay his price. I wasn't that desperate. Yet.

"Let me see you out," Mick said. My pride bristled, but the practical side of me knew his presence would keep us safe. At least until we left the building.

As I walked next to Mick through the club, I kept my gaze forward. When we reached the front door, he gave me a lingering kiss on each cheek and bowed his head to Sunny.

"I'll be in touch." He shoved his hands in his trouser pockets and walked away.

Sunny and I stepped outside. Although it was fully dark out, the heat didn't let up.

Abby and Neil waited for us by my rental. "How did it go?" she asked. "I saw Sharpe speed out of here."

"Not too well. But I don't think he bit London Sanders. Abby, do you think you could ask around, see if she was talking to any other vamps?"

Neil peered up at the sky. "Oh, man."

Abby nibbled at her lip. "I don't really like getting involved in all this shit, Holly. I just want to have a good time, suck a little blood, and party, you know?"

I tugged on my scarf. "Yeah, but your boy here hurt me. And Monty wants me to be happy. So…"

Her eyes grew big, and her mouth turned down at the corners. "Look, I want to help, but things are kind of weird right now. Some of us have disappeared, and I don't want to turn up missing, too."

"What are you talking about?"

She hastily shook her head. She seemed spooked, but what would scare a vamp? They were at the top of the food chain. "I'll ask around about this London chick," she said, "but I can't promise anything." She walked toward the club's entrance, and when Neil followed, she spun around. "Ten paces, Neil. Stay behind me at least ten paces." Then she walked inside.

I grabbed Neil's arm and stopped him. "What's going on with Abby?"

"Her best friend, Wendy—or as I liked to call her, Tweedle Dumber—went missing a couple of weeks ago. Probably had enough of Abby and wanted to get away. I've got to go." He yanked his arm from my grasp and shambled off.

Horrible James Sharpe didn't bite London. He seemed too shocked for me to believe otherwise. So who had? Who left her bruised? Every time I thought I knew something about these killings, I got the rug jerked out from under me. Frankly, I was tired of falling on my ass.

#

When I arrived home, my Honda sat in the driveway. Cade was back.

I hastily signed the expense report in the car, shooing Sunny home before I entered the house. My nerves were jangling, and my hands wobbled slightly as I opened the front door. I knew when I went to The Raven that I'd have to deal with Cade's anger. Facing it in theory wasn't that frightening. Reality on the other hand…

Cade sat on the sofa. Waiting for me. "Where have you been?" He must have gone grocery shopping because an empty beer bottle sat on the coffee table, right next to the grimoire.

Shit was about to hit the fan, so I went on the offense. "The next time you want to borrow my car, ask first." I hung my purse by the door. "Also, use a coaster." I fluttered around the room, closing blinds, plumping pillows. Basically keeping my hands busy.

His hazel eyes watched my every move, but he remained still. The pressure in the room expanded. His anger rose to explosive levels. "Where were you?" he asked softly.

I stopped all my nervous movements. "The Raven."

He was off the sofa and standing before me in an instant. "You went to The Raven by yourself?" I took a step back, my heel brushing against the leg of an end table. "I went with Sunny."

He advanced. "You went to The Raven."

"You're repeating yourself again. James Sharpe was there. He didn't bite London. Also, Jasmine True used to date that werewolf, Nick Alpert. She was jealous of London, so that's another motive for her. Stephanie Carson catered London's Solstice event. And vampires are missing. What's up with that? How about you?" I asked as calmly as I could manage. "Any news on Vane Aldridge?"

The scar on his cheek jumped as he hauled me up by my shoulders. "Do you have a death wish, Null? What a stupid ass move, questioning a vampire."

"Go to hell, McAllister." I squirmed against his tight grip. "I found a clue. If James Sharpe didn't bite London, that means someone else nearly drained her. The sooner I find out who killed London and Stephanie, the sooner I'm free."

"How do you figure?"

I sputtered. "I can get on with my life. Put all this Other crap behind me."

His laughter was tinged with bitterness. "Do you really think Others will just forget about you? Leave you alone? Mick Raven sure as hell won't."

"What do you mean?"

"I went to Texas today, looking for Vane Aldridge. Got a hot tip from an anonymous source. Turns out, it was bullshit. No sign that Aldridge was ever in Dallas. How did you find out James Sharpe was at The Raven?"

"Abby. She called and told me."

"It was a setup. Mick got me out of the way so he could get to you."

I thought back over the day. Mick giving me an expensive bag, asking me out, conveniently having drinks with James Sharpe. Damn. He was right, it was a setup.

"You heard Abby," Cade said, "even the other vamps are scared of Sharpe. Yet you just strolled in there and asked him questions like you're goddamned Nancy Drew. He could have ripped you in half. Even without his fangs, the man's a psycho." He abruptly dropped my shoulders and stepped back.

Crossing my arms, I stared at his wrinkled t-shirt. "Mick offered protection from James. He vowed it."

"I'll just bet he did. You keep getting deeper and deeper in this shit. You never listen." He scrubbed a hand over his head.

"What about you? You could have taken me to Dallas with you if you were so worried about my welfare. Why did you drive to Texas without me?"

"Because it's my job, and it doesn't include you." He pinned me with a glare. "I keep trying to do the right thing by you, Holly, but you fight me every step of the way."

I placed a hand on my chest. "I have no choice. Don't you get that?" The idea of finding my mother was never far from my mind. But I had to admit, the thought of catching this killer consumed me. I'd started down this path, and now I couldn't stop. Even if I wanted to. "I have more important things to worry about than fighting with you every ten seconds. You only care about your stupid rules and precious evidence. You're a robot, McAllister."

His eyes went from freezing ice to scorching heat in a flash. "You think I don't care? That I don't give a fuck what happens to you? You're wrong." With a swift move, he lifted me at the waist and threw me over his shoulder. Just like the first night we met.

The sorcerer was barbaric. But his domineering ways made me tremble in anticipation.

He stormed into my bedroom. Shadows slatted across the room from the open blinds. With a twist of his shoulder, he dropped me onto the center of the mattress.

Bouncing a couple of times, I glanced at Cade, who stood in silhouette at the foot of the bed. Before I could regain my balance and composure, he was on top of me, all heat and muscle and delicious scent. I couldn't get enough of it.

With my hands on his chest, I looked up at him. "This is your answer to everything, isn't it?" I asked breathlessly.

"With you it is. And I'm not a fucking robot." He kissed me then, tasting my lips like he was starving for them. When I felt his tongue lick at mine, I wanted more. I wanted everything McAllister had to give.

I tugged at his t-shirt until he pulled his lips away and dragged it over his head. Then my hands glided over him. His hot skin, his hard muscles.

Cade's lips were back on mine, not gentle, not coaxing. Instead, they demanded a response.

My tongue touched his, my fingers slid from his cheek, down the side of his neck, around to his back. I dug my nails into his shoulders and scraped them across his smooth skin.

He released my lips and pulled back an inch. "Again, Little Null."

I scratched his back once more. "Like that, Sorcerer?"

He opened his eyes and stared into mine. "Yes."

I turned my head and bit his shoulder. Hard. "And that?"

"Yes."

I dug in, raking my nails past his shoulders down to the waistband of his jeans. His hips jerked, making his cock twitch against my leg. Now it was my turn to groan.

"More of that," I said.

He aligned our bodies so that his length rested against the juncture of my legs. With deliberate slowness, he thrust his hips forward, rubbing himself against my sensitive pussy.

"Good?"

I nodded.

With a flash of teeth, he shifted away and grabbed the hem of my blouse. Whipping it off, he quickly reached under my back and unhooked my bra. I was bare to the waist in seconds.

Cade stared down at my breasts and licked his lips. "Beautiful." After swiping his tongue over one of my nipples, he concentrated on getting me out of my shorts and panties. Then he slowly unwound the scarf from my neck. Using a butterfly soft touch, he stroked the bruise. "I could kill that asshole for doing this. Still hurt, baby?"

"A little."

He kissed my mouth, then bit at my lower lip. "Put your hands above your head," he commanded, his voice sandpaper rough. When I did, he wrapped the scarf around my wrists, binding them together. My pussy throbbed as I tried in vain to pull my hands apart. I didn't know what McAllister would do next, and it excited me more than anything ever had.

Lightly, he traced my skin with the pads of his fingers, starting with my shoulder, across my collarbone. His mouth followed. He skimmed his index finger down to my bellybutton and dropped soft kisses in its wake.

"Cade."

When I said his name, his tender touch became rougher. He massaged my breasts and pinched my nipples. God, it felt fantastic. "Harder," I breathed.

He obliged, rolling them between his finger and thumb, pulling them, squeezing them with just a little too much pressure. *So good.* Then he set his mouth to the task. He took turns sucking on them. The frisson of his hot tongue circling my nipples had me moaning his name over and over. With his teeth, he tugged on one to the point of glorious pain while his hand cupped my other breast. "Don't stop," I panted. "Please."

But he did. I groaned in frustration. "Cade."

"My rules, my pace." Moving his big, calloused hands further down my body, he gripped my hips and squeezed.

I dug my nails into my palms. Of course he was a control freak in bed, too. Probably goddamned rule number four.

Suddenly, he was off me. My naked body missed his heat. He stood beside the bed, staring down at me and yanked his wallet from his back pocket.

I turned my head to watch him as I arched my back. Digging my hips into the bed, I rubbed my legs together to find some measure of relief from the empty ache deep inside me. His gaze skittered to my tits and stayed there while he unzipped his jeans.

He reached in and pulled his cock free. Long. Hard. Thick. My mouth watered at the sight of it. "There's no turning back after this, Little Null," he whispered. He tugged his jeans over his hips until he stood before me naked. God, he was beautiful.

"No turning back," I said.

He grabbed a condom from his wallet and sheathed himself. Then he was on top of me again. Gentler now, he trailed little kisses along my jaw and throat, careful not to touch my vamp hickey. His lips swept over my chest, made their way back to my breast and lingered there, nibbling at the underside of it while his hand barely touched the other nipple. The torture was almost unbearable. Then he switched breasts.

Since I ached to have his mouth on me and couldn't use my hands, I tried to thrust my chest toward him. He pulled his head back. "My pace."

"Seriously? You're killing me here."

He rubbed his chin along the soft skin of my belly and looked up at me. "I'm going to lick you before I fuck you. I've been dying to do that since the night we met. When I threw you over my shoulder, your hot little ass bounced next to my face. And I wondered what your pussy tasted like."

His rumbly voice increased my need. I closed my eyes. "You're all talk, McAllister. Not enough action."

He chuckled, his mouth nipping at my waist. He moved his way down my body, licking, sucking, biting at my skin until he got to my pussy. He grabbed both of my legs and positioned them over his shoulders. When the tip of his tongue traced my slit, I almost leapt off the bed. I wished my hands were free so I could play with my breasts. I did bring my wrists down, ran the smooth material of the scarf over my nipples. It felt good, but not as good as Cade's mouth, his hands, his fingers.

When I thrust my hips toward him, urging him to quit dicking around and let me come, he didn't hasten his movements. In fact, he slowed down. His tongue lapped at me in a gentle, smooth rhythm and he slipped two fingers deep inside me. When those long fingers pressed upward, I came unglued. I tried to pull my hands apart, moaning as Cade's tongue continued to circle my clit. I came so hard, I grew lightheaded.

I lay there, panting, as he slowly pulled his fingers from inside me. "You taste even better than I imagined." Rising to his knees, he placed my ankles on his shoulders. It was then I realized that I still wore my beaded sandals. I smiled, and wonder of wonders, Cade grinned back. He had a gorgeous smile. Radiant.

He plucked one shoe off my foot and tossed it over his shoulder and did the same to the other. His hands slid down my calves. I was spread wide open, but I didn't feel shy or self-conscious. When I saw the way Cade looked at me, with heat and tenderness, I felt beautiful.

As he reared over me, placing his hands on either side of my head, the tattooed dragon's red eyes watched me. My gaze fluttered to Cade's, and I ran my bound hands along his chest, tracing the dragon's scales. Then I dragged my tongue across McAllister's nipple and bit his chest. "Do you like that, Sorcerer?"

"Do it again," he said. I complied, licking at his skin before nipping it between my teeth. He positioned himself at my entrance. With one long stroke, he was inside me. He stayed like that, unmoving for a few minutes.

I tried to wiggle my hips, but he growled, "Don't move, Little Null."

I tried my best to hold still for him. When he did start moving, he filled me up, pulled out almost all the way, and shoved back in to the hilt.

Cade started slow and steady as he pistoned in and out of me, but soon he sped up, pounding hard and fast. So hard, his movements shoved me closer to the headboard where I hit the top of my head against the wood.

He leaned down and kissed me. "Sorry," he said against my lips.

Without warning, he pulled out of me, flipped me onto my stomach, drew me to my knees and reentered me. This new position felt even better, deeper. He kept one hand on my hip, and the other stroked my clit. I shattered then as another orgasm rocked me. Little aftershocks tingled through my body.

When Cade came, he bit down on my shoulder blade—not too hard, but I felt the sting. He shuddered and groaned my name while he kept pumping. After a few moments, his body went slack. His torso rested against my back.

"I've been wanting to do that forever." He shoved the hair off my nape and nuzzled my skin.

"Me, too, Sorcerer."

Pulling out of me, he moved to the side of the bed and walked into the bathroom. He returned a minute later, but I hadn't moved, was still on my knees trying to recover.

When he climbed on the bed, he eased my body down to lie next to his, spoon style, and untied the scarf. He smoothed back a strand of hair from my face, threw one leg over both of mine. "Okay?"

"Better than." I rotated my wrists and relaxed against him. I thought the first orgasm had been a doozy. The second one had all but knocked me out.

"You know this doesn't change anything, right?" I asked. "I'm going to keep pestering Others until I find the truth?"

He stroked my hair. "I know."

I gave a tired, satisfied little smile. "Good. I'm glad that's settled."

"That's why from here on out, I'm not letting you out of my sight."

CHAPTER EIGHTEEN

"What?" I pushed at his leg and rolled over.

"You were right. I shouldn't have left you today. I thought after my truck blew up, I should keep my distance. Someone's gunning for me, and I don't want you to get hit in the crossfire. But since I can't trust you to stay out of trouble, from now on we stick together." He closed his eyes like that was the end of the conversation.

I slapped his chest.

He opened one eye and grabbed my wrist. "Wouldn't try that again if you want to keep this hand."

"What if I'm the target, not you, McAllister?"

When he kissed my pulse point, a delicious little chill slid along my skin. "All the more reason to stick by your side. We need to go over to my place in a few so I can pick up some clothes."

"I haven't invited you to stay." I liked having him here, but I was reluctant to admit it. Besides, I needed to set some boundaries, or Cade would walk all over me. There was no give and take with him. He did what he wanted and expected me to nod obediently.

"I've been traveling all day, Hol," he said around a yawn. "Let me sleep and we'll talk later." He dropped my hand, rolled over, and was breathing deeply in seconds.

I stared at him in disbelief. Wham bam, thank you, ma'am, and cue the snoring. Not that he snored. In fact, he was pretty damn hot, lying there naked. Sleeping peacefully.

Naked.

I crawled off the bed and threw on fresh clothes. When I went hunting through the kitchen for something to eat, I realized I hadn't been to the store in a week. The only thing Cade had picked up was a six pack. I figured he'd be hungry when he got up, so I ordered a ton of Chinese food. I also called Gran again and reassured her I was fine.

After the food arrived, I crept back into the bedroom to see if Cade was still asleep. He lay on his stomach, the red nail marks on his back visible. I clenched my hands to keep from reaching out and tracing them with my fingers. Then I touched the back of my own shoulder. Cade had marked me, too.

Placing one knee on the bed, I whispered in Cade's ear, "Wake up, Sorcerer."

He sleepily turned over and gave me a sweet smile. It almost broke me, that smile.

He propped one hand behind his head, touched my cheek with the other. "I thought I was dreaming for a second." His thumb caressed my lips. "I like waking up to you, Holly James."

My heart did a flip flop. *Don't get excited, it's just the after-sex-hormones talking.*

I pulled away. "I ordered some Chinese food. Hungry?"

He sat up and, snaking an arm around my waist, pulled me on top of him. "Starving."

By the time we ate, the food was cold.

#

It was after one a.m. when we left the house. The temperature hadn't dropped much, and the muggy air remained heavy. Crickets filled the night with their chirping.

On the way to the rental car, Cade grabbed my hand, pulling me to him to deliver a swift, hard kiss. Then he opened the passenger door and waited until I got comfortable.

"I had lunch with Herbert Novak today," I said, once he climbed behind the wheel.

He glanced at me as he started the ignition. "I saw the grimoire. I'll save the lecture."

"Thanks. He told me the same thing you did about witches' signatures and patterns."

"Hmm." He backed out of the drive and took off down the street.

"He just got back from Texas, too. Some telekinetic went on a killing spree."

"I know," he said. "I caught the crazy bastard. That's why I thought the tipster might be telling the truth about Vane Aldridge being in Dallas."

His words brought me out of my drowsy lull. A bolt of unexpected fear shot straight to my heart. "My God. You're in danger every day, aren't you?" It sounded asinine when I said it out loud. Of course he was in danger—he was an Other cop. I always thought of him as Cade, the all-powerful sorcerer. I didn't get it before, was too preoccupied with my own crisis. Now that I'd fallen for him, it scared the hell out of me.

"Worried about me?" he asked.

"Of course I am."

He reached out and rubbed my knee. "I can handle myself. Been doing it a long time. And now you know how it feels. I worry about you, too."

I redirected the air vent upward. Thinking about Cade on the trail of a telekinetic heart crusher chilled me clear to my bones. "So, where does Aldridge fit into all this? Who is he, really?"

Cade sighed and braked at a stop light. "What I'm going to tell you is private, Council business. It goes no further, understand?"

"Sure."

"Aldridge metes out punishment set by the board. You know how Nick Alpert is an enforcer for the wolf pack?"

"Yeah."

"Well, Vane Aldridge performs the same function for the Board."

I shifted in my seat to look at him. The headlights from oncoming traffic flashed across his face, illuminating his expression before leaving him in the shadows. My sorcerer looked different somehow, harder, more aloof than he ever had. "What Board?"

He took the highway and drove in silence for a few moments. "Sure you want to know this?"

"Yeah," I said, suddenly not sure at all.

"The Council, they're politicians basically. They get the differing factions together, keep everyone playing nice, but the Board of Twelve makes sure Others stay in line. Like this spree killer in Texas. He'll be dealt with once he's been tried by the Board."

"Like a real trial, with a prosecutor and a defense lawyer? But with twelve judges?"

He hesitated. "Not exactly."

"Then what, *exactly*?"

"As the investigator, I'll present evidence to the Board, and they'll make their decision."

He turned down a side street. We were leaving the populated section of Broken Arrow and moving to the outskirts. I looked back at the bright lights behind me, feeling as if I had crossed over into a different world. "And this Board, their decision is final?"

He dipped his chin a fraction.

"So how does Vane Aldridge enforce it?"

He remained quiet.

"Does he kill them?"

Again with the chin nod.

"He's an assassin? Is that what you're telling me? *Vane Aldridge is a Council-sanctioned assassin?*" No wonder Gran was terrified of them. I rubbed my tired eyes. "And what about you? Do you kill for the Council, too?"

"No," he said, his voice hoarse. "No, Holly, I just investigate and report my findings to the Board."

Relief flooded through me. I didn't like to think of Cade as a killer. I knew he was capable. He might have even had to take a life, but somehow that felt different than carrying out a kill for this Board of Twelve.

Cade flipped on the brights as he drove the car down a rutted country lane. "Others have to be kept in check, follow the rules. If not, Norms could get hurt, and we'd all be compromised. What Vane does, it's dangerous. That's why there's a certain amount of secrecy involved when he's on a job."

"A kill, you mean?"

"Yeah, a kill." He pulled to a stop in front of a two-story white house. The wide front porch held a wooden rocking chair, and I could see by the headlights the shutters were a cheery red.

"This is your house?" It looked so un-Cade like. I didn't know where I pictured him living, but this wasn't it.

"What's wrong with it?" He sounded cranky.

Unbuckling my seatbelt, I looked over at him. "It's homey, but I can't see you sitting on the front porch, sipping sweet tea. That's all."

"I sip beer and listen to the ball game. It belonged to my parents."

"What happened to them?"

"They were killed." He stated it without emotion.

Killed? Naturally, I had questions, but if he didn't want to talk about his parents, I could respect that. I didn't like talking about mine either.

He moved to get out of the car, but I didn't. He peered back at me. "You coming?"

"Why don't I stay here? I'll ruin all your wards and protection spells." I could have sex with the guy, but I couldn't go inside his house. This was so messed up.

"Holly."

I glanced up at him. "What?"

"Get in the damned house. Wards and spells can be replaced." Not the most gracious invitation, yet it warmed me just the same.

I got out of the car and followed him up the porch stairs. Cade unlocked the door and motioned for me to enter. The place was pitch dark, but after he flipped the switch near my head, the small room flooded with light from an overhead fan and two floor lamps. One black leather loveseat, a big screen television, an end table. The walls were painted a soft taupe and the floors boasted original mellow hardwood.

"It's nice." With just one loveseat, it didn't look like Cade did a lot of entertaining. "Sorry about your parents." I glanced at him.

His expression gave nothing away as he touched my elbow. "Come through here." He escorted me through a small dining room that had been set up as an office to a white kitchen. It looked as sterile as an operating room, and I couldn't imagine Cade standing at the stove cooking. Making a sandwich and eating it over the large stainless steel sink, yes.

He walked to the fridge. "Want something to drink?"

"No, thanks." I glanced at the white walls. Most people have some kind of decoration in their kitchen. Curtains, or a wall clock, or a big jar filled with cooking utensils. But Cade's kitchen was completely barren. Only a white shade covered his kitchen window. "Love what you've done with the place."

"First, it's too homey, now it's not homey enough. Make up your mind." He twisted the cap off his beer and took a swig.

I walked to the counter and leaned against it. "What kind of cases have you seen as an investigator?"

"Obscure curses, strange illnesses, mystical robberies, anything criminal or out of the ordinary. Anything that draws unwanted Norm attention." He took another drink, but his gaze stayed on me.

"So, you go investigate and present evidence to the Board of Twelve. Then what?"

"Then they make a ruling."

"Without the accused?"

He nodded once.

"That hardly seems fair."

"Others know the score. It's worked this way for thousands of years."

"You know people are guilty because you can read their magical signatures from the crime scene?"

"Yeah." He swallowed the rest of his beer, threw the bottle in the trash.

"And Aldridge kills the guilty? How?"

"He causes a series of mishaps or screws with electrical wiring. He's subtle. All looks perfectly legit. The criminals deserve it, trust me. The guy who killed those Norms in Texas? He needed to be stopped."

He was right, but I didn't have to like it. It seemed unfair, like the deck was stacked against the defendant. "Why was London hanging out with Vane? Was she sleeping with him, too? She liked a thrill, maybe fucking a hitman was the ultimate score."

"Maybe. If we ever find him, we can ask. I'm going to get some clothes together. Had to buy new ones on the road this morning. Did you know your blood nullifies magic?"

My gaze flew to his. "No."

"I couldn't cast a spell this morning. I was wearing clothes from last night and had your blood on my t-shirt. Thought I'd lost my powers for good until I figured it out." He turned and walked out of the kitchen. "Come upstairs if you want," he said over his shoulder.

I felt numb. The reality of our situation just slapped me upside the head. "No, you go on."

Cade was afraid I'd rubbed off on him. Stolen his powers. Herbert Novak had said giving up power was like having an arm amputated. That was a good analogy.

I could never be with Cade. No matter how attracted I was, or how many orgasms he gave me, he couldn't function in my presence. A wave of sadness hit me, made me want to double over with pain.

Which was ridiculous. I barely knew him. I had gotten along just fine before he came banging on my door, and I'd be fine when he left. So why did the thought of never seeing him again fill me with utter despair?

I straightened my shoulders and pushed off the counter. I would have to get over McAllister. What was the alternative? Curl up in a fetal position? Go through life with an empty place in my heart that no one else would ever fill? *Yes.*

I shoved a strand of hair behind my ears and left the kitchen, walking with heavy feet to the dining room/office. I absently studied Cade's desk. It was as tidy as the rest of the house, devoid of personal items, just like London Sanders' place had been. He had to have a memento somewhere. Everyone did. And suddenly I was desperate to know what it was.

I began madly rummaging through the top drawer, tossing items aside. Pens, paperclips, a few rubber bands. I slammed it shut and opened the drawer on the right. Bright yellow Post-it notes sat on top of an upside down picture frame. I dug it out and stared at it. A younger Cade stood next to a beautiful blonde girl. They both smiled at the camera, full of happiness. I'd never seen that carefree expression on Cade's face. I never would. His hair was much longer, down past his ears, and the scar was absent.

"What the hell are you doing?"

I jumped at the sound of his booming voice. "Who is she?"

He jerked the frame from my hand, dropped it back in the drawer, and slammed it shut. "None of your goddamned business."

"Who is she Cade?"

With a duffle bag in one hand, he pounded to the front door while I scampered after him. He opened it and shut off the light, jerking his head toward the porch. "Time to go, Null."

My cheeks grew hot, and I told myself not to cry. Goddamn it. I wasn't this girl. The one who falls for a guy, then becomes a weepy doormat.

Cade McAllister was a bad-tempered, hot-headed, arrogant sorcerer. My life would be better without him in it. Easier. Less complicated. I could orgasm all by myself.

I slung my purse over my shoulder as I strode out of the house. "Did you love her? Do you still?" The words were out before I could take them back.

Staring down at me in the darkness, he opened his mouth, and then something pinged against the porch railing. Splinters flew at my upper thigh and hand.

Cade dropped the bag and threw his arms out in front of him. "*Nebula.*"

Another ping and something sharp stung my leg. "Ouch."

Cade tackled me off the porch and had me flat on my back, lying in the grass beneath him. I couldn't breathe, so I gently pushed at his shoulder.

"Goddamn it, Holly, lie still. Someone's shooting at us."

CHAPTER NINETEEN

"Yeah, I got that," I hissed.

"Shit, I could really use my powers right about now," he muttered. "I can't even cast a damned blanket of fog to keep us hidden."

Turning my head to the side, I scanned the area where the shot had come from. Cade didn't have any close neighbors. His house was surrounded by empty land. I saw no lights, no movement of any kind.

He held his finger to my lips. His eyes darted in the same direction mine had. He leaned and whispered in my ear, "Stay here. Don't get up, don't move."

I nodded.

Slowly, he climbed off me and crouched low on the balls of his feet. Still searching the area, he reached for my purse, stuck his hand inside, and pulled out the gun he'd bought me.

I realized I was shaking. Fine tremors rattled through my body, and my teeth started to chatter. This was the second attempt on our lives in two days. Only this time, we might not survive.

Cade cocked the gun, then keeping low, he ran toward the side of the house. Fortunately, no one shot at him. I watched him disappear and kept perfectly still except for one hot tear that seeped from the corner of my eye.

I said a quick prayer for the both of us. Gran would never forgive herself if anything happened to me. Not that it would be her fault, but I knew she'd find a way to blame herself, and I didn't want that burden on her.

After what seemed like hours, Cade was back. Still low to the ground, he ran to the car and opened the driver's side door, then reached in, quickly shutting off the interior light. He tossed the duffle bag in the back seat. Keeping the gun pointed toward the ground, he trotted back to me. With his head swiveling back and forth, he searched for any signs of movement.

"Get up, baby, slowly and stay behind me." As I rose, I snatched my purse off the ground and crouched behind Cade, using him as a shield, my hands resting on his back.

We sprinted to the car. I still didn't hear any noise other than insects. No engines, no running feet. On the plus side, no more shots.

"Stay low," Cade said. "Crawl to the passenger side. Sit on the floorboard."

I did as he commanded, crouching next to the seat with my knees pulled to my chest.

Cade slid swiftly into the driver's seat. He hunched down, left the headlights off, and peeled out of the long drive so fast my stomach lurched.

He used a lead foot until we hit Aspen Avenue. He slowed down a bit. Then he flipped on his headlights and used his knees to steer as he hooked his seatbelt. "Get up and get buckled in, Holly." He never glanced at me, or took his eyes from the road.

I did as he said, then clutched my purse strap with both hands. "Where are we going?"

"The Raven."

With a frown, I turned to stare at him. "What? Why?"

"Because Mick will provide backup."

"You kept telling me to stay away from him, and that's where you go for backup?"

"Yep."

"What about the fact that I'll nullify everyone in the place?"

"Tough shit."

As we drove across town, I wracked my brain over who might be shooting at us. The person who killed London and Stephanie seemed an obvious choice. But I'd ticked off so many Others lately, who knew? James Sharpe, Nick Alpert, or one of the pack? Maybe Vane Aldridge wasn't just hiding, maybe he was the killer. Spurned, jealous lover? Angry that London was seeing other people? It was possible.

I didn't have any answers, and I felt powerless right now. Completely out of control. I hated that feeling. But there was one thing I could do. Tonight at The Raven, Abby had mentioned missing vamps. Neil said her friend, Wendy, had recently disappeared.

I thought about the rogue vamp that had bitten London. What was going on in that community? Monty, Master Sebastian's personal assistant, might have an idea.

I decided to call him. I might as well do something constructive rather than sit here, thinking about all the people who wanted me dead.

Cade didn't even look in my direction as I pulled out my phone and dialed. My call went straight to voicemail. "Monty, this is Holly James. A few weeks before she died, London Sanders was bitten so severely, she almost bled out. Her boyfriend, James Sharpe, said he didn't do it, so I wondered if you might have any ideas. Perhaps the culprit is one of the vamps that recently disappeared? Oh, and by the way, Abby and Neil stopped by to apologize. Thanks for that. Bye now."

"What the hell was that about?" Cade asked.

"I told you earlier, there are missing vamps."

"Not sure getting the vamps involved right now is a good idea. We have enough to worry about without those blood whores sniffing around."

When we arrived at The Raven, it was three a.m., and the place had just closed. Tired-looking dancers in their green wigs and fur boots made their way to the back of the room. Normally, it would be jarring to see topless women parading around, but tonight it barely even registered.

Grabbing my hand, Cade made his way quickly up the stairs, past the empty privacy booths, down the hall to Mick's office. Without hesitation, Cade walked through the door.

Mick Raven sat behind his desk, a drink in hand, holding a thin, black cigar between his fingers. He looked from Cade to me without ever changing his bland expression. "Holly, you can't seem to stay away from me tonight. I'll try to take that personally."

"Someone shot at us," Cade said, not letting go of my hand.

I clung like a child. Right now, he was the only person who made me feel safe.

Mick raised a brow. "How bothersome."

"Don't fuck around with me tonight, Mick. It won't end well for you."

Mick smiled, his teeth gleaming white against his bronzed skin. "Perhaps I could fuck around with Miss James." His eyes slid to me and slowly took me in from head to toe, before glancing back at Cade. "But I guess you beat me to it."

Cade dropped my hand and was over the desk in a heartbeat. With Mick's suit lapels clenched in his hands, McAllister lifted him off the chair, pinning him to the wall. But Mick brought his hands up between Cade's arms, freeing himself. Then he punched Cade in the nose and blood spurted everywhere.

Mick had dropped his cigar on the desk, and it was smoldering through a thin stack of papers. While Cade delivered a kidney punch, I ran to the desk and placed the cigar in the ashtray.

"Stop," I yelled.

They both ignored me. Mick shoved Cade's head into the wall, making a good sized hole in the sheetrock, then slammed his fist into Cade's midsection. These two had some issues to work out, and I was a catalyst, not the cause, but that didn't make it any easier to watch.

They both landed on the sofa. Cade punched Mick's jaw one more time, but it was a half-hearted attempt. They were running out of steam.

Cade slowly climbed off Mick and leaned back, panting from exertion. He held his ribs protectively. The entire left side of his face had been pummeled.

Mick lay diagonally on the sofa, his legs almost touching Cade's. His lip and nose were bloody, one eye had started to swell.

"Do you need to stay here?" Mick asked, wincing with each word.

"Yeah," Cade said.

"Take the green room on the third floor. I'll close up for a few days."

"Thanks." Cade staggered to his feet, and with one arm still wrapped around his middle, walked stiffly toward me. "Can you grab my bag for me?"

"Grab your own shit, Sorcerer. I've had enough of the both of you. I'm not a bone for you two assholes to fight over." I left the office and jogged up to the third floor. After looking in every room but two, I finally found the green room, so named because of its sage colored walls. It held a queen bed, side table, and small chest. There was a tiny bathroom attached.

I locked the door behind me. I didn't really think it would keep anyone out, but it would send a message. I didn't want either sorcerer anywhere near me tonight. I felt like I'd been put through the wringer. Somebody shot at us. That bullet grazed my leg, no more than a bee sting, but still—someone fucking tried to kill us! *Again.*

Then there was the whole Cade thing. One minute I was having hot sex with him, the next he was giving me a dose of his pissy attitude over the photo from his desk drawer. Yes, I had been wrong to go snooping, but the questions and doubts remained. Who was that woman? Why did Cade look so happy with her?

I was wiped out, emotionally and physically. I couldn't take anymore tonight. Worst of all, I had fallen for McAllister. Hard. I needed to keep my distance from him. This wasn't a movie where we'd overcome our differences and have a happy ending. This was real life. And in real life, hearts got broken. Mine was already there.

In the bathroom, I unwrapped a bar of soap sitting next to the sink and washed my face. Back in the bedroom, I curled under the blankets and pulled the notebook out of my purse. I made a to-do list of the people I needed to talk to and the questions I wanted to ask. Now I had a plan. All I had to do was stay alive long enough to complete it.

I set my book aside and lay down, punched the pillow a few times to get comfortable. I'd never felt so wired and so exhausted at the same time. I left the light on and finally drifted off.

#

I awoke disoriented. With my eyes half closed, I glanced around the room and wondered where I was. Then I remembered the night before. Sex. Shooting. Mick and Cade punching the crap out of each other.

Sun filtered into the room, throwing shadows across the floor. It must be late in the afternoon. No wonder I was starving. The last thing I had eaten was cold Chinese food the night before. With Cade. Naked.

I pushed the thought aside and got out of bed. I winced as I checked myself out in the bathroom mirror. *Hot mess.* Pulling a brush from my purse, I dragged it through my tangled hair, then hunted for a toothbrush. I found one along with a tiny tube of toothpaste in the bathroom drawer. Next, I checked my phone. It was dead, and I really needed to call Gran again. Damn.

Grabbing my purse, I went to the door, unlocked it, and stuck my head out into the hallway, peering up one end and down the other. When I decided the coast was clear, I slipped out of the room and made my way to Mick's office on the second floor.

He wasn't there, so I took the opportunity to peek around a little bit. I looked through his desk drawers and file cabinets. There was a disappointing lack of anything un-business related.

I left the office, heading down to the first floor. From the stairway, I spied Mick and Cade perched on stools in front of the bar. They each had a drink in their hands and appeared to be in deep conversation. When they caught sight of me, they fell silent.

"Well, aren't you two chummy all of a sudden?" I came to a halt in front of them. Mick's right eye was swollen. He had a cut on his lower lip and an abrasion along his cheek. Cade's nose was probably broken, the bridge discolored to a purple-black while the entire left side of his face was mottled with bruises. If they'd performed healing spells earlier, I'd just wiped them out.

"I need to go home," I said.

Mick stiffly slid off the stool. "This is my cue to leave. Would you like something to eat, Holly? I'm sure Jasper knows how to make a sandwich or open a tin of soup."

"No, thanks."

Once he left, I turned to Cade. "I'm going home. You can take me, or I can catch a cab."

He stared at me for a long minute. "You can't stay there, Little Null. I'll take you to pick up a few things, but then we're coming back here."

"I'm not stupid, Cade. I get that someone is trying to kill us, but honestly, this murderer has pissed me off. I'm going to catch this son of a bitch before he gets either one of us, and I have a list of things I need to do in order to make that happen." I held up a hand when he opened his mouth to argue. "It's not up for discussion. Until we find out who killed those girls, I won't be safe and neither will you."

"I know that. Which is why you'll stay here with Mick, and I'll find the killer."

I lifted my lips in a bitter smile and glanced at the bottles of liquor lining the wall behind him. "You don't make decisions for me, Sorcerer. You don't have that right."

"I could force you to stay here, Holly." He said it softly, his deep voice barely a whisper.

"Then do it." I held my hands out in front of me, wrists up. "Tie me up, toss me in a room." He looked like he was considering it. "I am not going to hide away and act like a fucking victim. That's not how I operate."

"If I take you, you agree to come back here and let Mick watch over you while I'm gone."

"Where are you going?" My gaze swept his battered face. I wanted to ask if he was all right. Had he put any ice on that nose? Did he have a headache? But I couldn't get in any deeper with him. I couldn't let myself care any more than I already did. It would be too painful in the end.

"Someone took a shot at you, Holly. Do you really think I'm going to let that go?"

"Why is it okay for you to continue, but it's not all right for me? I'm not helpless."

He slid off the stool. "No, but you are powerless. I can't use magic when you're around. It makes both of us vulnerable." When he reached out to stroke my cheek, I stepped back. Cade rubbed his eyes. "C'mon, Little Null, I'll drive you home."

Liability. That's all I was. Cade could go off on his own and use his powers, but that didn't mean I was going to stop asking questions. It might be dangerous, but I didn't think parking my ass here in this bar and turning into a sitting duck was a smart move either.

He walked in front of me, motioned for me to stay put while he stepped outside. Then he held the door open for me. "Looks clear."

I squinted at the bright, hot, afternoon sunshine and wished to God we'd get a break from this merciless heat. I hopped into the rental car and the leather seats burned the backs of my bare legs.

We drove in silence to my house. I jumped out of the car, unlocked the front door, and strode inside. I made tracks to the bedroom where I hooked my phone up to the charger. While Cade watched from the doorway, I grabbed some fresh clothes and went into the bathroom, locking the door behind me. I couldn't even look at him. It tore at my heart, just gazing into those hazel eyes. The sooner we parted, the better.

Once I took a shower, dried my hair and put on fresh clothes, I felt like I could face the world again, but I still didn't want to face Cade. As I left the bathroom, I glanced at the bed—the rumpled sheets, the abandoned purple scarf, the indentation in the pillow where Cade had slept.

Shit. I was in love with him. And these feelings weren't going to go away.

Closing my eyes, I took a deep breath. When I opened them, I donned my game face. I could get through this. I had to stay alive, find the killer, and get a lead on my missing mom. Everything else had to fall in line. Even my heart.

I followed the smell of coffee to the kitchen. Cade leaned against the sink, staring out the window. When he spun around to look at me, he pulled a face. I could tell his ribs were bothering him.

"Come with me." I held out my hand, and he stared at it like it might be poisonous before taking it. I led him to the main bathroom and pointed to the toilet. "Sit."

He lowered the lid and sat down.

"Take off your shirt." I rummaged in the largest drawer until I found the Ace bandage. "Are your ribs broken?"

"I don't know. I think I'm just bruised."

"As soon as we separate, you can perform a healing spell." I glanced up at him, but his face held a blank expression.

I got down on my knees and started wrapping the bandage around his torso. Every time I had to wind it around his back, my nose touched his smooth chest, right where the dragon breathed out fire. "Too tight?"

"No." There was a slight hitch in his breath. He smelled wonderful. I had to fight the urge to put my arms around him. I missed touching him. Missed having him touch me.

"My mom abandoned me," I said. "Just a few days after I was born. I never knew who my father was. Wallace supposedly found out about me for the first time six months ago."

Cade stroked the top of my head. "I'm sorry."

I jerked away from his touch, even though I craved it. "I don't need your sympathy. I'm telling you this so you'll understand. My Gran gave up everything for me, quit the craft to raise me. She's been searching for my mom all these years, but never found a trace. Wallace promised he'd find my mom. Alive or dead, he'll find her and bring her home."

When I was done wrapping him, I stood.

Cade's eyes darkened with compassion. "That's the favor he promised you?"

"Yeah. Lift your arms." I helped him into his shirt. Then I walked out of the room.

In the kitchen, I poured a cup of coffee before popping a frozen waffle in the toaster. I heard Cade enter behind me. "Why Mick?" I asked. "You've been so hell-bent on my staying away from him, now you trust him?"

He stood in the doorway watching me. "I know he'll keep you safe, Little Null."

I shook my head. "That is bullshit. Enough with the cryptic. Just tell me why, of all people, you went to Mick Raven."

He sighed, the muscles in his jaw working overtime. "I've known Mick for years. I can trust him with shit like this."

"Shit like what, a null who's getting in your way?"

"No," he growled. "If I had to trust my life to someone, it would be Mick."

I grabbed my waffle out of the toaster, tossed it on a plate, and smeared it with peanut butter. "Then why act like you hate him?"

"Because I do."

"What makes you think I'll be safe at The Raven? Considering wards and spells won't work when I'm in the vicinity, what's to keep someone from throwing a bomb into the club? Or storming in and shooting up the place?"

"He has guards patrolling the perimeter. Surveillance cameras set up inside and out. It's the safest place I can think of unless you get out of town. Look, Holly, you don't have to do this. You don't have to depend on Wallace to find your mom. He's holding that over your head like the asshole he is. I swear to you, baby, I'll do everything I can to find her. *I'll* bring her home."

I shook my head. Giving up wasn't my style. I wanted to find this killer. No, I *needed* to. Stephanie Carson's eyes haunted me. "I'm not running away, Cade."

"Fine." His face hardened. "Then you stay at Mick's."

"Fine."

CHAPTER TWENTY

Turning my back, I ate my waffle and ignored him. My shutout didn't seem to affect him though. I heard him in the living room, talking quietly on his phone.

I rinsed my dishes and hied off to the bedroom to throw a bag together. I grabbed all the essentials along with my cell and charger.

Cade seemed to accept that I wasn't going to quit investigating, so I would give in on staying at The Raven. Sounded like Mick had things under control over there. At least I hoped so.

"Hey," I said, walking into the living room, carrying my bulging Ralph Lauren wicker tote. "I'm ready to go."

Cade glanced up from his phone. Our gazes held for a long moment. I lowered my sunglasses to shield my expression and headed to the front door. Before I could open it, he grabbed my bag. Shoving past me, he opened the door first, made sure the coast was clear.

We took the rental once more, in case the shooter wanted to try again. Since I'd just paid off my Honda, I considered that sucker a bullet-free zone.

We drove down my street, and I noticed a bright green lawn van. It jarred my memory. Happy Grass. "Cade, the day you took me to London's, there was a lawn service van just like that one, parked at a neighbor's house."

"So?"

"What if the lawn guy saw something the day she died? What if he saw who delivered the package?"

Cade's lips thinned. "Seems like a long shot."

"It's worth a try."

"You said you had a list. What's on it?"

When I opened my purse, I noted that Cade had put the Sig back. I gently shifted it to one side and dug out my notebook, flipping through the pages. "Warn Nick Alpert that James Sharpe is coming for him. Contact Tamara Dermot about Stephanie Carson's place of employment. Stuff like that."

"I've already talked to Stephanie's coworkers." He drummed his fingers on the steering wheel. "They don't know anything about her personal life. She kept to herself."

I wasn't ready to cross it off my list just yet, but maybe it wasn't as pressing as the other tasks.

"I'll call Dawson Nash if you want," he said. "Warn him that Nick should watch his back."

"Thanks."

"Hey, did you say something last night about Jasmine dating Nick? I got a little distracted by all the sex."

Well, that was nice to hear. I'd distracted the sorcerer. How about that? "Yeah, Jasmine's in love with Nick. She was pissed that London got sloppy seconds."

"She didn't tell me jackshit, and I interviewed her twice. I think it's time I pay Jasmine True another visit."

"Sounds like a great idea, but I'm coming with you. And let's check with the lawn service first."

The corners of his mouth twisted slightly. "Yeah, okay."

On my phone, I found an address for Happy Grass. Cade drove a few miles to a brick building that used to be an old Taco Bell. Three green vans sat in the parking lot.

As we exited the car, Cade turned to me. "Don't get your hopes up. In an investigation, you work a lot of leads with very little payoff."

Nodding, I strode through the glass door. A woman with short blonde hair smiled as I approached the reception desk.

"May I help you?" Her smile dimmed a bit when she noticed Cade's bruised face.

"My name's Holly James." I withdrew a business card that officially deemed me a generic consultant. "My associate and I need to speak to the person who handles the lawn on 69th Street. The luxury homes."

Her posture became less relaxed. "What is this about?"

Cade crossed his arms. "We have reason to believe one of your employees may have seen something related to a crime. We're working for the family of London Sanders." He rattled off her address. "If you'd prefer to speak to the police—"

Her mouth dropped open for a couple of seconds, then she pulled herself together. "Hang on." She tapped her keyboard. "Mike Adams takes care of that street. He's in the back, I'll go get him." She returned a moment later with a sandy-haired man in his mid-forties.

"How can I help you folks?"

"Did you happen to service the 69th Street homes on August eleventh?" Cade asked.

Mike glanced at the receptionist who didn't even pretend she wasn't hanging on every word.

"Let me check." She typed in the information. "No, you were there the day before, from two in the afternoon to five forty-five."

Mike focused on us again. "Guess not."

"How often do you spray the lawns?" I asked.

"We don't just spray, we landscape, too. We're a full package service. I have six houses on that street, and I'm usually there once a week. Our wealthier clients maintain their yards despite the heat."

"Did you see anything out of place in that time frame?" Cade asked. "A strange car or suspicious activity?"

"No." He scratched his chin. "But I do remember seeing a lady in a yellow SUV going into the house across the street. I don't know if it was that exact day or not, but it was a few weeks ago. She had this wild, curly hair. That's why I remember her, because of the hair."

Cade pulled a business card and a fifty from his wallet. "Thanks. Give me a call if you think of anything else."

Mike pocketed both. "Will do."

#

On the ride to Blessed Be, I wondered out loud at all the possibilities. "What was Jasmine doing in London's house? The reason could be completely innocent. They were business partners, so why hide it?"

Cade, of course, remained mum.

When we reached the shop, Jasmine wasn't happy to see us. She met us at the door with a faintly pained look on her face. "What the hell are you doing here?" she whispered.

"We need to talk." Cade's sharp gaze took in a couple looking at candles and the lady perusing the crystal necklaces.

Jasmine appeared rattled. Her eyes swiftly darted around the room. "I can't believe you brought her here." She nodded in my direction. "Do you know how much that's going to cost me?"

"Listen, everyone," Cade raised his voice, "shop's closed. Get out."

The couple gazed at him with wide eyes, and the woman jerked her head back as though he had slapped her. They remained rooted to the floor.

Cade strode past Jasmine. "Get. The fuck. Out." His voice was much softer now which, coupled with the sneer on his bruised face, made it all the more frightening.

The three patrons hustled to the door. Cade locked it behind them and flipped the closed sign.

Jasmine twisted a strand of red beads dangling from her neck. "You can't do this."

He stepped toward her. "I just did. And if you lie to me again, I'll close you down for good."

Her blue eyes slid to me.

I shrugged. "He gets real pissy when people lie to him. It's a thing."

"I haven't lied," she said.

Cade casually walked over to the crystal balls lining a glass shelf. "You didn't tell me shit. London dated a vamp *and* a werewolf. You were seen at her house around the time of her death. Lies by omission." He picked up the clear ball and threw it at the candles mounted on a glass table next to Jasmine. I wondered if he'd played ball as a kid, too, because he had great aim. The table shattered, sending the candles to the floor in a shower of wax and glass.

Jasmine screamed and leapt away from the broken fragments.

"See? Pissy," I said.

"You fucking bastard," she gritted out. "The Council will hear about this."

Cade raised one brow, then picked up another crystal ball, this one larger with an elaborately carved brass base. He hefted it in his hand, testing the weight. Pain radiated from his eyes at the movement. His ribs had to be killing him, but he was soldiering through it.

"All right." Jasmine thrust her hand toward him. "All right, please."

He paused, looked at the ball and back up at her. "What were you doing at London's house?"

"I was looking for paperwork she took home. I needed it for the quarterly taxes."

Without any noticeable emotion, Cade threw the crystal ball at the front desk, shattering the display cases that held crystals and geodes. I jumped. Jasmine screamed.

"Let's try again. And this time, the truth."

Beads of sweat popped out on her brow as she licked her lips. "I was looking for some embarrassing pictures on her computer, okay? It was the day before I found her body. She was at the shop, so I told her I had to run an errand. I used the key, disabled the alarm system. I deleted them from her laptop, end of story."

"What pictures?"

"They were just some embarrassing pictures from a night when I'd had a little too much to drink." Every muscle in Jasmine's body seemed tight, coiled, and ready to spring. Just like her hair. "London thought they were funny. She wouldn't delete them, so I took care of it."

I looked at Cade, who turned to the shelf of dragon figurines. He seemed to be carefully picking out his next weapon of destruction. "Nah, this is getting old. I think we should see what Jasmine has in the back room. What do you think, Holly?"

"No, please." Jasmine ran forward and clung to his arm.

Cade extracted himself from her grasp. He strode to the door behind the front display case, his boots crunching over the broken glass. Kicking a couple of trinkets and a hunk of quartz out of his way, he opened the door, disappearing inside.

A second later, he poked his head out and waved an old book of incantations. "Look at this. Eighteenth century." He flipped it open, jerked free a thick page, and crumpled it in his fist. He gazed at Jasmine with a cold intensity that would have scared the shit out of me. "I could do this all day."

Jasmine clasped at her throat and looked a little green like she could puke any minute now. "Please," she whispered.

"It's up to you. Do I keep going, or are you going to talk?"

Her head bobbed so fast, I thought it might pop off. "Fine, I'll tell you everything I know." Tears spilled down her cheeks, and she wiped them away with one hand.

Cade placed the book on a shelf next to the door. "Make it quick." He pointed to his watch.

"London was out of control. She liked to push the envelope." Jasmine gave a small, bitter laugh. "She liked to push people, see how much they could take. And she always wanted to win."

She walked to the front door, looked out to the street beyond the shop. "I dated Nick Alpert, and I thought things were serious. But then he suddenly wanted to take a break. That's when London stepped in. Nick was crazy about her. He broke up with me for good.

"London acted like it wasn't a big deal, but it was to me. A couple of weeks later, she invited me to a party. She liked going to sex parties. It wasn't my thing, but she dared me to go with her. She said that's why Nick had broken up with me because she was imaginative in bed and knew how to keep him interested."

While I felt pity for Jasmine's heartbreak, Cade's expression remained inscrutable.

She crossed her arms and turned to us. "To prove that I could loosen up, I went with her. That night, someone drugged me. I think there was a ritual of some kind. I have flashes, vague memories of what happened. I'm pretty sure I was bloodlet, but there wasn't any evidence of it. When I awoke the next afternoon, I was in my own bed with the worst hangover. I asked London what happened. She claimed I had a great time, that I was the life of the party." Jasmine lifted her head, tears shimmering in her eyes. "I began asking questions, and she tried to put me off, but when I pressed her, she told me she had pictures of everything. She said I looked like I was having a great time." A fine tremble ran through her. She wrapped her arms around her waist.

I walked to her and tentatively placed a hand on hers. I was surprised when she threw both of her arms around my neck and began sobbing on my shoulder.

"I'm so sorry that happened to you, Jasmine."

"You saw these pictures?" Cade's voice cut through her sobs.

Jasmine took a ragged breath and pulled away from me. With the back of her hand, she wiped her nose. "Yeah, she showed me a couple. Some man in a mask was fucking me, *raping* me. So, yeah, I went over to her house to delete those photos. And no, I'm not sad she's dead. In fact, I'm pretty damned happy about it. But I didn't kill her." She straightened and looked Cade in the eye.

He dipped his chin. "Good to know. Where was the party?"

She shrugged. "Out in Owasso somewhere. A huge house, but I don't remember the address or anything." Owasso was popular with the wealthy set. Mini-mansions on vast acreages.

"Jasmine, why is London's house so sterile?" I asked. "She didn't have pictures or personal items. What was that about?"

She shook her head. "That house was like a hotel for her. It belongs to her parents. Since they spend most of the year in Florida, they keep it as an investment. London drove out to Skiatook almost every weekend. She owned a cabin on the lake. That was her real home."

"Thank you. Sorry about the mess." I shot Cade a look.

He walked toward us, crunching over the damage he'd caused. Pulling out his wallet, he removed several hundred dollar bills and shoved them into her hand. "Let me know if this doesn't cover it." Then he left the shop.

"Jasmine, will you call me if you think of anything else?" I asked.

She nodded. "Yeah. Sorry I was bitchy before. I'm just so ashamed, and I didn't want you to think I was a suspect."

CHAPTER TWENTY-ONE

"What do we think?" I asked once I climbed into the car. "Was she telling the truth?"

"Maybe. She seemed pretty convincing." Cade pulled away from the curb.

"London sounds like a psycho bitch. Her friend Tamara said she had a dark side, but Lord have mercy, that's beyond dark." I clenched the seat on either side of my legs.

"If we can believe her, it gives Jasmine True another good motive for killing London," Cade said.

"There's still the question of Stephanie Carson. What does she have to do with any of it?"

"It's possible Jasmine's lying about the whole thing." He smoothly spun the steering wheel with one hand as he turned left. "She hasn't exactly been forthcoming with all this information."

I shuddered, remembering the look of anguish on Jasmine's face. "I don't know. If I'd been drugged, raped, and someone who was supposed to be my friend had pictures of the whole thing, I might keep quiet about it, too. What if the ritual Jasmine experienced had to do with London's practice of black magic? Maybe London wasn't a dabbler at all. She could have been a full-blown black magic woman."

Cade skimmed his thumb over his scar. "There should be evidence of it somewhere. I've been to that shop twice now, and I've never seen a trace of black magic."

"Unless she practiced at the cabin in Skiatook."

We stopped by a burger place and grabbed enough food for us, Mick, and all the bodyguards before heading back to The Raven. When Cade pulled up to the front of the club, he turned to look at me. Reaching out, he stroked my hair. "I want you to stay here. Mick will protect you while I'm gone, which hopefully won't be for long."

"Where are you going? You never did tell me."

"I have another lead on Aldridge. I can't give you any specifics. I'll be in touch, though."

"What about London's cabin?"

"I'll check it out as soon as I get back."

I stared at him, feeling that familiar frustration. "I'll spend the night here, but that's the only promise I'm making." I didn't like that he was still shutting me out, but my arguments would be useless. Cade had his list, and I had mine.

Inside, the club was deserted. Cade and I dropped the food on top of the bar. Then he turned to me. He caressed my cheek before bending down to bestow a kiss that took my breath away. "I'll be back. Please, Holly, stay put." His eyes held mine for a moment longer, then he sauntered out the door.

I should get used to seeing the back of him. My heart may hurt right now, but it was nothing compared to the load of pain I'd feel when he walked away for good.

With a weary sigh, I dialed Gran. I lied and told her I was doing fine. I'd just tucked the phone back in my purse when it rang. Wallace. I hopped up on one of the bar stools and answered.

"Holly, what is going on with this investigation? I've been in Florida for the last two days with London's parents. They're beside themselves with grief, and I don't have any news for them."

"Well, sorry about that. We're doing the best we can." I propped my elbow on the bar, resting my cheek on the palm of my hand.

His sigh was full of impatience. "That's not good enough, darlin'."

"Cade's truck blew up, and someone tried to shoot us. We're questioning the hell out of everyone. I don't know what more you expect."

"I expect results. I want you to find who did this, so I can tell London's parents the killer will be punished."

"Why? Because you want to win another election? Or because you actually give a damn that a girl was murdered? Because frankly, Wallace, I don't see much concern over Stephanie Carson's death."

"Naturally, I'm concerned." The honey flowed from his words. "When our young witches aren't safe, it affects everyone in the community."

I rolled my eyes in disgust. "You sound like a politician right now. Why don't you call me back when you can act like a real person—enchanter—whatever." I hit the end button and tossed the phone in my bag.

I hopped down. Standing alone in the dark empty club with no music, no hateful Others, no go-go dancers, the silence was getting on my nerves. So I went looking for Mick. I found him in his office, nursing a glass of scotch. The only light came from a floor lamp on the far side of the room.

"Did you need something, Holly?"

"I brought you a burger." I set it on his desk and flopped down on the sofa. I pulled a fry from my own sack and nibbled. "Drinking by yourself? That's always a bad sign."

His dark eyes flashed over my face. "I'm not by myself now that you're here." His accent was thicker than usual. I didn't know if it was because he'd been drinking, or because we were alone and he'd lowered his guard.

Mick stood and ambled toward me, holding his crystal tumbler. When he lowered himself on the sofa, he sat awfully close. I wiggled away to get some space.

"Did you like my present?" he asked. Maybe coming to find him wasn't one of my better ideas. "Why aren't you carrying it?"

I opened my mouth, but he beat me to the answer.

"Because Cade doesn't want you to?"

"Cade doesn't know about it. And I've been a little busy the last couple of days. I'll send a thank you note when people stop trying to kill me."

I studied him—his classic cheekbones, his sensual lips. And he had really long lashes for a man. Beautiful eyes with pretty girl lashes. Women must throw their panties at him like he was a rock star or something. "Where are you from, Mick?"

He smiled. "Not from Oklahoma."

"No shit. So where did you come from and how did you wind up here?"

"That's an interesting tale." He took a sip of whiskey.

I waited. "Well?"

"What will you give me if I answer?" With his eyes on mine, he ran his finger down my bare thigh, circled my knee and then rested his hand on my leg. His touch was warm on my skin. Did sorcerers run hotter than other people? I caught a whiff of the alcohol on his breath, but his woodsy, spicy scent surrounded him, too. It was different from Cade's, but smelled insanely good just the same.

I grabbed his wrist, removed his hand from my leg. "I'm not giving you a damned thing." Mick was possibly the hottest man I'd ever met, but I didn't want him to touch me. The only person I wanted was Cade, and since

I'd decided we should never have sex again, a long, dry celibate road lay before me. "I have boundaries, Raven."

"I'd like to cross them." He stroked my arm. "One at a time."

"You know I've slept with Cade."

"I don't mind. After me, you'll forget his name."

I smacked at his hand. "How do you know him? And why do you two hate each other?"

"Why are *you* so full of questions, Holly James?" He set his glass on the coffee table and angled his head toward me.

I wasn't going to get anywhere with him. He'd screw me in a heartbeat, but he wouldn't talk to me. Sounded like another sorcerer I knew.

"Are things serious between you and McAllister? Or is it just sex?"

I tossed a cold, uneaten fry in the bag. I didn't want to talk about this, especially with Mick. Cade was personal, and my feelings were too raw. "He's a sorcerer, I'm a null. What do you think?"

"Opposites attract."

"Right. So, what are we supposed to do until he gets back?"

Mick smiled, slow and sexy. "I could think of a few things."

"For crying out loud, take it down a notch, would you?"

He laughed at that. "All right, what would you like to do?"

I thought about it for a minute. "I want to know more about Stephanie Carson. Who was she? Where did she work? I know she was a client of Blessed Be, but why was she killed?"

"Let's go find out. We can stop for some real food along the way." He stood and walked his long, lean self toward the door.

I tossed the fast food bag on the table. "Where are we going?"

"To Stephanie Carson's house, of course."

"I don't know." I scrunched my nose. "We'd be going against Cade's rules."

Mick grinned. "Rules, my darling, were made to be broken."

"See? That's what I said."

#

I insisted on driving Mick's Porsche. Because, duh, a Porsche. And also because he'd been drinking. I didn't think he was over the limit, but it gave me a nice excuse to get behind the wheel. After giving it a spin—which included doing ninety down I-244—I never wanted to drive anything else.

I wasn't hungry, but Mick insisted we eat something of substance as he put it. We wound up at an upscale grill. I impatiently ordered a steak sandwich and Mick ordered a Kansas City strip so rare it looked raw.

Now that we'd decided to check out Stephanie's place, it was all I could do not to squirm in my seat. But within a few minutes, Mick skillfully had me telling him all about the case. London and her secrets, Jasmine and the photos. I laid it all out there.

"How did you get involved in this?" he asked. "It seems unlikely Cade would ask for help from an outsider."

That summed up my position nicely. "He didn't ask. My grandfather did."

Mick's eyes sharpened. "And who is your grandfather?"

"Wallace Dumahl."

"Ah."

"What does that mean? Is there something I should know?"

"He has a certain reputation for...how should I put this?" Mick paused and cocked his head to one side. "Having a rather ruthless streak. But you would know him better than I."

Not really, but I didn't want to get into my family history. Not only would it take too long, it depressed me.

I picked at my sandwich. Once Mick finished eating, he paid the bill. When we left the restaurant, I hit the fob to unlock the Porsche's doors, but Mick snagged the keys from my hand.

"My turn." He adjusted the seat and mirrors, then smoothly navigated through the side streets. Somehow, he kept within the speed limits. Evidently, he had a lot more willpower than I did.

He parked along the curb across from Stephanie Carson's yellow house. We exited the car and Mick subtly checked up and down the street. "We'll go in the back entrance. Don't turn on any lights. I'll make sure all the blinds are drawn before we shine a torch, yes?"

"A torch?"

Mick glanced down at me. "A flashlight." He dug into his trouser pocket and pulled out a small penlight.

Night had set in, leaving the sky a shade of dark purple which lightened to violet where it met the horizon. The temperature still hovered in the upper nineties.

We crept to the back of the house—okay, I crept—and Mick strolled with graceful steps. He held open the gate of the white picket fence and allowed me to enter first.

When the yappy little dog next door started barking, Mick pulled me toward the house and deeper into the shadows. His hand drifted to my ass, and in retaliation, I pinched his arm. He gave my cheek one firm squeeze before releasing me.

After a couple of minutes, the owner yelled at the dog to get inside. Taking my hand, Mick pulled me to the back door.

Since he couldn't use his sorcerer powers, he broke in the old fashioned way—by wrapping the flashlight in his suit jacket and breaking a pane of glass. We paused to see if the noise alerted any neighbors before he reached in and turned the lock. "I'll follow your lead," he said softly.

I swallowed, and after hesitating, walked into the house. It smelled a little musty from being closed up for several days. The last time I was here, Stephanie Carson's body lay in the living room. I shivered at the memory.

Mick walked through the house making sure all the blinds and shades were drawn so that our snooping would go unnoticed. I stepped into the kitchen and looked around. The flashlight wasn't big, but its powerful light shone on the gray tiled backsplash, white cabinets, and an apartment sized fridge.

"What are we looking for?" he asked, stepping into the kitchen.

"I'm not sure."

"Then we'd better check everything."

I moved to the fridge. It was filled with fruits and veggies. The kind you had to cook. The cabinets and drawers contained nothing of interest.

Mick stood in the corner, silently watching me.

When we entered the living room, I skirted the edges, giving a wide berth to where Stephanie's body had been. I checked under furniture, seat cushions, and in the drawers of the entertainment center. Nothing.

I stepped down the hall, flashed the light over the iron scrollwork wall hanging and walked into the bathroom. Since it faced the back of the house and had one tiny window over the shower, I decided I'd risk the light.

Mick leaned against the wall in the hallway and continued to observe.

The tiny room had been decorated in black and white tile. A pedestal sink stood between the tub and the toilet. I noted the lack of a mirror.

I shut the door on Mick in order to open the linen closet. A few black and white towels were stacked on one of the shelves. On the floor, a box of tampons and a bag of pads sat next to a package of toilet paper. Pushing aside the towels, I noticed a Band-Aid box.

That gave me pause. A witch needed Band-Aids? I pulled the box out of the closet and held it upside down. A small, hand-sewn bag made of velvet dropped into my palm. I untied the knot and gave it a sniff. Then I poured some of the contents into my hand. Wolf's Bane, mint, eucalyptus and a large chunk of agate. Obviously, this was a protection spell. Not a very effective one, either.

I poured the contents back into the bag, stuffed the satchel inside my purse. I opened the bathroom door, and Mick raised his eyebrows at me.

"Protection spell," I said.

I stepped past him to enter the first bedroom. A colorful quilt draped the queen-sized bed. Floral curtains hung at the windows. I flashed the light around and saw a black cloth covering the dresser mirror.

I turned to Mick. "What do you think?"

He lifted one broad shoulder. "Maybe she was trying to keep someone from spying on her?"

That had been my thought as well. A powerful witch or sorcerer could turn a mirror into a looking glass. Who, besides the murderer, would spy on Stephanie? She had to have known something about London's death. It was the only thing that made any sense.

I searched each of the dresser drawers and didn't find anything unexpected. I looked in her closet and went through the pockets of every garment. Looked inside the shoes, too and didn't find squat.

While I was on my hands and knees, I crawled over to the bed. Something lumpy was duct taped under the edge of the mattress frame. I glanced up at Mick. "Got a knife?"

He withdrew one from his pocket, opening the blade before handing it over. I sawed back and forth until a jar dropped to the carpeted floor. I held it in front of my flashlight, completely at a loss. A tiny potion jar filled with yellow liquid, rusty safety pins, and nails. Black wax sealed the cork stopper. A red ribbon had been tied around the bottle's neck. "What is this?" I stood and thrust it at Mick.

He took the flashlight from my hand and examined it. "It's a witch bottle." He handed it back to me.

"I've never heard of it."

"Old wives' magic. Fill a jar with urine, salt, and rusty, sharp objects. Seal it with wax and tie the string for protection." Stephanie's powers had been weak. She must have relied on various kitchen witch concoctions.

I set it on the bedside table. "Disgusting. And useless." Old wives' magic wasn't necessarily magic at all. Just mumbo jumbo Norms conjured up for the most part. I wiped my hand on the seat of my shorts.

With a sigh, I moved back to the hall to check out the second bedroom she used as an office. I cast my light over a framed picture of baby Stephanie and her parents. It brought to mind the one I'd found in Cade's desk.

"I saw a photo of Cade and a blonde girl. What's the story?" I couldn't help myself. I had to ask. Mick and Cade obviously had a history, maybe Mick could fill in some of the blanks. I shone my light on his chest and glanced into his dark, fathomless eyes.

"Shayna." The way he said her name, with a mixture of pain and longing, told me a lot. Had he and Cade been in love with the same woman?

"Who is she? A girlfriend?"

"No, she *was* Cade's sister. I shouldn't be surprised he didn't tell you."

Sympathy for McAllister washed over me. He must feel so alone. No parents, no sister—at least I had Gran. Who did Cade have? "What happened to her?"

He paused for a beat. "Cade killed her."

CHAPTER TWENTY-TWO

I felt like someone had just punched me in the stomach. All the air whooshed out of my lungs, and I collapsed into the desk chair. "How? Why? How?" I babbled, then slammed my mouth shut.

Mick leaned against the office door. "He was working a case six years ago, hunting down a firebug. Shayna went to see him and waited in his motel room. The man he was investigating thought Cade was inside and torched the place to the ground." His words were scripted, hollow. No emotion at all, unlike the first time he'd uttered her name.

"Oh, my God." I clutched the armrest with my left hand. "Cade must have been devastated. He felt responsible, didn't he?"

Mick glanced at me without moving his head. "He *is* responsible."

Pieces were clicking into place. "You loved her, didn't you? You loved Shayna."

"Yes."

I was silent for a moment. "But Cade loved her, too. He didn't kill her. It wasn't his fault." Something else dawned on me. "Does her death have something to do with his scar?"

"I gave him that scar. I don't know why he kept it. Finish up in here." He strolled from the doorway and out of sight.

Poor Mick. Knowing about Shayna made him seem...vulnerable. He still grieved for her, that much was obvious.

I pitied Cade as well. I knew why he kept that scar. Cade's need to protect was strong, but he hadn't protected his sister. That scar was a constant reminder that he'd failed. I was certain he felt responsible for her death, hence all his rules and regulations. And now he felt responsible for me.

Did he have any affection for me, or was I an obligation mixed with simple attraction?

Inhaling deeply, I pulled myself together. I wasn't going to fall to pieces. Not here, not now.

Deliberately forcing my mind from Cade and his sister, I flashed the light around the room, checked the desk drawers and moved to the filing cabinet, which contained Stephanie's birth certificate and bills.

I opened the small closet. There were a few winter clothes hanging inside. Just to be thorough, I checked the pockets and found nothing.

I was about to close the door when I noticed the flipped edge of the carpet in the back corner. I knelt down and pulled. It came away easily from the subflooring. Under the carpet was a rectangular space roughly cut in the plywood. Inside the little hiding place was yet another pouch. Blue velvet this time. I upended it to discover a silver amulet, very similar to the one that killed London—a circle larger than a quarter with a bloodstone cabochon in the center. I turned it around and ran my thumb over the faded runes inscribed on the back.

I placed it in the bag and stuck it in my purse along with the protection satchel, then put the carpet back as I'd found it. When I stood and closed the closet door, Mick was standing there. I gasped in surprise and clutched my chest. "God, you scared the crap out of me."

"What was taking you so long?" His gaze flickered over my face. "Did you find anything?"

"Yeah, an amulet."

"Good. Let's go." He led the way to the kitchen and out the back door.

The glowing moon hung low in the sky. Mick held the gate once again, and I had to squeeze past him. On the way to the Porsche, he strolled confidently whereas I furtively glanced at all the houses near Stephanie's, making sure we hadn't been observed.

We climbed in the car, and Mick turned to me. "Did you find what you were looking for?"

"I don't know." I shifted in my seat. "I'm sorry about Shayna."

"I do not wish to speak of her, Holly." His smooth voice held a hard edge.

Mick drove to the highway and headed north. I glanced at him out of the corner of my eye. "Where're we going?"

"You wished to know more about Stephanie Carson's place of employment. I am taking you there."

"You know where she worked?"

"I do. There's one club in town that gives The Raven competition."

"The Raven is notorious." I wrinkled my brow, doubting him. "If there were an Other club as popular, I'd have heard about it."

He caught my hand and brought it to his lips. "You say the nicest things, darling."

I jerked free from his grasp. "Quit touching me. Do you keep tabs on your competition or something?"

"I don't have competition. I eliminate it. I bought the club two years ago."

I was beginning to realize Mick Raven was a master game player. And he was always three steps ahead of me. That made him even more dangerous than I'd originally thought.

We drove fifteen minutes until we reached a rundown commercial area in the northern part of town. Mick hooked a left into an abandoned strip mall, and several cars shimmered into view. By the time he parked, I saw the lot was actually full. The buildings which had been boarded up moments ago spilled strobe lights and music into the night.

"Sorry about ruining your invisibility spell." I unlatched my seatbelt.

Mick turned and looked me in the eye. "Never apologize for being what you are. You have no idea of the power you wield. However, I'd be happy to teach you."

His words frightened me. I didn't want to be powerful. I wanted to live off the grid as far as Others were concerned. Even if that meant closing down my business. I'd had my fill of their world.

Mick smoothly climbed out of the car and came around to open my door. "Now, it's very important that you show no fear, no astonishment. Don't gawk. Just stick by me, and you'll be fine."

"What are you talking—"

Taking my elbow, he propelled me forward into a building filled with a writhing mass of people. Where The Raven featured topless girls dancing on daises, this place had masked, naked women on display in suspended cages, their arms pinned above their heads, held there by manacles. They gyrated to the music.

I glanced over the mostly naked crowd—men clad in studded leather, women wearing nothing but collars. This was an Other sex club. Mick owned it. Stephanie Carson had worked here. Little, mousy Stephanie Carson. Cade had to have known about this. He said he'd questioned Stephanie's coworkers. He might have mentioned it was in an S&M den. That sorcerer had me so past irritated, my blood was starting to boil.

Once again, every head swiveled in my direction. The bright violet, flashing orbs suddenly flickered out as I advanced. When I walked by a suspended cage, it dropped six feet to the floor, causing the nude girl inside to gasp.

Mick ushered me through the room, nodded to people as he walked, never breaking stride. I matched my steps to his, and the rest of the cages fell to the ground, one by one. I hitched my shoulders at the sound of each crash. Murmurs and a few startled screams followed in my wake.

I passed an older gentleman whose eight-pack abs morphed into a pudgy beer belly. More than one magically enhanced monster boner wilted and resumed its original size. I wasn't going to win points with this crowd.

The walls between the strip mall had been knocked down, creating one large space, but areas had been blocked off, making smaller rooms. Some had doors while others were completely open to spectators. This club made The Raven look like wholesome family entertainment.

I lingered at a window and watched a woman get tag-teamed by two men in leather face masks. Her upraised arms were shackled with chains that dangled from the ceiling. Several people stood around and silently watched, the men visibly excited by the performance. My stomach lurched, but it was hard not to stare.

Mick's hand squeezed my arm. "No gawking, remember? Unless you find it exciting?"

"I don't."

We moved on, passing a room with some kind of bench apparatus where a woman bent at the waist was getting her bare ass whipped by a bulky, bald guy. Large welts formed along her cheeks and upper thighs. Her long, dark hair dragged the ground, but I caught a glimpse of her face and skidded to a halt. Tamara Dermot. Excellent. I had questions for her.

A man in a leather vest and a g-string blocked my path. No gawking, Mick said. But come on, who wouldn't steal a glance? His well-sculpted muscles were impressive, and he seemed to be packing some serious damage in that cock hammock. Must be real, too, because my presence didn't cause shrinkage.

"What is she doing here, Mick?" He jabbed his thumb in my direction. "I pay a hefty fee. Having a null ruin my fun isn't part of the deal."

The bald guy with the whip had stopped hitting Tamara. He held it aloft while he watched Mick deliver a public verbal smackdown.

I glanced around the room. Men and women, some with barely covered sexy parts, stared at me. Their expressions ranged from vaguely confused to savage anger.

Mick regarded the man. "Are you dictating to me, Justin? That's not a very healthy attitude to take, my friend." Then he smiled pleasantly.

Beads of sweat formed along Justin's forehead. "Sorry. Sorry, Mick."

Mick nodded regally. "I will accept your apology. This time."

Cade would have stormed in here, fists flying, intimidating people with his snarls. Mick's steel hand encased in a velvet glove was equally effective.

I took the opportunity to walk up to Tamara. I bent over, grabbed a handful of her hair, gently pulling it away from her face. "Hi, remember me?" I gave her a friendly smile. I wasn't sure how that looked upside down.

"Yeah, you're the null."

"Can I talk to you for a couple of minutes?"

"I'm on the clock, but I can take a break. Unhook me, will you?"

I unfastened the straps binding her to the bench. But as I started to unhook the last strap, the bald man grabbed my arm, jerking me up.

"No one said you could do that."

"She did." I pointed at Tamara.

"No one told you to move, sub."

"I'm sorry, Master," Tamara said. "But I have to talk to her."

Mick was now surrounded by four men, one of whom wore assless chaps. While Raven appeared to be amused, I'd have been grossed out. Way too much impersonal nudity for my taste.

I glanced back at Tamara. "Don't you have a safe word or something?"

"Fire engine!"

Master sighed. "Fine."

After unfastening the cuff, I helped her stand up. Her hair was a wild tangle, and her face was as red as a ripe tomato. "You okay?"

She reached back and rubbed her ass cheeks. "Yeah, just sorry I couldn't finish the session."

I reminded myself not to shake hands. And I intended on taking a scalding shower as soon as I got back to the club. With antibacterial soap.

Mick cleared people out of his path and made his way to my side. Curving his arm around both our waists, he walked to the back of the club with Tamara and me. The sex people scooted out of the way.

He smoothly maneuvered us into a room that stated it was for employees only. This small office was nothing like his opulent cave at The Raven.

Tamara sat on a chair and winced.

Mick parked on the desk in front of her. "Holly has a few questions. I'd like you to answer them truthfully, yes?"

Her gaze darted between Mick and me. "Of course. But if this is about London, I've told you everything."

I propped myself on the metal desk next to him. "You work here, Tamara?"

"Yeah. It leaves my days free. The tips are awesome. Much better than a nine to five office job."

I was speechless for a moment. "And you get paid to have your ass whipped?"

"No, I consider it a bonus," she said, crossing her legs.

I closed my eyes and gave my head a little shake. Moving on now. "Why didn't you tell me that you and Stephanie worked together?"

"Um, you didn't ask. I don't see what it has to do with London getting cursed to death."

"Stephanie was cursed, too," Mick said.

Tamara huffed at me. "You never told me that. Besides, it's not like Stephanie and I worked *together*. She was the kitchen staff."

"She came in every morning and prepped for dinner," Mick said. "She was gone by one in the afternoon." That made more sense than shy, little Stephanie serving drinks in a leather bikini.

"You might have mentioned this earlier." I glared at him, irritated at his lack of candor. "You know I've been asking about Stephanie."

He simply shrugged. "I might have done a lot of things."

Fucking arrogant sorcerers. "Tamara, you told me London had a dark side, and here *you* are, getting your ass whipped in front of a group of people."

"This isn't a dark side. It's not about sex. Not for me, anyway."

I was starting to get a headache.

Mick shifted his leg. "I believe what Tamara is trying to say, is that there are levels of sexual contact. She doesn't associate being submissive with sex. Is that correct, Tamara?"

Then someone explain to me why she was wearing a pushup bra and lacy underwear. I called bullshit. "Tell me the difference between what you do and what London did."

"London liked rough sex, like really rough. I'm not that hardcore." She gestured toward her chest with one hand. "And she'd quit using the club's Dom. Said it was too controlled. Then she started dating a werewolf, and they're unpredictable, especially around the full moon. I'm sure the sex was riskier. She was going to private parties, too, but never invited me. This isn't a lifestyle for me, I just let off steam. Master Ron likes to be in control; I like to play the submissive once in a while. Plus, it keeps the customers happy."

None of this added up. Had London been lying? "That doesn't jive with what the werewolf told me. He said that he was very, very careful not to leave bruises on London."

Tamara chewed her lip in thought. "She showed me the marks on her arms and wrists. She had a really big bruise on her neck one time." She nodded at me. "It looked a lot like yours."

My hand flew to my hickey. Shit, I'd forgotten all about putting on a scarf. "But she never specifically said it was the shifter who'd marked her?" That neck bruise had been the result of London getting sucked by a mysterious vamp—if Sharpe was telling the truth.

"No, I guess not. I just assumed," Tamara said. "Maybe she got passed around at a party. Like I said, she never invited me. I told you something weird was going on with her."

"Could the vampire have left London bruised? Was she into that stuff with Sharpe?"

"Maybe. She told me they had great sex, but she never said he got rough with her. I got the feeling it was all about bloodletting with him."

This was all old news, so I switched it up. "What about Stephanie? Did she have any boyfriends?"

Tamara pressed her lips together. "I don't know. We weren't friends. We hardly saw each other, even though we both worked at the same place."

"And the Solstice party?" I asked. "Stephanie was working in the kitchen that night."

Tamara's eyes widened. "She was?"

I wanted to pound my head against the concrete wall. I was getting nowhere. Either Tamara was as bright as a nightlight, or she was a brilliant killer. I was going with the nightlight.

"Do you know anything at all about her? Some insight that can help?" Mick asked.

"She wasn't very powerful. I ran into her at Blessed Be once."

Stephanie had to have stumbled onto the killer, somehow. "Was Stephanie into black magic?"

"Not according to her aura," Tamara said. "She was so quiet and shy. I can't imagine her going dark."

"Is there anything you can tell us about London that will lead us to her killer?" I stared her dead in the eye, trying to impress upon her how important this was. "Even something small, something she said in passing. Think hard."

"Um, there's one thing I didn't mention to you that day at the café, Holly. London and I had a huge fight the night of the Solstice party." Her lower lip jutted out. "I kept bugging her, asking her to tell me what was wrong. I knew she was in trouble, and I warned her it wouldn't end well." As she began crying, mascara rimmed her large, brown eyes. "London finally told me to mind my own business or get the hell out of her house. I left early, and I didn't speak to her again before she died. The last words we said to each other were angry ones."

I dug a tissue out of my purse, handed it to her. "It wasn't your fault, Tamara." I leaned forward, rubbing her knee. After a couple minutes, the tears dried, leaving her eyes red and her face puffy.

"What about Jasmine True? Did London get along with her?"

"Jasmine's kind of a bitch, but they got along okay."

"How did they get into business together?" Mick asked.

"London's and Jasmine's parents were best friends. Like I said, she stopped talking to me, so I don't really know her reasons for doing anything this last year."

I frowned and tried to make sense of all the pieces. "London was into black magic," I reasoned. "Did the rough sex tie in somehow?"

Tamara's jaw fell open. "What? No. She couldn't have been dabbling. I would have sensed it. Sure, her aura was dark, but it wasn't stained." Her eyes slid to Mick. "You're wrong. Something was going on with her, but not that. I'd have known."

Mick stood and taking Tamara's hand, helped her to her feet. "I'm sure it's a misunderstanding. Thank you for speaking with us. Why don't you go home now, hmm? Take the rest of the night off."

Tamara nodded, sniffing as she stumbled out the door.

Mick watched her go, then glanced at me. "What do you think?"

"I think I'm grasping at straws."

CHAPTER TWENTY-THREE

Mick didn't speak much on the ride back to The Raven, and I was lost in my own thoughts. According to Cade, Stephanie's house held faint traces of magic from her own signature. London's sterile, showroom house had been wiped clean, save for Jasmine's healing spell.

Jasmine had reasons to kill London. Lots of them. But if she were the killer, would she have been able to use blood magic and remove all evidence of it? We were talking about powerful mojo here. How could she get rid of every single trace?

God, all these questions made my head hurt.

When Mick pulled into The Raven's parking lot, I spied four men, one at each corner. The bodyguards gave me an extra measure of safety, but if I thought about it too hard, I'd remember all the ways a killer could outwit four bodyguards.

I noted the rental car parked close to the door. Cade. My heart flipped at the thought of seeing him. Then I sternly reminded myself he didn't belong with me.

I nodded at a stretch limo parked in front of the club entrance. "Yours?" I asked Mick.

"No. It seems we have a visitor. And Cade is back. What joy."

When I walked into the club, my eyes immediately found Cade. He looked so battered with all those bruises and the broken nose. His gaze flew over me. I started to walk to him when I noticed someone standing to my right. As immobile as a mannequin, Monty Ridgecliff took up space near a round table. There was nothing distinguishing about him, except for his impeccable fashion sense.

In fiction, vampires were sexy. Sinful. They were that way in real life, too. But Monty bucked the stereotype. He looked about thirty, but he must be ancient to hold such a trusted position as Master Sebastian's mouthpiece. With a dark suit tailored to his long frame, he embodied formality.

He smiled, but on him, it never looked quite natural. "Holly, so pleased to see you. Please, join me."

Mick, who had stepped in behind me, placed a hand on my lower back and whispered in my ear, "Looks like we're late for the party."

I moved away from him and walked toward Monty. Two men melted out of the shadows, flanking him. Vamp bodyguards. Both stared straight ahead, hands clasped in front of them. Though they didn't seem very imposing without their powers, I was sure they could smack me around if they thought I posed a threat.

"Hello, Monty," I said, my head lowered slightly. "How are you?"

"I am well. Thank you for asking. Have a seat, please." He held out a chair for me.

Cade sat opposite me, and Mick took a seat next to him.

"Although I always find it delightful to hear from you, Holly, I was concerned when I received your message about missing brethren. Would you care to elaborate?"

Brethren, that's what vamps sometimes called themselves. "I hear things. And when brethren disappear, it's worrisome. Out of respect, I wanted to bring this to your attention."

"I thank you. And as Master Sebastian's liaison"—he placed a hand on his chest and stared at me through cold, blank eyes—"I do need to be informed of any rumors."

"Why don't you answer her question," Cade said. "Any missing vamps?"

Monty glanced at Cade and tilted his head. "Mr. McAllister, I hear you're looking into the tragic deaths of those unfortunate witches."

Cade's jaw tensed.

"I think we need a drink," Mick smoothly interjected. A bartender appeared, holding four glasses and a bottle. "I remember you like Scotch, Monty."

"What a memory you have. For a sorcerer."

Mick seemed to take no offense as he smiled and poured out a measure into each tumbler. Then raised his glass in a toast. "To…interspecies cooperation."

Monty took a sip. During this whole exchange, his expression never changed, wavered, or shifted. "All right, Holly, yes, four brethren went missing last spring. It was quite a mystery at the time."

Cade shifted in his chair. "Is it still a mystery, or did you figure out what happened to them?"

"We're mostly satisfied with our conclusions."

"Mostly?" Mick asked. "Does that mean some ends are still loose?"

"These things take time." Monty gestured with one pale hand. The motion was jerky. It was like he'd forgotten how to be human.

"Why wasn't the Council called?" I asked Cade. "Don't you guys investigate that type of thing?"

"We like to police our own," Monty said.

"A newbie vamp bit Holly the other night. Why isn't he a pile of ash?" Cade asked.

I ran a finger over the bruise. The pain was fading.

"Again, my humblest apologies." Monty briefly bowed his head. "Abby and Neil have been censured, I assure you."

Pushing my glass away, I placed my hands on the table. "Back to the missing brethren. Who are they?"

"I still don't know why you're curious." I sensed icy disdain beneath his polite demeanor.

I didn't want to out Abby as my source, but I couldn't see a way around it. "I heard Abby's BFF is missing, for one."

"Abby's beef?"

"Her best friend."

"Ah, yes. Although it's tragic, sometimes one has difficulty making adjustments. Suicide is rare amongst our kind, but not unheard of."

"So, all the missing brethren killed themselves?" Mick's tone was mild, but there was a hint of steel underneath. "And Abby's friend makes number five."

"That seems like a high number in such a short period of time." Narrowing his eyes, Cade crossed his arms. "Why don't you let the Council help you? We have excellent resources."

"While I appreciate the offer, as I've said, we're still looking into it." Monty glanced at each of us in turn. "Thank you for your concern." He shot a look at one of his guards and started to rise.

I took a deep breath. "I have another concern."

"Yes?"

"London Sanders was bitten by one of the brethren, almost to the point of death."

He slowly returned to his seat. "Unfortunate, but I believe she was involved with one of us at the time."

"The boyfriend didn't bite her," I said.

The pupils in Monty's light blue eyes widened, other than that, no reaction. "How interesting. What does this have to do with one of our missing?"

I shrugged. "I'm not sure it does. But if one of the brethren was drinking from someone else's property, that's a serious breach of etiquette."

Monty stared at me, unblinking. "If you're implying that James Sharpe killed his rival—"

I held up a hand. "I'm not implying anything. But isn't it forbidden to poach on another's possession?"

Monty was silent a moment, and then he spoke slowly, as though he were choosing his words very carefully. "It is frowned upon, but I had no knowledge that James Sharpe and London Sanders had a formal relationship. That type of thing is officially recorded."

"Meaning London wasn't marked?" Mick asked.

"Quite." Monty gave a stiff nod.

"You didn't know she was bitten?" I propped my elbows on the table. "That she almost died?"

"No, Holly, I did not."

"The names of these missing, who are they?" Cade grabbed his glass, and in one swallow, downed his scotch.

Mick winced and poured him another.

"I'm not comfortable giving names of brethren to a Council representative. However, I will keep you informed of our findings. Will that do?" It didn't really matter what our answer was, Monty would do whatever the hell he wanted.

He stood, buttoned his suit jacket, and bowed. Then he took my hand and pressed it to his lips. They were warm. I wondered how he felt about being human again, even for a few minutes. Did he enjoy having a heartbeat or resent it?

"Always lovely to see you, Holly." This time, his smile widened. It still looked weird, like it was painted across his face, but at least he was making an effort.

After he released my hand, I stood. "Thank you so much for coming by."

When he and his entourage left, I sank back down into the chair and glanced at Mick. "Can't I have a real drink? Something with tequila or fruit juice?"

He leaned toward me, a predatory grin on his face. "You, my darling, can have anything you desire."

Cade growled.

"A margarita would be nice."

"Yeah, why don't you go make it," Cade said, "before I bust that pretty face again?"

Mick's grin dropped and he turned toward Cade, his expression cold and scary. "Do not come into my house and presume to threaten me."

"Enough, you two," I said. "Mick, do you mind if I speak with Cade in private?"

Though still facing Cade, his gaze slid toward me. "Yes, I do."

Cade pushed away from the table and grabbed my hand. "Tough shit."

I barely managed to grab my purse before he marched up the stairs. I assumed we were going to Mick's office. Instead, he led me to the third floor green room, where I'd slept the night before.

He switched on the light and slammed the door so hard, the walls shook. "What were you doing with Mick?"

"Investigating. That's all I've been doing for the past five days, you know that."

His eyes searched mine, but he said nothing.

"You were so adamant about me questioning people by myself, I thought you'd be glad I took him along as backup."

Cade propped his hands on his hips. "Don't push it."

"Mick told me about Shayna." As soon as the words left my mouth, Cade's whole body changed. His face shut down, and the line of his shoulders became taut.

"Not talking about her. Where did you go with Mick?"

"Stephanie Carson's house."

"What?"

Tornado survivors say it's dead quiet in the eye of a twister, and with all the air pressure, it's impossible to breathe. Being in the room with Cade felt just like that.

He slowly stalked toward me. "You did what?"

"I wanted to look for clues. I found some."

"Tell me you didn't remove them from the house."

I glanced up at the ceiling. "Well—"

"Damn it, Holly," he yelled.

"I know, I know. I fucked with the evidence."

CHAPTER TWENTY-FOUR

I scrambled to my purse and pulled out the two velvet pouches. "Here. Also, her mirrors were covered."

"I know that." He opened the protection bag. "Where did you find this?"

"In a Band-Aid box. What was a witch doing with Band-Aids?"

He grunted. "She was a weak witch, so I didn't think much about it. Good catch." Then he opened the other bag. "Shit. This amulet is almost identical to the one that killed London. Where was it?"

"Hidden under the closet subfloor in her spare bedroom."

"How did you find it there?"

I shrugged. "Just lucky. Why would she have that?"

"I don't know." Stress lines framed his eyes, and he looked pale.

"How are your ribs?"

"Fine. Was this all you found?"

"Yeah. Let me rewrap you." I moved toward him and started tugging at his shirt. When I lifted the hem over his abdomen, my gaze captured his. "Did you really think I'd be with Mick after last night?" I asked softly.

His eyes shifted away. "I know how persuasive he is. Women fall for him. Never figured out why. He's an asshole."

I helped him take his shirt off. "I don't want him. Sit on the bed."

Cade cupped my face, his thumb traveling the seam of my lips. "Who do you want?"

I leaned into his hand, kissing his palm. Right then, I didn't give a damn that we were opposites or that any attraction between us would wither and die in the real world. Being in the same room with Cade made me forget all the valid reasons we'd never make it as a couple. When he touched me, my brain shut off and my heart took over. "Who do you think, stupid Sorcerer? Now go sit on the bed."

He eased down on the mattress, and while I rewrapped the Ace bandage around his torso, I told him about the sex club. "Shit. He actually took you there? Anything else you need to tell me before I break Raven's skull?"

I secured the bandage, and Cade's phone rang. He dug into his pocket, and I stood, getting my fill of that solid chest, the fierce dragon tattoo, the thick muscles of his shoulders and arms. He was all masculine strength and sharp edges. Just studying him gave me a little thrill.

After listening briefly, Cade held the phone away from his ear and glanced at me. "Dawson Nash. He says Nick Alpert's ready to talk."

Finally. Maybe the werewolf would have info. Anything to point us to London's killer. I was weary of searching for answers and coming up empty. "We passed a Denny's along the highway about thirty minutes from Dawson's house. That's a good halfway mark."

Cade flattened his lips and hesitated, but eventually held the phone back to his ear and repeated my suggestion. When he hung up, he grabbed his t-shirt and pulled it over his head, grimacing in pain. "We meet in an hour."

"What do they want to talk about?"

"London. Listen, Little Null, Mick and I could go—"

"Forget it."

"Yeah, that's what I figured."

#

It was ten o'clock when we stepped into the nearly empty Denny's. It smelled of coffee and pancakes. And although I was hungry, I couldn't eat. I was too keyed up. I needed to uncover what Nick Alpert knew, then get the hell out of here. Cade didn't know it yet, but I planned on heading to London's cabin in Skiatook next. That was the logical place to search since we'd found nothing in her sanitized mansion.

I spotted Nick and Dawson in a corner booth. Dawson, relaxed and rumpled in a disgracefully wrinkled blue t-shirt, tipped his chin at us. Nick was tense, his shoulders hunched to his ears. His big hands gripped his water glass so tight I was surprised he hadn't reduced it to particles.

"Hey." I slid into the booth. "So what's up?" I tapped my nails on the table.

Cade slid in next to me and clamped his hand over mine, forcing me to stop fidgeting.

A waitress brought us all coffee then left us alone.

"Thanks for meeting with us," Dawson said. "Nick here has some information for you. And an apology." He jerked his head at the enforcer, causing his sun-bleached hair to fall over one brow.

"I'd like to apologize for the way I acted the last time we met," Nick's voice was rusty. "I should have had more control."

Dawson stared pointedly at me. Cade kicked my foot under the table. Okay, I could take a hint.

"Thank you," I said. "I apologize for being so insensitive."

Nick shifted in his seat. "I'd like to help if I can. I want to know who killed London. In return for my help, when you find out who killed her, let me deal with him personally."

"Can't promise you that," Cade said. "I speak for the Council. There's no room for a personal vendetta, but justice will be meted out. I can promise you that."

Nick's nostrils flared, and he clenched his fist on the table. "That's the deal, Sorcerer."

"No."

Nick bared his teeth. "Then forget it."

"Really?" I asked. "You're not going to help us solve London's"—I lowered my voice—"murder because you want to get into a pissing contest about who gets to off the culprit?"

He looked like he was wrangling with himself before nodding. "Fine. Ask what you want."

"Did you know London was seeing Sharpe?" Cade asked.

Nick shook his head. "No. I thought we were exclusive."

"Do you know about the club she went to?" I asked.

"The sex club?" Nick swung his dark eyes in my direction. The intense look on his face was frightening. "Yeah, but after we got together she stopped going. Are you saying she lied about that, too?"

Dawson put his hand on Nick's arm. "Steady."

Nick shut his eyes and breathed deeply for a few seconds.

"Lately, she'd been going to private parties," I said. "Know anything about those?"

"No."

"She had bruises, Nick. One of her friends thought that maybe she got passed around."

"To other Doms?" I could hear the pain in his words. "No, that can't be."

"I thought that was your appeal for her, your dominance. She was all bruised up, and she liked it."

He shook his head violently. "No, I was careful with her. I would never *harm* her. And she wouldn't trust anyone else the way she trusted me. We had a bond. It was…it was more than sex. She had to trust me not to hurt her."

"But you hit her, right?" Cade asked.

Nick sighed and rubbed a hand over his eyes. "No. It's not hitting, not like you think. It's not abusive. I left her unblemished. It must have been that asshole vampire." He pounded his fist on the table, causing the other four patrons to stare at us.

Once again, Dawson laid his hand on Nick's arm, calming the enforcer.

Nick's eyes met mine. "I never hurt her."

"What about Jasmine?" I asked. "The two of you dated. Did you share the same *bond* with her?"

"No, she wasn't into that. That's one of the many reasons we didn't work out. She was too aggressive, too dominant."

"She still seems upset by the breakup."

Nick's gaze shifted to the table. "I feel bad about that. We dated for a few months about a year ago, but once I got to know London… We tried to keep it quiet from Jasmine so we wouldn't hurt her feelings."

"Do you think she could have killed London? How powerful is Jasmine, anyway?"

"Average, I guess. And no, I can't imagine Jasmine doing something like this." Nick placed his elbows on the table, resting his mouth on his fisted hands. He stared out the window. "I miss her. London. Was going to ask her to marry me."

I glanced at Cade then. He'd never feel that way about me, and it hurt. Even if he did, it would never work. A desolate, hollow ache settled in my heart. I licked my lips and looked away. Dawson was staring at me, his eyes full of compassion. I took a sip of coffee to wash down the lump in my throat.

"What about the bite London received?" Cade asked. "Do you know anything about that?"

Nick's eyes flickered from the window to my neck. "She said she'd been attacked. She didn't remember how it happened."

"And you believed her?"

"Of course. A powerful vamp could have wiped her memory. It never entered my head that she'd lie about something like that. Now I know she lied about everything." Nick's eyes went dark, almost black. "Sharpe did this to her, and I'm going to kill him."

Dawson's handsome face became a frigid mask. He straightened in his seat, suddenly every inch the pack leader. "No, you're not. We're not about to start a war with the vamps. Not for any reason."

Nick turned to Dawson. "Then what do you suggest? When I thought it was a random attack, I went to Monty about it, and he didn't do jack shit."

"Say what?" With my mouth open, I stared at Nick. "You told Monty?"

"Of course I did," he said with a scoff. "You think I was going to let something like that slide? Monty promised he'd look into it, but I never heard another word about it. Even Dawson called him twice."

Dawson nodded. "Monty said it was an ongoing investigation, and when *he* knew something, *I'd* know something."

Well, shit. So, Monty Ridgecliff had known London almost died from a vamp bite. I guessed I shouldn't have been surprised at his reticence. Vampires kept themselves to themselves. They were a very secretive bunch.

I shoved Monty and vampire politics to the back of my brain. "Just so you know, James Sharpe is as pissed off about that bite as you are. Swears some other vamp did it." I watched Nick closely, but couldn't tell what was going on behind those scary eyes. "Did London ever take you to her Skiatook cabin?"

"No, that was her personal time to practice the craft. She needed solitude for that."

I'd run out of questions, and Cade had too. We said goodbye and once in the rental car, he cranked up the AC while we sat quietly for a couple of minutes.

"What do you think about Monty?" I flicked the edge of my purse, running my finger over the side seam. "He knew what happened to London, that she almost died, but he sat there and said nothing. What does that mean? On a side note, what about the missing brethren? That's weird." I was a rambling stream of consciousness. Whatever popped into my brain came tumbling out of my mouth. "I want to know more about those parties London attended. She was getting bruises from somewhere. Tamara said London wouldn't include her in the parties, she'd changed in the last year. Did you know Stephanie—"

"Enough! Can't you shut up for five goddamn minutes while I think?"

"There's no time for you to think, McAllister. We need to get to Skiatook and check out London's real home—the cabin. Now."

"You're right." With a sigh, he backed out of the parking spot. "Got an address?"

"No, but Sunny will." I dialed and listened to her bitch for five minutes about all of the appointments she'd had to cancel. She finally ran out of steam.

"What do you want now?" she sniped.

"London's cabin in Skiatook—what's the address?"

"Can you say please?"

"I can say *you're fired*. Want to hear what that sounds like?"

She promised to text me the address and hung up.

In the meantime, Cade drove west. "The two of you are something else. You fight like sisters."

"If we were sisters, she'd have never made it through puberty. I'd have smothered her with a pillow. But she's good at her job. A total pain in the ass—"

"Not at all like you. All right, let's hear it."

"What?" I absentmindedly rapped my knuckle against the window.

"Your theory about Monty. You must have one. Or five."

I shifted in my seat to face him. "Maybe Monty's trying to cover up the fact that a vamp's gone blood crazy on his watch. Look at Neil. He attacked me at The Raven, the only sacred spot in the city. Doesn't sound like Master Sebastian has a tight rein on his people. The point is, Monty lied to us. If he's lying about that, what else is he lying about?

"And I keep circling back to poor, little Stephanie Carson," I continued. The dark hid Cade's facial expressions, but he reached up and fingered his scar. "Why the hell was she killed? Why have that amulet and why hide it? Did she overhear something at the Solstice party? At London's store? What other reason could there be?"

"I want to know *where* she got that amulet," Cade said.

"Have you looked through the inventory list at Blessed Be?" I asked.

"Herb has it. He said there's nothing that links the amulet to the store. Jasmine says the first time she laid eyes on it was the day she found London's body, but she's lied about so much, she may be feeding me another line of bullshit."

"What was London doing with Vane Aldridge?" I asked. "I'm aching to know the answer to that. You never told me what happened today. I assume you didn't find him?"

"Another dead end. I kept calling that number you found at his grandpa's house, but no one answers."

I suddenly felt so tired, I wanted to curl up and sleep for a week. "Maybe we'll find something at the lake house."

Sunny texted an address which I tapped into Cade's GPS. After twenty minutes, we left the highway onto an exit. We finally turned down a one-lane road that skirted the lake. The moon's reflection bounced off the waves, making the water sparkle. The stars were more visible out here. I could see why London liked coming to this place. Even at night, it was beautiful. Peaceful.

When the GPS claimed we'd arrived at our destination, Cade stopped the car and cut the engine. Ahead, resting on a shallow hill stood a narrow two-story house. He grasped my chin, planted a hard kiss on my lips. "Stay here while I check it out. If I find any signatures or evidence, I'll have to call Herbert."

"Okay. Good luck."

He stroked my cheek with the back of his hand. "I don't know what I might find in there. I don't want anything happening to you, Little Null. So for once, do as I ask and stay put?" Then he kissed me once more, tenderly this time.

His damned sense of responsibility had reared its head again. What he felt for me was nothing more than a strong sense of duty. Yes, he was sexually attracted, but how long would that last? As long as we were thrown into each other's company. After this was over, I'd be out of sight, and he'd never give me a second thought.

I leaned back and forced a smile. "I'll stay right here. Promise."

He grunted, touched his lips to my forehead. As he got out of the car and jogged up the drive, I rolled down the window. The night was full of sound. Bullfrogs and cicadas vied for attention in the oppressively humid air. I slapped at a mosquito that darted toward my head.

Cade slowed as he got closer to the house. He whipped out a flashlight and shined it over the porch. But just as his boot hit the first step, he fell to the ground, hitting his head on the railing. I could hear the painful thud from forty yards away.

Forgetting my promise, I was out of the car in two seconds, running for him. "Cade?" I'd almost reached him when something sharp stung the back of my neck.

CHAPTER TWENTY-FIVE

I awoke on my back and gently probed the goose egg above my ear. Groaning, I rolled over, but a wave of nausea stilled my movements.

The stars seemed to be spinning. I closed my eyes, swallowed convulsively, trying to keep the puke at bay. But the sickness was overwhelming and despite the pounding in my head, I quickly flopped onto my stomach, hurling all over the stone pathway that led to the house.

When I was through, I wiped my mouth with the back of my hand and slung my hair back, which not only caused my head to throb viciously but now my hair was wet. Gross.

It finally dawned on me that Cade was gone. It took a minute, but I remembered he'd collapsed near the porch. Where was he?

"Cade?" I called and staggered to my feet. I spun around, making myself dizzier as I looked for him and the flashlight. Both had disappeared. The moon was higher now, making me wonder how long I'd been unconscious.

The loud screams of the cicadas made my ears hurt. "Cade?"

I stumbled toward the car. But it was gone, too.

"Oh, God." Reeling, I sank down onto a porch step and glanced to where Cade had hit his head. I could make out a dark stain. I reached out with two fingers, touched the damp, sticky spot. Blood.

Since the car was gone, that meant my purse and my cell were gone, too, so I couldn't call for help. Despite the pain in my head and neck, I stood, almost fell, and righted myself on the wooden railing. I forced my feet up each stair. A sense of urgency gripped me, yet I could barely move.

I tried the front door and, naturally, it was locked. When I bent down to peek under the welcome mat, another wave of nausea hit me. I took a deep breath and kept my cookies this time. I didn't find a key under the mat, so I tossed it aside. Key, key, where would London hide it? Furthermore, why would she hide it if she could use an unlocking spell? My brain wasn't functioning at its normal speed. The pounding ache made it hard to think clearly.

I was going to have to break in. Gazing around, I looked for something, anything to help me. I spied a large watering can in the corner of the porch. It was heavy and made of tin. I took a deep breath, fighting against the brutal headache, and with all my might swung it into the window next to the front door. The glass from the first layer shattered. Turning my face away, I pounded at the second layer. After three or four good whacks, I stopped and looked at my handiwork.

Ragged shards clung to the edges of the pane. Once again, I turned my face away, scrunched up my eyes, and tried to make a clean hole to climb through. I faced forward and saw that most of the long pieces were gone. This was as good as it was going to get.

To keep my body from touching the jagged glass, I carefully crawled through the window, one leg at a time, and ducked my spinning head. I wasn't careful enough because I scraped the side of my face and shin pretty badly.

In the living room, a huge fireplace stood to my right. The moonlight streamed through the window, granting enough light that I could make my way through the room and not trip on anything. I carefully stepped over the broken glass. My leg bled freely, pooling into my tennis shoe.

Knowing I couldn't do anything about the wound until I called for help, I ignored it and quickly jogged through the house, pain lancing my head with every movement. I staggered through a small dining room to the kitchen. I flipped on a light switch and gazed around at the pine cabinets. No phone here either. Damn it.

Just then, I heard an engine at the front of the house. Crap. This was bad. Still feeling dizzy—both from blacking out and the blood loss—I was more vulnerable than ever.

Terror amplified my panic as I darted around the room, searching for a weapon. I found a nice long knife in the drawer next to the sink and dove for the light switch.

When the house was dark once more, I peered around the kitchen doorjamb. A flashlight bounced around the front yard. Then heavy footsteps pounded on the porch.

When the light flickered over the broken window, I shrank back into the kitchen and waited, wondering if I could hide in the cabinet beneath the sink. I was sure I could fold myself in there, but as I glanced down at the blood dripping from my leg, I knew hiding wasn't a good plan. Any idiot could follow a bloody trail. I'd have to stab this motherfucker and run.

With a shaky breath, I clung to the knife and closed my eyes. I could do this. Maybe this person had a cell phone and after the stabbing, which I didn't really want to think about, I could call for help.

A key slid into the lock. My heart thudded against my chest so hard, it almost hurt.

"Holly?"

I didn't recognize the deep, masculine voice.

Heavy boots trod through the living room and made their way over the hardwood floor to the kitchen. His steps slowed as he strode closer to the doorway. I had to do this now, while the element of surprise was on my side.

I leapt out and stabbed at the stranger. I grazed his arm with the blade before he twisted my wrist in his big hand. Tears of agony flooded my eyes. I tried to keep my grip but dropped the knife next to his booted foot.

I struggled to free myself, slapping out at him with my other hand. He quickly grabbed that arm, too and performed some maneuver that had my back against his chest with his arms wrapped tightly around me.

"I'm Vane Aldridge."

My thundering heart refused to slow down. Fear shot through me. "Where's Cade? What did you do to him? If you hurt him, I swear I'll kill you." I meant it, too. I snapped my head back, banging it against his chest. It didn't seem to faze him at all, but I almost passed out as the pain grew stronger.

"Calm down." His arms tightened their hold on my torso. "I thought Cade was with you. I got ahold of Mick, and he said you were coming to the lake house."

"How the hell did Mick know we were here?"

"I don't know." He continued to bear hug me and eventually, my pulse stopped racing. "Have you simmered down?"

"Yeah."

He let go and stepped back. I spun around and got a look at him, but not a good look since it was still dark and he'd dropped his flashlight in our tussle. He was tall and broad. Long hair flowed to his shoulders.

He picked up the flashlight, waving it over me, but kept it out of my eyes. "You're a mess, and you smell like vomit."

I lifted a shaking hand to a matted strand of hair and winced from the stench.

"Let's get you cleaned up." Before I could blink, he scooped me in his arms, carried me out the front door and down the steps toward his truck.

The jostling made me want to hurl again, but I was empty. "We have to find Cade. He hit his head, and there's blood on the step. The car's missing. Someone took him."

"I think you might have a concussion." Vane opened the door of the truck, and the light hurt. I squinted as I gave him a once over. His eyes were beautiful, turquoise, like the Caribbean Sea. He had a straight nose and high-ridged cheekbones. His shampoo commercial hair held a little wave and was so shiny.

He flashed the light in my eyes, which sent a wave of searing pain through my skull. "Yeah, you're concussed." He grabbed a first-aid kit from the back seat and started cleaning the gash on my leg. Though his touch was gentle, it still hurt.

"Why does a sorcerer have a first-aid kit?"

"I'm not just a sorcerer, you know. I'm also a telekinetic." He had dual powers? I'd never heard of that. Gran never mentioned it, so it must be a rare quality. "Just like a Norm Boy Scout," he said, "I like to be prepared for everything. This cut is deep." He swabbed my shin with disinfectant. "But I don't think you need stitches. Now, tell me what happened to London."

"She was killed by a cursed amulet." I studied his face, noted that he didn't appear surprised by the news. "Her house was empty, wiped clean. Cade couldn't find a signature, so we came here to look for clues."

"That doesn't add up. London did practice here, but she practiced in her house in Tulsa, as well. All the time."

He poured some more disinfectant onto a pad and dabbed at my cheek. "Tell me what happened when you got here?"

I remembered the kiss Cade had given me, and my hand drifted to my lips. I was losing focus, and I needed clarity in order to find Cade. But my head, leg, and neck ached. I was so damn tired.

"Holly?"

"Right. He got out of the car and walked up to the house. When he hit the first step, he just collapsed. I ran after him, then lost consciousness, too. That's all I remember."

He carefully placed a Band-Aid on my cheek. "How did you feel when you woke up?"

"Sick, dizzy. My head and neck hurt."

He placed his large hands on my head and prodded it. I pulled away when he touched the bump. "Ow."

"Turn around, let me see your neck."

I gave him my back. Vane lifted the hair off my nape and ran his thumb over my skin. He was amazingly tender for an assassin.

"Looks like a puncture wound. Probably a tranq dart." He let my hair fall back in place. "That and the concussion made you throw up."

I turned back around and swatted at the bugs that had filled the car, drawn to the light. "We have to find Cade."

He packed up the first-aid kit and stuck it in the back seat, then handed me a bottle of water. "Drink this. Don't gulp it, though." He twisted the lid off for me.

It tasted like heaven. I hadn't realized how thirsty I was, but heeded his warning and stopped with a sip.

"Where should we start looking?" he asked.

"I don't know. Either someone followed us, or they knew we'd be here and were waiting."

"That should make it easy. Who knew you'd be here?"

"Apparently Mick Raven. Though I still don't know how he found out." Was Mick behind all this? Did he hate Cade enough to kill him? I didn't want to believe that, but maybe he'd been playing me all along. "My assistant, Sunny Carmichael, knew. She gave me the address, but she's on my team." Sort of.

CHAPTER TWENTY-SIX

On the ride back to Tulsa, I fell asleep. I had questions for Vane, and I would have asked them all, but I just couldn't keep my eyes open.

He shook my shoulder when we arrived at The Raven. The parking lot was deserted except for the four guards holding their position in each corner of the property. Two more had taken up residence in front of the door.

A weird taste coated my tongue; my mouth was desert dry. I grabbed the bottle of water, took a long drink.

Vane trotted around to my side of the truck and helped me out. As I carefully stepped to the ground, I asked, "What's your role in all this, anyway?"

"Wait until we get inside. Then I'll just have to tell it once."

The guards eyed Vane but didn't let him enter until one of them called Mick and got the okay. Then the second guard held the door open for us. With his hand under my elbow, Vane ushered me inside.

Mick, usually so cool and smooth, hurried toward me, his brows drawn together, a frown marring his full lips. "Holly, are you all right? What happened?" He slid his hand around my waist and whisked me from Vane's side. Leading me to a chair, his dark eyes scanned my face, my body. "Say something."

"How did you know we'd be at the cabin?"

He jabbed a thumb toward the bar. "This one."

Sunny crinkled her nose. "You look awful."

"Your assistant showed up with a suitcase," Mick said. "I wasn't sure what you wanted to do with her. She was here when you called for an address to the cabin."

Sunny slid off the stool and glared archly at Vane as she made her way to the table. Pulling out a chair next to me, she perched on the edge of it. "You were receiving protection here. I figured I deserved the same courtesy."

"Cade's missing," Vane said. "Holly was tranqed. That's probably what happened to Cade, too."

Sunny lifted a brow. "Did I, or did I not, warn you about this Council business?"

I ignored her, focused on Mick. "Monty lied to us. He knew that London had been attacked. Dawson Nash reported it."

Mick's eyes narrowed, then he glanced at Vane. "And you?"

"I'll tell you what I know." Vane stalked to the table and sat. "Maybe we can piece this together." Mick signaled the bartender. He stepped forward and poured Vane a shot of whiskey. Vane nodded in gratitude and knocked it back before continuing. "London was doing a little undercover work for me. Vamps have gone missing. And while they usually take care of their own shit, a couple Council members were getting calls. Marked ones had grown concerned. Their vampires had disconnected from them. That rarely happens, and it usually means the vamp is dead. The marked ones weren't happy over the lack of concern Monty showed. They wanted action. While the Council can't involve themselves in vamp business officially, they told me to keep my eyes and ears open."

"But Monty said that only four of the brethren had gone missing," I said.

"No. There've been at least a dozen. And they all disappeared on the night of a full moon."

"The Esbats?" A full moon enhanced magic, made it stronger. Was a witch or sorcerer using vamps in a ritual? Their blood would be a powerful addition to any spell. Alarm bells started ringing in my head. Or maybe that was the concussion.

"Why was London working for you?" Mick asked.

"She and I dated a couple of years ago. We remained friends, and when I mentioned the missing vamps, she said she'd help. She was always craving her next big rush. Infiltrating the vamps provided that."

"She wasn't worried about becoming a vamp snack pack?" I asked.

"London likes…" He looked down and corrected himself. "She *liked* to live on the edge. She was an adrenaline junkie. And I couldn't interfere without alerting Monty or Master Sebastian, so she volunteered."

"Why were you so hard to pin down after London died?" I asked. "Cade's been trying to find her killer, and you had valuable information."

Vane pushed back from the table and stood to pace the room. "I didn't know about London. I've been trying to track down a necromancer for the last few weeks. When I hadn't heard from her, I just assumed she was still trying to gather intel." He threaded his fingers through his long hair. "It wasn't until you called from Gramps' house that I learned she was dead. This shouldn't have been a dangerous assignment. She was supposed to hang out with a few vamps and ask some questions. Instead, she made a connection with Sharpe. At first, I was worried and told her to stop, but she assured me that his interest would keep her from becoming a blood buffet for other vamps."

"What about the bite she received?" With my index fingers, I rubbed my temples in an effort to alleviate the pain. It didn't work.

Mick snapped his fingers, and the bartender appeared. "Coffee and Tylenol for Miss James."

Vane waited until the man set a mug of steaming brew and a bottle of pain relievers in front of me. Then he continued, "London went to a party about a month ago. She was drugged, and when she woke up, she'd lost a lot of blood. I think she may have been raped, too, but she didn't come out and say it. I told her she was done, that she *had* to stop. But she insisted she was close to finding the truth." He fell back into the chair. "I shouldn't have brought her into it."

I swallowed the pills with a mouthful of hot, undoctored coffee. "From what I've heard about London, she was headstrong. You wouldn't have been able to stop her if she was determined." Sounded a lot like me. A very sobering thought. "And that story you just told, about London getting drugged and assaulted, that's the exact same story Jasmine told Cade and me. Except in her version, Jasmine was the victim."

Vane shook his head. "No way. London was barely conscious when she called me. I went to her, nursed her through it, did a lot of healing spells. She wouldn't let me take her to the hospital. She refused to tell Sharpe what happened. She'd broken up with him because he kept urging her to take his mark. She was in love with Nick."

"Okay, let me get this straight," I said, trying to put the pieces together. "London was working for you. That's why she started dating Sharpe."

Vane nodded.

"But she went to a party and got fang banged one night."

"Yes."

"In the meantime, she was still dating Nick Alpert, and she cared about him. Sharpe was just business."

"That's about it," Vane said.

"So where does Stephanie Carson come in?" That same question kept tripping me up. "Why was she murdered? And who had enough black mojo to curse the objects that killed both her and London? Did you know London had started practicing dark?"

Vane held up his hands, palms out. "Whoa, one question at a time. I don't know why Stephanie was cursed. I don't know anything about her. As to who killed them? I don't have a clue. And London would never get involved in dark magic. Never. She liked a rush, but there was a line she wouldn't cross. That evil shit does lasting damage to your soul."

"I'm beginning to think you're right," I said. "The only evidence that London dabbled was a box of paraphernalia under her bed, but it didn't contain her signature. Also, London didn't have herbs or brooms in her house. Not even the most rudimentary ingredients for spellcasting, let alone healing potions."

Vane leaned forward and looked into my eyes. "Yes, she did. I cast spells and nursed her for almost a week. When I left, I loaded her up with a ton of supplies. She still needed to perform healing rituals because she was so weak. I left a full box of herbs, a bundle of birch wood and four chunks of amethyst for her to use during meditation. I made batches of pain elixir and put it in her cabinet."

"So the box under her bed must have been planted there." I glanced over at Mick.

"Obviously by the murderer," he said. "But why?"

I briefly closed my eyes and wished away the pain shooting through my head. "The killer had enough power to clear the house of any magical evidence. London's, Vane's, the killer's own signature—all of it wiped. It must have been Jasmine. The Happy Grass lawn guy saw Jasmine at London's house the day before she was killed. She lied about everything. And I bought it."

Mick leaned over and rubbed my shoulder. "Cade said he didn't detect a stain on her aura."

"He said that some people hide how powerful they are. Maybe she cleansed enough of the stain off and glamoured over the rest. Could fool some sorcerers."

"I agree," Vane said. "Especially if she's using vamp blood in her rituals. With that much innate power mixed with vamp juice, she could be damn near invincible."

Sunny, who'd been silent and motionless until now, squirmed in her chair. "Do we think Monty actually knows something, or is he just covering up his ineptitude in finding these missing brethren?"

I nodded and immediately regretted it. "Good question."

Vane sighed. "I think we need to ask him."

I stood up, weaved on my feet, but held steady. "And we have to find Cade."

"You're concussed," Vane said. "You shouldn't go anywhere."

I looked him over, noticed my blood on his shirt. "You need to take a shower and change clothes. My blood will nullify your powers." I grabbed Sunny's arm and checked her watch. "It's after midnight. If Monty's involved in taking Cade, we have less than six hours until dawn. But my main suspect is Jasmine. She could have taken Cade anywhere." I clapped my hands and pushed past my splitting head. "Let's go."

"Vane's right," Mick said. "You're not in any condition to do this. And no offense, darling, you're not the best choice of companions for this mission." He took my hand in his. "Besides, if anything happened to you, I would be most distressed."

"I'm going with or without you," I said, jerking free. Just as Cade felt responsible for me, I felt the same way about him.

Mick stood. "You will go nowhere without me." He looked me over, but I couldn't read his thoughts. His expression remained blank, but he narrowed his dark eyes.

"I will help you, Holly. But we need to decide on a course of action."

"I'm in," Vane said. "After I've had a shower. Raven, you got some clothes I can borrow?"

Mick didn't look at him. His gaze stayed fixed on me. "Don't move. I'll be right back." I'd heard those words more than once lately. It was getting old.

The two men jogged upstairs, leaving me alone with Sunny. A small sense of calm stole over me. I had Mick Raven and Vane Aldridge in my corner, and they were good allies to have, but I needed all the support I could muster. "Sunny, do you have your tablet? Then I need to use your phone."

"Of course." She studied my face. "Are you sure you can do this?"

"Yeah, I'm good. I'm going to find Cade and bring him back."

She pulled the tablet from her purse and handed it over. Fortunately, I backed up all my numbers. It took a few minutes, but I managed to retrieve Abby's and Dawson's.

Mick lightly ran down the steps, and I waved Sunny's phone at him. "I'm going to gather everyone together. Can they come here?"

"Of course."

I phoned Abby and explained the situation. Since her friend, Wendy, was one of the missing, she was willing to help. I told her to bring Neil, too. While he wasn't a warrior type, frankly, we needed all the bodies we could muster. Next, I called Dawson and told him to grab Nick Alpert. Mick gave me Sharp's number, and I rang him, too.

"Who is this?" the vamp answered.

"Holly James. The null. I found London's killer. We're meeting at The Raven in twenty. You in?"

"Just tell me who the arsehole is, and I'll deal with him."

Mick grabbed the phone. "Be here in twenty." He hit the end button and handed it back to me. "He responds better to direct instruction."

"I'll remember that."

#

After my phone calls, I trudged to the green room to grab a shower. I gave myself ten minutes. Sunny cut into my time when she insisted on wrapping my bandaged leg in a trash bag so it wouldn't get wet, which was actually very thoughtful of her.

My body ached and being pelted with hot water wasn't helping my skull, but feeling clean was worth it. I used up all my energy drying off and had to sit on the toilet for a minute, wrapped in a towel. My temples throbbed so hard, my eyes watered. I wasn't sure how I'd make it through the rest of the night. I just knew I'd have to summon the strength. Cade needed me. I finally got it, how he felt when I was vulnerable, in danger. It felt a lot like hopelessness.

A knock sounded on the door. I hoped it wasn't Mick. I couldn't deal with him right now. "Go away. I'm not dressed."

Sunny stepped into the room. She turned on the fan to disperse some of the steam.

"Do you have a hearing problem?" I asked, but there was no heat behind the words.

"No, I have perfect hearing; it's my eyesight that's a problem." She picked up a brush and a ponytail holder, motioned for me to spin so that my back was to her. Then grabbing another towel, she very gently squeezed the excess water out of my hair. She brushed out the tangles, taking special care not to hit the bump on the side of my head and pulled my wet hair into a low ponytail.

It was the kindest thing she'd ever done for me. I turned back around. "Thank you."

She jerked her shoulders and glanced away. "Of course."

Before she turned to leave, I grabbed her hand. "Listen, seriously, if I don't make it back, will you check on Gran? At least once a week, okay? Help her with the garden. And contact my grandfather, Wallace Dumahl. He made me a promise. Make sure he keeps it. I'm counting on you."

"Stop it this instant, Holly. You're going to be just fine and live long enough to give me the raise I deserve." Her hand tightened on mine before she pulled away and slammed out. If I didn't know better, I'd say she liked me.

The bedroom was empty when I entered it a moment later. After getting dressed, I slowly navigated the stairs, my head pounding with each step. Mick met me when I reached the bottom.

"Do you have a plan?" He stroked my bandaged cheek.

"I'm open to suggestions."

His eyes searched mine. "Are you sure you're up for this?"

"Yep." I walked around him to the bar, grabbed another cup of coffee and was heavy-handed with the sugar this time. Five minutes later, Abby arrived with a glum Neil in tow.

"Hey, Holly." She strolled in wearing what could only be described as the shortest skirt in history. In its former life, it may have been a spangly tube top. "I'm glad you called. I've been stuck with lame-o Neil who can't find a willing meal to save his un-life. He's been at it for *hours.*" She put three syllables into the word.

Neil glared at her beneath his bangs. "I'm just picky."

"Yeah, keep telling yourself that."

Vane, long wet hair pulled into a bun, jogged down the stairs. He wore Mick's clothes, and the trousers were a couple of inches too short.

"Who's that?" Abby couldn't take her eyes off him.

Vane strode up to me. "Where is everyone?"

"On their way," Mick said. He sat on the stool next to me and occasionally squeezed my shoulder. His attention wasn't sexual, just comforting. "Let's take a seat, hmm?" Mick stood and steered Abby to a table where Sunny had already snagged a chair. The rest of us trailed after them.

Nick and Dawson walked in the door soon after and found a seat. Mick played host and made the introductions. I was about to give up hope on Sharpe when he strolled into the room, ten minutes late.

Sitting to my right, Abby caught her breath at the sight of him. "You didn't tell me he was going to be here." She slapped my arm.

Sharpe fell into a chair and propped one sockless, Gucci-loafered foot onto the table. "Let's do this. Don't got all night."

"You," Nick Alpert growled. "You're that bloodsucker she was cheating with." Standing, he started to leap across the table toward James. "You're a dead man, asshole."

Dawson and Vane restrained him. "Calm the fuck down, Nick. That's an order," Dawson said, pinning Nick's shoulder with both hands.

Sharpe didn't move a muscle except for one flick of his brow. "Does this one need a shock collar, then?"

"That is quite enough," Sunny said, standing up and rapping her knuckles on the table. She pointed at Nick. "You're not a shifter here. Behave yourself." Then she turned to Sharpe and knocked his foot to the ground. "Sit up. Show some respect." The men froze as she calmly resumed her seat.

Nick sat, and Sharpe tugged at the edges of his jacket and sniffed.

"We have all calmed down, yes?" Mick asked. "Thank you for coming. As you know, Cade and Holly," he gestured toward me, "have been trying to find the killer of two young witches. Now, Cade has been abducted. We need to find him immediately. Holly will explain everything that's happened." He looked at me and bowed his head.

I told them everything I knew, all my suspicions about Jasmine and that Monty was somehow involved—covering up the missing brethren if nothing else. Vane broke in a couple of times to give more details.

Abby looked at me, her eyes wide. "The last time I saw Wendy was the night before the full moon. When I couldn't find her the next night, I asked Monty about it. He said he'd sent her on a secret assignment. I haven't heard from her since."

"Right," Sharpe said. "I've had a couple of mates pop off as well. Mentioned it to Monty. He imagined they'd got themselves killed in a hunt."

There was an awful lot of talk about Monty. Absolutely none about the Master himself. I looked at each of them in turn. "Out of curiosity, when was the last time anyone saw Master Sebastian?"

Sharpe glanced at Abby. "I've never seen him. Been in this territory for more than twenty years. Monty always says he's busy or traveling. Lot of the old ones don't like to interact, so I didn't think nothing about it."

Abby nodded. "I've never met him. I've always spoken to Monty."

Dawson stirred in his chair. "Same here. Just Monty. Says Master Sebastian doesn't like to deal with Others."

I glanced at Vane and Mick. They both appeared troubled. "Do you think Monty killed Master Sebastian?"

Sharpe scoffed. "Don't be daft. Too hard to kill a Master. Damned near impossible. They're protected from the sun, their powers are much greater than ours. That's why there's so bloody few of them."

I grabbed Sunny's phone and brought up the Blessed Be website. I tapped on the picture of Jasmine. Since London and Sharpe used to be an item, I assumed he'd met

Jasmine. The only two who didn't know her were Abby and Neil.

Abby studied the picture. "I've seen her. She's been to a few donor parties."

Neil reached for the phone. "Oh, yeah. I know her. She's friends with Monty."

CHAPTER TWENTY-SEVEN

We all stared at him. Waiting.

Finally, Mick snapped, "Elaborate."

Neil's gaze darted around the table. "Oh, sorry. I um, I followed Monty one night, because I wanted to talk to him, you know, in private. In the end, I chickened out, but I think they went to his resting place together."

"What?"

"Where?"

"When?"

Our voices rang out at the same time.

Neil had been sitting on some very powerful information. A resting place was the biggest secret a vamp had. By telling Jasmine where he lay during the day, Monty showed his complete trust in her.

"So, they *are* in it together," I said.

"Why didn't you tell me?" Abby smacked the back of his head. "God, you're useless."

"We need to find Monty." It was all finally starting to come together for me. "He provides the brethren for her dark magic. Maybe the cursed amulet came from Blessed Be, despite not being on the inventory list, and Stephanie realized it. That's why Jasmine killed her, too."

"Where is Monty's resting place, you little tosser?" Sharpe jabbed a finger at Neil, who crossed his arms.

"If I tell you, I want something in return."

Dawson stood, towering over the young vamp. He was so laid back most of the time that when he went all alpha, it shocked me. Bunching Neil's shirt with both fists, he pulled the kid out of his chair. "I could kill you, even with the null here. I could crush your windpipe or smash your head into the wall until your brain is soup."

Neil swallowed. "I want a different sponsor. I can't take being with Abby anymore."

Sharpe rapped on the table. "Oy, we'll find someone who can stand you, you little wanker. Now, where does Monty sleep?"

"Where?" Dawson asked through clenched teeth.

"In the Philtower. First floor."

Dawson dropped him, craned his neck to the side to stretch the muscles and then sat, slouching in his chair as though nothing had happened.

Sunny pushed at her glasses. "The first floor of the Philtower houses offices, not apartments."

"But a first-floor suite may grant him access to the tunnels," Vane said.

That had been my thought as well. In the twenties, oil barons built Art Deco skyscrapers as monuments to their wealth and status. The tunnels beneath the buildings served as a freight system for hauling supplies. But somewhere along the line, they became a shortcut to get from one downtown building to another. Many of the tunnels were still in use, but certain branches had been closed off for decades—a perfect place for a vamp to hideout during daylight hours.

"The Philtower tunnel is inaccessible," Sunny said. "Has been for years."

"When have rules ever stopped an Other?" I asked.

Vane gave Neil a steely-eyed glare. "Do you know the office number?"

Neil gulped. "One-oh-two."

Mick stood, and placing his hands on the table, leaned forward. "So we go to the Philtower and check it out.

My purse had been taken when the rental car went missing from the cabin. Hence no gun. "Who has firepower? I can nullify Monty's and Jasmine's magic, but that's about it."

Vane scraped back his chair and stood. "I've got a cache of guns, but it'll take an hour to get there and back."

"Forget it. We don't have an hour. If Jasmine's performing a ritual, we might already be too late to save Cade." My breath caught in my throat, and I choked on his name. It was almost one o'clock. Time wasn't on our side. What if we couldn't save him? I placed a hand over my eyes, willing the tears back. "I'm going in. Now."

Abby jumped to her feet. "I'm with you. Wendy was like my sister. I want to know what happened to her. You're coming, too, Neil."

"I'm so in," Nick Alpert said, cracking his knuckles. "I'm going to make them pay for killing London."

Sharpe remained silent.

"Let's go." I began marching toward the door with Abby by my side when Mick's voice stopped me.

"Wait, Holly. We can't go there unprotected. We need at least a rudimentary plan of action. I have a few handguns and a sword." He looked over his shoulder to a dark corner. "Jasper."

Five minutes later, Jasper and another bodyguard returned with a katana, two handguns, seven Bowie knives, and one scythe. What the hell was Mick doing with all this?

He met my gaze. "Martial arts. The Bowies are collector's items, and the guns are for fun."

Vane nodded at the pile of weapons. "The scythe?"

"Don't ask," Mick said. "We must assume Monty's sycophants are protecting him and his lair. Probably some marked humans as well. We'll see how tough they are when their powers are nullified." He tipped his head to me.

We all filed out. Mick handed me a gun. "You know how to use this?"

"Sort of. Cade tried to teach me."

"He will not go down without a fight."

I held onto that thought and refused to let doubt seep in. I couldn't afford to get bogged down in grief and pain. We had to go in strong, kicking ass, taking names.

#

In two cars, we drove downtown to a hotel parking garage where we could access the tunnels. Once we climbed out, Sunny, Neil, Dawson, and Abby each took a Bowie knife. I hoped I remembered everything Cade taught me about shooting an automatic.

Vane opted for the scythe. "Grim Reaper. I like it."

Nick Alpert decided on using his bare hands.

Since the toys were his, Mick claimed the second gun and a sword.

I looked around for Sharpe, but he wasn't there. "Anyone seen James?"

Everyone paused, looked at our group and shook their heads.

"Fucking coward," Nick said.

Why would he leave us? He'd seemed hell-bent on catching London's killer earlier. Maybe he *was* a coward, but I didn't think so. However, he was a dick. He probably took one look at Nick—his werewolf rival—and got his man panties in a jealous knot. Whatever. I couldn't think about him or his issues right now. We had a mission to accomplish. And Cade. I couldn't lose him. Even though he was never really mine in the first place, none of that mattered. His life did.

I gripped the gun handle with shaking hands and tried to steady myself. Fortunately since it was late, we were alone in the parking garage. Otherwise, some concerned citizen would have called the police. And rightly so. We looked like a group of crazies waving sharp objects.

Mick and Vane, the advance team, took off through the tunnel entrance. They'd be able to sense any Others nearby. Mick would use a glamour to keep from announcing their presence. Once they found the right tunnel, they'd text the rest of us, let us know which way to go.

During their absence, Neil whined about being hungry, Abby checked her reflection in a car window, Nick paced silently, Sunny stood with her back to the wall, and Dawson Nash plopped down next to me on his truck's rear bumper.

He smelled like the outdoors—sunshine and fresh air—despite gasoline and exhaust fumes floating around us. His long blond hair could use a brush.

"You worried?" He nudged my shoulder with his own.

"What's there to worry about? Cade's at the mercy of Monty and that bitch, Jasmine, and we could all be walking into a death trap."

"Good to see you're looking on the bright side."

I shot him a glare from the corner of my eye.

"Want a piece of advice?"

"Sure. Lay it on me, Nash."

"When I was a kid, some asshole issued my dad a challenge for the Alpha position in our pack. If he lost, he wouldn't just lose his title, he'd lose his life. I was scared shitless for him. But he told me something I'll never forget."

"What was that?"

His blue-gold eyes turned serious. "As long as you have breath, keep fighting. That's how we wolves live our lives. Keep fighting and avenge the ones who don't make it."

I scowled at him. "Is that supposed to make me feel better? I can't think about losing Cade. Saving him is the only option."

"He may not make it, Holly. You need to come to terms with that. If that's the case, I'll help you on the vengeance front. You have my word." He held his fist up for a bump.

Still frowning, I thought about his offer. "What if you don't make it either?"

"Then you're fucked. C'mon. Fist bump."

Instead, I covered my eyes with my free hand. What the hell had I gotten us into?

Sunny's phone beeped. "They're in. Right beneath the Philtower. Unused red doors, it says."

"Let's go." Dawson patted my back.

"Hey." I tugged on his sleeve. "What happened with your dad? Did he win?"

"No, he lost, and my family was banished from the pack. But I avenged him. His successor's head is mounted on my wall. Right across from my desk, so I can look at it every day."

Okay, then.

Single file, we tromped through the exit marked *Third Street Tunnel*. The tiled walls and floors reflected rows of lighting on one side of the low ceiling, illuminating the way. The tunnels were full of smells, water, rot and then suddenly a garlicky stench when we walked near a restaurant.

We followed the path, curving left then twisting to the right. I was in the middle of the group, along with Sunny. I glanced her way to make sure she was hanging in there. Her pinched lips and furrowed brow told me she was a nervous wreck. Sunny liked order and structure. Not the promise of violence.

"Hey, if it looks like we're in trouble, run," I told her. "Don't look back. Just run. You can turn around now if you want. I wouldn't blame you."

"I've worked with you for two and a half years," she said with a huff. "I'm used to trouble." I'd never seen this courageous side of her until now. It was impressive. She definitely deserved a raise.

We trekked along and ten minutes later, made it to the Kennedy building where we ran into Mick and Vane.

"They're using a closed-off entrance," Mick said. "It has been shut down for years. There's a mystical lock on the door. As soon as you get close to it, Holly, we should be able to bust in. We will shoot our way through it if we have to."

We quickly jogged through the Mid-Continent Tower and the Atlas Life Building.

"Don't they keep these doors locked after hours?" I asked no one in particular.

"Key card. Pretty simple to break through," Vane said. "Couldn't use magic because you'd nullify the spell."

I kept glancing over my shoulder to make sure we were alone. So far, we hadn't seen anyone, but of course that could change. When we stepped into the arched lobby of the Philtower, my heart started beating double time. Surely there had to be a doorman.

As we passed the front desk, I saw two feet sticking out from behind it, toes up.

I glanced at Mick. "You didn't kill him, did you?"

He sighed. "No, Holly. We merely knocked him unconscious." Mick ducked through a door at the far end of the lobby.

We followed him to a narrow stairway that led to a warren below the building, finally ending at a ceiling-high chained link fence. The gate had already been busted off the hinges.

Mick strode through it to a set of double metal doors painted institutional green. "Beyond here is where we felt their presence. We need to go in hard and fast. Take them by surprise. Anyone other than Cade needs to be killed."

My stomach lurched. God, I felt sick. But Monty and Jasmine had to be stopped. I could shoot someone in the gut if I damn well had to. I just hoped it wouldn't come to that.

"How close do you have to be to nullify Jasmine and Monty?" Vane asked.

"I may have to touch them. The more powerful a person, the closer I have to be. It sounds like Jasmine's mighty powerful."

"Let's get on with it." Nick bared his teeth and growled.

"Save it for the bad guys, dude." Dawson held the door for us. It made a loud scraping protest against the concrete floor.

One by one, we hustled inside. I blinked against the darkness, then suddenly green arced lights flickered on, shining on random areas of the tunnel. They must have been triggered by motion.

"Hurry," Mick whispered. "Holly, stay behind me. Let's move."

Sweating and nervous, I stayed almost on top of Mick. I hastily glanced back and saw everyone else right behind us in a two-person formation. The smell was rank, damp, the walls chipped and crumbling. Mold crawled up from the floor and clung to the ancient tile.

Suddenly, a hand grasped mine. Sunny didn't look at me, simply squeezed my fingers then let go.

I didn't know how long we wound our way through the tunnel. Seemed like forever, though it was probably only a few seconds. Finally, we came to an enormous vaulted door.

"Shit," I said. "Now what?"

Mick reached out and tried to turn the handle, but it didn't budge. He glanced at me. "Touch it."

I nodded and stepped forward. I grasped the cold metal and pulled with one hand. The heavy metal door moved an inch.

Vane and Mick quickly stepped around me and yanked it open.

Dawson slapped my back. "Good job."

No, it wasn't. It was luck, pure and simple. And it all seemed too easy. Why wouldn't Monty have a vault door locked with something other than magic? Was he that arrogant?

Vane shone his light on the tunnel ahead. "This is it. Our element of surprise will probably be a short one."

"Everyone," Mick said, "have your arms at the ready."

Mick and I cocked our guns. Everyone else held up their weapons and prepared for battle. I silently said a prayer.

Then we were off again, with Vane leading the way this time. His flashlight bobbed off the floor as we followed it like a floating ball of light.

We walked downward, circling our way toward Monty's resting place and hopefully, to Cade.

Without warning, the hall filled with fluorescent light. My eyes narrowed from the brightness.

Three tall, muscular men stood in front of us, assault rifles pointed at our heads.

"Drop your weapons."

CHAPTER TWENTY-EIGHT

With two steps, Neil separated himself from our group and walked backward toward the armed men. "Sorry, guys. I did what I had to do."

Abby's mouth hung open. Then, as the truth of Neil's betrayal sank in, she snapped her jaw shut. "You little asshole. You're so dead, Neil."

He smiled and held his hands out. "I don't think you're in a position to threaten me anymore, Abby." He sneered her name.

"I said, drop 'em." A blond man with a crew cut held the gun butt to his shoulder.

We glanced at each other and let go of our weapons. Echoes from the clatter filled the narrow space. They quickly frisked each of us at gunpoint. I didn't so much as twitch.

After they were through, Neil smiled. "Let's go. Monty's waiting for you." He turned and led the way through the last bit of tunnel to a set of polished wood doors. The brass handles shone as he grasped them and pulled.

I didn't know what I expected. More dark, water-eroded brick probably. But the room looked like something from a movie set. Bright lights showcased eight columns made of lapis lazuli. Golden sculpted leaves decorated the tops of each near the ceiling. The floors were polished marble with inlaid semi-precious gemstones of red, green, blue and black, which created a large compass in the center. There were two sets of doors on either side of the vast room.

I looked for Cade, but didn't see him. Where the hell was he? Then my eyes settled on Monty, who sat on a high dais before us. Stiffly perched on a golden throne, he was dressed in his usual natty way: tailored suit, knife-pleat crease in the trousers. A dozen burly men held semi-automatics and stood on either side of him. Smart. He had marked bodyguards. Even though I'd nullified their mystical bond, they obviously remained loyal to him. Now he had protection, and we had nothing.

Jasmine stood next to him, her riotous curls towered above her like a giant headdress. She wore a beautiful black dress with a crisscrossed bodice. Too bad about the hair.

Monty waved us forward. "Please, do come in." He shook his head at Abby. "I'm so disappointed in you, my dear."

She said nothing, just glared at Neil.

"Holly, I'm so very sorry it had to come to this. Truly."

"Sure you are, Monty. Where's Cade?" I prepared myself for the worst. Taking a deep breath and holding it, I waited to hear the news that he'd already killed Cade, and I'd never see my sorcerer again.

Monty shook his head as if the whole situation was tragic, and he was just as sad as he could be. "He's being kept, as these Others will be, until three a.m.

Cade was still alive. My breath hitched, and my knees almost buckled. Thank God. Then the rest of his words sank in. Three a.m. The witching hour. Magic at its strongest.

I glanced around the throne room, hopeless. Bereft. I'd failed. We were all going to die.

I glanced at Dawson. His eyes connected with mine. In spite of my splitting headache, the painful gash in my leg, and fear coursing through me, I clung to his earlier words. *As long as you have breath, keep fighting.*

I tamped down the despair that threatened to engulf me. I had to fight, and I'd keep on fighting until Cade and these people were safe. That was *my* vow.

"I should thank you all," Monty said. "You've been very helpful by delivering yourselves to me."

Stillness washed through me. A calm determination. I was ready to meet my death. Dawson, if he was still alive after all this, would avenge me. *Game on.* "Monty, you psycho freak, tell me where Cade is. Now."

"That wasn't nice, Holly." He frowned at my bad manners. "Take the Others," he said to his marked slaves. "Leave the girl with me."

Jasmine smirked, and I itched to yank those god-awful curls out of her hair. By the fistful.

Mick's eyes were shuttered, revealing nothing. Sunny blinked at me behind her frames. At least she was immune to whatever magic they would perform. I wasn't sure that was a good thing at this point.

The marked slaves moved forward and corralled everyone. Vane hauled off and slammed his fist into one's nose. Four of them pounced on him immediately. He took the butt of a gun to the kidney and a couple of hits to the face. I held my breath and waited for him to get up. He didn't. Blood gushed from his nose and puddled onto the shiny floor as they dragged him away.

Two of the men grabbed my shoulders and held me still as my group, the people I'd led into this slaughter, got shoved and pushed through a set of doors.

"I'll get you for this, you little shit," Abby yelled at Neil. A guard picked her up and tossed her into the mysterious room as if she were no more than a sack of garbage.

Once my people disappeared, I was on my own. Two guards remained, flanking me in case I tried to make a run for it.

Neil stood to one side of the room, watching. He tapped his fingertips against his leg. He seemed nervous. Yeah, I would be, too, if I just made a deal with the devil.

I faced Monty and Jasmine. "Where's Master Sebastian?"

Monty motioned me forward, and the two thugs dragged me to the bottom of the dais.

"Closer," Monty said.

They hauled me up the steps and forced me to my knees. When Monty reached out to pat the top of my head, I tried to pull away. One of the guards grabbed my ponytail, forcing my head upward. Since it was still in excruciating pain, I froze.

Then Monty took a deep breath. "I love that I can do that when you're around. Breathe. It's been so long. You remind me what it's like to be human." He covered his chest with one hand. "I can feel my heart."

"Where's Master Sebastian?" I asked again.

"He's being mystically contained. You have no idea how dangerous he is, how much destruction he'd cause if he were free. I'm doing what must be done."

"That's what dictators throughout the history of ever always say. And it's bullshit. What *you're* doing isn't destructive? You're killing your own people, Monty."

"The sacrifices are for the greater good. Do you think I like killing my fellow brethren?"

I glared at Jasmine. "What about London? She didn't get sacrificed. Nor did Stephanie Carson. They were murdered."

Jasmine twisted a curl around her finger. "Monty gave London to me. She deserved to die."

"Because she took Nick?" I asked.

"Yes." She continued to wind a springy curl around her finger. "But I knew she was up to something when she started dating Sharpe. She was mad for Nick, so why sabotage her relationship? I told Monty about it." She gazed at him and smiled. "He said I could bring her to a party. Her blood went into a spell I made. Then I let the vampires have her. I thought they would kill her, but she managed to survive."

"Vane Aldridge saved her."

She let go of the curl. "I *knew* she had help."

"You sent the cursed amulet?"

"Ah, that was inspired. Now London is out of my way, and the store is all mine. It's a prime piece of real estate, you know."

With the bodyguard still holding my head still, I glared up at Jasmine. What a psycho. She had no remorse. And I still didn't have all the answers. "Why did Stephanie have a similar amulet?"

"She bought one a few months ago, so when she heard the cursed amulet contained a bloodstone and runes, she came to see me. She knew there were two similar amulets in the store. Stephanie was so clueless, she asked if she should call her Council representative and let them know." Jasmine shrugged. "She had to die."

"Why did you hide the box of black magic paraphernalia beneath London's bed? Just to ruin her reputation?"

Jasmine rolled her eyes. "You're an idiot. McAllister needed a rabbit hole to chase. Plus, if it ruined her reputation all the better."

"Look at who you're dealing with," I said to Monty. "She's evil."

"Yes," he agreed, "but she serves the greater good."

Greater good, my ass.

"Who blew up Cade's truck? Who shot at us? It sure as hell wasn't you." I sneered at Jasmine.

"One of my Marked Ones planted a bomb in Cade's truck," Monty said. "We were expecting the two of you to be inside it, of course." Monty clutched the throne's armrests. "One of my newer servants shot at you. When he missed, he grew frightened and ran away. He was punished for his cowardice. Pity. He had such potential."

My gaze roamed over the pair of them. "The two of you are crazier than a couple of outhouse rats. I'm talking fucking, certifiable whack jobs."

Monty frowned, and it looked as abnormal as his smile. "Such a mouth, Holly. I expected better from you."

"I get to kill you, Null," Jasmine said with a shit-eating grin on her face. "Monty said I could. But I'm going to wait until I've killed all your friends first. Until you know that Cade died slowly and painfully. How's that sound?"

My gut clenched. I'd never had a violent streak, but I really wanted to leap for her throat and rip it out. If she touched a whisker on Cade's stubbled cheek, I'd gut her with my fingernails.

From my peripheral view, I watched Neil shove his hands in his pockets and shift from one foot to the other. "You're good with this, Neil?"

"I can't take one more day with Abby. She's such a bitch."

I glanced back at Jasmine. "She's not the only one."

Monty pointed at me. "Please take Miss James, now." He bit his lower lip. "I am sorry, Holly."

My two burly friends literally dragged me, kicking and screaming, to the opposite set of doors from where the group had been taken. Jasmine smugly watched me get carried out of the room.

#

I sat on a packed dirt floor, and by the light from the dim hallway, watched water trickle down the brick cell wall. That got old after a couple of minutes.

I stood and tried each of the bars again, but they weren't going anywhere. Walking to the wall, I used my fingers to dig away at the brick, hoping it had been compromised by water damage. But they built these suckers to last. I got nowhere.

Were Cade and the rest still down here or had they been taken to a different location? And where the hell was Master Sebastian? If he were close, I doubted my presence would be enough to nullify his mystical containment. Jasmine was très powerful. Neither Cade nor Mick noticed a stain on her aura, and she was eyeballs deep in dark magic

Guilt and anger gnawed at me. I'd led everyone right into Monty's hands. I had been taken in by Jasmine and her crocodile tears and false stories of rape and bloodletting. Well, I wasn't going down easy. She was going have to work to kill me.

Before I could come up with a brilliant escape plan, the doors at the end of the corridor banged open. Footsteps approached my cell. My breath hitched, and my palms grew clammy. Was this it? Execution time? Chances were I was going to die here tonight, beneath the streets of Tulsa. My grandmother would never know what happened to me.

Goddammit, Holly, quit thinking like a loser. Fight until you're dead. No breath. No heartbeat. Keep fighting.

I pressed my body tight against the bars. Out of the corner of my eye, I spied wild hair. The bitch slinked up, wearing a self-satisfied grin, her glassy eyes betraying her serious level of crazy. "How do you like it? It's a real dungeon, huh?"

"Yeah, it's super scary." I gave a fake shiver. "Not as terrifying as your hairdo, but…"

That made her scowl. Which made me smile even more.

"I'm going to torture you so bad. You're going to beg me to kill you."

"I wouldn't beg you for a drop of water if I were on fire, sweetie."

She placed a finger to her pursed lips. "Hmm, now there's a thought. I like it. I was going to go with something like torturing you with knife wounds until I got bored. But you're right, fire's better."

"Jasmine, honey, Nick must have been so happy to get rid of you. London was pretty and wild and fun. You're just...sad." In a lightening quick move, I grabbed her by that tatty hair, slamming her face into the bars. Blood spurted out of her nose as I tried it again, but she managed to jerk away.

"You bitch." As she cupped her nose, blood seeped through her fingers. "Guard," she screeched, her voice echoing through the hallway.

Two of them ran toward her while her gaze held mine. "Hold her."

"Monty said—"

"Do you want to live?" She pointed at him. "Open the door and hold her."

One guard unlocked the door, the other stepped into the cell. Grabbing my arms, he pinned my elbows behind my back.

Shit. I already had a concussion. I wasn't sure how much more head trauma I could take in one night. But if I managed to bleed on her, I'd wipe out Jasmine's powers. It was the best plan I could come up with. Time to take one for the team. "You're really brave with two guards and no magic." I grinned. Though I was shaking in my shoes, it gave me great satisfaction to see the blood running down her chin.

She swiped at her nose with the back of her hand and stalked forward. "What did you do to your face, Holly?" Reaching out, she ripped the bandage from my cheek, uncovering the cut I'd gotten from sneaking into London's cabin. It hurt like hell, and I gritted my teeth against the pain.

"Ah, you have a boo boo," she said, cocking back her arm. She rammed her fist into my wound. The ring she wore on her middle finger cut into my skin. Warm blood cascaded down my face.

I forced out a laugh. "That all you got? I hate to break this to you, Jazzy, but you hit like a little girl." When she punched me again, my neck snapped back and caused bursts of agony to shoot through my head. Crap. I might pass out for real and not wake up. *No more head shots.*

When she tried for a third blow, I pushed my back against the guy holding me and threw my feet up in the air, grazing Jasmine's chin. "That one looked like it hurt." I smirked at the hatred shining in her eyes.

She bent her fingers into claws and went for my throat, scratching deep grooves into my skin. That wiped the smile off my face. The vamp hickey hadn't healed. It hurt even worse now.

The second guard, the one who'd unlocked the door, pulled her off me. She was crazed—bloody and grasping to get at me, her talon-like hands reaching for me. The man held her firmly around the waist. Her wild hair sprouted from her head like coils, bouncing with every swipe she took.

The guy pinning my arms towed me backward, away from her.

Jasmine now had my blood trapped in her ring and under her nails. Unless she thoroughly scoured every bit of it off, she wouldn't be able to perform any magic tonight. A ray of optimism, bright and glowing, kindled inside me.

God, every part of my body ached. My neck was on fire, my cheekbone felt shattered, my head throbbed so badly I longed to face plant on the dirt floor, just to get some relief. But I started laughing. Couldn't stop. I heard the hysterical edge in it, but I laughed until my sides ached. My knees gave out, and the guard had to hold me up.

Jasmine stared at me like *I* was insane. After a few minutes of watching tears stream down my face, she pushed her way out of the guard's arms, turned on her heel, and left.

Well, that was fun. But now I had to get out of here.

CHAPTER TWENTY-NINE

I sat on the ground and kicked the wall. Then I paced for a while. Time passed. How much, I didn't know, but each minute that ticked by ate at me. Jasmine might figure out what I'd done to her. Or maybe she'd take a ceremonial bath before the ritual. I couldn't count on my blood working forever. Eventually, they'd all die. Because of me. I had to stop focusing on it, or I'd stop functioning altogether.

Sitting on the floor, I again tried scraping the concrete with my nail. I heard a creak. Scrambling to my feet, I flew to the bars. I hoped Jasmine wasn't coming back for round two.

Out of the gloom, Neil appeared. "Hey," he whispered.

"Thank God. Get me out of here."

"Shh," he whispered. "I can't. I'm sorry. I didn't know it would go down like this. I only wanted a little power of my own. I needed to get out from under Abby. I didn't realize they would kill everyone. Just that sorcerer you were with."

I wanted to hurt Neil. Badly. He thought it was all right if Jasmine only sacrificed Cade, but spared the rest? *My* Cade? Still, I needed Neil if I wanted to get out of here. Since he was my only chance of escape, I appealed to his rational side. "Jasmine is crazy. She's unpredictable. You're in danger, too."

"I don't know what to do."

"Where are they performing the ceremony?"

"One of the guards said there's a piece of land and a pond. Monty owns it. I guess they do all the sacrifices there." He stuck his thumb in his mouth and started chewing on a hangnail. He bit off a piece of skin and spat it out on the floor.

"What about Master Sebastian?"

He looked up and down the short corridor. "I don't know. I think they talked about him being in some underground club."

I stroked my hand along a bar. "What club? Where?"

He shook his head. "I don't know, man. I keep telling you that."

"Listen, Neil. Get me out of here. If you help free me and the others, I'll make sure you're under Cade's protection. Please?"

He looked at me in silence. Then, "No. Jasmine is wicked pissed that you broke her nose. If I help you, they'll kill me."

Frustrated and angry, I did the first thing that popped into my mind. I started screaming my head off.

Neil looked like he was going to shit his pants. "Shut up. All right, I'll help you. Just shut up!"

I stopped screaming. One of Monty's slave bodyguards opened the door, and a slice of bright light penetrated the murky hallway. Neil plastered himself against the bars. He was skinny enough that the thick brick wall between the cells hid him from sight.

"What's going on? Why are you screaming?" a deep voice called from the door.

"A mouse," I squealed. "I saw a mouse."

"No shit. Keep quiet." He slammed the door.

"Are you going to help me get out of here or what?" I asked Neil, who started wheezing.

"I have asthma. Or I did before I got vamped." His constricted lungs had him gasping and clutching his chest.

"Neil, get me out of here, and you can run off. You'll be a non-asthmatic vamp once again. Please?"

"Okay, I'll try to find a key or something." He wandered down the hall opposite the door and disappeared.

Master Sebastian was in an underground club? Like the club Mick took me to? But that wasn't underground, it was right out there in the open. Others knew all about it. Honestly, that wasn't my problem right now. Getting out of here was.

In a moment of frustration, I pounded my fist against the bars and immediately regretted it. I cradled my sore hand for a moment before I went back to picking at the mortar.

Time was speeding by, and I didn't want to die here, not without telling Cade I loved him. It probably wouldn't matter to him, but I wanted to say it. Just once.

I heard a soft chink and once again, I hustled to the bars, peering into the dim hall.

Sharpe strolled up with Neil, clamping down on the younger vamp's ear. "'Ello, love. Looks like your plan's gone tits up."

"Ow. Let go of me." Neil batted at Sharpe's hand.

"Do be quiet before I kill you," he said.

I crossed my arms. "You disappeared on us. What the hell, Sharpe?"

He let go of Neil's ear and bent toward me. "Lucky for you I did, or they'd have me trussed up like a Christmas goose as well, eh?"

I gripped the bars. "They're tied up? Did you see them? Where are they?"

Sharpe brushed his hands together. "Keep your knickers on. I didn't see them, my lad here did. Tell her." He nodded to Neil.

"They're tied up on the other side of this tunnel. They're alive. For now."

Sharpe cuffed him on the side of the head. "Oy, you're just a little ray of light, you are."

"We need to get them out," I said. "Did you bring the keys? What are you waiting for?"

"Just hold up there, love." James quirked one brow. "If I get you out of here, what are you going to give me?"

He had to be kidding. Everyone was about to be sacrificed by an insane witch and a kidnapping, murderous vampire, and he wanted to make deals? "What do you want, asshole?"

He reached through the bars and caressed my undamaged cheek with his thumb and shook his head in mock disappointment. "You've got a right filthy mouth, you do." Then he grinned. "I love it. Don't ever change."

I pulled away. "What do you want?"

"I want Cade McAllister, Mick Raven, Vane Aldridge, Nick Alpert, Dawson Nash, and you, my love, to owe me." He rattled off the list so quickly, he must have been practicing.

"Owe you what?"

He shoved his hands in his pockets. "One favor each, to be determined by me. No questions asked; no offer refused."

I tapped my foot, not seeing any way out. Owe this jerkwad a favor or let everyone get killed. These were my choices. "Fine," I growled, sounding a lot like Cade.

He nodded in satisfaction. "That wasn't so hard, now was it? Barely hurt at all, I'll wager." Plucking the old fashioned skeleton key from his jacket pocket, he slipped it into the lock and pulled open the door.

I thanked him by smacking his face as hard as I could. "Damn," I said, shaking my fist, "that was my sore hand."

"Oy, that hurt." He rubbed his bloody lip.

"Good, it was supposed to. Now, let's go."

#

They led me down the corridor, stopping at the door to the throne room. "You stay here," Sharpe told me. "I hope you're far enough away to not cock up my mojo. The lad and I will kill the guards and free your mates." Sharpe started to walk off.

I grabbed his jacket. He turned back with a raised brow. "You're touching me."

"That wasn't the plan. I want to go with you. I need to make sure everyone's all right."

He removed my hand from his sleeve. "Trust me, love, they'll need their magic to stop Monty and that raving bitch."

"What time is it?"

Neil dug out his phone. "Two-thirty."

I didn't know what would happen when Jasmine couldn't use her magic. My blood was her only deterrent. Shit. "How do I know you're not going to leave me here? Or the rest of the team?"

Sharpe gave me a cocky grin. "The team," he said with a snort. "Don't you trust me, Holly?"

"Not at all."

"Yeah, yeah, all right. But I want another favor from you, Null. You owe me two."

"Yes. Now give me your word you won't leave anyone behind."

With a smirk, he held one hand over his heart. "You have my super duper, solemn slalom vow. Band of brothers, no man left behind, and all that bollocks."

They headed off, leaving me in the corner of a cold, mold-filled hole in the ground with nothing but a tiny pen light Sharpe had shoved into my hand right before he left.

I tried to send good thoughts to Cade. And I paced. Finally, after several minutes, Neil and Sharpe returned.

"Where are the others?" I flashed the light on them. Neil appeared very pale and gaunt. Sharpe looked irritated.

"Sorry, love, they're gone."

"What the hell do you mean, they're gone?" My voice contained a shrill edge of panic.

"They've already been taken to the sacrificial place," Neil said. "Don't kill me, okay?" He held up his hands and backed away until he hit a wall.

I stalked toward him. "I will kill you, I swear to God, unless you tell me where the field is."

"They never said," he whined.

"I'd kill him just on that poncy voice alone," Sharpe said.

I spun and flashed the light over him. His gold hoop earrings glinted. "You're not helping. Do you know where Monty has a field?"

He shook his head. "No, love."

I turned back toward Neil. "What about Master Sebastian? You said they had him in an underground club?"

He nodded convulsively. "Yeah, that's all I know, a club."

I felt Sharpe's hand on my shoulder. "Let me have a go at him." He moved forward and punched Neil in the balls. It wasn't a hard punch, but the kid doubled over in pain.

"Now, Neil, my lad, you're going to think really, really hard. Master Sebastian. Where is he? Because the next time, I won't hold back."

Neil cupped his junk and groaned. "Please, man, please. I don't know. They said he was underground in a club."

Sharpe pried Neil's hands away and brought back his arm for another ball pounding. I covered my eyes with one hand.

"Stop," Neil pleaded, "they said it was some building."

I peeked between my fingers.

"No shit, mate. All these tunnels are under buildings."

"Wait," I said. "Did they say Tulsa Club Building?"

Neil swallowed. "Yeah, that sounds right."

"Are you sure, Neil?" I asked. "Be very sure."

"Yeah, they're holding him in an underground club building."

"The Tulsa Club Building over on Fifth Street has been abandoned for years," I said. The building was a city eyesore. It was an architecturally stunning piece of Art Deco, but with liens on the place, the owner didn't have the money for renovations. So there it sat, dilapidated. A homeless Hilton, the locals called it.

"I know it," Sharpe said. "Junkies used to hang there. Easy peasy when you needed a quick snack."

I shook my head at him. "What happened to you, dude?"

"I'm a vampire, sweetheart. Now, can we get there from here, lad? Or would it be easier to go above ground?"

Neil bobbed his head. "I can get us there from here. I have a decent sense of direction."

"Very good. Because if you're mucking us about, I'm going to suck you dry and leave your undead husk in the ground. Now, get us out of here."

"Wait," I said. "We need to see if they left any of our weapons. We dropped them in a tunnel off the main room."

"Go, then. Don't have all blooming night."

I retraced my steps, ran through the double doors and into the beautiful throne room. In the vaulted tunnel, I found the katana and the scythe. The guns and knives were history.

I scooped them up and ran back to the vamps. Sharpe immediately went for the scythe. "Haven't seen one of these in a long, bloody while."

I handed the flashlight to Neil. We followed him, half-jogging, half-running through the underground corridors.

Sharpe had to kick in several, unused doorways which sometimes took a while. Finally, we arrived at a red door with peeling paint and warped wood.

"I think this the one-hundredth block," Neil said. The trail ended here. No more tunnels. We'd reached a dead end.

"Stand back." Sharpe brought up his booted foot, and after a few tries, cracked the wood above the handle. We all looked at one another then Sharpe took the flashlight out of Neil's hand and strode into the room.

We were deeper underground. It smelled of rotting soil. Sharpe flashed the light around the large room. Graffiti covered the walls, and a pile of old wooden chairs were stacked on a table in the corner.

My heart sank, and tears filled my eyes. I wandered aimlessly around the room. Cade and the others were going to die tonight. Fuck!

Livid, I kicked out at the table, sent the chairs toppling. Ignoring the pain thrumming through my head, I picked one up and threw it against the far wall. I reached down to pick up another when I saw a figure slouched in the corner.

"Oh, my God." I began shoving chairs out of my way to get to him. "Help."

Sharpe and Neil rushed to my side. Sharpe swept his arm out, clearing a path so I could dive over the table and touch the unmoving person.

I brushed my fingers across one of his broad shoulders. He groaned. His chin, which had been slumped against his chest, barely lifted.

Sharpe ran the light over him. The man blinked his dark eyes and muttered deeply in a language I didn't understand. After a few seconds, he gracefully rose to his feet. He wore a shabby, threadbare suit with unfashionably wide lapels. I wondered how long he'd been down here.

He wasn't the least bit stiff. Must have something to do with the containment spell.

He was tall, easily seven feet. A thick, long beard covered the lower half of his face. With scraggly hair hanging down his back, he was half biker, half serial killer. One-hundred-percent frightening.

Sharpe immediately fell to one knee and bowed his head. Neil observed him then quickly did the same.

The man pointed at me and spoke again. I still didn't understand him.

I pointed to my chest. "I'm Holly. You're Master Sebastian? We're here to free you." I said all the words slowly.

"What am I doing here, Holly?" His voice sounded scratchy, and he said my name as though it was an interesting new flavor he was sampling for the first time. He also had a broad accent I'd never heard before.

"Monty Ridgecliff had you mystically contained. He's about to kill a bunch of my friends to keep you here."

He nodded thoughtfully. "Yes, Montgomery." He glanced at the men who were kneeling before him. "Rise."

They did but kept their heads bowed.

He glanced at me again. "Why do I feel so strange?"

"Sorry about that. I'm a null."

"Ah. Where is Monty now?"

"That's what I don't know and time is running out. Do you know where he'd be performing a blood ritual?"

He lifted his head and scratched his jaw with one hand. "There's a field with a pond near Broken Arrow. Earth, water, air, and of course they'll have fire. No ritual would be complete without it."

My heart pounded as fear and hope warred in my chest. "Can you take us there?"

He nodded. "Yes, of course. A ritual like this is best performed at the witching hour. Come, gentlemen. You can introduce yourselves on the way."

Sharpe and Neil finally lifted their heads. Neil led the way out of the tunnel to a stairway. We climbed to the lobby of the building. Decayed and torn apart by vandals, the floors and walls had been destroyed, but a few classic moldings framing the ceiling remained intact.

Sharpe grabbed an old keg that had obviously been used for a party and pounded at the chain-wrapped doors. After several minutes while Neil and Master Sebastian looked on, he finally broke through.

We stepped out onto the street. The moon was lower in the sky. A sense of desperation made me panic. "It's after three. We need to go. Now!" I stood, my feet planted on the sidewalk, swiveling my head from side to side. We didn't have a ride.

Sharpe, keg still in hand, found an older Ford sedan a half a block away, bashed in the passenger window, and unlocked the door. He hopped in, dipped his head out of sight, and in seconds, the car was running. He looked back at us. "You lot going to stand there all night?"

We sped toward the car. Master Sebastian swept glass aside before climbing in the passenger seat. Neil and I scrambled in the back. With Sharpe driving like he was a Formula One racer, we sped off to Broken Arrow.

The master vamp calmly gave directions, taking us to the outskirts of town, then out of the city. Sharpe made fast, wide turns that had Neil and me either careening into each other or the car doors. My concussion wasn't going away anytime soon, and I was nauseated when we stopped a quarter of a mile from the ritual site. Over the hill, a huge fire of orange and red flames licked the night sky. Smoke rode the hot, humid air.

We'd had a big discussion on the way about whether or not I should accompany them or let them handle things magically. Ultimately, we decided I should tag along since Sebastian wasn't at his usual strength. My presence might level the playing field.

I grabbed a sword from the floorboard and glanced at Neil. "You flip on me again, kid, I'll turn you into a shish kebab. Got it?"

He nodded.

Piling out of the car and keeping low, we ran across the field toward the base of the hill. The sharp tang of smoke stung my nose.

Sebastian strolled behind us, arms crossed over his chest, his long hair a tangle down his back. "I see a human that way." He tipped his head to the left.

Sharpe and I spotted the guard at the same time, but he was much faster. With a *swick* of the scythe, the man's head rolled away from his body.

I averted my eyes and breathed through my nose to keep from throwing up or passing out. I couldn't afford to do either right now.

Sharpe moved forward and snagged the assault rifle for himself and checked the headless corpse's pockets. "Found you a gun, love."

"Great."

He trotted back to me. A revolver. I hadn't practiced with that. "Just get close to someone and pull the trigger."

"Yeah, I know the basics." We ran back to where Sebastian and Neil stood. I couldn't believe I'd just seen a man beheaded. I was living a surreal nightmare. I handed the sword to the ancient vamp.

"Why does she get a gun?" Neil whispered.

Sharpe smacked the back of his head. "Shut it, muppet. Spread out, and together we go up the hill. Holly, you're going have to storm the castle, darling. Get as close to the witch as you can."

She'd fucked with Cade, busted my cheek, and scratched ribbons of skin from my neck. *Payback time, bitch.* "Got it."

Sebastian sighed. "Let us go now, children. I grow weary of this. My meeting with Montgomery is long overdue."

Ducking, the four of us clambered up the hill. I glanced to my right at the Master. His eyes were narrowed, and his face appeared alien strange in the moonlight. I glanced to my left. Sharpe had a sick look of anticipation on his face. He was actually enjoying this.

Poking my head over the ridge, I caught sight of Jasmine. She stood facing me, naked and close to the fire. The crazy curls on her head weren't the only hair she needed to tame. In her hands, she raised a long, lethally sharp athame toward the sky. The fire glinted on its silvery blade. I couldn't hang around, waiting to see what she'd do next. I had to reach her before she used that knife.

I ran up the hill, shooting at three guards. I knew I hit one because he grabbed his ear. Not the appendage I was going for, but I'd take what I could get.

I heard gunfire behind me and expected to feel the sting of a bullet any second, but it never came.

Jasmine's eyes flew open and locked on me. "No. This is not happening." She brought the knife downward. Mick lay at her feet. Firelight turned his skin bright red. Sweat glistened on his handsome, unconscious face.

Fear propelled me forward. I stopped in my tracks, cocked the gun, and gently squeezed the trigger.

I was aiming for her forehead.

I hit her hair.

Dammit.

Her face became a snarling mask of rage. With the knife in one hand, she ran toward me, her lips moving in a curse. What a dipshit. I was a null. Hello?

As she advanced, I heard gunfire all around me. Once more, I took a shot at Jasmine but wasn't able to aim this time. A look of surprise crossed her face as she fell to the ground.

I wasn't sure where I'd shot her, didn't much care. I ran past her, my gaze searching, hunting for Cade. There. Back to back against Vane Aldridge. His hands were tied behind his back, his mouth duct-taped shut. His head lolled to one side. Was he unconscious or dead?

I ran to him, threw down the gun, and felt his neck for a pulse. He had one. I closed my eyes in relief. When I opened them, I noticed all of my Others were bound, gagged, and semi-conscious as well. They must have been drugged because I'd have deactivated a spell by now.

But Cade was alive, and I was grateful. So grateful.

I ripped the tape from his mouth, tapped at his jaw. "Wake up, McAllister. Wake up, baby."

His eyes fluttered. "Holly?" He was groggy, could barely mumble my name.

I looked around for something sharp, a knife or a rock to cut the ropes binding Cade's wrists. Three feet away from me, I spied a craggy rock, the size of a tennis ball. The angles looked sharp. It would have to work.

I glanced up and watched Sharpe shoot a guard in the head. Not far from Sharpe, Monty turned tail and began running away from the fire and carnage. Sebastian's booming voice halted his retreat.

"Montgomery. You will come here at once." Like a child listening to a stern parent, Monty obeyed. He pivoted, as though compelled to follow Sebastian's order, and scurried to his Master.

When Monty reached him, Sebastian dropped the sword and shoved his huge paw into Monty's abdomen, ripping out a rope of his assistant's intestine. Fuck me. That was brutal.

"Holly!"

Sunny.

I lifted my head, looking beyond the fire. Jasmine, her hand coated in blood, held the athame to Sunny's throat.

CHAPTER THIRTY

"Stand up nice and slow, or I'll kill her," Jasmine said.

I could barely breathe. Poor Sunny. She never wanted to do this in the first place. I'd roped her into this. My stomach muscles tensed and fear sliced through me, sharper than that athame Jasmine held.

I did as the witch instructed but clenched my fists, hoping she wouldn't notice the rock in my right hand.

"Walk toward me, Holly. Slowly. No sudden movements."

I stepped over two dead guards, never taking my eyes off Jasmine. "Just let her go."

"You shot my hip, you bitch." I sure did. It was bleeding steadily, flowing down the side of her leg, looking dark and slick in the firelight. "And you did something to my magic. You said my powers would come back, but you stole them."

I tried to placate her with the truth. "They will come back." I was only ten feet away from her now. I risked a glance at Sunny. Her eyes were as wide as her frames. "It's my blood, Jasmine. You have it under your nails from scratching me."

Jasmine lifted her hand slightly, jerking at Sunny's ponytail. Sunny winced in pain. "You're lying."

"I'm not. I swear it."

Her lips turned up in a cold smile. She was going to slit Sunny's throat. I could see it in her eyes. And she was going to enjoy it.

"Sunny, hold still," I commanded. I only had one weapon at my disposal—the rock. I hoped my third base softball skills were like riding a bike. With no time to aim properly, I cranked my arm back and let it fly. Somehow, the rock managed to do what my bullet couldn't—hit Jasmine right between the eyes.

She let out a shriek, and Sunny bit her wrist until Jasmine dropped the athame. Then Sunny turned and punched the other woman in the boob before sprinting to me.

I pulled her into a hug, didn't care if she wanted it or not. "Are you all right?"

Before she could answer, I heard a shot. Jasmine's expression froze. Blood trickled from her mouth. She tried to speak, but no words came. All life fled from her eyes, and she fell to the ground.

Sharpe stood behind her, wearing a vicious sneer. Lowering his gun, he walked over and kicked her in the ribs. Her lifeless body jerked. "That's for London, you slag."

Sunny burst into tears and hugged me back.

"I'm so glad you're okay." I pulled back, ran my hands over her cheeks. "Sunny?"

"That fucking bitch was going to kill me," she whispered.

I'd never heard Sunny cuss, but if she were going to do it, now was the perfect time.

"I'm glad she didn't."

Sunny huffed out a laugh. "Me, too."

"I have to get to Cade. Help me free the others, okay?"

She stood, unmoving, unyielding.

"Sunny. Help me. I need you right now."

She blinked and snapped to. "You always need me. You'd be lost without me."

I smiled, my lower lip quivering. "Completely."

I ran to Jasmine's lifeless body, avoided looking at her, and grabbed the athame. Then hand in hand, Sunny and I walked back to the rest of our group. I sawed through the tape binding Cade's hands. Then I worked on Vane and gave the knife to Sunny.

They were all starting to wake, some more slowly than others. Abby and Vane both threw up in the grass.

I sat on the ground and cradled Cade's head in my lap. He hovered in and out of consciousness. At one point, he glanced up through half-lidded eyes. "Never thought I'd see you again."

I stroked his forehead. It was the only part of his face that wasn't bruised. "I love you, Cade," I whispered the words, knowing he'd never remember them. Yet I'd promised myself I would have the courage to say them.

Seeing movement to my right, I watched Neil help Abby up, put his arm around her waist, and half carry her past the fire. Sebastian stood, staring down at Monty. Sharpe slung the assault rifle over his shoulder then pulled the Master's former assistant up by the back of his lapel, forcing him to stand despite the vamp's intestinal problem.

Monty's dying gaze sought me out. "You have no idea what hell you've wrought, Holly. I served…the greater good."

"Pipe down, you twat," Sharpe said. "You killed my best mates."

"Don't worry, Monty," Sebastian said, "we'll get you out of here, and you'll regenerate. Oh, but how you'll wish you hadn't." When he smiled, the firelight cast an orange glow over his features. It was the most frightening grin I'd ever seen. He turned to Sharpe. "Get him out of here and take him back to his lair."

Sharpe picked up Monty, hoisted him over his shoulder, and started down the hill with him.

Master Sebastian's piercing eyes met mine. "Thank you, Null. We will meet again, you and I."

Not if I had anything to say about it. I was out of the null for hire business. Out of interfering in the lives of Others.

"Who was that?" Cade asked.

"I'll tell you everything. Later."

#

Mick recovered faster than the rest. He shuffled toward me, holding the side of his head. Squatting down, his gaze took me in, the bruise on my cheek, the deep scratches at my throat. "Hello, brave Holly. We made it." His eyes flew over Cade. "He had a double dose of sedative, I believe. Might take him a bit longer to recover."

I nodded.

Eventually, they all recovered but were hung over and shambling about, unsteady on their feet. Mick and Vane dragged Jasmine's body to Monty's limousine.

Dawson and Nick said they'd stay and take care of the guards' bodies. I wasn't sure about the details, and I didn't really want to know.

Sunny sat quietly next to me. She was never quiet, and her demeanor had me worried.

At last, Cade woke up fully. "What happened? The last thing I remember…" He rubbed the top of his head. "Shit, I can't remember much of anything."

Mick and Vane strode back to us, helping Cade to his feet. With Cade sandwiched between the two men, Sunny and I followed, slowly making our way down the hill.

Vane climbed behind the wheel of the limo and rolled down the window. "We'll take him to the Council. Your car's over there." I glanced where he pointed. "Your purse is still inside."

Mick tucked Cade's body into the back seat. He stood, holding onto the door and glanced down at me. "I'm sure he'll call you when all this is over."

I nodded. "Where did Neil and Abby get to?"

He looked around. "I'm not sure. But they can fend for themselves." He slid two fingers beneath my chin. "I'll be in touch." He climbed in the car, shut the door, and Vane drove off in a cloud of dust.

So that was it. My sorcerer was gone.

It was all a bit anticlimactic.

Sunny stood at my elbow. "Give me a lift back to The Raven so I can get my car?"

"Sure."

We remained silent on the drive back. Cade was all right. Everyone made it out alive—except for Jasmine, and she didn't count. I should be relieved. Instead, I just felt sad. Probably the adrenaline crash. *Or your broken heart.*

We arrived at Mick's club, and I wearily climbed the stairs to the green room to gather my stuff. It didn't take long.

With my bag in hand, I stood there as tears pricked the backs of my eyes. I would be all right. I kept repeating that phrase to myself, hoping it would prove true. Batting my eyes, I held the tears at bay.

When I trudged back down the stairs, Sunny waited for me by the door, her suitcase near her feet.

"How are you holding up?" I asked.

"I don't care for field work."

I laughed. "I don't care much for it myself. Especially when the field is a spot for black magic rituals."

"Especially then." She looked rumpled, tired. Sunny didn't belong in this Other world any more than I did. We were in-betweeners—neither Other nor Normal. I wasn't sure where we fit in.

"I'm going to dissolve the business," I said. "We'll split whatever is in the account fifty-fifty. You've been my partner in all this, not just an assistant. And you've been my friend. Thank you for that."

"You're in no emotional state to decide anything right now, but we'll discuss the partnership later." Her body stiffened. "I...consider you a friend, as well." She pointed a finger at my nose. "But I'm not fixing to make you a bracelet or anything. Get that out of your head right now."

We walked to the parking lot. With a wave, she hopped in her car and sped away. I took the rental to Gran's house.

It was time to tell her the truth.

#

My cocoa grew cold as the whole story—Wallace, the dead girls, Cade, and tonight's almost tragic ending—tumbled out of me. I got the order of events mixed up because my head still hurt, and I was exhausted.

Gran didn't say a word, and after I finished, sat back in her recliner. "You should have told me."

"You'd have only worried." I rubbed a hand over my gritty eyes.

"I can't believe your father knew about you from the start and never made contact. What a little asshole." She pursed her lips and adjusted her glasses.

"Yeah, I don't think the fruit falls far from the tree. Wallace is kind of an ass, too."

"Do you think he'll keep his promise?" she asked.

Before entering Gran's house, I'd sat in the driveway and called Wallace. I explained everything, letting him know Jasmine was dead, and Cade was squaring things up with the Council. The old man swore he'd start looking for my mother immediately. Not sure I believed him, despite his oath.

Now, I set the mug down on the coffee table then pulled the afghan tighter around my shoulders. "I don't know. But I'm going to hold his feet to the fire. He's not that crazy about having me in the Dumahl family. You know I'm not above blackmail, and it *is* election season. People might not want to vote for him if they knew he had a bastard null grandchild."

"Don't talk about yourself that way, you hear me?" She leaned toward the edge of her seat, reached out and patted my leg. "Anyway, I don't believe your mother's out there, honey. If she were, I'd have found her by now. Goodness knows I've looked hard enough."

I wasn't ready to accept that. Not yet. "Maybe she doesn't want to be found. Maybe she's so ashamed…" I sobbed on the last word, and the tears finally came. Gran rose to sit next to me, cradled me in her arms.

"I don't believe that, either, Hollyhocks. Who in their right mind would be ashamed of you?"

I pulled away. "How can you say that? You gave up magic for me, Gran. I *stole* your life. I turned out wrong." I swiped at the tears streaming down my cheeks. I winced, forgetting for a moment that my left cheek was bruised and cut.

"Look at me. You didn't steal diddly. Magic was never my life. If I've done one thing right, it was you. You're not wrong, you're special."

Her words comforted me. We both cried for a while and clung to each other.

"So, what about this sorcerer?" she finally asked, petting my hair. "You care about him?

"Yeah, but he doesn't feel the same. It's just, you know, physical."

"Physical attraction can lead to deeper things. I may be getting old, but I remember that much."

"He's so complicated. Cade blames himself for his sister's death. He has this whole protective vibe going on. I'll get over it. I've known him for less than a week. The whole situation is ridiculous." I was doing it again. Lying to her. Trying to lie to myself.

Gran harrumphed. "Is he arrogant?"

"Yeah. And bossy. And he likes rules."

"Sounds like another sorcerer I know. It only took me two hours before I was head over heels for your grandfather. He'd be so proud of you. If he hadn't wrapped his car around that tree. Damned fool."

"You've lost a lot, Gran. I'm sorry for that."

"That's life honey, but I have you, and that's what matters." She squeezed my hand. "Go on up to bed. You look like you're dragging."

"Love you, Gran." I stood and bent down to kiss her cheek.

She straightened the belt on her leopard print bathrobe. "You, too. Now git."

CHAPTER THIRTY-ONE

Gran shook me awake. "Come on, get up."

I cracked my eyes open. "What?"

"He's downstairs, pacing the floor like a caged tiger. Get yourself together, Hollyhocks." She bustled out of the room.

Cade? Did she mean Cade?

I threw back the covers and jumped out of bed. What was he doing here?

While brushing my hair and teeth, I ran through a dozen possible scenarios. All of them ended with Cade walking away forever. I didn't see any other outcome.

Nervously, I threw on a pair of pink shorts and a matching cami. There wasn't much I could do about my face. I looked like I'd run into a brick wall a few times, thanks to Jasmine.

When I'd dawdled for as long as I could, I left my old bedroom and headed for the stairs. Taking a deep breath, I walked to the living room.

Cade was indeed prowling around, and Gran was nowhere in sight.

He looked even worse than I did. His entire face was one big contusion. The bridge of his nose had turned a sickly purple-green. The rest was a mottled shade of blue and black. He stilled when he saw me.

"How are you?" he asked.

"Alive. You?"

"Pissed off. That was goddamned stupid what you did, walking into Monty's lair." The words were angry, but his voice was a soft rumble. "Bringing all those Others with you. What the hell were you thinking?" Stepping toward me, he carefully ran a finger down my sore cheek.

"I was thinking about you. You'd have done the exact same thing. Don't pretend otherwise."

"That's not the point, Little Null. I can take care of myself."

"Yeah, well so can I, Sorcerer. I may not have magic, but I've got moxie."

Planting his hands on his hips, he clenched them into fists and glanced out the window. Afternoon sunshine poured into the room, revealing just how shabby Gran's plaid blue sofa really was. "I counted on Mick to stop you. Bastard couldn't even get that right."

"Hey, I'm a grown woman who makes my own decisions. Mick knows that." I jabbed my finger toward his chest. "When are *you* going to get it through your thick skull?"

Instead of slinging angry words back at me, he cupped my chin and looked at me with such tenderness, it made me gasp. "Last night, I knew Jasmine would kill me. The only thing that gave me any comfort was knowing Mick would take care of you. When I lost Shayna, it damn near killed me. The thought of going through that again scares the shit out of me, Holly."

I knew that admission was hard for him. Cade didn't like showing any weakness and seeing him vulnerable like this made me fall in love with him just a little bit more. "I'm not lost. We both made it out. We're here."

With the back of his hand, he caressed my brow. "But it was damn close, Little Null. I may have been drugged for most of it, but Mick and Vane filled me in on what happened last night. You freed Master Sebastian and took on Jasmine."

"I had help."

"You put everyone's life in danger, especially your own."

"I believe the words you're looking for are *thank* and *you*." I smacked his hand away.

"I don't want you to put yourself in that position ever again. I'm not worth it, believe me."

"Is this because of Shayna?"

He looked away.

"What was she like?"

He was silent so long I thought he wouldn't answer me. After a few minutes, the words came. "She always pestered me when we were kids, wanted to tag along. I miss those days. Shayna was funny and smart, talented. She had a thing for music. Classical music, Beethoven and all that shit. God, it was awful. And she had a mouth on her." He breathed out a laugh tinged with bitterness. His gaze washed over me. "She was a lot like you.

"After my parents were gone, it was just the two of us. Until Mick came into the picture. He was different then."

"What happened, exactly?"

Cade stared at one of Gran's antique cross stitch samplers hanging on the wall, but his eyes were unfocused. "I'd been in the field for a week, trying to catch a pyromancer. I made the mistake of telling her where I was staying. I shouldn't have, it was against protocol. But Shayna always worried." He turned his back on me, strode to the fireplace and fondled one of my high school trophies sitting on the mantle. "It's my fault she's dead. Mick's right. I killed her."

I walked to him and reaching out, brushed my fingers across his back. Cade stiffened at my touch but didn't pull away. "It wasn't your fault."

He shrugged my hand off then. "Well, if you say so, that makes it all right."

"You're not perfect, Cade. You're not a god. And if you're to blame for telling Shayna your whereabouts, it was her fault for showing up."

He whipped around, anger flowing from him in waves. "You don't know what the hell you're talking about."

"And it was the killer's fault for trapping her in that fire. And Mick's, because he didn't stop her from going in the first place."

"Shut up," he growled.

I gently wrapped my arms around his midsection, careful not to squeeze too tight. His body remained rigid. "You didn't kill her."

He rubbed his eyes and stayed quiet.

"You didn't kill her. It's not your fault," I repeated.

Slowly, Cade wrapped his arms around my shoulders. I placed my uninjured cheek against his chest and listened to his heartbeat. We stood like that for a long time, then he kissed the top of my head while he stroked my back. Eventually, he withdrew his arms from my shoulders. When he stepped out of my embrace, severing our contact, I almost shivered from the loss of his big, warm body.

"Holly, I'm not sure I can protect you. I'm not always in town—"

"*I don't need your protection.* How many ways can I say it?"

"No, you need someone watching out for you, now more than ever. You've got the Council's attention and that won't go away."

"I also have a grandfather on the Council." Yes, Wallace was a political hack, but I wasn't afraid of exploiting our connection. I'd do what I had to in order to protect myself.

"You're on Master Sebastian's radar, too."

"I'll handle it. He owes me." I wanted this sorcerer until I ached with it. But I didn't want to keep putting his life in danger. I sure as hell didn't want to become his obligation, his responsibility. "I'm no longer your problem."

I turned away so he wouldn't see me blink back tears. Swallowing, I took a deep breath and forced a smile before throwing one last glance over my shoulder. "I'm out of your hair for good. Take care of yourself, McAllister."

As I began walking away, he grabbed my arm and spun me to face him. "That's it? That's all you have to say to me? Take care?" He wagged his finger back and forth. "And what about this thing between us? You think that's going to disappear?"

"Yeah, I do." I couldn't look him in the eye, so my gaze settled on the collar of his black t-shirt. "Once you go back to your life, you'll never have to worry about me again. You can go on being an Other. You can cast spells and see magical signatures and solve crimes without me there to screw it up."

"Look at me."

Licking my dry lips, I slowly glanced up at him. He was angry, his lips compressed into a thin line and a vein beat visibly at his bruised temple.

"You honestly believe I'd forget about you? That even if we're not together, I won't worry about you? What kind of an asshole do you think I am?"

"I don't think that, Cade, but you can never be who you really are when I'm around. I'll take years off your life. Ask Gran. She gave up magic for me, and it guts me every damned day."

"I'm not giving up magic for you, Holly. You're not sacrificing your business for me. Even though I hate it, I'm not asking you to give it up. If I did, you'd tell me to go to hell."

"I don't want to become your project, the person you have to protect and save. I understand why that's important to you, but that's not what I want."

"What do you want? To call it quits?" His sharp gaze pinned me to the spot. "Never see each other again? You're okay with that?"

I raised both hands and gestured in frustration. "I nullify everything that makes you special."

"Magic doesn't make me special," he scoffed. He was silent a beat. When he started speaking again, he slowly shook his head. "I never pegged you for a quitter."

"It's not that easy."

"It doesn't have to be complicated," he said.

I was at a loss. I had good arguments, valid ones, but he kept shooting them down. "Then what's *your* big plan, McAllister? Are we going to date or something lame like that?"

"Yeah." He nodded. "Why not?"

After everything we'd been through, dating sounded so…normal. "Because we can't. We're on different sides of the magical coin. Because you're a control freak. Because—"

"Because I make you come until you can't move. Because you like it when I toss your ass over my shoulder." His eyes bounced down to my chest. "Because your nipples get hard, like they are right this second, whenever I'm within reach. Because I want you even now, when I'm so fucking battered it hurts to breathe."

Biting my lower lip, I turned it over in my brain. I'd never felt like this before. This love stuff was new and exciting. Also terrifying. I'd always worry about Cade's safety. We had that in common. But was it possible to be in a relationship and not have to give up who we were? He'd still have his sorcerer's gig. We'd see each other on weekends. If Others weren't actively trying to kill us, it might take some of the pressure off. I'd been ready to sacrifice my life for him last night. The least I could do was go out on a date. "We're going to drive each other crazy, you know that."

"Having a lot of hot, nasty sex might make up for it."

I fought a smile. "Arrogant sorcerer."

He grabbed my hand and pulled me closer. He kissed me softly, causing my heart to stutter. Standing on my toes, I touched his tongue with mine and was very careful not to lean against him.

When he lifted his head, he gave me a smug grin. "See, you like me."

"You like me more. I have one question, McAllister." It had been nagging me since the night Neil bit me in The Raven parking lot. "You said Neil violated rules two and three. I know rule number two—don't piss you off. So, what's number three?"

Red flooded his neck and probably his face if I could have seen past the bruises. "Don't touch my shit."

I paused. "You think of me as your shit? Like your property or something?"

"Sounds kind of negative when you say it like that."

Although I liked his primitive side, I didn't want to encourage it too much. "I'm my *own* shit, McAllister."

"If you say so, Little Null." He fingered a strap on my cami, toyed with the little pink bow. "Do you want to go to a movie with me next week?"

"Why wait for next week?"

"I'm back on the Council clock. Got a call on the way here. Someone's been conjuring spirits, scaring the locals. Shouldn't take long to straighten it out. I'll call you."

"Fine." I traced a nail over a dragon scale at his neck. "But I get to pick the movie. Nothing with superheroes or explosives. I've had enough of that crap in real life."

"Can I at least feel you up?"

A little smile played on my lips. "Maybe. If you're lucky and obey rule number two."

"Is a hand job completely out of the question?" When I rolled my eyes, he grabbed my wrist and kissed my palm. "I'll call you later, okay?"

I walked him to the door where he gave me one more kiss. As I watched him drive away, I still felt a twinge of guilt, knowing that I'd nullify his powers whenever we were together. But real life was going to be a lot different than the drama we'd encountered over the last few days. Still, I couldn't look too far into the future, or I'd keep seeing all the problems. Maybe he was right. I made things too complicated.

I closed the front door, intent on helping Gran in the garden when my cell rang on the small entryway table. Sunny's ringtone. "Hey, how are you feeling, Sunshine?"

"Perfectly fine. We've got a funeral. A whole clan of feuding harpies. I told them you were recuperating, but when they insisted on your attendance, I charged an extra two thousand. Can you be there by three?"

I sighed. Deeply.

Author's Note

There are tunnels still being used to walk underground from building to building in Tulsa, Oklahoma, but they don't descend, and they don't run under the Tulsa Club Building. I took a little artistic license with that one.

Thank you

Thanks so much for reading Dispelled. I hope you enjoyed Holly's story, and there's more to come in the Null for Hire series. If you'd take the time to leave an honest review on your favorite site, I'd greatly appreciate it.

I love to hear from readers. Contact me at **TerriLAustin.com** and sign up for my newsletter while you're there.

His Every Need

Allie Campbell is determined to take care of her family, no matter the cost. But when her father loses their home to British tycoon Trevor Blake, Allie finds herself forced to plead for more time to pay off the loan...and if she has to use her own body as collateral, then so be it.

Trevor isn't moved by Allie's story. But when Allie impulsively offers to do anything to keep the house, he's intrigued enough to raise the stakes: for the next two months, she must cater to his every need, no matter how depraved. To his amazement, she agrees.

Allie has no intention of enjoying her time with the arrogant, domineering Brit, but it doesn't take long before he's got her aching for his touch-and he'll do whatever it takes to make her beg...

Praise for His Every Need

"I was so into it... I read it all in one night - so I think that means it's a winner." - *Diary of an Eager Reader*

"Is it possible to give a book more than five stars? If so, this book would be at the top of the list to deserve those extra stars... Its a wonderful story, full of surprises and love. " - *One Final Word*

"Easily one of the best books I've read this year and possibly ever. The characters are brilliant and the love story is extraordinary; truly a whimsical modern day Beauty and the Beast tale testing the bonds of family and the fragility of love... I've been irrevocably enchanted." - *Expressions of a Hopeful Romantic*

"From nicknames to bizarre wedding plans, this is a story that will stimulate your funny bone...in between moments of extreme heat." - *Romancing the Book*

Diners, Dives and Dead Ends

As a struggling waitress and part-time college student, Rose Strickland's life is stalled in the slow lane. But when her close friend, Axton, disappears, Rose suddenly finds herself serving up more than hot coffee and flapjacks. Now she's hashing it out with sexy bad guys and scrambling to find clues in a race to save Axton before his time runs out. With her anime-loving bestie, her septuagenarian boss, and a pair of IT wise men along for the ride, Rose goes from zero to sixty and quickly learns when you're speeding down the fast lane, it's easy to crash and burn.

Praise for Diners, Dives and Dead Ends

"Austin's debut kicks off her planned series by introducing a quirky, feisty heroine and a great supporting cast of characters and putting them through quite a number of interesting twists." - *Kirkus Reviews*

"I predict this will be a long and successful series...I strongly recommend picking a copy up to read this summer. I know I am looking forward to reading more books by this author. FIVE STARS OUT OF FIVE." - *Lynn Farris, National Mystery Review Examiner at Examiner.com*

"What a blast! Diners, Dives & Dead Ends is a fast-paced mystery loaded with wonderful wit and humor that had me laughing and loving every page. Terri Austin will hook you right away and keep you riveted until The End. I want more!" - *Ann Charles, Award-Winning Author of the Bestselling Deadwood Mystery Series*